The Oblate's Confession

for Bob,

Many thanks!

Bill

WILLIAM PEAK

Secant Publishing, LLC
615 North Pinehurst Avenue
Salisbury MD 21801

www.secantpublishing.com

Excerpts from THE JERUSALEM BIBLE, copyright © 1966 by
Darton, Longman & Todd, Ltd. and Doubleday, a division
of Random House, Inc. Reprinted by permission.

First Edition

ISBN 978-0-9904608-0-0

Book design by Six Penny Graphics
Maps © 2014 by Neil Boyce

for Melissa

the sun, the moon, the earth, and the stars

CONTENTS

Britain in the Seventh Century A.D.

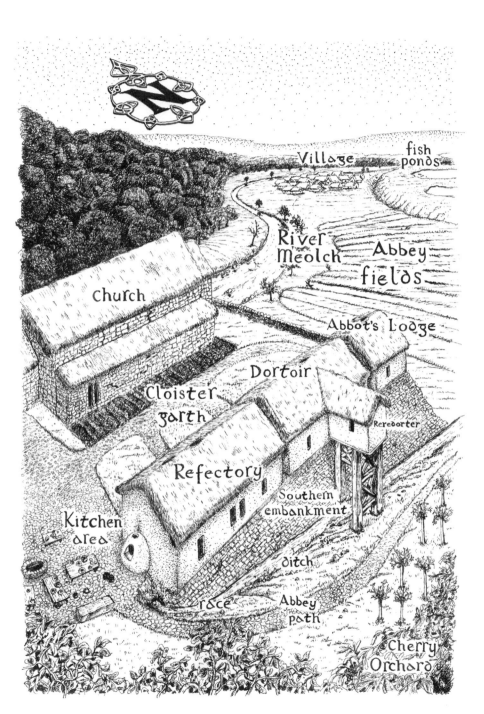

The Monastery at Redestone

There came a mighty wind, so strong it tore the mountains and shattered the rocks before Yahweh. But Yahweh was not in the wind. After the wind came an earthquake. But Yahweh was not in the earthquake. After the earthquake came a fire. But Yahweh was not in the fire. And after the fire there came the sound of a gentle breeze. And when Elijah heard this, he covered his face with his cloak and went out and stood at the entrance of the cave.

1st Kings 19: 11-13

I

The snow makes a sound as it falls. It is a slight sound, as if the air the snow is falling through were muttering to itself, but it is a sound. And there is something else too, another sound, muffled, distant. Practice? Are they practicing? But it is gone now. Whatever it was, the sound is gone now, the cloister silent. Except for the snow. The snow falls and falls. Like sleep it settles around the figure of a man and holds him there, as in a dream, silent, still. It is Father Dagan. Father Dagan. Father Dagan is standing in the middle of the cloister, hood up, arms at his sides, a gray and silent figure surrounded by falling snow.

There was a door. I remember that. A large door—big, dark, and, as I recall it now, new I think, the smell of fresh-cut oak creating a sort of refuge, a place into which I just fit. I was crying. The men were gone. The dark men in their dark clothes had marched off somewhere else, but I was still afraid. My father had left. It was almost nighttime and my father had left, and the dark men in their dark clothes said he wasn't coming back.

But this man came back. He looked behind the door and there I was. He smiled at me. As if this were part of a game, as if his finding me behind the door had been part of some grand elaborate game, he smiled at me. He held a finger up before his lips which made me like him and made me want to laugh but I did not laugh. I wondered what he was going to do. He didn't tell me a secret. He took me by the hand and, gently, he led me outside.

It was snowing. The air was soft with snow. It whispered in my ears and was cold and then wet on my face. I laughed. Again the man brought a finger to his lips. The smile made me shy. Why did he like me? He knelt down. Like a mother checking her little boy's shoes, the man knelt down. Only he wasn't a mother, he was a man, and he should have checked my shoes earlier, before, while we were still inside.

I held my foot up for the man but, instead of checking the shoe as he should have, he began to scrape at the snow on the ground before him. With big red hands the man scraped at the snow, raking it into a pile. A part of me wanted to kneel down beside the man, play in the snow with him, but I didn't. I was shy. I didn't know the rules. When the pile of snow was big, the man gathered it up into his hands and, working quickly, crushed it into a ball. The man placed the ball on the ground between us.

A second time the man raked snow into a pile and a second time he crushed the snow together into a ball, set it on the ground between us. Then he stopped. Instead of making a third ball, the man stopped; he looked at me. I smiled. The two balls resting side by side were pretty. You could see where the man's fingers had pressed into them. But he wanted something, I could tell. He pointed at the balls and then he looked at me, eyebrows raised. Why didn't he just say what he wanted? Why was everyone so afraid to speak here? Had something happened? Had something really bad happened?

The man's eyes grew large. He smiled at me, shook his head. Like a mother he shook his head, forbade me to cry. Then he reached out as if to comfort me; but instead of patting me or pulling me toward him, he pulled my hand out as if checking to see if it were clean. With his other hand the man now picked up some snow and placed it in the hand he held. He looked at me, looked back at the snow in my hand. I looked at the snow. It was pretty, one or two loose flakes just catching the light. The man looked at me again. He brought his now empty hands together and pretended to make another ball.

I knew what he wanted!

I brought my hands together as the man had and crushed the little pile of snow into a ball like his. I was surprised by how cold it was. Something about packing the snow tight seemed to squeeze the cold from it.

The man took the ball I had made and laid it on the ground between us. My ball looked small next to the ones he had made. Then the man did something that surprised me. He pulled two sticks from his sleeve. Like an uncle pulling eggs from his ear, the man pulled two sticks from his sleeve. Sticks and not sticks: long and pointed like sticks but also shiny, polished, like overlarge needles. The man placed the two needle-stick things on the ground beside the balls. Again he looked at me. His eyelashes and beard were now white with snow but beneath the flakes I could see that he was smiling. I smiled too. He looked funny.

Gently, like someone stacking pots, the man placed one of his balls on top of the other. On either side of the uppermost ball the man inserted one of the stick-like things so that now they really did look like sticks, sticks sticking out of a tree whose trunk was made of two big balls of snow.

The man looked at what he had made, and then he looked at me. There was a question in his eyes but I didn't say anything. I had no idea what he was doing. The man smiled. He raised a finger and I understood that he wanted me to be patient. Then carefully, very carefully, as though it were the most important thing in the world, he lifted my ball from the ground and held it in his hands. He looked at the ball and his face became serious. He looked at the two balls he had made, the one stacked on top of the other. He cocked his head. I was afraid he didn't like my ball, that it was too small. Then the man leaned forward and, with infinite care, placed my ball on top of his.

It was a man. A little man. We had made a *snow man*.

I have no more memories of that night. Did we go into church afterwards? Was that where the other monks had gone? Did Father leave the little snowman standing as he had created it, out in the middle of the garth? Or did he knock it down? I don't know. I don't remember. All I remember is Father Dagan standing in the middle of the cloister, tall and silent, a gray figure with his hood up, snow falling all around him. At his side stands a tiny form, equally still and mute, white and simple—my first snowman.

II

here are, of course, other memories from that first year at Redestone, though Father Dagan and the snowman remain my earliest. Working on this confession, trying to remember everything I can, I am sometimes surprised to find myself recalling what appears to be nothing more than a simple lump of wax, doubtless the trimmings from someone's tabulum. The memory surfaces, when it surfaces, unattached to any other. I don't know who would have given me such a thing or why the thought of it after all these years has the power to move me so, to make my mouth water as though I recalled not a useless bit of wax but a particularly choice piece of food. Perhaps, in the world of rules and obedience I had been dropped into, the thing's magic lay in the fact that it was malleable, that warming it in the palm of my hand I could force it to adopt whatever shape I liked…though I think color played a part as well, the subtle changes in hue wax may undergo if you observe it closely in the light. At any rate, whatever the attraction—and though I know it would have been wrong of me—I think I must have kept the thing, hidden it away in my bed, for the memory is often accompanied by a dim recollection of the scent (old, familiar, comforting) of my first mattress, a smell replaced almost immediately by the lighter more volatile scent of the wax itself, a fragrance which, nowadays, I associate with words, tabula, the material upon which I scratch out this draft.

When I try to remember how the abbey itself looked in those first days, it is not at all as you would expect. When we picture Redestone, we see the cloister, don't we, the green of the garth, the church on one side, the refectory, dortoir, and abbot's lodge on the other? We

create in our minds a clear, if simple, view of the place. But this is
not the way a child sees it, or at least not a very small child. When I
remember my first days at Redestone, I see not a grand plan of abbey
and grounds, but, rather, a series of seemingly insignificant images
(the view from a window I was just tall enough to reach, a mossy
bit of flagstone walk, the place in the church's south wall where, at
mid-morning, the stones became warm and rosy), these were the reference points of my life, the little places that, in the aggregate, added
up to my idea of the world. If the sun passed behind Modra nect
each afternoon then as it does now, dousing the garth in shadow, I
made no connection between the mountain and the change in light
(if asked, I would have guessed, I suppose, that everywhere the world
grew dim at the approach of Vespers). I must have been aware of
the great terrace our monastery sits upon, must have seen the fields
below, the village beyond, but I don't remember ever looking at these
things—at least not in that first year or two—certainly don't remember ever thinking about them. I thought about food. I thought about
the place at table where I sat. I thought about my bed. I thought
about the spot along the church wall that on sunny mornings grew
warm and rosy in the light.

As using a stylus to scratch out my tale upon this wax has reminded
me of Father Dagan (the styli he used to make the arms on my first
snowman), so, in a similar fashion, remembering my earliest images of
Redestone brings Oftfor to mind, the absurd little tour I gave him the
day we met, the things I said. As it happens, this is the same Oftfor
that would eventually become so famous, though on the occasion I
am remembering he was still just a boy like me, looking, as I recall it
now, rather small and underfed. Though I can't be sure, my guess is it
was the day of his oblation. It makes sense. I have a vague memory of
strangers having been at the abbey at that time, the intense interest I
always felt in grown-ups that weren't monks. And making it the day
of Oftfor's oblation would explain why the two of us were out there
alone on the garth like that, unobserved by anyone but the young
postulant set to watch over us. Doubtless everyone else was inside,
in the church, participating in the rite of donation—something we

would have been judged too young to understand. The postulant was, I believe…. Yes. Yes, of course it was. It was Dudda.

Dudda said we weren't to run, which seemed unfair as we hadn't been running, only walking fast.

I looked back at the little boy. He looked happy. His cheeks were red, either from the cold or the exertion, and, if he wasn't smiling, at least he wasn't actively crying anymore either. I wished he would wipe his nose. He could get into trouble for that if Brother Baldwin saw him. But there was so much the boy could get into trouble for; he was really quite hopeless. And loud! The brothers were always complaining about how loud I was, but until today I hadn't realized just how loud and noisy a little boy could be. I pointed at the refectory.

Oftfor looked at the building and then took two quick excited steps toward it. He stopped, looked back at me.

I shook my head.

He frowned, looked once more at the refectory, then back at me.

Again I pointed at the building; then, flexing my hand at the knuckles while keeping my fingers straight, I made the first of the two signs. It looked more like a roof when Father Dagan did it.

Oftfor's forehead grew surprisingly wrinkled, like an old man's.

I frowned, shook my head: *Pay attention!* Again I made the roof-shape Father Dagan had taught me, then I brought my fingers to my lips, opening my mouth wide to make it clear what I was doing.

Oftfor's eyes grew large. "What have you got?" he asked, the question booming off the cloister walls.

I tossed a quick glance over at Dudda and was relieved to see he was no longer watching us, was, instead, peering in at the church door. I looked back at Oftfor, shook my head. "No!" I whispered. "It's how we're supposed to talk."

Puzzlement.

"With our hands!"

Oftfor looked at me as if I'd told him hot was cold, cold hot.

"Because of the silence!" I said aloud, wishing Dudda *would* look over here now, see how hard this was, how hard I was working to bring the new boy into line.

"The silence?"

I smiled, a teacher proud of his pupil's first success. "Yes. The silence." I began to whisper again. "We can't talk because of the silence, so we have to use our fingers."

The boy frowned. "Why can't we talk?" he asked, whispering himself now. "Have we done something wrong?"

"No, of course not. Unless we talk."

Oftfor looked suddenly frightened, as if I'd said something mad.

"No, no, it's all right!" Why was this so difficult? Why did it make perfect sense when Father Dagan said it and none at all when I did? "We can't talk because we're monks, because monks don't talk, they chant. It's what monks are for."

"We're not monks. We're little…"

"No, no I know. I mean I know we're not monks, we're oblates."

"We're…?"

"Oblates," I said, proud of the ease with which I now pronounced the word.

"What's a…an…."

But I hurried on before Oftfor could finish that question (let Father Dagan answer that one). "Monks don't talk because they chant instead. That's what monks are for."

"Monks are for chanting," Oftfor said dubiously, a child repeating his lessons.

"Chanting and praying."

The boy cast a wide-eyed glance over at Dudda. "That's all they do!?"

"Well no, of course not. I mean they work too. Listen, do you want to learn this or not?"

"What?"

"The signs!" I said, "The way we talk with our hands!" I indicated the cloister with what seemed to me a particularly grown-up sweep of the arm.

Oftfor flinched as if from a blow.

"What? Did you think I was going to hit you?!"

Oftfor just looked at me, chin thrust forward bravely but dimpled now, quivering.

"No, it's all right," I said, confused by this, the unexpected feelings it engendered (Father had said I was to look after this boy, that he was now, in a sense, my little brother). "Look, it's simple. The way you make a building's name is by making first the sign for roof, and then the sign for whatever you do in that building."

Still on the verge of tears but trying hard to be a good little boy, Oftfor gave me a bit of a nod.

"We *eat* in the refectory," I said, watching him closely now, not at all sure he was following this. "So the way you say 'refectory' is...." I made the roof-shape again, then, careful to make the movement seem non-threatening, brought my fingers to my lips. "See...? Like someone eating?"

Oftfor looked from my hand to my mouth and then back at my hand again, utterly bewildered.

"So this," I said, repeating the signs a second time, "means 'refectory'!"

Oftfor watched my hand a moment longer, as one might a snake, then, frowning, looked back at the refectory. "The reflectory," he said thoughtfully.

What could you do?

But I didn't give up, wouldn't give up (Father expected this of me!). Since the boy was clearly slow, I'd have to start with something a little easier. I pointed at the church. "You know what that is, don't you?"

Oftfor looked at the great stone building, the breathy sound of the chant just then rising from its interior. "The church?" he said.

"Right. The church. So the sign for it is.... Remember? First you make the sign for roof...." I did so. "Then you make the sign for what you do beneath that roof...." I brought my hands together, palm-to-palm, before my lips. By my calculation even the dullest of boys must know the sign for prayer.

For the first time, Oftfor smiled. "The church!" he said with a little laugh.

I held a finger up but smiled too. "Yes," I whispered, more sure of myself now, "the church."

Once more I made the two signs and, this time, Oftfor repeated them for me. The boy's roof looked more like a turtle than a roof, but, still…Father Dagan was going to be so proud of me!

"All right, now look back at the refectory," I said, thinking it was time to try something a little more difficult.

Oftfor turned and looked.

"See the building next to it?"

Oftfor glanced from the refectory to the dortoir and then, uncertainly, back at the refectory. I had never noticed before how much the two buildings resembled each other.

"The refectory's the one on the right, the one on the left's the one I'm talking about. It's the dortoir."

"The…."

"The dortoir."

For a moment or two Oftfor studied the dortoir's simple earthen façade as one might a great mystery, then, apparently growing tired of this, let his attention wander to the diggings next-door. "Why's there that hole?" he asked.

"Oh, that," I said, pleased to show off my newfound knowledge. "That's where they're going to put the abbot's lodgings."

"What are those?"

Truth be told, I hadn't a clue. When I'd first heard the phrase, something about the way it had been said made me think of hurdles (then, as now, no one liked making hurdles), but since they'd dug this surprisingly square and shallow hole I'd begun to wonder if "lodgings" might not mean something else, a kind of food maybe, something only abbots got to eat, a category of nourishment so delicate and delicious it had to be stored, like grain, in its own special pit. "Wouldn't you like to know," I said. "But it's the building next to the hole that we're talking about."

"The reflectory."

"No, the reflec…the re*fec*tory is the other building, the building on the right. The building on the left is the dortoir."

"The…."

"The dortoir's where we sleep. So the sign for dortoir is…. Remember? First we make the sign for roof…." I did so. "Then we make the sign for what we do beneath the roof...." Once more I brought my hands together palm-to-palm; then, making sure Oftfor could see what I was doing, I placed the sign for prayer against my right ear, turning it into the sign for sleep.

Oftfor nodded as if impatient now with any and all instruction. "Why's it called that?" he asked.

"Why's it called that?"

"The door place. Why's it called that?"

"Because that's what dor*toir* means. It's the building where you sleep."

"But I mean, why? If it's where you sleep, why don't they call it the bedchamber? I mean, that's what it is, isn't it? There're beds in there, aren't there?"

"Well, yes."

"Then it's the bedchamber, right?"

"Look, you want to see something else?"

And so it was that Oftfor and I, grown tired of playing pupil and pedant, became again what in fact of course we had been all along, just two little boys trying hard to entertain themselves in a world entirely not of their making. Naturally enough, I showed him all my secret places straightaway: the spot by the refectory door that had been damaged when they carried the table in, the stain on the base of the lavabo which looked, if you stood in just the right place, rather like a cow, the treasures to be found in Brother Kitchens' rubbish heap, and, of course, the place along the church's south wall where, in the early spring, it was nice to sit in the sun and feel the stones warm at your back.

As I remember it, Oftfor enjoyed our little tour. Though it seems hard to believe now, he was in those days a boy like any other, small for his age and a little timid, but otherwise perfectly willing to accept and even enjoy whatever circumstances the world presented. I remember he particularly liked the west walk. To this day I can see the look of delight that spread over his face as he stood on its flags and, for the first time, realized what he was feeling through the soles of his feet. Later I showed him a place where, if you put your eye close to an opening between two of the stones, you could see, as well as feel and hear, the dark rush of the water beneath you. It was as we knelt at this spot, the fresh smell of the race scenting the air around us, that Oftfor, in all seriousness, asked if someday we might catch fish there; and, child that I was, for a moment I remember I allowed myself to think we might.

There is of course, or at least there was, another story told from that day. Funny I should remember it after all these years. I didn't care for the thing at the time, didn't care for the way it made us look, Oftfor and me. The brothers who repeated the story were known to chuckle among themselves as they made the signs. Truth be told, I can't even promise it is true; certainly I have no memory of the exchange it pretends to describe. But I write under obedience, so let me record here, simply and without qualification, what was said. The postulant Dudda (who—it should be pointed out—was young himself then and therefore quite possibly prone to exaggeration) claimed afterwards to have overheard a portion of the instructions I gave Oftfor that day. According to this Dudda, I was saying something like "Father Dagan is Father Prior, Father Agatho is Father Abbot, Brother Baldwin is Brother Sacristan, Father Cuthwine is Father Cellarer..." when, supposedly, Oftfor interrupted me. "Are there any mothers?" he asked.

III

have other memories from those first years. I could, I suppose, fill an entire book with such childish remembrances. But so could many others, and I write under obedience: Father Abbot has ordered me to give an account of the events that led up to my sin. And so I move now to a day, perhaps a year or two later, when I received my first inkling of the role I would someday be called to fill, the mission I would so basely abuse. By that time there were four of us. I came first. No one, not even Waldhere, would deny that. When we oblates marched into church, I stood at the head of our little line. But in truth, if not in precedence, Waldhere came first. He was the oldest among us and, at least for a while, the tallest as well. Not surprisingly then it was he who led us that day—all eyes and expectation—out onto the garth, pointed us toward the mystery that would, in time, lead to the writing of this account. Which is not to say that it was Waldhere's fault. No. No of course it wasn't. The fault was mine. I do not claim otherwise.

I wonder now what he told us. It can't have been much. Waldhere would have understood next to nothing of what he had seen. A secret then, a hint, the suggestion of something marvellous, and we would have followed him out to the edge of the terrace, followed him to the edge of the world for that matter, followed him because he was Waldhere and we always followed him, followed him because—though secrets may be common in a community that keeps the silence—few of any consequence are known to oblates.

Though I loved Waldhere, though I loved and revered and, at times, wanted to be Waldhere, still there was a part of me that resented

Waldhere. I was first. I had lived at Redestone longer than any of them, could tell stories of a time before the abbot's lodge, before the dortoir, before even the reredorter; and so, doubtless, a part of me would have resented that excursion as well, would have resented the ease with which Waldhere had taken command, the impertinence of it, the implied reproof. It would have been like me to have said something. It would have been like me to have—in this if nothing else—taken the lead, been first to break the silence.

"Such a surprise—here it is morning and, behold, the sun rises!"

Waldhere ignored me. Like a grown-up, like one of the exalted personages that ruled over our lives, Waldhere ignored me, leaned out over the edge of the terrace, cast a long self-important glance down toward the ditch. But there was nothing there—grassy banks, the abbey path—certainly nothing to warrant my attention.

I looked back out at the fields, the village beyond. The sun had already reached the wheat, turning its surface into something soft, rosy, a gentle relief of the ground hidden beneath. Among the peas the sparrows had begun their day as well, bickering as they gleaned. But the village still lay in shadow, the sunny tops of the Far Wood rising from the haze of its cook-smoke like something in a dream, something conjured up, hardly real.

"Look!"

It was Ealhmund and he was pointing toward the village.

I shaded my eyes against the sun but at first could see nothing; then the figure of a man detached itself from the shadows, waded out into the wheat. I glanced over at Waldhere but was not surprised to find him uninterested. This was not the secret.

With little else to do, I watched as the man made his way obliquely across the field. Twice he stopped and knelt down as if looking for something. When he did this, the surface of the wheat seemed to swallow him whole, only the dark line of his progress through the dew remaining to tell you where he had to be. Each time he reëmerged, head and shoulders rising suddenly into the light, I found myself pleased, as if I had both predicted, and then personally performed, something of a miracle.

Presently the man worked his way over to the ditch. With an exaggerated step, he leapt to the other side. I expected him to turn back then toward the village, or maybe walk up toward the abbey, but he ignored the path altogether and continued on into the tall grass beyond. Which told me where he was going. Should someone run to the refectory? Should someone tell the brothers? Should I?

Two ducks rose squawking from the nearer of the ponds and flew out over the village toward the river. The man seemed only mildly surprised by the ducks. He watched as they turned over the Meolch, flying east into the cover provided by the Far Wood. As if in some obscure way he approved of the course taken by the ducks, the man gave a quick nod in their direction, and then, turning back toward the pond, began a series of elaborate gestures that made him look like a monk talking with his hands. But of course he wasn't a monk and he wasn't talking with his hands: he was pulling a net from his blouse. The four of us stood up as tall as we could but it made no difference; the man knew perfectly well where the community was at that time of day, that he need not worry about the abbey. And of course we could not yell.

"Some secret, a poacher."

Waldhere shook his head but I could tell he was beginning to have doubts himself. Which disappointed me. Though I hadn't wanted him to succeed, I also didn't want him to fail. I wanted to see something I hadn't seen before; I wanted to learn a secret.

I looked back toward the village. There were mothers in those houses. Mothers and fathers and their children. And somewhere south of here there was a house like these, a house that held my family. Or at least my father. I was Winwæd, son of Ceolwulf, and Waldhere couldn't say that. Ealhmund and Oftfor couldn't say that. No matter how many aunts and uncles they had, everyone knew they were really only orphans. Aunts and uncles didn't count: I was the only real oblate.

"There he is!" said Waldhere, and even as he said it we saw him, saw the monk emerge from behind the terrace wall, continue on his way down the abbey path. Though he shaded his eyes against the sun, the man made no attempt to disguise his walk.

"Brother Ælfhelm," said Oftfor gravely; then, apparently unsure of the importance of this, added, "He's probably just going to work in the peas."

"During Chapter?"

It was, of course, impossible. And immediately I loved Waldhere again. How had he found this out? How could anyone have discovered anything so wonderful?

"Oh he'll get a beating now," said Ealhmund, who liked beatings.

"No he won't. He goes every week."

I looked at Waldhere.

"He does! Every Sabbath!"

And for some reason I believed him. Not, I think, because Waldhere was believable or it made sense, but because it wasn't, because it was impossible, incredible, and therefore in absolute keeping with what I watched. A grown man, one of the brothers, perfectly healthy and, so far as I knew, in complete possession of his faculties, was walking down the abbey path right in the middle of Chapter. And what was more he was doing so without subterfuge. When he crossed over the ditch bridge and turned back toward us, the sun behind him now, eyes raised, he made no attempt to pull his hood up or avert his face. Anyone could have seen him! Anyone could have known!

But, then again, they couldn't, could they? They were all in Chapter. And would a villager report such a thing if he saw it? Would a villager even recognize such behavior as wrong? Villagers didn't come to Faults. Villagers weren't allowed in Chapter. How would anyone ever know?

Ælfhelm regained the terrace wall, threw a glance up at the abbot's lodge, turned and began to walk along the base of the wall toward the river, toward us.

"It's all right," whispered Waldhere. "He doesn't look up."

We all held our breath.

Ælfhelm passed beneath us.

Without looking up, Ælfhelm passed beneath us and then, crossing himself absently, passed beneath the church.

We all breathed again. Then, just as we were beginning to feel comfortable, Ælfhelm did something completely unexpected. Instead of turning back east and following the river down toward the village, he stepped out onto Wilfrid's bridge.

"He's going for wood," whispered Oftfor, and, just as quickly, Waldhere whispered back, "Without a cart?"

"But I like Brother Ælfhelm, I like his stories."

"Too bad," said Waldhere, "he's going anyway."

And he was. Without even stopping to think about it, Ælfhelm crossed the bridge and walked right into the belly of the great North Wood.

Of course there was quite a debate after that. The four of us stood at the end of the garth and argued the case like four old farmers arguing over a cow—each of us sure he was right, sure he was the one who knew what Ælfhelm was up to. Not that it really mattered. Apostate or spy, the man had broken the Rule—one of the adults, one of the spotless ones, had a spot, a secret, and we all now knew it.

For weeks after that I thought about Ælfhelm, pictured him as he made his way down the abbey path, passed beneath the refectory window. I could imagine what it would be like, the sounds that would come from that window, the voices—maybe Prior Dagan asking a question, Father Abbot clearing his throat, saying something you couldn't quite hear. It was pleasant lying in bed and thinking about that, picturing Brother Ælfhelm, secure in the knowledge that he (and he alone) would suffer the consequences of his actions. Many's the night I drifted off dreaming of trespass and the great North Wood.

IV

I suppose the bad times really began with the furnace master's speech. I mean, when people think about the bad times—if they allow themselves to think about them at all—that is probably what they think of first, the speech, the fact that it was the furnace master who told them what was going to happen. Indeed, I sometimes wonder if that was the beginning of Victricius's own personal bad times as well. It makes sense. No one likes to hear such news, and especially not from a foreigner. But I write under obedience. I must record only what I can attest to, and I cannot attest to this. I was still too young for Chapter then; I never heard the famous speech. No, when I remember the bad times, I think not of the furnace master but of the little one, of poor little Oftfor. And not for the reasons you think. I remember Oftfor not for what he became but for what he was, the boy I knew, the living breathing child.

That was a wet year. The rains came early that spring and continued well into the haying. When it rained hard we knelt in church and prayed for better weather, and when it rained less hard, we pulled our hoods up, gave thanks to God, and marched out into the peas, our woolens still weighted with the previous day's mud. By the end of that summer there were brothers whose feet were so swollen and white from the damp it was said they looked more like fish than feet. Brother Tunbert lost some toes.

Still, when I think of that year, the end of that summer, I think first not of bad weather but of good, of a day that dawned so bright and clear it seems now to mock all that came after. I remember colors—turf, lichen, moss—I remember a high blue almost winter sky.

I remember Oftfor. Oftfor stands in the angle created by sanctuary and apse, russet walls steaming at his back, sunlight everywhere,
sparkling. The boy raises an arm. He must have been wearing woolens too big for him for, in my memory, as he raises his arm, the opposite shoulder (frail, bony, white) always slips incongruously from the
neck of his garment. He smiles. As if embarrassed, as if unsure of the
importance of what he has to show me, Oftfor smiles. It's a squirrel.
A dead squirrel. Oftfor is standing in the angle created by sanctuary
and apse and he is holding a dead squirrel up by its tail. The thing
hangs in the air by Oftfor's left ear, its eyes caked, useless, perfect
little feet clutching at nothing.

And then, always, whether I like it or not, a second memory
intrudes upon the first. This time we are in the reredorter and I am
feeling disappointed. Despite myself, despite conscience, the horror
of what Oftfor has shown me, I am thinking of myself, realizing that
I've been tricked, betrayed, that this had nothing to do with food,
that I shall not be gorging myself anytime soon on illicit food.

Not that it began in the reredorter. No. No, of course it didn't. It
began in the dortoir.

Which probably explains Waldhere and Ealhmund's absence.
I mean we must have left them in the dortoir. Doubtless I didn't
want to share, doubtless this too reflects an essential poverty of spirit.
Still, if that is true, if they were there—convenient, handy—why
choose me? Given Waldhere's natural gifts, the obduracy that made
Ealhmund as trustworthy a receptacle for secrets as a wooden box,
why did Oftfor turn to me? Why burden me with this memory? I do
not know. It makes no sense. Yet that is what happened. Even now
I can see him standing there, back to the wall, hands behind him as
if hiding something. I think I must have given him a look or signed
something derisive because I remember his forehead crumpling—and
that does make sense, does fit with my memory of the boy, Oftfor's
forehead having been, in its way, as supple an organ of expression
as most people's eyes or mouth. And on this occasion it crumpled
uncertainly. He looked at me. Forehead crumpled, Oftfor looked at
me, raised a hand, walked two fingers quickly through the air.

I shook my head, *No*. Dudda had already explained that. The dead animals were a sign, he'd told us, an omen. They'd said so in Chapter. All the little corpses meant Death was coming, that Death was coming and it rode on the air like a horse. The part about the horse hadn't made sense to me, but Dudda said he was just repeating what the furnace master had said. Dudda said the furnace master told them there were different kinds of airs, just as there are different kinds of horses, and that bad airs, like the one Death rode, were heavier than good airs. He said this was why Oftfor had found so many dead squirrels and mice, and why all the village dogs were dying. He said that, being smaller than people, living closer to the ground, these animals were more susceptible to heavy low-lying airs. But now that Death had killed all the little animals, it was going to rise. According to Dudda, the whole valley was filling up with Death like a bowl filling up with water. He said the bad air was at our knees now but soon would rise to our necks and then our heads. Waldhere had made a joke about this. He'd said that Oftfor would die first and then me and then Ealhmund. He said he would last the longest because he was the tallest. He laughed when he said it but you could tell he didn't really think it was funny. Which was why I didn't want to go to the reredorter. *No!* I shook my head, *No!*

Oftfor closed his eyes, opened them again. He turned his head, looked down the length of the wall at his back. I looked down that way but there was nothing to see, just beds, a few windows, the gray and rainy light. Oftfor looked back at me, his expression different now, changed, a decision of some sort apparently made. He brought his hands from behind his back. He was holding a piece of bread.

I glanced over at the door, made sure it was closed, then stood up, walked to the nearest window. The garth was reassuringly empty. I looked back at Oftfor, smiled. He entered the reredorter ahead of me.

We'd been using the necessarium ever since Hlothberht caught us digging graves behind the lavabo. I had no idea why Oftfor took such pleasure in searching out and finding the dead animals, but, whatever the reason, the resulting funerals had provided something of a diversion. Or at least they had until now. Now that we knew what each of these deaths signified, how much closer they brought us to Dudda's full bowl of water, I was—I think for understandable reasons—less interested in make-believe. A few brief words, maybe a priestly gesture or two, and then I was going to tip whatever bundle of fur and bones Oftfor had found this time down the nearest hole *and eat that bread!*

Oftfor took up a position by the window, arms firmly at his sides, neither bread nor beast in evidence. Something about his posture made me think he was planning on being the priest, but—food or no food—I wasn't going to let that happen. Heretofore Waldhere had filled that role; this time it was my turn.

Oftfor raised an arm.

Before I could stop him or object, Oftfor raised an arm and—his sleeve slipping down toward his shoulder—the little room filled suddenly with a bad smell.

"What's that?!"

The skin on Oftfor's forehead drew taut like the skin of a drum. He pointed at the inside of his elbow.

I took a hesitant step closer (the smell was really quite offensive) and was able to see a small dark spot where Oftfor pointed. The thing looked too black to be part of his skin.

"Did you burn yourself?"

Oftfor shook his head.

I came closer still, breathing through my mouth. "Did something bite you?"

"I don't think so."

"Well cover it up and we'll show Father Prior."

Oftfor pulled his sleeve down and I turned to go, the bread crowding once more into my thoughts, making me a little angry with Oftfor, this smell, the fact that now, hungry as I was, I was going to have to go without, help him with this.

"Wait."

I turned around, ready to say something.

The skin on Oftfor's forehead drew taut once more, then, abruptly, curdled. Looking at me, never taking his eyes off me, he reached down and jerked up his woolens.

I turned away in disgust.

A small hand grasped my sleeve.

More disgust, and, with it now, the first touch of horror. I jerked away. Was there something wrong with Oftfor? Did he think he needed me to stand guard while he made water? I jerked away, spun around, the look on my face daring him to try that again.

Oftfor appeared as shocked as I, eyebrows raised in a show of almost comic fright.

I stared at him.

Oftfor glanced down and, despite myself, despite the fact I knew I didn't want to, that I would do almost anything to avoid looking down there, I followed his gaze. Along the crease created where Oftfor's left leg joined his body, a small line of welts stood out like the sting of a whip, rebuke to my curiosity.

"A rash?" I asked, my voice sounding suddenly different, wrong, a voice belonging to someone else.

"I don't know. They weren't there yesterday."

I shrugged, anxious now to leave, to get out of there, the room suddenly too small, its roof too close, the once pleasant sound of rain on thatch now become something else entirely, a mad irreligious chant.

Oftfor looked back down at his groin, woolens held up around his chin like a bib. "I don't know Winwæd," he said, shaking his head like an old man shaking his head over an apple gone bad, "but I think I'm going to die."

V

n my memory of that night the moon makes a sound as it rises. I know that cannot be, that it's impossible, but that is the way I remember it. The thing is big, too big, and it seems to make a sort of noise as it rises over the Far Wood. In a fever you can sometimes get a noise like the noise I am remembering. It is a steady sound, constant, irritating, as though someone were humming beneath his breath right behind you. But in a fever of course no one is really humming. You can stop your ears with your fingers but it will make no difference for the sound is not in your ears, it is in your head. This is the sort of sound I remember hearing that night as we came out of Vigil. I don't think we really heard it. I don't think it was possible we could have heard the sound that soon, that far away. But that is the way I remember it—the garth, the moon, the mindless sound of someone humming.

And then of course we entered the dortoir and whether or not we'd really heard the humming out on the garth we certainly heard it then. Though Eadnoth sat at the far end of the hall, there is no doubt in my mind that we heard the humming from the moment we first stepped through the door. And that nothing happened. For that is another strange thing about that night, the fact that, so far as I can recall, no one did anything about it. No one said anything or went down to where Eadnoth sat to remonstrate with him. No one even seemed upset by the fact that Brother had so clearly missed the Vigil.

Which, looking back on it now, makes a sort of sense. I mean, when you think about it, you can see how this could have happened. The older monks, all the senior monks, certainly all the obedientiaries, would have been keeping the long watch: they would still have been in church, praying. The community that marched with me across the garth that night would have been young, novices and postulants for the most part—children really, children unprepared for such a thing, children taught daily to do as they'd been told, to follow orders, not give them.

And so they went to bed. Despite the sound, despite the sound and the vision of what sat at the far end of our hall, the grown-ups did nothing, behaved as though all of this were perfectly normal, knelt, said final prayers, went to bed. I'll never forget that. I'll never forget what it was like to walk down that hall (longer then than at any other time in my life), dim figures on either side of me casually going about their business, moving in and out of the moonlight, the fire-light, climbing into bed, pulling the covers up, while down at the end of the hall, down where all could surely see him, (*down where I must go*)—Brother Eadnoth sat covered with spots, humming to the moon.

Later that night others came down with the illness. I came down with the illness. At some point someone must finally have sent for the obedientiaries, or at least for Brother Sacristan, for I remember that, remember the sweet scent of incense blooming suddenly upon the air of that place. I think it was then that Brother Hewald stood on his bed, stretched his arms out like the Christ's, began to pray aloud. I had never seen anyone pray like that before and so I remember it— the unsettling scent (wrong, out-of-place), Brother standing on his bed, back to the wall, legs and feet bathed in moonlight, upper parts vague, indistinct, something as much imagined as seen.

I remember little else from that night. We must have gotten up for Matins, chanted, returned to bed—but I don't remember doing so. At some point I slept. I know that for I remember waking, remember the odd sense of dislocation I experienced, the smell, the feeling that something was not right, that something was out-of-place, missing; and then the even stranger sensation when I realized what it was. Except for the sounds one expects to hear at the end of the interval (the rustling of bedclothes, the quiet tread of feet), the dortoir had returned to its normal state of silence; Eadnoth had stopped humming. I looked over at his place but was not surprised to find him gone. Father Abbot must have him. Father Abbot must have him and now everything would be all right. There would be punishments of course. There would have to be—punishments, expiation, Faults—but that was as it should be. And everything would be all right. Eadnoth would be well again. He had stopped humming.

It wasn't till we were outside, lining up for Prime, that I saw what had really happened, saw the two bodies leaning up against the wall of the dortoir. It had begun to rain again. After the clear night, it had begun to rain again, and I remember how strange it was to see Eadnoth and Sigeberht sitting there like that, side by side, staring down at the water pouring off the roof onto their feet. I thought they might say something. To my childish mind it seemed likely they might speak. They looked that way. Their faces I mean, they looked as though they might say something, as if, after all those years of quiet forbearance, now, here, sitting with their feet in the rain, they might have something to say.

But it was Ealhmund who broke the silence. As if struck himself by the nature of the dead men's predicament, Ealhmund—poor slow-witted Ealhmund—laughed.

And we turned on him. Anxious, wet, afraid—Waldhere, Oftfor, and I spun around there at the end of the line, glared at the most junior member of our company. But Ealhmund was unimpressed by our disapproval. Laughing shamelessly, he raised a finger, pointed it at me.

But *I* hadn't done anything! I spun back around, faced the rest of the community: *I didn't do anything!*

A movement, a jostling further up the line, brothers stepping aside, making way for someone, heads bowing, whole bodies, monks stepping out into the rain, hoods up, heads down; and then Father Dagan was among us, looking from me to the corpses, to Ealhmund, then back to me again.

I started to raise my hands but before I could sign to him, make my lord prior understand that it wasn't me, that I hadn't done anything, he took hold of my chin as one might take hold of something that belongs to one and, not ungently, turned it to the side, exposing a portion of my neck.

I reached up.

Father flinched, but I reached up anyway, touched what he had exposed. There was a crust. There was a tumescence. I released it. Repelled, I released what I had touched and, even as I did so, felt it respond, resume some sort of loathsome shape.

Father smiled. Not looking at me, still studying that which he had found, Father smiled, acknowledged what we both now knew.

I turned my eyes from him. Telling myself I did not care, that it was all right to have one's head held like this, that Father knew what he was doing, that I could trust him, I turned my eyes from him, stared down at a puddle bubbling in the rain.

But it wasn't true; I did care. And for once I wasn't entirely sure I could trust Father Prior. I was afraid he was going to tell me I must die. I was afraid he was going to make me go and sit next to Eadnoth and Sigeberht.

Father released my chin. He looked at me, smiled in a way that did not seem quite right. "You're going to be all right," he said, pulling my hood up, smoothing it down around my face. "But I want you to go back to bed now." He nodded as if in answer to some question I had not asked. "It's all right," he said, "we'll say the office for you."

I assumed custody of the eyes, bowed, turned, stepped back toward the door. Though I knew I shouldn't, though I knew Father would think it an impertinence, I nevertheless glanced down one last time at Eadnoth as I passed over the threshold. On Brother's neck lay a black and crusty-looking excrescence.

VI

fter that the memories become vague, confused, Vespers following Vigil, the Vigil Prime. I awoke at midday, again at dusk, slept through the night, perhaps the next day, only to awaken again in full dark, febrile colors, shapes, moving about the dortoir, the smell of incense mingling uneasily with that of disease. I saw things. I heard things. What dreams I had swam so far beneath the surface of sleep—and I had to rise through so many layers to escape them—they seemed upon waking more like memories than dreams, something that happened long ago in a world both wrong and, at the same time, somehow, moaning.

Still, the memories persist. The suggestion of a correspondence—a sound, the scent of incense detected in the wrong place at the wrong time—and I am back there again, the memories as fresh and vivid, as unavoidable, as the air one breathes, the sin one is born with. And some of them, surely some of them, are true. What happened to Oftfor for instance—other people saw that, other people were there, can, and readily will, attest to what I record here. But as for the rest, well, who's to say? I think these things happened. At the time I was almost certain they were happening. But now…well, now all I can say for sure is that when I call them to mind, dredge them up from wherever it is such things live, they look like truth, bear, if not its conviction, at least a good imitation of that virtue's manner and dress. I remember well, for instance, the way my eyes ached when I opened them that day, and how, more than anything, I wanted to close them again, to bathe them in sleep, forgetfulness, but that I couldn't, *couldn't*, because, it seemed, someone was there.

But that was impossible.

I opened my eyes again, forced myself to look.

And there did seem to be someone there.

So maybe he was dying. Maybe Oftfor was dying and someone had already been sent to keep watch by his bed, to wait and see if he saw anything, reported anything, as he passed over.

I pulled myself up on an elbow and—though my head ached—I could see that it was true, that there really was someone lying on the floor by Oftfor's bed. Though it couldn't be, it looked like Brother Baldwin.

I lay back down, looked up at the ceiling, watched as, one by one, the rafters took flight, began to turn slowly in the air over my bed. I closed my eyes and the rafters were replaced by the spaces that lay between them, pale ghostly rafters that took up the dance precisely where their partners left off.

I opened my eyes again, tried to focus on the far wall. As if leveling my gaze also in some way leveled my spirit, the spinning came to a halt and my eyes rested on the figure of Oftfor. For some reason something about the way the boy lay on his bed touched me and I found myself subject to an unexpected emotion. I sat up a little, looked once more at the tiny body lying across from my own. Oftfor's eyes were closed but I could tell by the way his lips were moving that he was saying his prayers. I remembered the time he had woken half the dortoir calling out for his mother in his sleep and I hoped that now, in his delirium, he wasn't praying aloud. A part of me wondered if I should get up and go over there, warn him of the danger that lay listening on the floor by his bed. But the thought itself fatigued me. I lay back down, closed my eyes, was pleased to discover the spinning now entirely at an end. I told myself I would rest for a while, regain my strength, and then—then I promised myself—I would get up and go over there, warn and protect my fellow oblate.

But the next time I awoke, I was surprised all over again to discover Brother Baldwin lying on the floor by Oftfor's bed.

I don't know how many times this happened, how many times I awoke to make such a discovery, but memory tells me it was often, a succession of like images repeating themselves down a long dark corridor. Of these, one in particular still haunts me, still holds the power after all these years to shock and, vaguely, to repel me. For I seem to have seen the skin at the back of Brother's tonsure move. Now I know this is unlikely. Surely no one—not even a child whose senses have been enhanced by fever—could hope to have seen so fine a movement at so great a remove. Yet that is the way I remember it, the old man's shoulders raised slightly as if bracing himself against some effort, the delicate muscles at the back of his tonsure causing his scalp to shift and wrinkle slightly. At the time it looked for all the world as if Brother were chewing on something. And though I knew such a notion preposterous, still I couldn't help thinking I'd caught him in the act, that, even as I watched, the good brother was worrying at something he'd found on the floor there by Oftfor's bed, trying to lap it up quickly, furtively, before anyone else could steal it away.

"You're going to live! Oftfor says so, you and Ealhmund too!"
I smiled.
"He did, Brother Baldwin told us."
I smiled, went back to sleep.
Someone shook me. "Did you hear me?"
It was Waldhere. Waldhere was sitting on my bed. He was talking about something.
"Did you hear me?"
I shook my head.
"I said you're going to live. Oftfor says you're going to live."
I'm going to live.
"Baldwin told us about it but Oftfor said it."
I just looked at Waldhere. He had said I was going to live.
"Yes, *Baldwin*. He likes him now. I mean I think he likes him now. You can tell, because he spends all his time over there on the floor by his bed."

By his bed?

"Like a supplicant."

"A supplicant?"

Waldhere nodded and I knew immediately there was something wrong, that there was something wrong with everything he was telling me (including, perhaps, that I should live) for Baldwin couldn't be a supplicant. Supplicants were bad monks. Supplicants had to crawl from table to table like babies and beg for their food. But not Brother Baldwin. Brother Baldwin never had to do anything he didn't want to do.

Still, there had been something like that once. A dream or something. I pulled myself up on an elbow, looked across the hall. The floor by Oftfor's bed was empty.

Waldhere smiled. "Sext," he said, as though he were used to people being unaware of the time. "I don't have to go anymore."

I looked at him.

"I don't, Father Prior said so. Except for Mass. Someone's got to look after things."

The way Waldhere said this scared me. The way he looked down the hall as if he were Father Dagan when he said it scared me. For the hundredth time that day, I touched the lumps beneath my arm. "He says I'm going to live?"

For a moment I thought Waldhere might be scared too, but then he smiled and nodded. "And he's seen heaven. Baldwin says so. He says everyone's there, everyone who's died."

"But I'm going to live?"

"Yes. Yes, you're going to live but..." Waldhere looked across the hall. Oftfor was asleep, the shape of his arms just visible through the bedclothes. "But he's going to die. Everyone else is going to live except Oftfor. He told Baldwin. He said he still has to die."

I don't really remember the viaticum. Waldhere says I was awake, but I don't remember it. I do remember the monks. At the end, in my memory, Oftfor floats on a cloud of upturned faces, the entire community come to kneel by his bed. I also remember the light. Of course that's impossible. Oftfor's bed lay along the north wall, mine along the south, so I must have dreamt that, imagined that. Still, in my memory, the windows are open and there is a little light coming through the one over Oftfor's bed.

For a long time nothing happened; then there was the suggestion of a movement, as if all the monks closest to Oftfor had, in unison, taken a breath of air. Father Prior stood up. He leaned over the bed and, like a man who has dropped a stone to judge the depth of a well, he placed his ear over Oftfor's mouth and listened. After a moment or two, he pulled back, looked over at Father Abbot, nodded. Father Abbot pursed his lips in that way he had, looked back at Oftfor. The boy's forehead was smooth now, untroubled, his eyes focused on something distant. Father Prior leaned forward again. He kissed Oftfor and immediately, as if a flock of birds had broken into the hall, the air of the dortoir was filled with the sound of wings. We all looked up but it was too late; Oftfor was gone.

VII

owadays everyone knows Oftfor's story, how he saw heaven and predicted the future. We hear such tales all the time and accept them without thinking about them, though it's not like that when the story itself takes place. When everyone told me I was going to live, that the little saint had said I would recover, I wanted to believe them. I wanted to believe them very much; but I didn't. Not in my heart. I knew Oftfor; he was no saint: he was the little boy who slept across from me, the one who liked to play with dead animals, the one who once stole a piece of bread.

But of course I was wrong to think that way. Oftfor *was* a saint, must have been, for we did recover. All those infected but still living at the time of his death regained their strength; however haltingly, we returned to our duties, our lives, the Rule. I can still remember the first time I was able to get up, go to the reredorter by myself, what it felt like to sit in that place and look out the window, watch a breeze move across the southern slope of Modra nect. At the time even so simple a thing as the way the trees turned and changed in the path of that breeze, going from dark to light and then back to dark again, struck me as remarkable.

We buried a little over half our community that year. All the able-bodied were needed to save what could be saved of the harvest, so we oblates had to help the older monks dig the graves. We didn't have time to sew up the hoods. We carried the bodies out one by one and buried them on the garth. Their names were:

Oslac, an old man.

Fursa, who had been cellarer under Abbot Folian.

Ælfwine, who sang well.

Hlothberht, who had charge of Redestone's oxen.

Cuthwine, priest and cellarer.

Cerdic, who had changed his name.

Wihtred, who snored.

Rædwald, who had a special devotion to the Blessed
     Mother.

Guthere, who was lame.

Eadbald, who had charge of Redestone's kitchens.

Osberht, said to have been among those baptized by
     St. Paulinus at the River Glen.

Byrhtnoth, a priest.

Eatta, another priest.

Ceolwulf, who carried my father's name.

Leofgar, who suffered from earaches.

Ælfhelm, poet and servant to Gwynedd.

Hrothweard, who had a scar.

Wulfred, whose name alone is now recalled.

Wiglaf, who was a Mercian.

Plegmund, whose spear and shield are buried in the abbey
     orchard.

Eadnoth, who slept in the bed next but one to mine.

Beornred, whom no one knew was ill.

Torhtmund, who was Sigeberht's brother.

Dudda, who liked pancakes.

Sigeberht, the first to die.

Ceawlin, who had only just entered the monastery.

Oftfor.

I do not know the names of the people who died in the village but there were many. Father Cuthwine watched over them until he too became ill. After that, some probably died without a priest. There were so many dying then and there were not enough priests.

That year, for lack of able-bodied men, most of our crop rotted in the field.

VIII

he abbot's lodge. The name alone signifies. Yet I who saw that building's construction may now live long enough to see its name, possibly even the building itself, fall into disuse! Should Father Abbot actually follow through with his plans, move permanently into the dortoir with the rest of us, what do you suppose will become of it? Guesthouse, granary, storeroom, shed—it can never be the same. Still, so long as we live, we who remember what a summons thence could mean, memory must lodge there if nothing else...the dark, the cold, the fear, the smell.

The smell.

I knew what that was.

But I didn't want to think about that.

I hugged myself. It was cold in here, colder than any of the other buildings. Where Father Abbot came from the Rule didn't permit fires except for cooking; monks in that land were stronger than us, tougher. Father Abbot probably didn't even need a fire. Which was why they stored the woolens in here, and the vestments, and, sometimes, a portion of the harvest, because it was cooler in the abbot's lodge, drier, because things were less liable to rot.

Which made me remember despite myself. I wondered if the smell would persist. Come the haying, when they handed out the fresh woolens, would the brothers remark upon it? Would they remember what had been stored here?

A noise as of teeth being ripped from their sockets and my heart skipped.

It was Father Dagan, hand still holding the curtain aside, eyes wide, questioning.

But he didn't say anything. He didn't ask if he'd frightened me. He looked at me, nodded once, and then, pressing the curtain further aside, the noise insignificant now, a commonplace, he indicated I should enter.

I stepped through, covered my eyes.

The figure of the abbot stood before an open window, light pouring in around it like cold air.

I knelt down and the floor was hard and cold but I could see better. No one said anything. The abbot's feet were flat and the spaces between his toes too wide. I wondered if the furnace master (who was from the same country as Father Abbot) had feet this flat, toes spread this wide.

"Do you know why you are here?"

I nodded. Ealhmund had started it, but there was no point in making excuses now.

Father Abbot said something I had trouble understanding for he spoke in the Roman tongue; but, thankfully, Father Prior replied in our own. "Winwæd," he said, "has no idea why he is here." You could tell from the way he said it that he was talking to me as much as to Father Abbot.

Father Abbot's attention returned to me. "You are called Winwæd?"

He didn't pronounce it right but I nodded anyway.

"A peculiar name."

I assumed custody of the eyes.

"Were you there yesterday?"

I nodded. The beggars, he meant the beggars.

"Someday they may not go so easily."

The beggars had appeared toward the end of winter. At first they'd seemed more spirits than men, hanging about the edge of the wood, shifting in and out among the trees. Then the villagers began to complain of them: a scythe went missing, a basket full of eggs. Yesterday, for the first time, they'd invaded the abbey precincts. By the time we oblates had gotten there most of the excitement was over, but you could still tell what had happened. A dun-colored spray of grain lay fanned out on the ground, one of Botulf's pits open beside it, broken bits of seal scattered all around. A group of beggars stood by the gate, empty-handed, eyeing the grain. A slightly larger group of monks stood between them and the pit. You couldn't really hear what the beggars said when they spoke to one another, but you couldn't miss what they said to the monks. Of course the monks paid them no heed. They were monks. They kept the silence. After a while the beggars simply gave up and went away.

"But of course you know about Ælfhelm."

I blinked, remembered myself, nodded emphatically.

"You helped with the digging didn't you?"

Again I nodded, trying to look like someone who'd been paying attention, wondering how Father had gotten onto this subject, wondering if he too was bothered by the smell.

"Well at first we thought they both were dead. When Ælfhelm didn't come back, it was…. Well it was only natural, wasn't it, what with so many dying? But Brother Tatwine surprised us." Father Abbot looked at me. "They brought only the one body down. Father Gwynedd's still alive."

I smiled for Father Abbot—who clearly thought I should be pleased with this information—while casting a desperate glance up at Father Dagan: *Father Gwynedd?*

Father Dagan frowned. "Have you been listening, Winwæd?"

I nodded but my lord prior didn't care. "Father Abbot," he said, "you asked for someone dependable, a boy who would listen and do as he was told. Forgive me, I have failed."

I lay down on my face before Abbot Agatho and then, for a while, no one said anything.

It was Father Abbot who finally broke the silence. In the voice he used when someone coughed in choir, Father asked, "Is he always so… so inattentive?"

"Occasionally," said Father Dagan. "It's been worse lately."

"Hunger."

"Yes. Yes, probably."

"Well I can't spare Tatwine anymore. I need him every day now."

Father Prior didn't say anything.

"How about one of the others? What's the tall one's name...
Wulfhere?"

"Waldhere, but I think Winwæd would be best. If he'll listen."

Nose flat against the floor, I smiled.

There was a sound as if someone had sat down and then Father
Abbot said, "Well, I don't know...it probably doesn't matter that
much either way."

Father Prior must have nodded because I didn't hear him say
anything.

"Winwæd," said the abbot.

I tried to indicate attentiveness with my back.

"Stand up and look at me when I'm talking to you."

I looked. It was Father Abbot who had moved. He was sitting on
the bed now.

"Go ahead," he said, nodding. "You have permission."

I stood up.

"Now look at me. I told you I wanted you to look at me."

I looked. Father's eyes were blue.

"Good. That's good. Now, will you listen to me?"

I nodded, *Yes*.

"Your life and the life of everyone in this monastery may depend
upon it. Do you understand?"

Everyone.

"Fine. Now you tell him Father Prior, I'm tired of your ridiculous
language."

Father Dagan smiled as if Father Abbot had said something amusing. He turned, looked out the window, eyes losing their color to the
light. "What I'm going to tell you about took place a long time ago.
Before you were born, before this building was built, before Father
Abbot even came to Redestone...." Father stopped, looked back
at me—eyes brown again, bright, commanding. "You must understand, this was a different place then. Different. It was Father Abbot
who built the Redestone we know—the terrace, the refectory, the

dortoir. But there was a time before you were born, before Father Abbot, when these things weren't here. In those days there was only the church and even it was smaller. Of course it looked big. I mean from down in the fields it looked big. Because of the ridge. In those days a ridge extended out from the base of the mountain a little way into the fields and our church sat up on its lower end. So it could look big. From down in the village it looked quite large. But it wasn't. Not really. Just a simple structure built of sticks and mud. We monks lived in a cave at the base of the ridge."

Father looked back out the window as if expecting to see the cave, that long-ago time. "Of course it's gone now, the ridge I mean, buried, like Oslac and Cuthwine, beneath our garth. Seven times we climbed that ridge, seven times we climbed back down; every day: year-in, year-out. No dortoir, no refectory, no necessarium.... It's hard to believe now. *But we weren't barbarians.*" He looked at me. "You mustn't think we were barbarians."

I didn't.

"We were monks. *Monks.* Life was hard but we kept our rule: we worked, we prayed. Every day. And on the sabbath we received our Lord. Those were good men back then, good men. We just didn't have Father Agatho yet, that's all."

I nodded and Father Abbot nodded with me. I had no idea what Father Dagan was talking about.

"Then Penda came." Father's voice grew soft. "Have you heard of Penda? Did your mother frighten you with tales of Penda?"

The suggestion of a fragrance, like flowers, and a face, like the Virgin's. I shook my head. No, no I couldn't remember any stories.

"Well she should have. Penda was a Mercian and a pagan, the cruelest, most wicked pagan of them all, and he joined forces with the Cumbrogi—not much better—to destroy our land. Many a morning we awakened to smoke on the horizon and, once, women and children spilling from the South Wood like frightened deer. Folian was abbot in those days, and Folian was afraid of Penda. He asked one of his monks, a man called Gwynedd, to climb Modra nect, keep watch from Dacca's crag. You know the crag?"

I nodded, amazed to discover there had been an abbot before Father Abbot.

"Yes, good. But it's different now. In those days it was an evil place, covered with runes and depictions of vile practices. Father Gwynedd was afraid of it. But he was a good monk. He climbed to Dacca's crag because his abbot told him to; but he was afraid."

Father looked at me. "You know, when you leave the cloister you are entirely on your own. No one keeps you safe; no one cares about you; you have no friends. The monks here at Redestone are more than teachers and masters, Winwæd, we are your family. But out there...." Father's eyes grew pale again as he looked toward the window. "Well.... And of course it was worse in those days, pagans everywhere, fighting, killing. Not that it's much better now. Father's right to send out his priests; the hill people remain a proud and stubborn race. But in those days they were also bold; we sometimes found dogs hanging from the rafters in our church, mare's blood upon the door. Gwynedd's fear was justified. Not only had the abbot sent him to live by himself in a forest full of heathen, but he had sent him to live upon one of their holiest sites, to sleep, eat, and relieve himself upon its ground. The first nights he must have had no rest at all. I remember, when the wind blew right, you could hear him up there, chanting, praying, beseeching God to protect him. It made everyone uneasy. All of us. Knowing he was up there, a goat staked out for wolves. But then a day came when we realized that, with or without the wind, we had not heard Gwynedd for some time. Of course we knew what had happened; something had killed him—pagan or wild animal, it made little difference, the result would be the same. So Abbot Folian sent a party up to retrieve the body. But the brothers came back empty-handed. Nothing was wrong, they said, Gwynedd was still alive. He had received them properly—washed their feet, begged for their prayers—but he had seemed just as pleased—content even—when they left. Very strange." Father paused to think about this. He shook his head. "Of course no one knew what it meant. Then, well, time passed, and, after a while, it became obvious Penda wasn't going to attack us that year. We've always been isolated up here, and there was no furnace then, no reason for him to take an interest in us." Father Dagan stopped, glanced over at Father Abbot to make sure it was all right for him to continue. But Father Abbot wasn't looking at Father Dagan just then, he was looking at the floor.

For a moment no one said anything. From the window came the sound of someone chopping wood. Then, as if Father Abbot had said it was all right, Father Dagan went on. "But I think it was more than our isolation that saved us; I think it was prayer. Prayer protected us then, and it will protect us now."

Father Abbot nodded at the floor. In church he sometimes called prayer "our buckler and shield."

Father Prior went on. "So, once it became obvious that Redestone was safe, Father Gwynedd came back down to the monastery. Of course everyone was glad to see him—as we are glad to see any brother after a long absence—and Gwynedd was glad to see us. But, after a while, another strange thing happened. Father Gwynedd began to miss Dacca's crag. I know it sounds incredible, to think that anyone could miss so wild and desolate a place, but Father did. And when we asked him why, he said that it was *because* it was wild and desolate."

Again Father stopped, seemed to give thought to what he had said. "You know he never even lit a fire. Of course in part this was because fire was the signal he had agreed upon with Folian, but he was afraid too. Who knew what fire might attract? Kinsman or not, the Cumbrogi would have made a meal of him. And in those days our side of the mountain was just as bad as the other. But Father liked it. Or at least he missed it. The loneliness, the lack of companionship. For the first time in his life he had placed his trust entirely in God. Entirely in God. There was no one else. No friend, no brother. But he said that was good for him, the poverty, that it forced him to abandon all attachments, to turn his face toward his Maker alone."

Father Dagan paused, shook his head. "Lying on the ground at night, afraid to sleep, afraid to even close your eyes; every sound a footfall, every noise the approach of...something. And so alone." Father looked at me. "If you cried out when they came for you they would find that amusing, entertaining, a proof of weakness. But otherwise there would be no one. No one to hold your hand. No one to kiss you good-bye. We all must die of course, but to die alone, unloved…. Well, we all thought him mad. And he looked terrible—skeletal, sun-burned, his tonsure grown in. But he said he wanted to return. He said he wanted nothing more in life than to leave it, to be left, like Isaac, on the mountaintop, alone with God."

"Careful Dagan."

Father was as surprised as I.

"Lonely mountaintops, terrible odds…. Boys love that sort of thing."

Father Prior looked back at me, surprise becoming astonishment. "Do you?" he asked.

I shook my head but Father wasn't looking at me anymore. "First it was hermits and now it's monks. Half the beggars out there claim to be displaced brothers, women clinging to them, children at their feet!" Father looked back at me. "Recite Chapter One."

Here? In front of our lord abbot?

Father's expression softened a little. "It will be all right, I'll help."

I looked over at Father Abbot and he looked back at me so I assumed custody of the eyes. For a while no one said anything and my ears grew warm. Finally, hardly believing it myself, I began.

"Louder please."

I glanced up and was horrified to see Father Dagan nodding, exchanges between abbots and oblates apparently a commonplace in his life.

I began again, my voice funny and distant but, I hoped, a little louder.

"The Holy Rule. 'Chapter One. Of the Kinds or the Life of Monks.

"'It is well known that there are four kinds of monks. The first kind is that of Cenobites, that is, the monastic, who live under a rule and an Abbot.

"'The second kind is that of Anchorites, or Hermits, that is, of those who, no longer in the first fervor of their conversion, but taught by long monastic practice and the help of many brethren, have already learned to fight against the devil; and going forth from the rank of their brethren well trained for single combat in the desert, they are able, with the help of God, to cope single-handed without the help of others, against the vices of the flesh and evil thoughts.

"'But a third and most vile class of monks is that of Sarabaites, who have been tried by no rule under the hand of a master, as gold is tried in the fire; but, soft as lead, and still keeping faith with the world by their works, they are known to belie God by their tonsure. Living in twos and threes, or even singly, without a shepherd, enclosed, not in the Lord's sheepfold, but in their own, the gratification of their desires is law unto them; because what they choose to do they call holy, but what they dislike they hold to be unlawful.

"'But the fourth class of monks is that called Landlopers, who keep going their whole life long from one province to another, staying three or four days at a time in different cells as guests. Always roving and never settled, they indulge their passions and the cravings of their appetite, and are in every way worse than the Sarabaites. It is better to pass all these over in silence than to speak of their most wretched life.

"'Therefore, passing these over, let us go on with the help of God to lay down a rule for that most valiant kind of monks, the Cenobites.'"

At first nothing happened. Then, with care—and what seemed to me infinite wisdom—our lord abbot lowered his eyelids and permitted his head to drop ever so slightly forward. Father Prior was going on about cenobites, about how much better they were than other monks, but I didn't care. Father Abbot had nodded; *he approved my recitation!*

"And anchorites, don't talk to me about anchorites! If half Northumbria's hermits were as holy as they are revered, we should all be saved. Small wonder everyone wants to be one—all honor, no rule, *no work!* But where would we be if Father Abbot let every brother who wanted to, wander off to live by himself among the trees? Who would plow our fields, sing the office, take care of you?" Father looked at me as if it were my fault he couldn't be a hermit, then looked back out the window. The chopping had stopped. Down by the peas I could hear someone encouraging an ox.

"The vow of stability is so important," Father said, "so very important. And Abbot Folian was no fool. He may have been wrong about some things, but he knew the importance of vows. So he tested Gwynedd. He told him that, in a year's time, if he still wished to live as a hermit upon Modra nect, the subject could be discussed. But until the year was up, it was not to be mentioned again. And Gwynedd didn't mention it. Not once. Not even subtly." Father looked at me. "You know, Winwæd, we don't leave all our faults at the monastery gate."

I nodded, it was one of Father's favorite expressions.

"Acts of piety aren't always done for the love of Christ. There are monks who will walk on their knees all day long for no other reason than to draw attention to themselves. But not Gwynedd. No nettles beneath his woolens, no undue fasting—he lived as he had promised to live: simply, as a monk. It seems such an easy thing—the Rule to follow, your abbot to direct you—but it requires great humility. Many attempt it, few succeed. That Gwynedd did, told Father Abbot everything he needed to know about the man. When the year was up and Gwynedd admitted he did still long for the mountain, it was old Father Abbot himself that climbed up there with him, helped to put the place in order, prepare it for such a life."

Father Prior paused, straightened a sleeve, began again. "To cleanse the site they fasted for three days, said many prayers, chanted day and night. On the fourth day they received the Host, broke their fast. It would have been a sad little celebration: Father Abbot unlikely to ever climb back up, Gwynedd forsworn from climbing down. Still, they did what they could I suppose—blessings would have been exchanged—final blessings in a sense—the kiss of peace, then the two would have parted. I don't think they ever saw each other again."

Once more Father looked out the window. "The years have come and gone since Father Gwynedd took that vow, and he has spent every single one of them by himself. Not once has he sat at our table or sung with us in choir." Father turned, looked at me. "But that doesn't mean he goes without. Though one could say he abandoned Redstone, Redstone has not abandoned him. The fraternal vow works both ways, Winwæd. Just as you have been given in perpetuity to us, so we have been given in perpetuity to you. Like Christ, nothing—not illness, not distance, not even sin—can keep us from loving and protecting you. And Father Gwynedd. Regardless of his status upon Modra nect, he remains a member of this community. Though he may be a hermit, he is our hermit and, so long as he lives, we will visit and care for him. And pray for him."

Father closed his eyes, nodded to himself. "Yes. Yes that is how I should say it. We pray for Gwynedd, just as he prays for us." The eyes sprang open again. "You mustn't think that because he is a hermit, Gwynedd's prayers are more effective than ours."

I didn't.

Father's eyes grew suspicious. "Because they aren't. God honors all prayer, farmer's or prophet's. Did Christ prefer the rich man or the poor?"

I looked at Father Prior.

"Go ahead, you have permission."

"The poor man." Twice now I had spoken in front of my lord abbot.

"That's right," said Father Prior happily, "and Father Gwynedd is rich in prayer. *Ora et labora*—you know what this means?"

I nodded.

"Prayer and work, the monk's simple call; but Gwynedd's work is his prayer. That's all he does up there, day and night. But does that make his prayer any better than ours?"

I shook my head.

"It's his craft, that's all. Does God love the mason more than the cobbler because he builds a better wall?"

Of course not!

"And so it is with Gwynedd's prayer, don't let anyone tell you differently."

I wouldn't, the idea seemed suddenly disloyal.

"Good," Father said, smiling as he did when I got my lessons right, "because simple people—people who don't understand the meaning of 'community'—can err in this way. They mistake the care we give our brother for evidence of his importance. He is excused from Chapter and allowed to live on his own. Though he neither sows nor reaps, he

eats: we bring him food; in their eyes, we wait upon him. Simple people—rustics, fools—see this as proof the man is special. They think he
is a holy man, some kind of saint." Father looked at me. "Foolishness,
vanity. Everyone wants to think they know a saint, it makes them feel
important. But Gwynedd is no more likely to be a saint than you or I.
You are to treat him with the same respect you owe everyone; nothing
more. There is nothing special about Father Gwynedd."

I looked at Father Prior. Was I to meet the hermit?

"Tell him Dagan." Father Abbot sounded impatient. "You make
everything so complicated."

Father Prior assumed custody of the eyes.

Father Abbot shrugged, looked back at me. "Ælfhelm's dead. You
know that, you buried him. He was Gwynedd's servant. Once a week
on the Sabbath he visited the hermit, brought him supplies, prayer
requests, what-have-you.... Since his death, we've sent Tatwine."
Father hesitated. His expression grew soft. "But I can't send Tatwine
anymore, you understand? I need him. I need him for the planting."

Oh yes, I understood. The eyebrows, the changed voice, the way
Father leaned toward me as he spoke. Things weren't good. Things
were so bad Father didn't have enough people to do all the work
that needed being done. It made me angry and it made me sad. I
wanted to help. I wanted very much to do something, anything, to
show Father how much I appreciated his speaking to me, how much
I loved him for talking to me, to me a mere oblate, to show him that
I understood, yes I knew, how deeply he cared for Redestone, how
much he loved us all. I smiled at him, *Yes, Father, whatever you wish, I,
Winwæd, shall accomplish it for you.*

"Good," said Father Abbot, smiling himself now, "because from
now on I am sending you in Tatwine's place. Tomorrow morning,
after Prime, you will climb to Dacca's crag."

IX

The beggars must already have begun to climb out of the Far Wood by the time Brother Tatwine and I set off, for their figures hover around my memory of that morning like the remains of some strange ground fog: gray, tattered, fading in and out among the trees. I think I also remember (though you could tell me this was the memory of a dream and I would not be surprised) crossing over Wilfrid's bridge and entering the wood for the first time: one moment walking in light upon familiar ground and the next, darkness, the air itself turned cold as the wood breathed upon us. It was this, as I remember it, that most impressed me that morning, the separateness of the wood. Everything I knew of life I knew from the abbey—its peace, its order, its goodness. But the wood stood apart from Redestone, had been defeated to make way for Redestone, and now I entered it. On my own two feet I walked into a place whose sign was gloom and damp, a place which said to my senses again and again: *I am different from all you know. I stand apart from sun and field and all that is right in an otherwise dangerous world. I am chaos. I am death. Welcome.*

For most of the morning we climbed without stopping, Tatwine walking so fast I was afraid he would leave me behind. At one point I remember our path followed the dry bed of what had once clearly been a great torrent, and I expected at any moment to be washed away upon the flood. Later still, the way became so steep we had to climb on all fours like horses, the pull of the world behind us palpable upon our backs. The bell for Terce, when, finally, it stopped our climb, frightened rather than pleased me. I would have preferred not to have heard it at all than to have heard the frail distant thing it had become. Surely it was too far away now to ever again shake me from sleep, call me to the table, save me from the fields. I can remember thinking we must have climbed too far too fast, that Tatwine had hurried us right past Dacca's crag, that now, surely, we stood upon the very summit of the world.

But of course we didn't. Though we were high up. I later came to know the place well, passed it many times on my way to and from the hermit's. The path there crosses a steep slope of brittle, slate-like rock. When you walk on it, this rock makes a sort of crunching noise underfoot, and, every now and then, pieces of it break off and slither away down the mountain. The path itself is a result of this weakness, a liver-colored line of broken bits of rock worn out of the lighter ochre of the slope. A species of pine—stunted, windblown—grows on both sides of the path, each of the trees clinging to its spot with roots that resemble small desperate arms. Normally I suppose Tatwine would have moved a little further on, chosen a place more suitable to our purpose, but on this occasion he must have wanted to impress upon me the importance of the office, that, even this far from Redestone, and regardless of circumstance, a brother was expected to hold to the Rule.

Carefully, I lowered myself onto the reddish-brown margins of the path. The surface, a mixture of dead pine needles and broken bits of rock, made a sound when I sat upon it. Before me, the slope fell away until I couldn't see it any more; beyond this, the tops of tall trees, and, beyond these, the valley itself, a great green waste of trees that, like a flood, fanned out mindless and indifferent to the horizon. Redestone was nowhere to be seen. The Meolch was nowhere to be seen. The bell had stopped ringing.

Having disposed of his scrip, Brother Tatwine turned slowly around, his body leaning in toward the mountain. Once he was facing me, his look of concentration changed to one of horror. "We are about," he said, in the first words I had ever heard him speak, "to address God."

I stood up again.

Neither of us had a great gift for song and, winded as we were, we must have presented a poor image there on the mountain that day, singing back and forth at each other like two men having an argument. Still, as we sang, the power of the chant began to have its way with me:

> Who else is God but Yahweh,
> who else a rock save our God?
> This God who girds me with strength
> and makes my way without blame,
>
> who makes my feet like the hind's
> and holds me from falling on the heights,
> who trains my hands for battle,
> my arms to bend a bow of bronze.
>
> You give me your saving shield
> (your right hand upholds me),
>   with care you train me,
> wide room you make for my steps under me,
> my feet have never faltered.
>
> I pursue my enemies and overtake them,
> nor turn back till an end is made of them;
> I strike them down, and they cannot rise,
> they fall, they are under my feet.
>
> You have girt me with strength for the fight,
> bent down my assailants beneath me,
> made my enemies turn their backs to me;
> and those who hate me I destroy.
>
> They cry out, there is no one to save,
> to Yahweh, but there is no reply;
> I crush them fine as dust before the wind,
> trample them like the mud of the streets.

Of course I knew it was spiritual enemies the Psalmist writes of here, but there on the mountain that morning the demons I imagined had more heft to them than that: I slew rim-walkers with my chant—Cumbrogi and Mercian, beggar and wolf, these were the beasts that fell before my sword. I liked these songs, I liked the feel of them, the crunch of them beneath my feet.

And then, in an instant, all the chant's courage drained from me: Brother Tatwine suggested I should close Terce.

Of course he must have thought he was doing me a favor, must have thought he was bestowing a great honor on me, yet the very idea took my breath away. Still, what choice did I have? A monk, a *solemnly-professed* monk, had given me a direct order.

Choosing for my benediction the one prayer I knew I could get through without error, I began, "Great and beneficent God, hear me. Bless Ceolwulf, companion and gesith of Oswiu. Give him rings to bestow and a strong right arm. Make his animals fecund, his fields fertile. Grant him victories and long life. Furnish him with sons, great God, grant him offspring to crowd the borders. And give him fame that his sons and companions might sing the name of Ceolwulf and recall his adventures for generations to come.

"Great and beneficent God, hear me. Bless Oswiu, ring-giver, ruler of all the land north of the Umber, rightful lord of Mercia, warrior among warriors, leader of men. Grant him victories and treasure, make him generous, Lord, that his name and the story of his deeds may have many tellings, his companions good reason to sing his praise. Fill his hall with drink, good food, happiness; let the sounds of harp and laughter ring in that place. Give him long life, God, for his followers would miss his voice as they do those of the great heroes long gone.

"Grant these gifts, good and generous God, in the name of Your Son, Jesus the Christ, Most Valiant of Warriors, Prince of the Sky."

Tatwine was looking at me in a way I didn't like. "Does Father Abbot know you pray such a prayer, that you pray for Oswiu?"

I nodded, unsure what I had done wrong.

Brother frowned, seemed to think about what I had said. Then he turned carefully, picked up his scrip, and began once more to make his way up the path. I hurried after him, puzzled and not a little afraid.

Had I lied? In my haste to respond to an elder, I had answered without thinking. Of course Father Abbot knew my prayer of oblation, Father Abbot knew everything! But now, as I climbed along behind Tatwine, I wondered...Did he? A part of me had always thought Father Abbot the source of my prayer. Someone had taught it to me; it was too grand a thing for me to have made up on my own. And that was part of its beauty too—when I thought about it—the fact that it had been a gift, that someone had taken the time to create it for me—just for me—a special prayer, something I could repeat whenever it got too dark or too lonely and everyone else was asleep. It had to have been Father Abbot who gave it to me, who else? And if not Father Abbot, then surely Father Prior.

The next time we stopped was at Ælfhelm's Shrine, though we didn't call it that then. There was no cross in those days, no circle of stones, and the only trees of any size were four or five oaks that grew at one side of the path. A spring rose from the ground among these trees to form a small pool—really little more than a puddle—its surface at that time of year sprinkled with catkins.

Still it was holy ground. Brother Tatwine said so, which made me feel both safe and a little sad. Father Dagan had said there was nothing worse than dying by yourself, all alone on a mountainside, no one to hold your hand, no one to kiss you good-bye. A part of me had always envied Ælfhelm because of his songs, but when I looked at this place, I was glad God had decided Ælfhelm should make it holy and not I.

Of course in those days everyone knew how Brother Ælfhelm had come by his songs because of the chestnut. Despite what the Rule says about possessions, Brother was allowed to—in a sense—*own* the thing (certainly it was considered *his*), wearing it openly on a thong around his neck. Father Dagan said this was permissible because the chestnut served as a reminder both to Ælfhelm and the community of God's power, and that its value, therefore, was essentially spiritual and not material. Lest some future generation think such a judgment specious, I will give a brief account of the story here.

Before he became a monk, Brother Ælfhelm had lived as a swine-herd in a part of Bernicia that was then otherwise uninhabited. The moon came and went, years came and went, but Ælfhelm hardly ever saw another soul. Then, one day, a snowstorm drove a band of lonely men to his hut. Now Ælfhelm was not a little afraid when he saw these men for they carried great shields and battle-axes. But the swineherd was not so far removed from civilization that he had not heard of the new faith, and—mindful he should "show hospitality to strangers, for thereby some have entertained angels unawares…."—he suffered them to enter, offering them what food and comfort he could.

After a while, the men—warmed by drink and Ælfhelm's fire—begged a favor of the swineherd. It was, they explained, a custom among their people to pass a brooch belonging to their host as they sang their drinking songs, whichsoever man held the brooch being the one whose turn it was to sing. Now at this news Ælfhelm was greatly affrighted, for he was a poor man, his cloak held in place by a simple knot: he did not own a brooch. Still, his guests insisted he give them something; so, fearful lest they hurt him, he picked a large unblemished chestnut from the stores he kept for his animals and let them use that.

Slowly, ever so slowly, that chestnut made its way around the fire, each man taking his turn, singing his songs, then passing it on to the next with all the honor due a great jewel. Eventually the chest-nut reached the man next to Ælfhelm, and it was then that the poor swineherd realized that he too would be expected to sing, that, indeed, this was likely the purpose of his guests' strange custom, for it assured their host the honor of the last song. But Ælfhelm did not want to sing. He was terrified of singing. The swineherd, as the saying goes, "had a mouth full of teeth," and his guests had been drinking. Who knew what offense they might take when they heard his ill-natured voice, his rough country songs?

Still, there was little he could do. Even as he thought these thoughts, the man next to him brought his lay to an eloquent inventive close. Toasts were drunk, compliments paid, more wood placed upon the fire; and then, quite simply, like someone passing a piece of bread, the man next to Ælfhelm handed him the chestnut. As he stood to sing, the poor swineherd offered up a silent plea that the new God might save him, give him a song that would please these men, keep them from killing him. Then, having no idea what would come out of his mouth, Ælfhelm began to sing:

> Great is the Earth,
> And He Who made it.
> Great the Sky,
> Great the Sea.
>
> The Night rolls back,
> Day is revealed,
> And all is as it should be,
> All is as it should be,
> Should be, should be.
>
> All is as it should be—
> That is my song,
> The song of the Earth,
> The dream of the Sky.

Of course the rest of the story is well known. The men, as it happened, belonged to Bishop Wilfrid. They were so impressed with Ælfhelm's song, they presented him to their lord, who, in turn, had the swineherd placed at Redestone that his poetry might please the community and convince the ignorant. For there was no doubt that Ælfhelm's songs were miraculous. The brother himself admitted as much. Father Prior asked him to sing for us once, and, afterward, he told us the story of the chestnut and the gift it symbolized. His songs, he said, always arrived without warning or effort. He would be washing or weeding or performing some other perfectly ordinary task when, suddenly, he would realize he had been repeating some phrase under his breath, something entirely new, something which, even as he repeated it, even as it assumed the rhythms of his work, would, apparently of its own accord, give birth to still more phrases, the phrases assembling themselves into lines and verses, until, before he knew it, before his very eyes, a song had appeared. It was always like that, he said, his songs arriving when he least expected them. It was as if God wanted to make it perfectly clear they were a gift.

"Don't you bother him."

A shiver ran down my spine. Was Tatwine speaking of Ælfhelm?

"When he prays I mean," said Brother, eyes studying the pool. "You leave the hermit alone. He has better things to do than worry about some boy."

I assumed custody of the eyes. It wasn't fair for Tatwine to talk that way. I never bothered anyone.

For a while we sat in silence. Then, quite unexpectedly, Tatwine said, "He could have stopped it you know. The pestilence I mean. He could have stopped it if, you know, if Ælfhelm had reached him in time." Brother glanced at the far bank of the pool and I guessed this was where the body had been found. He looked back at me. "You'll ask him to pray for me, won't you? I mean, he should pray for everyone of course but, whenever you think of it, a little prayer for me?"

I looked at Brother and nodded. No one had ever wanted anything from me before.

Tatwine regarded me for a moment longer, then he looked back at the place Ælfhelm had made holy. "I first noticed it about a month ago," he said.

The spring?

Tatwine nodded at a small sapling and held his hand out, palm-down. "It was only about this high then." He looked at me. "It's a chestnut," he said. "I don't know what happened to the thong."

We didn't stop for Sext but climbed on, singing as we went. After a while the air grew cold and dark and—the overhanging wood notwithstanding—you could tell that the day had become cloudy. A fine mist began to fall and then, rather abruptly, Tatwine stopped. When I caught up with him, I saw that we had happened upon someone's camp—one or two broken pots, the remains of a shelter, and, hanging from a pole by a small stream, a tattered piece of cloth, black markings on a white field. Despite the mist, the fire was still smoking. Someone had left this place in a hurry. Had they heard us?

All the noise we'd made as we'd climbed came suddenly clanking and clattering back to me.

How could they not have heard us?

And if that were true, didn't it mean they must still be nearby, that, perhaps even now, they watched, readied their leap?

I leapt, and then realized it had just been Tatwine turning around to say something.

Brother seemed distracted. He made a show of bringing a finger to his lips.

What?!

He indicated the stream with his chin and I froze. *There was someone there, someone sitting by the stream!*

I looked back at Tatwine wanting reassurance, some reason for hope, but Brother continued to stare grimly at the figure by the stream.

Carefully—fearful lest the turning of my head make a noise—I looked back that way. The man appeared to be asleep—eyes closed, head forward, hands resting in his lap—but I knew this could just be a trick. And I wondered if that was it, if the men who had made this camp—Cumbrogi, beggars, what-have-you—if they might not have left this ancient as bait, the perfect bait for religious sworn to help such creatures—the poor, the old, the halt and blind. And there was something about his head I didn't like either, something wrong and, at the same time, vaguely—perhaps even disturbingly—familiar.

And it was then that I noticed the stubble and a great sense of relief washed over me: The man wasn't bald, just poorly shaved! This was our hermit—our hermit in need of a razor, but our hermit nonetheless!

I looked over at Tatwine and—proud of myself now, secure, one adult speaking to another of a child—I raised my hands and placed them palm-to-palm against my ear, *Asleep?*

Tatwine's hands rose in a similar gesture but stopped before his face, *Praying.* Then a single finger broke free to tap, once more, his lips.

We unpacked the loaves and tabula and placed them in neat piles by the fire. Then we sat and waited for the hermit to finish his prayers.

He prayed for a long time. Watching him, I found myself wondering about hermits, wondering what their prayer might be like, my speculations growing vague, indefinite, as the waiting extended and I grew drowsy, the hermit's figure slowly merging with its surroundings, becoming first a pot, round and gray, then a stump, an old gray stump sitting by an old gray stream.

When I woke up, the hermit and Brother Tatwine were standing by the fire, talking quietly. It had stopped raining and I was cold and tired. I wondered when we would eat.

"It won't take that long, really."

"Father, look at your fire. It's going to take some time to get that going again. Maybe if the boy hadn't dawdled so...."

The hermit glanced over in my direction. He was taller than I had expected. And dirtier. His woolens looked as if he had slept on the ground.

"But a welcome, a proper welcome. Even the Rule requires as much."

Brother Tatwine shook his head. "Forgive me, Father, we can't. If we're to make it back before dark, we must leave now."

I stood up, liking the idea of making it back before dark.

The hermit noticed me move and a row of teeth appeared in his ratty, unkempt beard. He looked back at Tatwine.

Tatwine held his hands out. "Besides," he said, "there'll be plenty of time next time. He's so slow, he'll have to spend the night."

Spend the night!

But an elder had spoken, a pronouncement been made: to question it now would only provoke a charge of pride, possibly even a mention at Faults. I said nothing. Tatwine handed me my now-empty scrip, we knelt before the hermit, received his blessing, and then we left. I remember, as we hurried off, he called after us. "Pray for me," he yelled. *Pray for me*, as though we were the holy men and he some farmer we'd passed in a field.

Climbing down Modra nect was easier than climbing up. Brother Tatwine called out to me regularly, apprising me of certain landmarks, ordering me to pay attention to the turns, to beware of false paths, but my mind was on the hermit. He hadn't been what I had expected. Far from it. Despite Father Prior's warning, perhaps even because of it, I had been expecting someone special. I had (it seemed silly now) pictured a man dressed all in white, a figure out of Scripture who would welcome us with milk and honey, speak differently from other men, more brightly, more gaily, perhaps even laugh aloud. Why there had even been a part of me that had hoped—being special himself—the hermit might recognize something special in me, a kindred spirit perhaps, one with whom his own might correspond.

But of course he hadn't. And so I decided Father must have been right, that this man was no different from any other. Indeed, now that I thought about it, I wondered if Prior Dagan might have been trying to tell me something more, if, possibly, he had wished to warn me that this Gwynedd, this reputed holy man, was not only not special, he was also not particularly nice, that, in point of fact, he might be mean, someone like Baldwin, a mean man who did not like children. Which, in turn, got me to thinking about the other thing, the thing I'd been trying so hard to forget, that soon—not too soon, but soon enough: seven days—I was going to have to go back up there, I was going to have to go back up there and stay with him, stay with this man Father might have been trying to warn me about, stay through the night (in the wood!) with this man who did not look special, did not even look like a monk, this man who, truth be told, looked like nothing so much as a beggar, one of the evil thieving beggars.

By the time we recrossed Wilfrid's bridge, the sun was down and Redestone sat quiet and dark beneath her stars. Prior Dagan met us at the kitchen gate, signing to us to keep our voices down while whispering rather loudly himself. We had missed collation but Father had set aside cold soup and bread for us. I remember he hugged me, though he wasn't supposed to, and listened while I told him and Tatwine about our day. After a while I grew sleepy. It was nice to be home.

X

The dream is always the same, I climb and I climb but, no matter how high I go, how desperate I become, I never can find the hermit. Later, when I awaken, the reason for this will become clear: the mountain I've been climbing isn't Modra nect; it's some other mountain, like Modra nect but not like it too. On at least one occasion it wasn't even a true mountain, just an unending series of hills. Nevertheless, and despite the obvious incongruities, I always resolutely climb on, certain only of my uncertainty, that things are not right, that these landmarks, while familiar, are, in some fundamental way, wrong: a spring at the top of a cliff instead of the bottom, a valley where the path was meant to rise. Once I even sought the wrong hermit. I remember how strange I felt upon waking to realize that, instead of Father Gwynedd, I had been sent after a Father Spoor. An interesting name when you think about it, as if I had searched after searching itself—the art of searching, its methods and tools.

My first trip up Modra nect by myself must have been very much like my dream. I must have been exceedingly afraid, exceedingly unsure of myself. No doubt I thought I was lost again and again. But I cannot swear to this, for I have no memory of that first climb. Indeed, nowadays, I cannot even imagine what it would be like to *not* know my way up that path—its bends and turns, its slopes and level places, having long since been laid down as surely in my mind as they are upon the mountain itself. Nevertheless, as the scar left by a wound otherwise long forgotten may still, on occasion, pucker and ache, so the mark left by that first trip still sometimes troubles my sleep and I awaken in panic, bedding wrapped round me like winding sheets, heart pounding in my ears, arms flailing about like those of a man trying to swim to safety. After a moment or two, sheepishly, I remember where I am, who I am, that I have no reason to fear losing my way on the mountain anymore, that, indeed, I have no reason to go there anymore. I lie back on my bed as relieved as I was when, on that first trip, I finally did reach the hermit's camp. For that I do recall, the giddy sense of accomplishment, the pride, the silly joy. "Father!" I remember shouting, "Father, I am here!"

The hermit looked up, all color drained from his face.

I stood where I was, hand still hanging stupidly in the air. I had done just what I had been told not to do, I had disturbed the holy man at his prayers.

For a moment or two the hermit just looked at me. Then, slowly, like a man getting up from a long sleep, he unwrapped himself from his sitting position and, awkwardly, climbed to his feet.

I smiled a little, but thought better of waving again. Should I prostrate myself? Did people do that sort of thing on a mountain?

The hermit took a few hesitant steps toward me, then stopped at a distance too respectful for the kiss of peace.

Again I smiled. Should I bow? No one had told me anything.

The hermit did not smile. He stood very still and very straight, looking at me as if he had forgotten something.

I was about to whisper, *Winwæd, I am your servant Winwæd,* when, cautiously, like a man lowering a fragile weight to the ground, the hermit lowered himself to his knees, looked at me one last time as if reconsidering, then lay all the way down, face-down on the ground before me, that great unshaven head of his coming to rest about a hand's width from my foot.

For a moment all was still. I think a bird called somewhere. Then, in a rough voice, a voice muted by the earth, the hermit begged for my blessing.

Of course I knew what he was doing. Messengers from the bishop, the man sent annually to collect the iron, even the first of the beggars to arrive at our gates had been welcomed by Father Abbot according to the Rule: "Let all guests...be received as Christ...the whole body prostrate on the ground, let Christ be adored in them...."

The hermit must have realized the effect he was having, for he waited only a short time for my blessing before proceeding as if I had given it.

"How are you called?" he asked.

"I am Winwæd," I said, my voice sounding strange in that place, small and weak.

The hermit just lay there.

"And how are you called?" I added hastily.

"I am Gwynedd," he answered, and my heart trembled, not so much at the ease with which he pronounced the Cumbrogi name as that he should pronounce it at all, that this hermit, this holy man, should respond to my question willingly, naturally, as though he thought it perfectly fitting to be questioned by a child.

"Winwæd," said the hermit, "will you join me by my fire?"

And so it was that Redestone's holy man, following the rule laid down for us for the reception of guests, washed the hands and feet of an oblate. He was very gentle. He used clean cloths and his best bowl. He warmed the water by the fire. I can still remember the way his eyes looked when first he brought the cloth steaming to my hands. *Too hot?* they asked, and I shook my head, reminded of an earlier occasion, some earlier washing I could not quite recall. When he washed my feet, the sensation felt so good I lay back and closed my eyes, wanting to remember this forever, the scents of forest and steam, the feel of someone washing my feet. Later I must have opened my eyes again for I have a memory of looking up through delicate spring leaves at a pale blue sky.

If the hermit's welcome was meant to reassure me, what he did next had the opposite effect. Instead of asking after me as Father Prior would have done—checking to see if I was hungry or needed anything—the old man seemed to dismiss me entirely from his thoughts. Looking back on it now, I think I know why this happened. In Gwynedd's day there were no oblates, and in all of his life he would have had little experience of children. Doubtless he was as shy of the homunculus that had invaded his camp as I was of the giant that ruled over it. But at the time of course I understood none of this. When Father put away his cloths and bowl and began to look through the tabula without so much as a glance in my direction, I was hurt, disappointed. Later, when he crossed himself and closed his eyes, becoming as still and solemn as a dead man, I was truly frightened. I had seen men die like this—suddenly, without warning—and the thought that he might have died, or could at any moment, leaving me to spend the night alone on the mountain (*seated next to a corpse!*) so terrified me I almost spoke, demanded he move, give some proof of life. But of course I didn't. And, when, finally, he did move, did open his eyes, it made me feel little better, for still he avoided mine, avoided any semblance of contact, or even of recognition.

The day wore on. Twice more the hermit performed his strange trance-like devotions, twice more was revived. None was chanted, a tasteless gruel served for collation; then, just after Vespers, the thing I most feared, most dreaded, began.

At first of course the change was nearly imperceptible: the declivities of the earth growing vague, indistinct, as if filling with a bad air, the line between a bush and the ground at its base blurring so that the one seemed to be melting into the other. Then, slowly, inexorably, the gloom began to rise.

A tree at the edge of camp was the first to lose its lights. I told myself the sun had passed behind a cloud, that the radiance must soon return; but in defiance of my wishes the tree continued to fade, grow dull, its edges becoming smudged, obscure, something changing into something else. Eventually it disappeared altogether and I found I faced not a tree or trees but a vague and murky wall of tree-shaped things. Desperate now, a man coming up for air, I looked skyward and was relieved to discover that here at least day lingered. Indeed, if anything, the heavens seemed more brilliant than before—pink clouds burning before a blue eggshell sky. There was time yet. It wasn't night yet.

But of course it was. Soundlessly, one by one, each of the clouds was snuffed, went out, only a dirty puff of smoke left to mark the place where, moments before, it had seemed an angel had burned. When stars began to appear, I gave up all hope and looked down; the fire—which earlier had seemed so small—now illuminating my entire world: three cooking pots, a small circle of flickering ground, my knees, the hermit's eyes, and little else. The size of the darkness that surrounded this sphere could only be guessed at—an occasional rustling in the near distance and, sometimes, farther away, the sound of the wind moving across empty slopes. There was no moon. Every now and then an owl called. When a second answered it I almost swooned, so large was the night that separated their keening.

I have always loved Compline, its simple sentiments, the feelings of security, domesticity, that it evokes. The Great Psalm itself has always signalled rest to me, bedtime, all things good and warm. But that night, for the first time in my life, I understood what it is that Compline unlocks, heard the words we sing, grasped exactly what it is that we praise:

> You made the moon to tell the seasons,
> the sun knows when to set:
> you bring darkness on, night falls,
> all the forest animals come out:
> savage lions roaring for their prey,
> claiming their food from God.

That was the long night. From Compline to Vigils, I don't think I ever once closed my eyes. Not that there was much to look at. The hermit's hut never did breathe well, and on that night in particular I remember a pall of smoke hanging over us like something alive, the way it twisted and turned, the curves described, the suggestion of intent. Later still, after the fire had died back, I tried to focus on the hermit's bed, telling myself I could still see him, that it was he that breathed so moistly there in the darkness, though in truth all I could really see was an indeterminate shape, more shadow than form, dark, slug-like, overlong—something pale, a hand or possibly a bit of beard, glowing faintly at one end.

It must have been toward the end of the first interval (though at the time it seemed later still, the night become eternal, morning a distant unlikely dream) that somewhere in the darkness outside the hut a stone struck another, skittered across two or three more, came to an uneasy rest.

I did not move.

I lay where I was and I did not move. I listened.

For a long time nothing happened. My bladder grew tight. My heart beat like a drum. But, otherwise, at least for a while, nothing happened, and I was just beginning to believe it, to tell myself every-thing was going to be all right, that we would live, when, closer now, I heard it again, a hollow sound of stone smacking stone that made me think something was working its way up the streambed, kicking the occasional rock as it came. I wondered what sort of beast could stroll so confidently through the night, unconcerned by the noises it made, and unbidden an image of Eadnoth rose before me, peered through the darkness. I shook my head, tried to think of something else, but the vision would not let go: Eadnoth's brindled form loping through the wood toward us, his eyes fixing upon our shelter as easily as, in my dreams, they fixed upon me. We really were ridiculously exposed up here when you thought about it. How could anyone have ever believed this place safe?

But of course they hadn't. That was the point. That was the reason the hermit lived up here, because he preferred it that way, he wanted to live by himself, unprotected and alone. If anything happened... well, he was a holy man, a hermit, either way he came out a saint. But what about me? There wasn't anything special about me. No one begged for my prayers; no one said I didn't have to work, sent me food whenever I wanted it. I was just an oblate; who was going to look after me?

As if in answer to this question a new sound now began to make itself known. At first I tried to ignore it, told myself I was hearing things, that it was a trick of the wind and nothing more; but the sound quickly became too definite to be denied (my hearing now as acute as vision, my ears eyes, my mind the darkness beyond the hut's fragile walls): whatever was out there had clearly changed direction, left the streambed, and was now audibly padding its way up through the wood toward us, its pace too irregular, too considered, for innocence, the thing apparently orienting itself, homing in on us, this place, the hermit, me.

Me.

I wanted to scream. I wanted to cry out for Father Prior, Father Abbot, our lord bishop, anyone. But of course I couldn't. To make a noise now would serve only to alert the creature to our location, bring it that much quicker to our hut, the end I now knew lay in store for me. I held my hands between my legs, squeezed them for comfort, prayed, held my breath. Outside I heard the swish and sigh of something large passing from brush to clearing, visualized the beast as it entered our camp, raised its ugly head, peered about. And then yet another sound reached my ears, a sound I could not quite credit, a damp puffing sound as if whatever was out there had placed its lips to the ground and, moistly, blown out hard. The sound was repeated, then, closer still, repeated again, and there was something about this new sound, its almost comic nature, that made the whole situation seem worse, unbearable, for here was something utterly stupid, utterly vile, snuffling and sniffling its way up to eat us.

And then as abruptly as the sounds had begun, they stopped, and I sensed—knew—that the beast had found something that interested it, a spill of food perhaps, or, maybe, the place where I had sat.

A moment's awful silence, then the snuffling noises began anew, this time eager, urgent, the animal no longer able to contain itself. I threw a final desperate glance at the hermit's side of the hut and was surprised to see a change in the shape that lay there. Was he sitting up? Had he awakened? Could the old man possibly save us?

The sound of one of the hermit's pots being knocked over was followed immediately by a report so loud and sudden it made me jump.

He had clapped. The hermit was awake and bravely, competently, *he had clapped!*

Silence.

Should he have clapped? I imagined the beast raising its head, testing the air, wondering if this new noise signalled prey. Then, wonderfully, down by the stream (Had the animal flown?), a confusion of braying and limb-snapping that even my untrained ear recognized as retreat. I looked over at the place where the hermit lay and though he couldn't see me, I smiled. The man was a saint, a miracle-worker, wild beasts obeyed his every command.

"Bear?" the hermit's voice guessed.

A bear.

"No," the voice decided. "More likely badger."

As the sounds of the bear's retreat grew distant, a new and distressing fact pushed all sense of deliverance from my mind. I looked around but there was no way out of this, life up here impossible, unendurable. "Father?" I said.

Silence.

"Father, I need to…."

"Anywhere," said the voice, and I thought I saw a vague wave of a hand. "So long as it's not near the stream."

For a while then I sat and looked at the place where I knew the door was. I wanted to get up, I wanted to obey my master, but I couldn't.

"You know," said the voice finally, "I think I need to too. Would you mind if I went with you?"

"No," I replied. "No, Father, that would be fine."

XI

That was a hard spring for Redestone. With the abbey's stores depleted after the bad harvest and our ranks reduced by pestilence, only one growing season stood between the community and famine. Nighttime offices were curtailed and Terce, Sext, None, and Vespers sung in the field. When we worked, we worked like men asleep, planting and pruning by memory. When we sang, we sang like old men crying. Hunger made us short-tempered. I remember on one occasion we even heard the village women quarreling down by the river. We were all surprised by this for we did not hear women often. Sometimes they sang at their wash, but if the sound of the singing reached us, one of their men was always sent to quiet them. But not this time. No one shook their heads this time, no one looked embarrassed, no one did anything. We just worked. Come rain or shine, cold weather or hot, we worked, we planted. We had no choice, this growing season must succeed.

Strangely enough, despite all the hardship, I have fond memories of that spring. After only two or three trips to the hermit's camp, I grew confident of my ability to get up and down the mountain safely. Not that I didn't still sometimes think myself lost. If a tree had fallen across the path or a portion of it been washed away in the rains, I could easily become confused. But, generally, the landmarks remained in their proper places. There was even a sort of logic to them: as Vespers followed None, so the mossy place in the trail always came after the high ridge, the cool place after the stream. You could depend on it. Indeed, I became so sure of my proficiency I began to enjoy the climb, looking forward to it, drawing it out, delighting in my ability to predict what lay around the next bend, over the following rise. The further away from Redstone I got, the better I always felt. It was as if I grew happier and healthier the higher I climbed.

But in reality of course I did not grow healthier the higher I climbed. By the time I reached the hermit's camp I was inevitably exhausted, the week's work having taken its toll. After receiving my master's blessing, I would go directly to bed, not waking again until after dark, my body stiff and sore, Father warming something by the fire. Sometimes the stiffness was so bad I couldn't grip a spoon and the hermit would have to feed me by hand. It shames me now to remember the pride I took in this. I would look at my hands, trying to bend the fingers, and I would think about the sacrifice I was making, how I was working as hard as any adult. And of course I was working hard, we all were, but that gave me no right to look at the hermit, as I sometimes did, as if I were better than he. He too did his work, he too made his sacrifice. To be quite honest about it, I think he sometimes missed the fieldwork. I'll never forget how sad he was when he learned old Dextra had died. He told me he had broken her to the plow.

Mornings on Modra nect were my favorite time of day. Though he wasn't supposed to, Father usually let me sleep through the Vigil, and, as a result, I always woke up feeling reinvigorated. Of course I should have been sent directly back down the mountain, but I never was. Rarely did I leave before Sext, and even then it was my own decision, not Father's. He treated me more like a monk than an oblate; and of course I didn't complain. Until that spring every day of my life had been defined by the hours. From the moment I woke up till I put my head down again at night, I always had some place to be, some chore I was meant to be doing. But now, once a week, I found myself, incredibly enough, with time on my hands. I could lie in bed as long as I wanted, or I could jump up and play in the sun, and no one, not Father Prior, not Brother Baldwin, not even Father Abbot, could do anything about it. I loved those mornings on Modra nect. The thought of them pulled me from sleep like the smell of something good cooking.

Still, there was little for a boy to do around that camp. I made up small games for myself but of course I had to be quiet: the hermit was always working. Sometimes he scratched at a tabulum. Sometimes he read from one of the books Father Prior sent him. Sometimes he busied himself with supplies. But, mostly, he prayed. The man had a capacity for prayer that was truly extraordinary. He could sit for entire intervals without moving—eyes closed, lips still, hardly even breathing.

Father Prior had ordered me not to think the hermit special, his prayers any different from any other monk's, but in this I had long since disobeyed him. No one could look at the way this man prayed, the length of his prayers, without realizing he was different, that what he did was different. And by then of course I had heard the tales. Living trees would bow toward the hermit as he prayed, dead ones sprout new growth. His water would attract butterflies, his night soil salamanders and snails. Doves would build nests in the eaves of any structure he built. Coals from his fire could cause stones to burn, water to burst into flame. I was told to watch him closely when he prayed, that he might float like a cloud, the air above his head fill with lights. And if that was not enough, there was the attention I received as his servant. Monks waylaid me on the garth, knelt by me as I weeded, woke me in the night; they whispered, cajoled, pleaded for a moment of the hermit's time, a prayer, a special blessing, a little help with "something I haven't wanted to bother Father Abbot with." Even Father Prior stopped me once in the peas and asked that the hermit say a prayer for him. He didn't tell me why. Indeed, I think he wanted me to think it perfectly normal, merely a matter of courtesy; but of course I didn't. You must remember that I was very young. The idea that grown-ups ever did anything out of the ordinary was entirely foreign to me. That they did, or seemed to, for this one reason, impressed me more than anything else.

And so, morning after morning, I sat opposite the hermit and waited as he prayed, certain I would see something miraculous. And—morning after morning—I saw nothing. Once there was something, a swirling in the air over the hermit's head as if a cloud of midges had suddenly been attracted to that place, circled for a moment, then as quickly departed. But, otherwise, nothing. No concourse. No angels dressed in white, no voices singing. Nothing at all really. The man just sat there. He might have been asleep for all I knew.

It was Waldhere who first suggested the hermit might be sleeping instead of praying. Of course at the time I thought he was just jealous of the attention I was receiving, but, as week after week passed without any miracles, I too began to have my doubts. Looking back on it now, I suppose it was inevitable I should get into trouble.

It was foggy that morning—as most mornings on Modra nect were—and concentrating on the empty air over the hermit's head had made me dizzy. Waldhere and Ealhmund sometimes made a game of dizziness, spinning and spinning until, unable to spin anymore, they staggered around like drunken beggars, wide-eyed and laughing at themselves. But I didn't like it. Being dizzy made me feel sick, and I didn't like anything that made me feel sick again.

I opened my eyes and the hermit was still sitting there: eyes shut, head drooping—looking for all the world like a monk asleep in choir. It was irritating when you thought about it, and not very smart. Didn't he worry someone might tell?

Unseen in the fog overhead, a tree rubbed against another, creaked and groaned. When I looked back down again I was surprised to see a small leaf, purple-red in color, resting on the hermit's forehead. For the first time that morning I felt a little excitement. Now he'll move, I thought, now he must move!

But of course he didn't. I waited and waited but, though I had to scratch my own head in sympathy, the hermit never so much as twitched. It was like watching a dead man pray.

The thought brought the predictable response: there again sat Eadnoth, rainwater pouring off the roof onto his feet. I looked away, tried to think of something else, and found myself thinking instead of the similarities, the resemblance between that image and this. Here sat Gwynedd, perfectly still, oblivious even to the fall of leaves, and there in my mind sat Eadnoth, equally still, equally oblivious to the rain. And maybe that was it. Maybe that was why I hadn't seen anything. Maybe I hadn't seen anything because there was nothing to see…*here*. Maybe, like Eadnoth, the slack-jawed, loose-skinned thing sitting before me now wasn't so much the hermit as it was the carcass he'd left behind, a skin shed and waiting, like me, for the return of its master.

Goose flesh ran down my arms. I was lying on my back in front of the hermit, my head resting on my hands, feet nearly touching his… and yet, possibly, not his. If I was right, those feet were empty, no more than cast-off shoes, those hands as lifeless as a pair of gloves. It seemed impossible but possible too. It would explain so much. Nothing escaped the hermit's notice. He could name the singer before I even realized a bird had called. Yet when a limb fell in the wood while he was at prayer, he never so much as flinched. Truthfully, *it was as if he wasn't here.*

The wind shifted toward the north and smoke began to get in my eyes. I got up and walked around to the other side of the fire, hardly bothering to be quiet now. The hermit remained perfectly still.

I found a stick and played for a while at plowing the campsite, one eye on the hermit.

Of course Waldhere wouldn't believe it. You could count on that. Not even that the hermit had remained still. Everybody moves, he'd say, sooner or later, even Father Abbot.

But he was wrong. Father Hermit didn't move. Even now, wood smoke streaming past him like water around a stone, he didn't move. Didn't even cough. And that was something, when you thought about it, the fact that he didn't cough. Like Shadrach and Abdnego.

I had never seen Victricius's furnace, but on clear days I sometimes saw the smoke it produced. I imagined it was like Brother Kitchens' oven only bigger and hotter. Nebuchadnezzar's furnace would have been even bigger still. I looked at the hermit's fire, trying to imagine what it would be like to stand in its middle, and then I looked at the hermit again.

Still thinking, I placed the end of my stick in the center of the fire. At first not much happened: the dirt and moss adhering to its plow-end turned brown, flamed up momentarily, turned white, then dropped off into the coals. I waited, a little shocked by the idea forming in my mind.

It wasn't long before the stick itself caught fire, but when I held the thing up to look at it, the flame went out. Still it was hot, you could tell, the burnt end papery and white. And smoking. Even the end I held in my hand felt warm. I looked over at the hermit, who remained as he had been, back to me, oblivious to my thoughts as well as the smoke. Which was just as well really; this didn't have anything to do with him. This was for Waldhere. This was to show Waldhere.

The yell, when it came, seemed louder for being so unexpected, as if, instead of the hermit, the skin itself had cried out at being treated so. Of course a part of me had known he would feel it, had known as soon as I had smelled the hair, seen the skin blanch and peel back, that no one could be touched like this, be burned like this, and not feel it. And yet still I was surprised—surprised and amazed—by how loudly he screamed, how easily he cried out not like a man or even a boy but like, and the thought astonished me, like a girl. And then, before I could recover from that shock, I was even more surprised to discover that terribly, and apparently uncontrollably, *I* had begun to cry.

"It's all right," the hermit gasped, "it's all right, it just surprised me." But for some reason the sight of the hermit holding his hand, eyebrows raised in concern for me, made me cry all the harder.

"What is it?" he asked. "What's wrong?"

"It's just that…just that…." but the excuses caught in my throat. I blinked, took a great gulp of air, and then—looking at the hermit as if to say, *See what you have done?*—gave in to the crying, not even caring anymore, because it was over, I'd burned the holy man, the *saint*, and I'd done it *because* he was holy, because…. But I would never be able to explain that. No one would listen to me, no one would believe me. Tomorrow, maybe even today, I would be expelled from the monastery, unloved and unregretted, gone like poor little Oftfor. And for some reason the thought of Oftfor made me cry even harder, his loss suddenly as important to me as anything, as if Father Prior had died or Father Abbot.

And it was then that—for the first time in my life—the hermit held me. One moment I was standing there, alone and afraid, and the next I was against him, the smell of wood-smoke and old man in my nostrils, scratchy wool against the skin of my face. I was so shocked I stopped crying instantly. I looked up. The hermit looked down at me, smiled at me from out of his beard. Beneath my chin, his stomach rumbled.

Afterwards—after he had patted me and given me some tea and assured me a hundred times that all was forgiven, forgotten, not to be worried about—the hermit asked me, gently, why I had burned him. "Were you angry with me?" he asked, and he looked at me as if it really mattered, as if he were really concerned he might have offended me. He was always like that. The man's capacity for prayer was equalled only by his capacity for charity. It shamed a person. At the very moment when you most deserved rebuke, the hermit assaulted you with love. Later, when I was older, this could make me angry, but on this first occasion it merely made me shy. I equivocated, not mentioning Waldhere at all but repeating how sorry I was and explaining I hadn't meant to harm him, that I had honestly believed he wouldn't feel anything, that, somehow, when he prayed, he would be impervious to pain. Of course the hermit had laughed at this, but that didn't surprise me. Whatever the secrets of his prayer, I couldn't expect him to share them with an oblate.

After that, as I remember it, I sat and sipped my tea, the enormity of what I had done—and what the hermit had done in response—silencing me entirely. Father busied himself about the camp, selecting the tabula he wanted taken back down the mountain, packing my scrip. When he was finished, he suggested a walk. He said he had something he wanted to show me.

Oddly enough I can still remember that walk. Of course I know now we didn't go far, couldn't have, yet I remember certain aspects of that journey as you might those of a longer trip, a pilgrimage that, for whatever reason, impresses itself upon you—the white bloom of the fog, the sense of a morning cast adrift, time unimportant, forgotten, trees looming suddenly into view, monstrous boulders, everything silent, mysterious, the world afloat; and then the unexpected halt, Father grinning as if he'd found something wonderful, asking if I knew where I was.

I shook my head. "We left the trail back there, didn't we? By the stream?"

"Yes, very good." Father frowned, thought about it. "Now the fog's breaking up, you should be able to see it even better on our way back. But what do you see up there?"

I had already been looking up the path but could make no sense of what I saw, dark trees before a lowering sky. Had we come upon a meadow?

The hermit nodded. "You go ahead, but be careful. It's Dacca's crag."

Dacca's crag! I could see....

"You can see Redestone from out there."

Thankfully something stopped me. Maybe the hermit yelled, maybe a peripheral awareness of the height intruded upon my mind, maybe God took my hand, but something, something firm and not to be denied, reached out at the last moment and stopped me before I could run out onto the rock. I clung to a tree at its edge and waited for the hermit to catch up, afraid to move, afraid even to look down.

"It is quite safe."

"Sir?"

"The crag. You can walk on it."

"Oh. Well. I don't know."

"Don't you want to see Redestone?"

With one arm wrapped securely around the tree, I glanced once more at the rock, its rounded surface stretching out before me like the back of a great fish. Above and beyond the crag, clouds raced from right to left so that, in turn, the crag itself seemed to be moving ever so slightly from left to right.

"I don't think so. It's nice though."

The hermit smiled. "Really Winwæd, it's quite safe."

I didn't want to look at the clouds again, so I looked down at my feet.

"I'll be right here in case anything happens."

"You're not going?"

The hermit only smiled.

"Why not?"

"There really is nothing to fear."

"Then why won't you come with me?" A part of me very much wanted to see Redestone, to look down at Waldhere, and now, by refusing to accompany me, it had become the hermit's fault I couldn't.

"My vow...."

"But Father says you can't go *below* Dacca's crag. *On it* isn't the same as *below it*."

The hermit's smile was tired. "You go on. You'll be fine."

Again I looked at my feet. My own indecisiveness made me edgy and, for want of anything better to do, I stuck a foot out and tested the surface of the rock.

It was cold. Cold and pocked like old iron.

I leaned a little further out and, still holding onto the tree, pushed down. There was no movement. The rock held steady.

The hermit smiled and I realized that, having seen me test the rock, he was already thinking how brave I was.

I took a quick step out onto the crag, fingers stretched out toward the tree behind me. For a moment clouds and view flew about like excited birds, then, thankfully, resumed their natural positions. I took a breath, looked around, arms held out at my sides for balance. I had done it: I was out on the crag, sky all around me, rock firm beneath my feet. This wasn't going to be so hard after all.

Then the wind hit me.

It wasn't much, just a breeze, but I swayed as if struck by a plank. Out of the corner of my eye I saw Father move but before he could get to me, I regained my balance.

"Maybe all-fours wouldn't be a bad idea," he said, "just this first time."

And so it was that I made my first trip to the end of Dacca's crag on my hands and knees, sweaty palm-prints fanning out behind me like prayers. But it was worth it, whatever shame and embarrassment I felt were worth it because, at the end of the crag, when, finally, I reached the place where rock stopped and air began, there was Redestone, the abbey and its lands spread out before me like a map of itself.

For a long time I remember I just lay there, chin on my hands, feet stretched out behind me, delighting in what I saw. It was like lying at the end of a great log hung up on the lip of a waterfall. Overhead, the sky rolled and tumbled. Below, rock and pine fell away toward the river, tattered patches of fog rising up like spray. And beyond, just the other side of the Meolch, so close and so perfect I could almost touch it, was Redstone, the place I had lived practically all of my life.

Looking at it from above was both wonderful and strange. At one and the same time, everything looked familiar yet different, unchanged yet entirely new. Walls which all my life had bound my vision, holding it safe and close, now opened up, joined others to form buildings, enclosures, the outlines of a plan. Fields which at best had been *next* to other fields, the orchard which had always been *over there*, the forest which had simply been the end of all things, these places now lined up in their proper order, took on meaning in relation to one another, contracted and expanded according to their true natures. The fields for instance became small, manageable (for the first time I saw why Brother Cellarer did not look at them and despair), while the forest, which had always threatened, grew now immense, nightmarish, out of proportion to, and clearly in danger of overwhelming, the world I lived in, the tiny world I had always thought large, magnificent, safe and enough.

In a way I suppose I had always known these things would arrange themselves in this manner, would perhaps have even been able to draw a poor image of such a place. But now I actually saw it. For the first time in my life I saw the place where I lived not as an idea, something I held in my mind like an article of faith, but as a fact, something I could see and point at, something I could understand, almost touch. It was like learning to speak a new language in an instant. Everything was changed, everything different. To this day, when I think of home, I picture what one sees from Dacca's crag.

As I have said, it is much smaller than you think. Our monastery is surrounded by a great forest. What we call the Far Wood and the Great North Wood are, in reality, a single wood, separated only by the river. Beyond the orchard they join the South Wood to form an enormous waste that covers the land around us and swamps the distant horizons. Our abbey sits on the high ground at the base of Modra nect looking out over this forest like a tiny lighthouse looking out over a vast sea. The Meolch, which drains the mountain at our back and seems so straight when you stand next to it, actually curves as it passes us by. Our lands lie on the inside of this curve, the monastery and the terrace it sits upon at one end, the village at the other, our fields in between. Beyond the village the river straightens out again before entering the Far Wood, falling through a series of short rapids which, at midday, sparkle from the crag. It is here, in the pools just this side of the rapids, that the women do their wash.

The village looks much as it does from our terrace, small, compact, a cluster of toy houses built for a child. On fine days the smoke rises from the roofs in thin gray lines so that the houses seem joined to the sky by lengths of thread. Sometimes you can see women moving about in the open area at the center. I suppose this is meant to be their garth though there is no grass on it. With all the drying racks, it looks more like kitchens.

The fields too are as you would imagine them, the wheat green and silver when the wind blows, the peas thin and straggly. Chapter was cut short that spring so there would have been people in the fields by the time I reached the crag, but I don't think I saw Waldhere. I remember this because I remember being disappointed. For some reason I had thought I would be able to reach out and touch him. It was foolish of course, but at the time I believe I had some idea that the picture of Redestone I would see from Dacca's crag would be like any other—things large would become small, things far away, close at-hand: touch the top of the picture and you touch the clouds, the bottom and your finger covers someone looking at the sky. In this way too I had thought I would see Waldhere. I had thought I would tower over him like someone holding his picture.

You can't really see the ditch from the crag. Between the fields and the abbey path, the weeds and grasses look thicker and greener than elsewhere, but you can't really tell it's the ditch. A stranger would never know unless they opened one of the dikes. When they open a

dike, water spills from the ditch and darkens all the rows in that part
of the field.

Beyond the ditch and the abbey path are the fish ponds. From that
high up you would think you could see the fish no matter how deep
they went but you can't. Sometimes the water reflects the sky and the
clouds overhead and sometimes a bit of the forest, but most of the
time it's too gray or shiny to see anything. Between the ponds and the
southern part of Modra nect lies the orchard. Part of the orchard you
can't see because the monastery's in the way. In the spring, when the
trees are in bloom, it looks as if the abbey's floating on a cloud.

If you stand in the door of the dortoir after Vigil and watch the
stars roll back over Modra nect, they all seem to disappear behind
the same line of trees. What you are actually looking at is the crest
of a long ridge that reaches down from the mountain's southern peak
like an arm. The lower part of this arm rests, elbow to hand, along the
abbey's side of the river, its length carrying the load of our church.
When Abbot Agatho had the retaining walls built and the area south
of the church filled in to create the terrace, he effectively buried all
evidence of this ridge. Except from the crag. From the crag it looks as
if the mountain holds our terrace close to its chest like a basket full
of earth. The buildings of our monastery sit on top of this basket like
four boxes set on top at the last moment: the smaller ones on the far
side of the terrace—the abbot's lodge, dortoir, and refectory—balanc-
ing the larger one on the north, our church.

The walls of our church have always struck me as little short of
miraculous: the stones too large, too perfect, their rosy color too uniform, to be the result of craft alone. Yet from the crag it isn't the
walls that impress so much as it is the roof. The thing stretches from
the front of our terrace all the way to the back, an impossibly long
and perfect pile of hay, its north side stained green by the weather.
The same mind that dreamt up such a roof, imagined whole marshes
stripped bare to create its length, had a series of crosses woven in at
the crest, a sign, apparently, for God alone.

Below the roof you can see where the stone of the church's north
wall joins that of the ridge, the two so alike in color and form it's hard

to tell where the one ends and the other begins. It is here, against the base of the ridge, that the Meolch ends its long fall down the mountain. This is the sound you hear when you kneel on the north side of the church. The stone of the ridge becomes darker where it is touched by the spray, almost purple. This dark color, along with a stain which I take to be moss, extends up onto the lower portions of the church. Sometimes the mist and spray drift out beyond the ridge and into the light of our fields. When this happens, a small rainbow appears in the air over Wilfrid's bridge. There is something in the nature of these rainbows that makes them visible only from the crag.

The coincidence that makes the earth at Redestone the same color as the rock makes it hard to tell our southern buildings are any different from the church. A stranger would guess they too were built of stone. The abbot's lodge, dortoir, and refectory line up opposite the church like children trying hard to please. From the crag at least, they conceal their faults: you can't see any of the cracks or weathering. The abbot's lodge is decidedly smaller than the dortoir and refectory. It sits out in front of the other two at the terrace's southeastern corner like the abbot himself, short and squat, his flock at his back, watching for the Thief who comes in the night.

You can't see the reredorter from the crag but you can see the kitchens. The drying racks look like gibbets, facing out toward the orchard the way they do. I have never liked the sound they make when the wind blows. It is a shame the cooking has to be done so close to the refectory, but where else? If you prepared the food down among the fields, it would be such a job to deliver it to the community, especially in winter. And of course it would arrive cold. So there the kitchens sit, muddy and disreputable, at the very entrance to our otherwise neat and tidy cloister. I have often thought we should put up a wall.

But there is an advantage to the kitchens' location, in addition to the convenience I mean. Have you ever sat in Chapter and wondered if Bica's baking was a personal test for you alone? Of course you have; we all have. It seems so unfair the way that smell invades the refectory just when everyone is hungriest. But I'm afraid it isn't a test. Not really. God I think has more important things to do with His time.

It was from the crag that I first realized this. I was sitting there one morning, thinking about everyone in Chapter, the air over the oven winking and curling with heat, when a chill ran down my back. I pulled my woolens close and, without even thinking about it, envied Father Abbot his seat at the west end of the refectory, his back against that hot and cooking oven.

Things become so clear when viewed from above. Someone— Father Abbot, Brother Eadbald, possibly even the bishop—placed that oven against the refectory's west wall not to tempt us, not to test our patience, but, instead, to give Father and the older monks at his end of the hall a nice warm spot to sit in. So simple, so kind. And undoubtedly instructive as well: a relationship which at ground-level had seemed arbitrary and even cruel turns out, upon examination from above, to have a reason, a purpose, to warm someone who, otherwise, might have suffered from the cold.

I remember I received one such lesson on even my first visit to Dacca's crag, though I doubt I realized it at the time. I had been lying on the rock for a while, enjoying the hermit's gift of the view, when the sky—which had hung low and heavy all morning—began to show signs of breaking up. Here and there, as I watched, beams of sunlight pierced the clouds, reached down and began to probe the earth. I was watching one of these troll a patch of gold through an otherwise dark wood when an unexpected movement drew my eye to the terrace. Someone was there. Someone had knelt down, was kneeling down, in front of the church—someone who had no business being there at that time of day.

When he stood up, I saw that it was the novice, Eosterwine, and that he had something in his hand that required him to get up carefully, gingerly. Since his admission to the abbey, Eosterwine had become attached to Brother Baldwin in his duties as sacristan. Which probably explained why he was up on the terrace at this time of the morning instead of out in the fields where he belonged. Brother must have seen something at Mass he didn't like, a candlestick improperly polished, an altar cloth in need of repair, and now Eosterwine had paid the price for his master's displeasure: he had been made to return to the church and fix whatever was wrong. I wondered if Baldwin had made a fuss about it in Chapter. Regardless, everyone must now know, as I did, that Eosterwine had erred. He was, after all, very late to the peas.

When the novice passed out of the church's shadow, he surprised me by casting a long glance across the garth as if measuring the distance to the abbot's lodge. From this I guessed two things. First, it was most likely paten and chalice he carried so carefully before him (in those days sacred vessels were stored in a chest by the abbot's door); and, second, Eosterwine was thinking about breaking the rules. I knew this because I'd been there. How many times had I looked at that grassy expanse, late for lessons or office, and contemplated a mad dash while no one was looking? It's no fun being late, temptations multiply.

And, interestingly, it was at this moment, when Eosterwine was most distracted and I most sympathized with him, that the sky opened up, a beam of light reached down, touched the garth, and, for an instant, turf, stones, daub, and thatch glowed like colored glass.

Then the light went out.

As quickly and as quietly as the world had been set afire, the light was extinguished: all colors dead, the garth just a garth again, the walls no longer aflame, the grass no longer glowing. But Eosterwine had seen it and so had I. For the briefest of moments the abbey had been transformed. And to give him credit, Redestone's newest novice had the grace to kneel and cross himself.

I remember I looked back at Gwynedd when that happened, hoping he had seen what I had seen, wanting to share it with him, share it with the man who had given me this pleasure. But Father was looking up at something else just then, staring up into the tree I had held onto earlier, studying a bird perhaps or maybe its nest. Still, when he felt my eyes on him, he turned, raised a hand to let me know he was still there, still watching over me; and it was then that I saw it, saw the angry red spot on the back of his hand, and, seeing it, remembered what I had done, the pain that I had caused him.

XII

No matter where I am or what I am doing, the smell of green wood burning always makes me happy. In this I am not alone. Everyone's step seems lighter when Father Abbot finally orders us out to clear the ditch, even we ancients up at the head of the procession laughing a little as we march down the abbey path; spring has returned, the winter ended, we have lived to see another year. But the pestilence changed all that. Not the first year. No, that year followed a normal cycle: in spring we cleared the ditch and planted; in summer we cut hay, weeded peas; and, come autumn, those of us that survived the illness brought in the harvest. Except for the pestilence itself, the year of its visitation was like any other. It was the next year, the year after the sickness, that the order of our work grew strained and unnatural: for the first time Sext and None offered no respite from one's labors, children did the work of men, and the smell of green wood burning meant not the end of winter and cold, but the end of spring and the beginning of wasting heat. It was Brother Cellarer who decided all this, decided the office could be sung in the fields, the ditch cleared after the seed was in the ground. You can see what he would have been thinking. Then as now, the men of the village were responsible for preparing the fields, the brothers the ditch. When both tasks had been accomplished, the two communities joined and the planting began. But that year there weren't enough villagers left to break and plow the soil by themselves. So, given the amount of rainfall we could expect in an average spring, Brother must have reasoned the ditch could wait till summer; the sowing couldn't.

Not that we oblates understood any of this. Two more years would pass before Waldhere and I were deemed old enough for Chapter, and poor Ealhmund never would get to see the community in session. All we knew was that, for some reason, instead of clearing the ditch in spring when it made sense, we were doing so now, after the planting, when our hands and backs were sore and tired, the weeds had grown tall and well-rooted, and the heat made the smell of the reredorter unbearable.

Still, it was hard not to find some pleasure in the task. Somewhere far up the valley, the furnace master had closed the gate that linked our ditch to the Meolch. Redestone's water supply was stopped: the mill did not turn, the lavabo did not flow, our reredorter stood over a dry and stinking ditch…and we oblates were up to our knees in muck. We were supposed to be pulling weeds (the monks had been issued shovels and scythes), but the novelty of standing in a place normally full of water made it difficult to concentrate on the task at hand. When Brother Osric (who was named cellarer after the death of Father Cuthwine) looked our way, we pulled and yanked with enthusiasm, but, for the most part, we spent our time searching the mud for treasure washed down from the abbey kitchens.

It was overcast that day and hot. The air was full of smoke from the fires and the smell of green wood burning mixed with that of the reredorter. I had just found a piece of fish bone and was about to show it to Waldhere when I noticed how quiet everything had gotten. I looked up.

It was a man on a horse. He had already passed through the village and was now nearly even with the first of the ponds. As I watched, a second man became visible behind the horse. He was on foot and hurrying to keep up. The man on the horse seemed unconcerned about the man on the ground, but he did ride slowly. At one point he reached down and scratched a knee. The man behind him was carrying two spears. As he hurried along behind the horse, the shafts of the spears bent up and down in rhythm with his movements.

The creaking of leather and the clicking of the spears became audible as the two men drew near. I couldn't see the horseman's sword because it hung down on the other side of his horse, but I could see his shield. It had been painted green and red in a design I had not seen before. There was something wrong with the man's face. One side of it was swollen.

When the horseman drew even with the place where Waldhere and I stood, I could see that I had been wrong about his face. A scar ran down the side of the man's forehead, crossed his cheekbone, and then buried itself in his beard. Whatever had caused the wound (I imagined a war-axe), had clipped off the end of the man's eyebrow and a significant portion of the right side of his beard. Neither had grown back and, as a result, the right side of the man's face looked somehow wider, fatter, than the left.

The man didn't look at us as he passed, nor really did he look at anyone. He glanced up at the abbey once or twice but not like most visitors. You could tell he had seen such places before.

It was Father Prior who broke the spell. He clapped his hands once and everyone jumped. I looked around and someone laughed. Father looked at the brother who had laughed and then, fairly quickly, the sound of shovel and scythe started up again.

I began pulling weeds but I also glanced over at Waldhere. He looked back and the two of us raised our eyebrows at each other to show how pleased we were with what we had seen. Then Waldhere's eyes grew larger still and a sudden shadow passed over the ground between us. I bent to my work, pulling weeds with a vengeance now, but it made no difference. Whoever was standing behind me, kicked me. I stood up, turned around.

It was Brother Baldwin. He was standing at the edge of the ditch, glaring down at me, his forehead and cheeks flecked with mud. When he was sure he had my attention, he pointed up at the rider and his companion who had just reached the abbey rise, their figures wavering now in the heat and smoke from the fires. I looked that way and then I looked back at Brother Baldwin. The old monk smiled in a way that scared me. Never taking his eyes off me, he moved his hand through the air before him like a snake.

I nodded.

The smile on Brother's face evaporated. He pointed at me.

I must have looked surprised because I remember Brother smiling again at that. Then, as if pronouncing judgment, he caused the fingers of his right hand to rain upon the back of his left.

The message could not have been clearer. *That snake*, Brother had signed, *is your father.*

Ceolwulf did not visit me on that occasion. I saw him once or twice in church but he did not speak to me and may not have known I was there. I remember only that he wore many rings and that when he came into church there was a smell that came with him. Waldhere said this was because of the oil he wore but I didn't believe him. The man who came each year for the iron wore oil but he didn't smell as good as my father.

I did not see Ceolwulf leave Redestone. One day his horse and man were simply gone. I did not see them depart.

XIII

everyone loves the story of the hermit and how he refused to accept food from Redestone at the height of that summer's hunger and actually sent provisions from his own stores back down the mountain to the abbey. Even Father Abbot tells the tale though he must know it isn't true. I wish Father himself could hear it. I can see him now, sitting by his fire, biting carefully into one of the biscuits I've brought him, tilting the cake just so to keep the honey in place, eyes closed, listening, enjoying the story and trying not to laugh for fear of the crumbs. Afterwards he would have reminded me of "crosses to bear." He always did. He said everyone has one and his were the ideas people have about hermits. "They like to think of us as cut off from the rest of the world, needing nothing and no one. When of course," he would have laughed, "you know as well as anyone how much I need Botulf's biscuits."

But Father did try to be self-sufficient. Often as not, when he wasn't praying, he could be found foraging on his mountaintop, looking for mushrooms or berries, whatever manna God and the wood would provide. He even used to fish on occasion, though I think he did this more for the love of angling than anything else: I never saw him catch anything. But you would hardly have called his larder full. I have no idea how the story of his charity during the hunger got started, but I can assure you I never carried any food back down the mountain. What little he was able to collect from the forest around him wasn't enough to sustain his own person and would have proven of little assistance (and even less palatability) to the monks of Redestone.

But he did try. I can still see the old man holding up some plant he's found, brushing the dirt from its roots with his free hand and asking if I remember its name. If I could then, I can't now. I learned many things from the hermit, lessons about the practice of a religious life, lessons about death; but when I try to bring back the name of the plant he made soup from, or the one he preferred for his tea, there is nothing, that wax having long since melted. Which is interesting when you think about it. Did I have my own ideas of what a hermit should be? Was there something about the pleasure the poor man took in finding some seed or herb that I found embarrassing, unmanly? I don't know. I hope not. I pray I wasn't one of the crosses he bore.

Still, I did go with the hermit whenever he went foraging, and it is for this reason that it should have come as no surprise—when he suggested a walk that morning—that I picked up my gathering basket, slipped its strap up over my shoulder. But he looked surprised. The old man's eyes grew wide and he shook his head as if he couldn't imagine anyone wanting to look for food on such a day. Of course I knew he was making fun of me. It was one of the things I liked about the hermit, the way he poked fun at me, but still I was surprised. We always carried the baskets when we went for a walk.

It is in the nature of mountains that, paradoxically, as one climbs nearer the sun, the air carries less warmth. But that morning, despite the chill, despite the fact I wore my hood up, kept my hands muffled in my sleeves, the hermit strode along bareheaded, his enthusiasm for the sights we passed along the way apparently all that was necessary to keep him warm. At one point I even remember him directing my attention to the sky, asking if I didn't think the clouds overhead looked like animals chasing one another. When I agreed, he said the hill people called such weather "The Hunt." I became quiet then. Father Prior said we weren't supposed to talk about the hill people.

After we had been walking for a while, the sound of some great large thing rushing through the wood built up suddenly behind us. Before I could get too scared, the leaves on the trees around us began to pop and dance and a lone raindrop broke fat and cold against my cheek. It had been dry since the haying and I was pleased at the thought of a shower but, as it happened, this one did not last. As if God had shaken a branch once and then moved on, the rain stopped. When the sun came back out, the leaves around us sparkled in the light.

We were in a part of the forest I didn't know when the hermit stopped to look at some tracks. I was always a little nervous when we entered parts of the wood I didn't know. On another such walk the hermit had announced, as if it were nothing at all, that we were now on the Cumbrogi side of the mountain. Hoping to hurry him along, I knelt down beside the old man to see what he was looking at.

There wasn't much. Or quite a bit I supposed, if you understood such things. The surface of the path was a fine gray dust, pocked here and there by the redder craters of raindrops. Pressed into the dust and scattered across it like leaves on a pond were innumerable tracks. I glanced back over my shoulder. Behind us two sets of prints, pure and white, floated unerringly up to Father and me. Why couldn't animals walk like that, straight and true?

I looked back at the ground in front of us. There was deer track of course, there always was, but I no longer took any pride in identifying deer track: deer track never made any sense—these for instance, each separate, individual, as if a herd of one-legged animals had spronged through here, each striking the ground once and at odd angles to its fellows before vanishing, apparently bodily, into thin air. And then there was the bird. The thing began bird-like enough at the side of the trail, scratching and scuffling along, but when I followed it, hoping to find the place where walking ended and flying began, the creature developed a subterranean nature, its tracks diving beneath those of a dog like some sort of bird-footed mole. It was always like this. Animal tracks made about as much sense to me as the patterns left by raindrops.

But not to the hermit. With an agility that surprised me, he was suddenly on his feet and pulling me onto mine. Before I could ask what was wrong, he had a finger to his lips and was pushing me, roughly, up into the wood. We went a little distance, tripping over fallen limbs and making quite a bit of noise, and then he made me lie down behind a log. Once he was sure I couldn't be seen from the trail, he lay down beside me. I looked at the hermit carefully but he didn't say anything. He rose up on one elbow and watched the path below.

For a while we lay like that—I more than a little afraid, the hermit watching. It was cold and damp where we lay and, more than anything, I wanted to be somewhere else. But we couldn't move, probably shouldn't even breathe, so I stayed where I was and tried, very hard, to be still. After a while, either from fright or cold or a combination of the two, I began to shiver. The hermit looked at me. Something in his face made me think it might be all right to speak. "Cumbrogi?" I whispered.

The hermit sat up as if stung. "Where?!"

I nodded toward the tracks.

He looked that way uncertainly and then, after a moment's hesitation, smiled. "No," he said, his voice relaxing, becoming again Father's voice at ease. "Not Cumbrogi. Something better I think. Something you're going to like."

I started to ask another question but the hermit just shook his head. For once this didn't bother me. Something good was going to happen, something I was going to like. And there would be no Cumbrogi, no knives, no axes. Father had said so. Obediently, like a good child, I leaned against the old man and waited, enjoying his warmth, the smell of his smell.

A little later on something made me aware again of my position. Reluctantly, like someone pulling himself from a good dream, I pulled myself up from Father's side and looked out over the top of the log. There was nothing there. The path sat as empty and dull as before. I settled back down again and was about to close my eyes when, once more, the hermit poked me. Annoyed now, I sat up and in the same instant saw something move at a little distance from us up the trail. I glanced over at Father and he smiled: this was what we'd been waiting for. I looked back at the place where the movement had occurred and once more a slip of color—vague, indecipherable—passed between two trees.

As the animal drew near, a peculiar rustling sound began to reach us, a sound such as chickens make when they scratch at the earth, and it was as I was trying to turn whatever was down there into a kind of large ground bird that the animal came momentarily into view, grew suddenly monstrous, the head too wide, the body too long, for anything that could ever hope to perch upon a branch, take wing, fly away. I threw a desperate glance up at the hermit, hoping that now we might fly, escape whatever it was his strange craft had conjured up, but Father continued to stare down at the path, inured, it seemed, to the grotesqueness of the thing that walked there.

And it was then, as I looked down that way one last time, that the animal came most fully into view, became, quite simply, what it was. A fox. A very old fox but a fox nonetheless, the poor thing feeling its way cautiously down an otherwise unexceptional forest path.

I looked at the hermit and he nodded, this was what he had been expecting.

I looked back at the trail, the animal just then drawing even with us. For a moment it seemed to hesitate, a patch of light touching the side of its face—ears up, whiskers black and alive, eyes wondering—and then, as if we'd committed some offense, the beast turned its back on us and leapt into the underbrush on the far side of the trail, its rear-end hanging in the air just a moment longer than seemed necessary.

Though I watched the open spaces along the line of flight indicated by that leap, I did not catch sight of the animal again. Still I had seen it. And despite its having been so old and ill, it was fun having seen a fox so close. I felt we had outwitted a very clever beast.

"Did you like that?"

I looked up at the hermit and smiled.

The hermit looked back at the place where the fox had been and I could tell that he had liked it too.

"Where did he go?"

The hermit shrugged.

"How did you know he was coming?"

Father smiled and, without saying anything, stood up and began to walk back down to the path. By the time I got down there, he was already on his knees, studying the dust.

"You see these here?" The hermit indicated the tracks I had mistaken for a dog's.

"The fox?"

"Yes, very good. Now what can you tell me about them?"

"Was he after this bird?"

"The thrush? No, that was earlier, you see how its prints start up again over here?"

Oh.

"But it was good you noticed that, it could have been that." The hermit's smile made me feel better. "You see how the fox's tracks go right through here without stopping, as if it were in a hurry, and then again over here?"

I nodded. "So he'd been here before?"

"Uh-huh, and do you see here, where the fox came back up the path?"

"Yes."

"Now why do you suppose it would do that? Why would a fox who's supposed to be so crafty keep coming up and down this path like that, when it could just as well travel through the wood?"

"Because it was old?"

Father looked at me.

"I mean, because it was so old, maybe it was easier for him to walk on the path than in the forest."

"What makes you think the fox was old?"

"Or sick. Maybe it was sick."

Father just looked at me.

"Well, because its undersides hung down like that? I mean that didn't look right. And it was so thin. He just didn't look right."

"Right. Good. Well, that's a good idea. So the fox is too old to walk through the forest, the path is easier, so what can you tell about these tracks?"

"That he came through here more than once? That he liked going up and down here?"

"Right…and what else? Look closely."

I was already on my hands and knees but now I put my face close enough to smell the dust.

"Careful, don't disturb the tracks."

I pulled back a little and looked again. The things appeared all the same to me, small dog tracks, some going down the mountain, some coming back up.

"What about this here?" Father pointed at a print that looked a little whiter than the others.

"Yes?"

"Notice the raindrops?"

"They're all crushed from where he stepped on them?"

"Right, and over here?"

"These must have fallen after he walked through here."

Father looked at me, waiting.

I had to think about it for a while—seeing the raindrops falling on the footprints, seeing other footprints falling on the raindrops— but when it finally came to me the solution seemed so obvious I couldn't believe I hadn't seen it before: "You can tell when things happened!" I cried. "You can tell when he passed through here by the raindrops!"

"Yes!" said the hermit, and I could see that he was proud of me. "Yes, that's very good. I believe you've got a talent for this, Winwæd."

I smiled. He was right. I *was* good at this.

"Now see these here?" Father pointed at a set of the whiter prints. "When we first got here, only these prints going up the mountain had tread upon raindrops, all the others going up and down preceded the rain. So that was how I knew the fox was coming. It had gone up and down the mountain several times, and now it was clearly up again. The likelihood that it would come down once more was good."

"What about these?"

"That's the set it just made, coming back down past us. See where it takes off there when it caught our scent?"

I smiled. I liked this. It was so easy. I was amazed I hadn't seen it all before.

"So I still don't understand though. Why's he keep using the trail when he could be going through the wood?"

"A good question." Father looked back down the way the fox had gone. "It's off and running now but maybe if we follow its tracks back up the mountain we could see where it's been."

I nodded.

"You lead. You're good at this."

Of course I wasn't, not really, and it wasn't long before I found out just how little I actually knew. At first, as we went along, the path remained dusty, the tracks, like little pictures of fox feet, easy to follow, but after we had gone only a short distance we came to a stretch of ground where the surface was hard, the dust almost non-existent. Here, except for the occasional claw mark or scratch, the animal had left little trace of itself. Sunlight made matters worse. Whenever we came to open ground, the few marks that did exist faded before the sun like shadows. I began to get frustrated. When, inevitably, I came to a place where, no matter how hard I tried, I could find no more prints, I looked at the hermit as if it were his fault.

The hermit just smiled. "Sometimes," he said, "you have to get down on the ground like the animal you're following."

I looked away. When I looked back again, the hermit was on his hands and knees, studying the ground carefully. When he saw that I was looking at him, he raised his leg like a dog.

I laughed.

The hermit smiled and went back to studying the path.

"What do you see?"

"Not much. You were right, this is a smart fox."

I smiled.

Then the hermit did something that surprised me. Quite deliberately, like a man eavesdropping at a wall, he placed his ear to the ground, held his hand up as if signalling for silence, then became entirely still. For a moment I was sure that he could hear the fox, that, somehow, he listened for footsteps long after they had been made;

but then he switched ears and I saw that he wasn't listening so much as looking: examining the surface of the path from the lowest possible angle so that no mark or scratch, no matter how small or insignificant, could be missed. I was a little disappointed. After so many months it would have been nice to see a miracle.

Presently the hermit's expression changed. "Look," he said, "a sort of cave."

I was beside him in an instant. All my life I had wanted to see a cave. "Where?"

The hermit pointed at the base of the bramble bordering the trail.

"Where? I don't see anything."

"There, see how the bushes are pushed apart there. The fox forced its way up through the thicket, making a sort of tunnel as it went."

For a moment longer I saw nothing and then, quite suddenly, I saw what the hermit was talking about. Beneath the green roof of the bramble there was a weaker understory of stems and dead brush. It was up through this underlying tangle that our fox had gone, snapping and breaking canes as it went but creating, in the process, a sort of fox-sized passageway. I looked at the thing—like a cave but not a cave—and wished I could enter it. Bending down I could see that, further back, it rose with the ground up into the body of the bramble. The cave I sometimes imagined Lot and his daughters living in rose at a similar angle as it climbed back up into the earth. And it was quite possible I would never see a real cave. Father Prior said the mountains around here held few of them.

"I don't think I could fit in there, do you?"

I looked at the hermit and smiled. Though he was as thin as the rest of us, he liked to complain I was making him fat.

"But maybe you could."

Again I stared at him, this time expectantly.

"Would you?"

"Of course, Master," I said, assuming custody of the eyes and trying to look serious. We both knew he had just provided my excuse should Baldwin complain of the state of my knees.

"Be careful."

I nodded and then, fearing he might change his mind, lay down quickly and reached up into the hole.

The first thing I touched pricked me. I drew my hand back and licked the finger, trying not to let the hermit see I'd been hurt. Then I reached up into the hole again and this time found something smooth and firmly rooted in the ground. Grabbing this, I pulled myself half-way up into the fox's tunnel, the bramble heaving around me like an animal disturbed in its sleep. It was a tight fit. Briars caught at my woolens and scratched the top of my head. With my body now blocking the entrance, the light became poor, like dusk, and the air smelled of dog. After taking a moment to assure myself that nothing terrible was going to happen, I began to work my way further in, using elbows and toes. The light grew poorer still and I felt my feet join me in the tunnel as a sort of coolness. After that the world grew quiet, but I wasn't afraid. I pushed with my toes and pulled with my elbows. Every now and then, from somewhere behind me, the hermit called advice, "Watch for the thorns!" "If you get stuck, it's all right. I'll get you out."

If truth be known, I pretty much ignored him. There was something about this I liked, something about pulling myself along on my belly like a snake, the hermit so close I could hear him but not see him, nor he me. I was hidden yet known, on my own but not unprotected. Except for Father's calls, which became more and more muffled the further I went, nothing reached me. There were only the sounds of my own exertions and the musty odors of fox and berry and something not quite identifiable. It was like being somewhere both familiar and strange, a fever in the comfort of your own bed. And of course there was the adventure of it. As I pulled my way along I couldn't help pretending I *was* the fox, mute and savage, working my way toward who knew what, answerable to nothing and no one, neither Abbot nor Rule, nor good Brother Baldwin.

After going what seemed a considerable distance (though it could not have been much more than that between the bottom of the abbey path and the kitchen gate), a strange noise began to filter down to me through the bramble. By now the hermit was no longer calling out instruction and I was able to concentrate on what I was hearing. It sounded a little like the note a bird makes when you get too close to its nest and a little like the squeaking of mice. Whatever it was that was making these noises, there was something in their nature that struck me as essentially harmless, and, bravely, I soldiered on. It was shortly after this that the passage I was following took a sharp turn to the right and, negotiating this curve, I found I could now make out individual branches and briars in the space around me, see the scratches on the backs of my hands. Ahead of me a circle of light— and what I took to be open air—beckoned.

I stopped just short of the opening. The noises were decidedly louder here and—though I knew I knew nothing of forests and their inhabitants—I was sure these weren't human. Still I wasn't afraid. Or not much. Father was near, and there continued to be something about the timbre of these sounds that, for whatever reason, convinced me of their innocence. But I was no fool. I raised my head into the opening only high enough to bring my eyes level with the light.

I was at the edge of a sort of clearing. A well-worn path no wider than my wrist ran from my hiding place up through thick grass to a mound of reddish earth at the very center of the open area. Playing on this mound and around the ground at its base were seven or eight fox kits, their coats golden and flossy in the light.

I'm not sure how long I lay there. That little clearing with its den lodges in my memory now as it did in that bramble, a bright place full of color and baby foxes. Again and again, I remember, an uncommonly ambitious, albeit roly-poly, little fellow climbed to the top of the parent mound and attempted to leap from that height onto the backs of his litter-mates, each time ending up in a cloud of dust at the base of the mound, undamaged but clearly surprised to find himself so far short of his goal. His brothers and sisters, for their part, always seemed equally astonished by this turn of events, gathering around the little fellow as if they had never seen such a thing before, pushing and climbing over each other for a better look. Then, in an instant, all curiosity satisfied, they would pounce on the target thus presented and the games begin anew.

Of course it couldn't last. At some point I began to hear Father quietly singing Sext somewhere back behind me, and when I looked back out into the clearing it was to find the mound deserted, all the little foxes gone.

Later, on our way back to camp, the hermit explained what I had seen. The fox whose tracks we had followed was not really old or diseased; it had appeared thin and its coat poor because all the food it was finding was going to feed its young, the pups I had discovered at the den. He told me this was why its undersides had hung down like that, that these were udders, like a cow's, and that on any animal such protuberances were proof of motherhood. This also explained the animal's repeated trips up and down the trail. In a hurry to find food for her young, the vixen had risked the open path rather than taking a safer but slower route through the wood. Father told me these things as if he found them as remarkable as I. It was a gift he had. Of all the masters I have ever known, none taught me so much while always making it seem *I* was the one who was wise, *I* the one who deserved approbation for having provided the reason for such a lesson.

XIV

xcept for the end, except for what happened, what I did, at the end, I have always remembered my days on Modra nect as good, healthy, a time of unrelieved innocence, of lessons learned, discoveries made, the slow and uneventful process of growing up. But now, as I record these memories for the first time, attempt to put them in some sort of order, place flesh upon their bones, air within their lungs, I find myself beginning to wonder. Is that the way it was? Were things as perfect as I recall? Or is it possible that the habit of mind that would lead to my offense was present even in the child? Are we so formed at birth that our lives are just an empty clap of thunder, the lightning having long since done its work, flashed and gone out? The sins of the father. I don't know. All I know for sure is that, as I labor here, I find myself again and again coming up against the same hard fact: Winwæd is about to abuse a gift. Someone in authority over him has given the child a gift—whether of trust or of knowledge—and now we shall watch him abuse it, watch him wander off not after God or Wisdom or even truth, but after chimera, after some pointless chimera of his own foolish making.

I don't really remember what sort of animal it was that led me to the grove. All I remember for sure is that I was tracking, practicing the new art Father Hermit was teaching me, trying to follow the print of some unknown and otherwise savage beast, to participate, at this small remove, in its daily round. I do remember the surprise I felt when I came out into the meadow, saw the trees at its upper end. I had not known there was a meadow there, had not realized until I saw it that I was now in a part of the wood with which I was unfamiliar. And it was above me. The meadow itself, and the grove. I was always suspicious in those days of places that were above me. Climbing, it was easy to pass—however unwittingly—from one side of the mountain to the other, to the wrong side. I didn't like going down the mountain—*down* meant home, Redestone, the Rule—but up was worse, *up* could mean Cumbrogi. So, generally, I stuck to level, restricted my explorations to those parts of the wood my mind told me more or less corresponded to the height of the hermit's camp.

But there was something about this place, this unexpected meadow in the middle of nowhere, that appealed to me. Like all things on the mountain, it seemed larger than it should have been, for I was always in those days finding myself surprised by the size and multiplicity of the landscapes Modra nect contained. I had thought I had known the mountain, but what I had known was only its image, the reassuringly compact view I held of it, had learned of it, from down below, down at Redestone. But Modra nect wasn't that view; no, Modra nect was something else entirely, a nearly monstrous place that, even as I roamed over it, grew and shifted beneath me, giving birth to new arms, new legs, new valleys, new slopes. And now here was this meadow opening out before me like a great and rolling loaf of freshly baked bread. How could I not explore it, how could I resist?

Whatever the animal was that brought me there that day—badger, fox, deer—the thing had not hesitated but instead walked directly out into the meadow. And so, in doing likewise, I was able to tell myself I was merely being obedient to my master—for Father Gwynedd *had* told me I should follow whatever track I commenced upon till I could follow it no further, never permitting myself to be distracted by unrelated print or phenomena (*age quod agis*). It must have been a large animal, probably a deer, for I remember having little trouble following it up through the tall grass. Large animals are easy to track in such places since their bodies as well as their feet leave evidence of their passing. But after the two of us had proceeded only a short distance up the meadow's slope, my absent companion's sign became agitated: the animal turning abruptly, then bolting for the wood from which we both had previously emerged.

Yes. Yes, the more I think about it, the more certain I am it was a deer, for I remember sighting along the line of that escape—the narrow, punctuated trough of broken grasses that only a deer can make—back down toward the wood, Redestone, home. Then I turned and looked back up the hill, wondering what it was that had so frightened the beast.

I couldn't really see much. The ground rose from where I stood in such a way that, further up, it obscured what lay beyond. Still, from this vantage point, I could now see that the grove—which earlier had seemed to occupy the highest part of the meadow—actually stood at the end of a long ridge that swept back toward me, toward whatever lay above me. I looked back up that way, wondering if I might be able to see the abbey from up there. It happened sometimes. Sometimes when you least expected it, Modra nect could reveal aspects of Redestone you never would have thought possible.

With little else to do, I began to climb toward the high ground, arms up, woolens catching at the grasses, releasing, then catching again. It grew windy the higher I went and, from time to time, the grasses around me whispered and sighed. Between me and the distant grove, the slope opened up, grew wide, acquired a dappled appearance: the white-blonde swells of grass giving way here and there to irregular patches the size and color of cloud shadow. Eventually I reached a place where I could see that the ridge did indeed cross above me, providing a sort of backbone for this part of the mountain. From here it appeared that the meadow encompassed the ridge, lay over it like a blanket thrown over the back of a horse, the grove a roofless cage resting atop distant withers.

I looked toward the faraway grove, back toward the ridge above me, both pleased by the prospect and a little disappointed; for I think I had secretly wanted to find something more than this, something different, unusual, a reason to linger, a reason not to go home. Telling myself there was still time, that it was not yet Sext, I began to climb again, working my way up toward something I had noticed near the crest of the ridge, a spot of color in what I was beginning to admit was really a rather empty and uninteresting landscape.

The lay of the land continued to change as I mounted the slope. When first sighted, the ridge above me had seemed higher than the grove, but as I climbed the two changed positions; or, rather, the grove maintained its height while the ground I was making for fell away, became increasingly level, its highest-most point now clearly lower than that of the distant trees. My spot of color changed as well, becoming green, a dark green I thought, and I began to make out what looked like an area in the grass around it that had been trod upon. Which made sense, for anything still green so late in the year was bound to attract deer; indeed, the animal I'd been following had probably been headed in this direction when it was frightened off. I was rather proud of myself for thinking this, for it sounded like something Father Hermit would have thought, reminded me of the way he would have described something like this had he been here.

But, as it happened, I was wrong in this, my self-praise premature. It hadn't been deer that had trampled down the grass. When I reached the place I saw that it couldn't have been, for the track these animals left was too straight for that. Deer don't walk in straight lines, never walk in straight lines: it was one of the first things Father Hermit had taught me. And they don't eat holly either. For that was what this was, my spot of color, a few horny leaves—blue-green and leathery with age—on a length of branch woven carefully into the tall grass at the edge of the path.

I looked around. Whoever they were, you could tell from the track they'd left there'd been many of them. The line of trod-upon grass came down over the top of the ridge at an angle, turned here to rise again, then fell and rose in a series of gentle loops as it crossed the slope of the meadow to my right. Eventually, as if someone had made up his mind, the path ascended a last time and buried its head in the grove at the far end of the ridge. At the bottom of each loop in the path it looked as if someone had stopped to place one of these holly branches.

I saw all this, realized the meaning of all this, in much less time than it takes to describe here, in an instant really, and in that same instant I suddenly felt myself terribly exposed, vulnerable, standing there in the middle of the meadow. I knelt down. I knelt down and was relieved to discover that, kneeling, the grass hid me from anyone who might be watching from the wood below, the grove above. Of course I knew I should return immediately to the abbey, report what I had found, warn the community that there were strangers on the mountain. But—God forgive me—I wasn't really thinking about the community just then; I was thinking instead of what the brothers might say, what Waldhere might say, if I brought everyone up here and there was really nothing to see, just a place where some people had beaten the grass down as they passed through a field. I raised my head a little, looked out across the meadow toward the distant grove.

The place looked safe enough. There appeared to be something moving at one end but it didn't look important, a branch or something blowing in the wind.

Though it could have been a sleeve.

Maybe someone's arm signalling someone down in the wood.

The more I thought about this the more I liked it. I could hear myself telling it, how I had knelt here, spying on the grove, and how, then, something had moved, maybe only once, and I had thought, feared, there was someone up there, someone signalling someone down in the wood.

Of course in reality I didn't think this at all. The way the thing moved—regular, desultory—made the place look even more deserted: safer, emptier. I stood up, checking the grove a last time but no longer really afraid. I would have a quick look-around, that was all, and then home to Father Prior and the wide eyes of my fellow oblates.

As I made my way across the meadow, I thought about the Cumbrogi that had created this path (for I was certain it was they), wondering what it would be like *to be* a Cumbrogi, to walk across a meadow like this with my mind full of evil. Such thoughts are in the nature of tracking. When you follow an animal's print, discover in its sign proof of the decisions it has made that day—the stops, the turns, the place it chose for its bed—it is only natural to find yourself sympathizing with the beast, recognizing its needs, walking, as it were, in its shoes. Moreover, such thoughts are necessary to tracking, to understanding and anticipating your quarry's intentions. But the holly branches surprised me. The things had been braided into the grasses here and there along the path with great care, even skill. There was almost a sort of beauty to it. Still, they were a puzzling people, the Cumbrogi—everyone said so—and I supposed even the wicked could be expected to take pains in their pursuit of wickedness.

By the time I reached the bottom of the last loop in the path, I could see there was a scattering of parchment-colored leaves still clinging to the outer branches of the trees in the grove, which meant they were oaks. Father Hermit said oaks were the wise old men of the forest for they sometimes retained their leaves like this late into the year, holding them close against the coming cold. And maybe that was what I had seen. Maybe it had just been some dead leaves blowing in the wind.

But, once again, the day would teach me that perceptions arrived at from distance are not to be trusted. When I was about halfway up that last section of path, the movement became visible again and there was no doubting then what it was: a small piece of cloth—undyed, weathered—beating from the top of a tall pole.

I knelt down again. I didn't like this. This was too much like my story, signals left for people, warnings. I looked back down at the wood, for some reason certain this was where my enemy lay. At this distance the leafless trees formed a single gray mass, marked here and there by the darker patches of pine. There was no way I would be able to see anyone hiding down there.

I looked back at the grove. The place certainly looked empty. Though I was still too low to see the ground they stood upon, I could see the trees well now, their limbs gesticulating in the wind. Beyond them it looked as if there was nothing, just moving sky. To my left the ridge dropped away from me, back down toward the point at which I had first seen the holly, first joined this path. Again I found myself thinking about the back of a horse, though now it seemed I stood near the animal's head, looking down its neck toward distant hindquarters. Which made me think this must be the ridge's uppermost point, that the grove must mark that point, sit upon it…. Which meant that beyond the grove, just the other side of these trees….

If I stuck to this path, crawled up there on my hands and knees, no one down in the wood would be able to see me because of the grass; and then I could slip through the grove, out the other side, and disappear down the far slope before anyone even knew I was gone!

I liked the idea. If there were Cumbrogi down there, it had every chance of fooling them; and, if there weren't, well, it would be fun to crawl up there anyway, pretending there were.

I started out, keeping low, the grass on either side of me so tall I was reminded of crawling up through the fox's tunnel. Though I was afraid, I was also a little happy. The farther I went without any sign or sound from the wood, the more difficult it became for me to believe there really were any Cumbrogi down there. After all, I hadn't actually seen anything. Most likely I was going to reach the top of the path, explore an abandoned encampment (or maybe even a fort!), and then hurry home with exciting news. There were worse ways to spend an interval.

As I drew near the grove, the sound of the wind blowing through the trees grew loud, a mad rattling of dead leaves that unsettled me. Still, Father Gwynedd had taught me to attend to sound, that you could learn from it, that it too was a form of sign. When the noise became very loud, I judged myself close enough to stand up, risk a second look.

And that was when I saw it. That was when I saw the wagon.

Of course I've thought about this before. I've thought about what might have happened, what perhaps would have happened, had my mind not been in thrall to the story I was telling it, the notion I had of myself as some sort of hero, the little boy who was going to warn everyone of the bad people traipsing about on Modra nect. If I hadn't been half-playing, half-believing, there were Cumbrogi down in the wood watching me, I wouldn't have crawled up there like that, wouldn't have waited till the last possible moment to stand, look at what lay before me. I don't think the wagon would have had such an effect upon me then, for it would have come into view gradually as things do when one climbs toward them. I would have had time to become comfortable with it, note the familiar shape, recognize and identify the thing long before I saw it whole. But standing up as I did close like that, almost on top of it, there was no time for thinking, no time for context or understanding.

I had an unbroken view of the thing. I'm sure of that. No branches, no leaves, intruded upon that vision. And immediately behind the wagon there must have been a corresponding break in the trees, for I remember it seemed to float before moving clouds like an image of itself, at once perfect and improbable, furniture of dream and of nightmare.

I walked up to it.

As if it *were* a dream, as if I were part of the dream, I walked up to the wagon. I walked up to it and carefully, almost reverentially, I reached out and touched it.

It was real.

I had been playing at driving my imaginary oxen for some time when it happened, when the sound of the wind blowing through the trees abruptly changed, and—as if a signal had been given—the spell was broken. I remembered myself, remembered where I was, what I was doing, whom I had feared. I glanced to the right, the direction my ear told me should concern me, and seeing something, seeing something I did not want to see, immediately looked forward again, tried to pretend there had been nothing there, that I hadn't seen the figure standing at the edge of the grove. Perhaps if he didn't know I knew he was there he wouldn't move too quickly. Perhaps—if I was very fast—there was still time, I could still escape, get away.

But then it was all too much for me and despite myself, despite what I thought it was, indeed because of what I thought it was, what I most feared, I turned and looked Death in the eye.

And it was Father Gwynedd.

Father Gwynedd was standing just inside the ring of trees—hair, beard, woolens, everything, blown sideways by the wind—eyes alone steady: looking at me.

When we returned to the grove, we brought three brothers and Father Prior with us.

Of course by then I had some understanding of what it was that I had done, what it was that I had trifled with. Father Gwynedd had begun my instruction immediately upon finding me in the grove. The ridge-top wasn't, he had explained, a Cumbrogi holding at all. The grove and wagon belonged to the hill people, served as a place of worship for them, were, in point of fact, what they worshipped. He had pointed at the wagon then and—rather sternly for him—declared it to be proscribed. "You must treat such sign as you would the bear's," he said. "Caution! Danger!"

Later, after we'd come back to the grove, I found myself thinking quite a bit about that warning. At the time it hadn't bothered me unduly—someone was always pointing out how perilous the world was to oblates. But since then everyone had been behaving so strangely. Weren't we supposed to seek out pagans? Weren't we supposed to find them, convert them to the one true Faith? Father Abbot was always sending someone out "to save the hill people," and here I'd found some for them close-at-hand and you'd have thought I'd told them the world was coming to an end. Brother Swidbert was so scared he trembled constantly, his hood pulled down over his face like a man already dead. He'd gotten ill during the night and, despite the wind, you could hear the sounds he made, like a skin bursting. And Brother Hewald was worse. Except for the office, he never moved, standing with his arms stretched out like the Christ's, staring down at the distant wood. He'd stood like that during the sickness too, and though I now knew it to be a form of prayer, I still didn't like it. I didn't like anything that reminded me of the sickness. And what did it say about our situation that he chose to pray again like this now, here, when everything else seemed otherwise so perfectly ordinary? These were monks. What could be so bad it could scare a monk?

I looked over at Father Prior. Eyes closed, back held rigidly erect, he was kneeling by the wagon as he had been ever since Terce, praying diligently. Behind him, clouds tumbled past the ridge-top like frightened sheep. I thought about this, wondered about the difference between what was going on behind Father and what was going on within him. The way he held his head reminded me a little of the time Waldhere and I had heard something and, peeking through the window at Chapter, seen Father Prior in earnest discussion with our lord abbot. And maybe that was it. Maybe Brother Hewald's stance, Father Prior's wrinkled brow, weren't so much signs of prayer as of discussion, even of argument. Maybe that was why the monks were so afraid, because they knew what they were up against, knew what God was capable of, what He might do to such a heathen place.

And it was at that moment—even as I contemplated the power that sets all things in motion—that the clouds behind Father Prior abruptly froze in place and everything else—wagon, trees, Father Prior, Brother Hewald—began slowly, gracefully, to revolve back around in the opposite direction, back around me.

I shut my eyes.

Of course it was probably the hunger. We'd been fasting for two days now, and when you went that long without food you had to expect this sort of thing to happen. Still a part of me wondered if it might not be more than that. There were those that believed fasting made one susceptible to visions—even Waldhere believed this. Was it possible that what I was seeing, witnessing, was real? Could this be what it would look like, the effect of so much prayer: the grove's profanity being unwound like a dirty bandage from around the top of this ridge?

Or, worse, might this be preliminary to Whirlwind?

I kept my eyes shut tight, joined my prayer to that of those around me.

Dead leaves rattled in the trees overhead.

A raven called somewhere off in the distance.

But, otherwise, nothing happened.

I opened my eyes. I opened my eyes and, mercifully, everything was as it should be: the circle of oaks had ceased to revolve, Father Dagan knelt where he had been kneeling, and though my forehead felt unusually cool and damp, I felt better. Surely everything was going to be all right.

And it was then, as if God had made a particularly good point in their argument, that an entirely new set of wrinkles appeared on Father Prior's brow. He looked puzzled, uncertain. He looked worse than that.

I waited.

For a moment or two nothing happened. A finger rubbed another, the upper part of a leg twitched, but, otherwise, nothing. Then—so quickly it frightened me—my lord prior's eyes flew open and, twisting his head around violently, he cast a wild glance down at the far wood.

Of course I looked that way too but there was nothing to see, neither painted men nor blinding light. I looked back at Father and was surprised to find him looking at me. He smiled. I smiled. Then, embarrassed for him, I assumed custody of the eyes.

Later that afternoon it began to snow. I crawled under the wagon but the monks remained out in the open. The snow came down in big wet flakes that melted as soon as they touched the ground. There was something in the nature of this snow (God's silence descending upon our own) that dampened all sound. A hill person would have thought the monks mad, that they looked like nothing so much as big dumb statues amid all that swirling snow; but I knew better. I knew that quietly, internally, they were calling down Power onto this place.

Prior Dagan was the first to give up, climb in under the wagon. He settled himself against the inside of a wheel, pulled his hood down over his face and became quite still. After a while I could tell from the sound of his breathing that he had fallen asleep. Which didn't bother me. The others were still awake and Father deserved his rest: he'd been keeping the long watch ever since he'd learned of the grove.

The snow continued to fall, big white flakes drifting down out of an unnaturally flat dark sky.

Brother Swidbert came in next, then Brother Edric. When Brother Hewald gave up and crawled in under the wagon, he looked at me as if I'd done something wrong. I looked away.

The afternoon wore on, our tiny shelter growing close, the stink of damp woolens and someone's fasting breath. At some point I must have drifted off because I seemed to be on another ridge, long ago, when someone jostled me and I opened my eyes. Brother Hewald had changed positions. He was looking at Brother Edric. Brother Edric nodded and then glanced out at the open ground. He shook his head.

I looked out that way too but could see nothing wrong. The snow had changed—the big feathery flakes gone now, replaced by a snow that was coming down so fast it made a sort of hissing sound as it fell. Around the grove, in the lee of rocks and trees, the snow was accumulating in little piles that looked like spills of salt. Otherwise though, everything remained as it had been: the ground dark, the air white and moving, the hermit gray. I looked back at Brother Hewald and was a little frightened to find him looking at me. He shook his head to keep me from looking down, then—eyes insisting I pay attention—he lifted his chin toward the open area out in front of the wagon.

I looked out that way again but still could see nothing wrong.

Hewald's jaw muscles knotted.

I cocked my head: *Sir?*

Brother Hewald crossed himself, glanced once at the sleeping Dagan, then, in a whisper loud enough for everyone to hear, said, "Your master! Have you no shame?"

"Sir?"

"Take something and cover him up!"

Hot tears filled my eyes. I pulled my hood down over my face and held it there. Someone shoved a blanket under my chin and for the briefest of moments I thought it was meant for me. Then I remembered myself. Holding the blanket against my chest, I crawled out from under the wagon and stood up. For a moment I let the snow sting my face, each icy missile welcome, a blessing. Then I hurried across to the hermit.

Father was sitting with his back to the wagon as he had been since None. Earlier such a position might have afforded him some advantage, but since it had begun to snow the wind had changed direction. Fearful the dripping tonsure and beard might really bring on some life-threatening illness, I raised my blanket, intending to drape it over the old man's head and shoulders. Then I remembered. The last time I had touched the hermit when he was praying, he had told me I must never do anything like that again. Admittedly I had touched him with a firebrand on that occasion but, still, he had been emphatic.

I glanced back at the figures resting under the wagon and held up my blanket: *I hate to disturb him.* A pair of hands—white against the shadows—gestured impatiently.

I looked back down at Father Gwynedd. Water dripped from the tip of his nose; an icy froth was developing on the whiskers around his mouth. Then I noticed the dry place. Though elsewhere snow was pelting Father at will, the right side of his face—the side I was blocking from the wind—looked dryer. I moved to my left and the effect increased: fewer flakes struck the hermit. If I raised my blanket....

I held it out behind me like a sail and, like a sail, it caught the wind and blew flat against my back, my body and the blanket blocking both wind and snow. If he was conscious of the real world at all, Father must have thought it had stopped snowing.

I spread my legs and assumed a more comfortable stance, rather pleased with myself. Now, instead of returning to the wagon, I would have to remain out here on the open ground. Like Father Hermit, I would brave wind and snow, do my part to help the grown-ups cleanse this place of evil. It was a nice thought. It made me happy. I hoped Father Prior would wake up soon so he could see what I was doing.

For a long time I stood as I had imagined I would stand. My arms grew tired, my heart beat in my fingertips, but I did not falter. The brothers under the wagon knew I was there even if Father Gwynedd didn't. A part of me wondered what Father *did* know. Usually, when one of the monks underwent a mortification, you could tell they were suffering. It showed in their faces and, sometimes, in the way they behaved. But the hermit was different. Despite the fact his woolens were encrusted with rime, his tonsure dripping, he looked, well, if not happy certainly content, a man sitting by his fire thinking about something, pondering. And maybe that was it. Maybe he was. Who knew where Father Hermit went when he prayed. Did it snow in the Holy Land? Did the wind blow in Heaven?

A crystal of snow landed on the upper part of Father's ear, melted and, following the curve of the ear, ran down to the tip of the lobe from which it then hung, refusing to drop. I shivered and found that the motion relieved some of the pain in my right arm. When I turned my head to stretch in that direction, I saw that the snow had picked up again, the flakes coming down so fast they looked more like needles than snow. As I was noticing this, thinking this, the ground (like a piece of cloth rising toward the hand that stitches it) rose into the sky.

I looked down, forced myself to concentrate on the hermit, concentrate on holding my blanket just so. It helped. The ground grew firm beneath my feet, the earth ceased to levitate, and, slowly, my knees began to relax. I closed my eyes and thought about the hermit. In my mind I saw him flying, like St. Peter, around the tower of our ridge, a gray man flying wingless through a gray sky.

When I opened my eyes, it was to find the hermit looking at me.

"Winwæd?" he said.

Father followed my glance over at the wagon. When I looked back at him, he was smiling. "Well," he said, "at least you can sit under the blanket with me."

"Sir?"

Gently, Father pulled me down onto the ground beside him. He took my blanket from me, shook it out, and then, with a flourish, draped it over our heads. From the wagon we must have looked a little like Modra nect, the back of my head representing the mountain's lower, southern peak.

For a long time we sat like that. Perhaps it was the fast, perhaps the enchantment of falling snow, but, for once in my life, I felt no desire to speak or fidget; I lay quietly against Father's side, smelling the smell of old fires in his woolens and enjoying the tinkling sound the snow made on the blanket he held over our heads. After a while I grew drowsy. When I spoke, it surprised me as much as it must have the hermit. "What do you see, Father? When you pray I mean, what do you see out there?"

Though my eyes were closed, I could hear the smile in the voice that answered me. "Well," said Father Hermit, "if I'm lucky, I see nothing at all."

We still have the wagon. It's the one Father Cyneberht uses to haul manure. We had to play the part of oxen to get it down the mountain, but it would have been a shame to leave the thing behind. It was a perfectly good wagon.

XV

The furnace path was different in those days—darker, wetter, more mysterious. A species of bird called back there then that called nowhere else, its song fey, haunted, ethereal. Nonsense of course, the birds that sing now are the same as those that sang then; the valley above the monastery remains just as dark and dank. Still, memory insists it was different. Waldhere and I used to lie on our bellies at the entrance to the path and make up stories about what went on up there, the mill and its creaking wheel, the foreigner, Victricius, and all his works. We knew the place was important. When the man from the bishop was expected, the hours themselves seem to slow in anticipation of his arrival: Chapter was lengthened, prayers said, the food got better. But it wasn't the iron that interested us, it was the path itself, the fact that it was forbidden, that it lay there open and inviting at the very edge of our realm; and we could not go there. No matter how much we might want it otherwise, the furnace path was one place that would, we knew, remain forever out-of-bounds.

And then one day late in Lent, a third of the way through what had been up until that time a perfectly ordinary year, Father Prior asked me to walk with him there.

It was morning I remember, Prime having just come to an end—Father pulling me from the back of what was in those days not a particularly long procession. He didn't speak, just took me by the shoulder and, gently, pulled me from the line. When he pointed at the furnace path, indicated I should accompany him there, I tossed a quick glance at Waldhere and was pleased to find him looking back over his shoulder at us, clearly wishing he were me.

In truth we didn't go far, just far enough to be out of earshot of the cloister, but where we stopped was interesting enough. As with the west walk, the furnace path marks both walkway and watercourse, its flagstones roofing and concealing our abbey race (here too one feels the gentle thrumming through the soles of one's feet). But the furnace path is different as well, for the monks who dug the race were forced by the steepness of the upper valley to cut their channel directly from the side of the mountain. On one side of the path where Father Prior and I stopped, a sort of manmade cliff rises dripping and lichen-covered to half again the height of a man, while, on the other, the ground falls away dramatically toward the Meolch. The air would have been full that day, as it was every day, of the scents of hemlock and pine; the river, at full spate, deafening.

Father said something.

I cupped my ear.

He spoke again, louder. "You know how much we care for you."

I nodded. This was going to be bad.

"Good. It is our duty to love our brothers, but Christ has placed an especial obligation upon us to love children. For some this may be easy, for others it is a great cross to bear. You understand?"

Of course, he was talking about Brother Baldwin. I nodded.

"Good. Well, I wanted to make sure you understood this, that we love you, that we will always take care of you."

I smiled but I was beginning to worry. Once before, when we were all very little, Baldwin had tried to get rid of the oblates. I remembered it only as a time of loud words and unhappiness, but Dudda had told me, if it hadn't been for Father Prior, we all would have been placed at the far end of the abbey path.

Father must not have liked what he saw on my face. "Really," he said, "we do care about you. *I* care about you."

Again I nodded.

Father looked at me for a moment, then shook his head as if changing his mind about something. "It's your father," he said, "your father Ceolwulf is here."

I looked at my lord prior.

His voice softened. "The stranger?" he said. "The man with the scar and all the rings? He's your father, your natural father."

The relief was so great I almost laughed. Father didn't know I knew who the visitor was. He'd just been preparing me for the shock.

"This is good? You are pleased the man is your father?"

Knowing that I wasn't supposed to be, I shook my head and bit my lip, trying to appear serious. But I was overjoyed. They weren't going to throw us out after all!

"Well," Father went on doubtfully, "he is your father and, right or wrong, he has asked to see you."

"Sir?" I said, forgetting myself.

"Your father has asked to see you. He's waiting for you now in the abbot's lodge."

I didn't say anything.

"It's all right, you have my permission to speak."

"Now?" I asked.

Father nodded. "But it's all right. You don't have to see him if you don't want to. You are a member of this community with the same rights and privileges as anyone else. This man has no claim on you. As far as the Rule is concerned, he is just a visitor to the abbey, a guest like any other."

I looked back down the path toward the cloister. He was there *now*. He was waiting for me *now*.

In my memory of that morning there are two small, unrelated things that stand out. The first was a bowl of soup Ceolwulf's man was eating. In those days children fasted during Lent like adults. I hadn't had anything to eat since collation the night before and I was very hungry. I wonder now if the man knew this. In my memory he was sitting on the ground by the door to the abbot's lodge and he looked at us when we walked up. Later I would find out he was my older brother but I did not know this then. He was just a very tall, very hard-looking man sitting on the ground next to the door to the abbot's lodge. There were two spears and a shield leaning against the wall beside him. And he was eating. It was still early, the sun just coming up over the Far Wood, and the light was very pure. The man's soup looked good. Its surface glistened. When the man noticed where I was looking, he smiled. He pulled a chunk of bread from his blouse, dipped it in his bowl, and brought it, dripping and soggy, to his mouth. My stomach turned at this extravagance and if Father Prior hadn't shoved me through the door I think I would have fainted.

I also remember the fire someone had lit in Father Abbot's private chamber. It's funny what you focus on when you feel confused, and I was feeling very confused that morning. Things were happening that weren't supposed to happen. Father Prior had invited me to walk on the furnace path. I had been given a choice as to whether I wanted to meet the man who was my father and was not my father. A stranger had looked me directly in the eye. And now there was a fire in Father Abbot's private chamber. Everyone knew there weren't supposed to be any fires in Father Abbot's room, the lord abbot himself had forbidden it. And yet someone had lit one. The man I was about to meet? If Ceolwulf had lit the fire, would he get in trouble for it? Could a man who was a guest (but was also my father) get in trouble for breaking a rule?

There were no introductions. Or, if there were, I don't remember them. All I remember is myself on the floor, kneeling, the sound of Father Prior's feet receding through the front room, the heat of the fire on my down-turned head. For a moment I knelt there, terrified, wondering what would happen next, and then, roughly but quite easily, a large hand pulled me to my feet.

I tried to look down but the hand wouldn't allow it. A finger caught my chin and forced it up. Red face, pale scar, big eyes, shining teeth. "There now," said the man who was my father, "we'll have none of that. If there's one thing I hate about these baldpates, it's the way they're always looking at my feet."

I tried to smile but I could feel the tears coming. I wasn't used to being handled so.

"That's a boy, that's a boy!" The big teeth got bigger and my father's face broke into a lopsided grin. "You're your father's own son!" The hand released my chin and for a while I could feel where a ring had pressed against the skin. The man who was my father noticed that I had to stop myself from looking down. He nodded to himself. "Uh-huh, uh-huh," he said, and then, as if he'd decided something, he turned and sat on Father Abbot's bed.

"There now," he said, smiling again, "warm yourself by my fire. You know there was no fire in this place when I arrived! Cold as a dead man's backsides!" Ceolwulf laughed and when he laughed it was as if his teeth would fly from his head. I had never seen anyone laugh indoors before and it frightened me. I wanted to step back, to assume custody of the eyes. I wanted to explain why there had been no fire in Father Abbot's chamber. There were many things I wanted to say, do, but, instead, I was polite. I kept my mouth closed and extended my hands toward the fire. I tried to look like someone who liked so much heat.

Ceolwulf smiled and rubbed his hands back and forth on his legs. "There now, there now. So, are they treating you well?"

I glanced at the door through which Father Prior had gone but could find no help there. I wanted this man to like me, to know I was a good boy, but he had asked me a direct question without first giving me permission to speak. How did he expect me to respond?

Ceolwulf's eyebrows rose, inviting me to get on with it.

Again I glanced at the door. No one had told me what to do. No one had taught me anything about this.

"Come on," said Ceolwulf, "I have a right to know. I'm your father."

I stood up straight. If I went slowly, very slowly, he might understand. Ceolwulf waited.

I pointed at myself. I placed my hands back at my sides. I smiled. I pointed at my smile. Still smiling, I raised my right hand and rubbed my belly contentedly.

"What's that supposed to mean?" said Ceolwulf, jiggling his fingers at me. "I'm no monk."

Despite myself I looked at my feet.

"Come on boy, don't be shy, speak up!"

I took this as permission. "I am Winwæd," I said, "oblate of the monastery at Redestone."

"Yes, yes, and I am Ceolwulf, son of Beornwine, companion of kings, slayer of Ethelhere and Tiowulf…. What of you, boy? What of you?"

Slayer of Ethelhere and Tiowulf.

"You look terribly thin."

I looked down at myself, embarrassed.

"Do they feed you enough?" Ceolwulf glanced toward the door. "Because if they don't, I will speak with them. You are my son, you should be treated with respect."

"They feed me enough…."

Ceolwulf looked at me. I had almost called him "Father."

"All right, all right," he said. "And what of your work here? Do you enjoy the life that's been given you?"

For a moment I just looked at the man. No one had ever asked me a question like that before.

"The praying, the Church, do you like it?"

I thought about Waldhere and Ealhmund, Father Prior and Father Gwynedd.

"It's not a hard life, now is it? No one, I think, would call it a hard life."

"There was a sickness. I had to help bury people."

"Um-hmm, um-hmm, and so you should. When people die, you have to bury them, don't you?" My father had a habit of playing with the whiskers next to his scar when he was thinking about something. I tried to keep my attention on his eyes.

"You're very fortunate you know. You know that don't you?"

Again I thought about Father Prior and Father Gwynedd. I nodded: *Yes, I was very fortunate.*

"Never having to worry about anything, never having to make any decisions; it's a nice life you have up here, a great gift I made you as well as God."

I had never thought about it that way before but, yes, I supposed he was right. I smiled.

"Of course your mother fought me every step of the way."

My mother.

"Yes, yes, I know it's hard to believe. Most of the women are so caught up in this," Ceolwulf indicated Father Abbot's room with his hand. "But when a man wants to do something, show he cares too, what do they do?"

I didn't know.

"'He's too young, wait another year.' 'Not this year, but the next....' And then another and another. Before you know it, you'd have been as big as Oisc out there." My father nodded his head toward the door. "Think they'd have wanted you then?"

My mother had wanted to keep me.

"Of course not, of course not, and that wouldn't have been right would it? I mean, Lord knows, you can't do any better than a monk, can you? I mean living life as a monk's the best thing you can do, isn't it?"

The scar formed a sort of crease on the side of my father's face. His whiskers bent in toward the crease so it looked as if they were being sucked into the scar.

"Of course it is, damned priests telling you all the time. And the woman going to deny you that, her own son! Can you imagine?"

I tried not to look at the scar.

"And of course a promise is a promise, isn't it? Especially a promise made to God."

I nodded. I knew the answer to that one.

"Well of course it is." Ceolwulf smiled. "And I had promised you to God. But I suppose they've told you about that haven't they, about Oswiu and me, Gaius Field?"

The question caught me off guard. I could tell from the way he asked it that I was supposed to know, that apparently everyone was supposed to know, but he had already struck me with so many new ideas—whether I liked it here, my mother, my work, Ethelhere, and now somebody's field—it was all too much for me.

Ceolwulf shook his head. "Silly priests. Well, sit down boy, sit down. You've a right to hear. No, not there. There, by the fire. Make yourself comfortable."

The fire was big, too big for the room, and I was already over-warm, but the man was a guest and my father so I did as I was told. I sat by the fire and looked up at Ceolwulf.

"There, how's that?"

I smiled at him. It was nice that he was so concerned for me.

Ceolwulf nodded to himself then placed his hands on his knees, sat up straight and looked at me. "You will have heard of Penda," he said.

I nodded, happy to show myself knowledgeable.

"A bastard. But did they tell you it was Deira he attacked, that it was sweet Deira caught the worst of Penda?"

I shook my head. Of course I had been taught about Deira, Deira and Bernicia. We lived in Deira and the bishop lived in Bernicia. But beyond that I knew little.

"Yes, I didn't think so. Twenty-two years Penda ruled Mercia and every one of them hell for us." Ceolwulf looked at me. "Killed your mother's people you know, wiped them out. Had their way with the women, stole what they didn't eat, then burned everything to the ground. Afterwards, when I knew they were gone, I took her there. Thought there might be something left but there wasn't. Post-holes, trash pits, nothing else. Not an animal alive." Ceolwulf shook his head. "Never seen your mother like that. Didn't cry, just got pale, white, all the blood gone to her feet. She picked something up—I can't remember what, piece of wood, a broken pot, something—and carried it around with her for a while. I don't think it really meant anything to her. After a while she dropped it again. The place stunk of fire. If you walked close to the house, little clouds of ash puffed up around your feet.

"Of course I was angry. Everyone was angry, but what could we do? Penda had friends, didn't he? Simple as that. Don't see why everyone has such a problem understanding it. Painted devils to the north, Cumbrogi to the west, Penda south, the sea behind. Simple." Ceolwulf looked at me. "Never go into battle with water at your back, boy"—he smiled—"we taught them that. But in those days everyone wanted to be Penda's friend, Penda's companion, even Ethelwald. We didn't stand a chance."

Ceolwulf got up and walked away from me. For a moment I was afraid the story was over but then I saw he was just getting more wood. It had been a wet winter and the wood was damp. When Ceolwulf placed it on the fire, the flames died down a little and, however momentarily, the air around my face grew cooler. "Don't know what's wrong with these people," said Ceolwulf. "Don't give you enough wood to cook your porridge then look at you as if you'd spat when you ask for more. Whole damned place surrounded by wood! Where was I?"

"You didn't stand a chance."

Ceolwulf smiled. "Right. We didn't stand a chance. So Oswiu did the only reasonable thing, offered treasure. Brooches and rings, dyes and salt, enough iron for fifty swords, a gold and ivory comb that had belonged to Queen Ethelberga, two hundred hides of land (most of it cleared), and his daughter, Alchfled, as bride to Penda's son. And what did Penda do?" Ceolwulf's grin grew fierce. "He waited a year, then burned half Deira to the ground. Bastard. Accepted our tokens, gave his pledge, then invaded anyhow, boasting of what he would do. He loved fire, Penda did, fire was his favorite. He'd as soon torch a field as harvest it, burn a virgin as do her. You could smell him coming on the wind, the smoke and the burning. Sometimes, when the air was very still, the ash would fall like snow when Penda was coming."

Ceolwulf looked toward the window and for a moment I could see only the left side of his face. He was handsome, at least that side, straight nose, thick hair, dark eyes. Of course the hair looked wrong—there being far too much of it—but otherwise I thought him handsome.

"But you have to give Oswiu credit. He didn't hole up at Bamburgh as some have when Deira burned. No, he raised an army and...." Ceolwulf paused, smiled to himself. "Or maybe the army raised him. We were all going up there of course. Puch and Tondhere, Beornhæth with what was left of his band, Ingwald and even Guthfrid. Anyone not cut off by Penda's march left Deira that year for Bernicia. It was late autumn when we arrived and I should imagine Oswiu didn't like the looks of us, camped around his walls like so many beggars. But he put a brave face on it. Cried out against the destruction, promised revenge, brought in his priest to pray for us. The priest probably wasn't such a good idea." Ceolwulf poked at the fire with a piece of wood. "Called Penda a pagan, all sorts of names, then, as if it were nothing, pointed out that the bodies of the burned now stood little chance of resurrection. That stirred 'em up." Ceolwulf glanced around the room. "Put up with all this, then lose it anyway because some bastard likes fire." Ceolwulf looked at me for a moment. "Do these priests know what they're doing?"

Again I was caught between two worlds, the one wanting to be agreeable, the other loyal.

But Ceolwulf didn't wait for an answer. "Anyway," he said, "Oswiu stepped in before the idiot made a complete balls-up of it. Reminded everyone Christ could do whatever He wanted, greatest prince of them all, the usual, could heal anyone, raise anyone, even someone as horribly burned and disfigured as their poor wives and children—the priest all the time nodding in the background, suddenly afraid of what he's done, all the murmuring, the ugly looks. So Oswiu convinces them they weren't complete fools to have become Christians (this having been *his* policy), and to show them how powerful this new God is, how He can do anything, defeat anyone no matter the odds, he offers to prove it with a bargain. If Christ will march at the head of his army and wipe the enemy from the field, then he, Oswiu, like the good king he is, will grant a boon in return for the favor performed." Ceolwulf held his hand up and made his rings glitter in the firelight. "Always a good idea to remind people of the gifts you can bestow when you're about to take them into battle. And Oswiu was no fool. No miser either. For us, gold; for Christ, a woman. Or at least a little girl. It was his daughter Ælffled, I think her name was Ælffled.

"So, anyway, in those days, when a man made a gesture like that, especially when he did it in his own hall, his guests were expected to do likewise. Especially when war was afoot. So, soon enough, everybody's drinking and boasting, promising to give Christ their daughters, their sons, what-have-you. Hell one fool even offered his ox." Ceolwulf laughed, shook his head. "Of course no one's as generous as a young man with his whole life in front of him. I thought I was immortal in those days, no one could touch me, no one." Again Ceolwulf shook his head. "I stood up, proud, all eyes on me, and promised my next-born *and* two hides of land. My next-born turned out to be you."

I smiled, pleased to be made part of the story.

Ceolwulf looked at me as if I'd done something wrong. "That was good land," he said. "Fine land, belongs to your abbot now. A little rocky perhaps but nothing wrong with it. Shame really. If he's not going to use it, you'd think he could.... You know what I'm talking about Winwæd, the land beyond the two oaks? Don't know what they call it around here but you might want to talk to the good brothers, see if...." Ceolwulf stopped and looked at me, shrugged. "Hasn't been cleared anyway. High ground, rocky, probably not worth the trouble." He glanced toward the door. "Though the baldies haven't done so badly with rocks, have they?"

I smiled. Guests always complimented our church.

"So, anyhow, pledges made, songs sung, we marched south to find Penda. Not hard really. Stay down-wind, follow the smoke. Supposed to have been something in the old days, Penda, a real warrior, but I wasn't so impressed. Couldn't have been easier to follow, no rear guard, no one left alive to put up a clamor, raise the alarm." Ceolwulf pulled at a thread on his sleeve. "Of course you can see what he was thinking. Thirty commanders. Called 'em 'legions!' Thirty commanders leading thirty *legions*. Must have thought he was invincible. Oswiu's own nephew to lead them in. But that was where he made his mistake." Ceolwulf looked hard at me. "Never fight with water at your back and never trust a traitor."

I nodded, pleased the way he taught me things while he told his story. It reminded me of Father Prior.

"If a man has betrayed once, he'll betray again. And Ethelwald was leaving his backdoor open. Oh I'm sure he told Penda it was because the valley was better, straighter, easier to keep his army together, plenty of water, provender. And of course he was right, more settlements along a river, always are. But he was keeping his options open too. You don't need a horse when you've got a river, one side safety, the other hell. When the battle finally came, Ethelwald was on the opposite shore. A traitor but no fool. Almost got away too. Would have if we hadn't been so quick.

"It was around Loidis…" Ceolwulf hesitated. "You know…maybe Christ really did want all those little girls, you think? I mean, why's he like little girls so much?"

"The Christ loves all children." Father Prior said so.

Ceolwulf cocked an eyebrow at me. "Well, maybe, it certainly did rain. Buckets. Two days, three days, might never have caught him otherwise. On the fourth day, still raining, Penda finally stopped. Why march in weather when you're winning?" Ceolwulf's smile wasn't nice. "Only desperate men march in weather. We marched in weather. Caught up with him at a place called Gaius Field. Just a bend in the river really, I don't know, maybe somebody named Gaius held it once. Anyway, they stopped there. Didn't burn the place this time because of the rain. Nice farm. Bottom-land. Two or three out-buildings, a granary, and the one main building. By the time I got there it was already dark. Tondhere took me up to the top of the ridge so I could see them, so many campfires down there it looked like stars, the main building lit up in the center. We sat there for a long time, sounds coming up to us—laughter, singing—the kind of sounds you hear when things are going well, no real resistance, plenty of women for the thanes, farm animals for everyone else."

Ceolwulf chuckled for a moment, then became serious. "We took them just before sun-up. Early morning. Just enough light to move without noise. It had stopped raining but everything was still wet, slippery. I remember we could smell them before we saw them, moving down through the trees. Armies always stink but this one was particularly bad—all that damp wool, the piss, and something else, we didn't know what, a terrible smell. As we got closer it got so bad you couldn't help feeling they were all around you, like the smell, all around you. Then, finally, the fog began to lift and we could see them, hundreds of them, thousands, the ground littered with bodies." Ceolwulf looked at me. "That's what they sing about it now, that it looked like a battle already won—smoke in the air, bodies littering the field, stench of death—but it's not true. People like songs like that but it doesn't really look like that, not at the time it doesn't. At the time it just looks bad, impossible—I don't care if they were sleeping. I mean I don't care if they were all lying around on the ground, sleeping. That many men, looking out at that many men: it'll put the wind up you.

"But we took them. Took them just before sun-up. Best time really. Catch a man in the middle of his dreams, bed still warm, air cold, spirits low. Catch a man like that he hasn't had time to remind himself of who he is, who his friends are, what they will think of him. Like a child really, all he knows is his sleep's been broken and more than anything else he wants it back. Like a child.

"It was sun-up, just before, mist everywhere, everything gray and wet. I remember there was a shout, I don't know, somebody caught a guard, somebody taking a piss, I don't know, but I remember there was a shout and everyone was running forward, and then I was running forward, swinging my sword, yelling. I killed four men before I had to face anyone standing up. Everyone did. Dead bodies everywhere, tripping over them, slipping in the blood. I saw a man trip over his own guts, stand up, trip again. I saw a man with one leg trying to get to his feet. Comical really, though at the time you don't think that. I was swinging at someone, the fourth or fifth man, when something hard hit me, stunned me really. For a moment it was as if I were somewhere else, the story of a battle instead of the battle itself, everything moving slowly as it does when you want someone to hurry up and finish the story, and then, all of a sudden, there was a great rush of sound and I realized the man I'd been hacking at was already dead and there was another man, a man with an ax, looking at me. I turned toward the man with the ax and it was then I felt the blood. It was all over me really—you know how facial wounds are—my beard must have been red, my neck. The front of my shield certainly was."

Ceolwulf smiled as if he'd remembered something funny. "Peculiar thing about wounds, some wounds, they help you instead of hurt you. But you have to work fast before the shock wears off. That was what was wrong with the man that hit me. Shock. Maybe he was young, maybe he'd never hit anybody with an ax before, maybe he was still half asleep, but instead of finishing the job as he should have, he just stood there like an idiot, eyes wide, mouth working. Used to be a one-eyed man in Oswiu's hall talked about it. Somebody'd hit him too, an ax, a club, I can't remember, but instead of gouging his eye or splitting it, the thing had squeezed it somehow, pinched it, because it had popped out." Ceolwulf chuckled. "'Like a plum from a pie,' he said, popped from his face 'like a plum from a pie.' And then of course it just hung there, by its cord, dangled against his cheek.

"Well you can imagine. Same thing happened to him happened to me—his opponent so surprised by a man standing there with his eye hanging out he hesitated for a moment, forgot what he was doing. Before he remembered, he was dead. That's the advantage. A wound like that affects the people around you more than it does you. And of course it makes you angry. The old man claimed he killed twenty before it was over, said he held his eye out in front of him like a lantern, turning it this way and that, seeking them out. Of course it didn't really work anymore. Later, after the battle was over, he tried to put it back in but it didn't work anymore, couldn't see anything with it. Used to laugh and say he'd probably put it in wrong, upside down or something. Anyway, he had to cut it off and after that he wore a cloth over that eye."

Ceolwulf fingered the whiskers along his scar. "Ugly isn't it? My eyebrow used to go all the way out to here." He pointed at a spot beside the crease. "Saved my life though. I'm not saying I remembered the old man's story, I'm not saying I didn't. All I know for sure is suddenly no one was moving around me, that idiot standing there like somebody waiting for orders. I gave him orders. I sank my sword into him, opened him up from top to chops, each eye watching me as it went down. Hell I don't blame him! My cheek was opened up to here, wasn't it, back teeth showing? Must have looked like my ear was grinning! Why I could stick out my tongue without ever opening my mouth, wiggle it like a snake. They shat all over themselves getting out of my way, cattle really, sheep. Never felt so brave, so sure of myself. But of course it didn't last, couldn't I suppose. Killed two more I think, maybe three, then I don't remember anything after that." Ceolwulf looked at me. "Flesh wounds do that to you. No matter how strong you are, how big, the strength drains from you with the blood. Anyhow, after it was over, they told me I'd killed eight men, Ethelhere among them, but I don't know. That seems like a lot of men."

Ceolwulf got up and walked over to the window. Earlier they had been working in the pollards but the sounds had stopped now. Ceolwulf looked out that way anyway.

"What about the smell?" I asked. "What about the smell you smelled? What was that?"

Ceolwulf looked at me, the light from the window making his face pale. "The smell?"

"The bad smell you smelled at the beginning."

"Oh, that." Ceolwulf smiled. "Well, I didn't find out about that till later, afterwards. There were Eyra women there that time, sometimes there are, sometimes there aren't. Anyhow, one of them nursed me. Not much to look at and her poultices stank, but she knew what she was doing." Ceolwulf looked at the fire. "It's the fire you want to keep out of a wound like that, the heat. It's when they turn red-hot you know you're in trouble. But the woman knew what she was doing. She bathed me and tended me and, slowly, the hole knit itself shut.

"Of course for a long time I couldn't talk. Tried to but half the time air just blew out of my cheek. She didn't like it. Said I shouldn't do it, it was bad for the wound, but I don't think that was it. I think she just didn't like the sound it made. Anyhow I lay there for a long time with nothing to do, couldn't talk to anybody, didn't have the strength for any work. People would come by and talk to me but all I could do was nod or shake my head, maybe point a finger at something." Ceolwulf had sat back down by the fire and now he looked at me. "It makes people uncomfortable you know, the not talking. It shows a lack of courtesy. No one wanted to sit with me, no one wanted to talk with me, or at least not long. I couldn't carry on my share of the conversation. But, even so, I began to hear what had happened."

For a moment Ceolwulf stared again into the fire. "It could have gone either way. I mean you can see that now, looking back on it, you can see how badly it could have gone. I wish you could have seen their fires that night, there were so many of them, like stars they said, like looking down into a pool full of stars. But we surprised them and that was an advantage. Maybe the numbers too, an advantage I mean. While all of us had our hands full, hack and swing, hack and swing, most of them had little to do, the second and third ranks caught between river and battle, no place to go, nothing to do—try to move forward and you shove your own men into the battle, move back and you're up to your ass in water." Ceolwulf smiled. "And it was then"— the smile grew larger— "it was then that the river began to rise.

"Of course it was your Christ did it, or that's what the priests all claimed. Hell I'd claim it too, the way it rained and rained and then, at just the right moment, began to flood." Ceolwulf studied the furnishings in Father Abbot's room. "You know sometimes they call Him 'Prince of the Sky', 'Heavenly Warrior', that sort of thing. The priests I mean. Notice they don't do it around here much but they sure do up at Bamburgh. And I don't know, when you think about it…I mean you have to admit it was a piece of work. Like someone knew what they were doing, knew the difference between the front and the rear."

Ceolwulf looked at me again. "Funny place, the rear, time on your hands. You can hear the sounds, the yelling, the clanging, you can hear the screams, but you can't do anything about it. All the fear, none of the action. Then, all of a sudden, your one advantage, the fact that you *are* in the rear, that behind you all is safe, is taken from you. A man who was sitting down, jumps up"—Ceolwulf jumped up, hands behind him—"hands on his backsides." He pointed at the fire, "A fire sputters, catches again, sputters, goes out. Then, right in front of you, the first small trickle of water runs across the ground." Ceolwulf sat back down, a funny look on his face. "They would have held up their feet at first. Laughed. Glanced at one another. But it wasn't funny. Not really. They all must have known what it meant. The river was rising, would probably continue to rise, and there was no place to go, no place to go but forward.

"Well you can see how it must have been after that, once it got started, the men in the back beginning to push forward, grumbling, trying to stay out of the water, the men in front of them pushing forward too, word spreading as it does, men at the very front beginning to realize something is going on, something behind them. You don't like that, the feeling something is going on behind you, nobody likes that, it makes you nervous. So, probably about then, probably not long after someone first noticed the water, someone way up at the front got the wind up and turned and ran. Probably someone didn't even know what was happening. Afterwards no one ever knows who it was. Funny, I mean you know someone was standing there, next to him, behind him, someone must have seen it, but no one ever tells." Ceolwulf laughed. "Maybe it's because they can't. Had to turn tail to tell tale."

Ceolwulf smiled to himself, then became serious again. "You can see it before it happens you know, little things. The eyes no longer on you, not really, the feet sidestepping. It's easy to kill a man when he's fighting like that, backwards, mind on the rear, thinking with his heels. Must have been strange though, men at the front beginning to shift backwards, press into those behind them, they in turn pressing into those behind them and so on until, finally, someone escaping us came up against someone escaping the water. There was a struggle maybe, men pressing forward, men pressing back, yelling, swearing, I don't know, swinging swords. Probably could have gone either way but it didn't. We must have seemed worse than the water. Anyway, the tide turned. Everybody began moving backwards, slowly at first and then more quickly, backwards, toward the river.

"Don't get me wrong, it wasn't a rout. There were too many of them for that, they couldn't move that quickly. Those in the rear would have had time to think about it, to wander in, wade in, eyes wide, feeling their way, praying for shallows. Maybe a spear fell among them, who knows, an arrow—there were arrows that day. Whatever, something began to hurry them along, they began to take bigger steps, forget where they were, what lay ahead of them, striding out to get away from the fighting. Then, one by one, they would have struck the deeper water—the shout, an arm thrown back, already too late, the channel already beneath them, the press upon them." Ceolwulf shook his head. "Ugly scene then, always is, men beginning to step on one another, climb over each other. Embarrassing what they'll do at the end, the way they'll claw at each other, do anything to get away—same men brave otherwise."

Ceolwulf thought about that for a moment, laughed. "When I came to, the place looked like someplace somebody's building a fort, you know, a big old fort, the water full of logs they've floated down." Ceolwulf chuckled. "Bobbing up against one another, turning, jamming up the eddies." He shook his head. "People tell you they sank are fools. Lots of people claim that, that the river's full of treasure, the bodies sank because they were weighted down with gold. Fools. There wasn't any gold. I'd have gotten my share, wouldn't I have? I don't know, I guess the other people had it, the ones that got away, or Oswiu. But the bodies floated. Hell everything floated—shit, blankets, firewood—you had to clear a place just to get a drink of water."

"What about the smell? The smell you smelled when you first got there?"

"What? Oh, yes, I was going to tell you about the smell. Well, that was the funny thing, that was the thing that made everyone laugh. Every battle has one, something funny happens I mean. Cow mistaken for the enemy, speared to death, a path that's supposed to take you to the rear, takes you to the front, that sort of thing. The best I ever heard was the man whose army ran away from him. I wasn't there, but the way they tell it he was standing on a little rise, shouting at the enemy, boasting of his superior numbers, of how he would carry the day, while all the while his men were deserting behind him, running away right and left in full view of the enemy, the fool still going on, unaware of it, giving his pretty little speech while, right behind him, one by one, his army was melting away. Finally I guess there was just him standing out there all by himself. I would have loved to have seen the look on his face when he finally realized what was going on, turned around and saw there wasn't anyone there."

Ceolwulf shook his head. "Anyway, that was the funny thing that time, the beans. When the light got better you could see them, they were everywhere. I don't know, I suppose the rain had gotten to them, spoiled them or something, fermented. You ever smell beans when they've gotten like that, gone off like that?" Ceolwulf closed his eyes and shook his head like a man smelling something he didn't like. "Shoo that stinks! Anyhow, I guess they'd distributed them anyhow, I don't know, maybe didn't know they were bad. But it hadn't taken long to figure it out. I guess some of the men threw theirs in the river and some up into the forest. That was what we'd smelled, what we'd marched through, it really had been all around us!" Ceolwulf laughed. "Beans! But a lot of them hadn't even bothered, just pitched them out wherever they were, beans everywhere, stinking up the ground, mashing underfoot. Whole camp stunk of it, and then afterwards of course there were the dead too. But it was the beans that were funny." Ceolwulf shook his head at the memory. "Whew was that a stink!

"But it was the river I was telling you about. It's the river that's important. The river saved the day that day, don't let anyone tell you otherwise. They had us three-to-one, some say five-to-one, and that river just sucked them down, wrapped her coils around them and pulled them down." Ceolwulf smiled. "That's what it was like, a snake, a big old mud snake swollen with food." He shook his head. "It was something. That river really saved the day."

Ceolwulf moved his shoulders once, loosening them, and then he stood up. He stretched—hands balled into fists, reaching up toward the roof. I watched him stretch and thought about getting up and stretching myself, though of course I didn't. I could tell the story was over but I didn't mind. It had been a good story, a very good story, and I knew that Waldhere and Ealhmund would like it. I could see myself telling it to Waldhere and Ealhmund, how they would look, how I would look. I was sure I wouldn't forget anything.

Ceolwulf walked over to the window. He didn't walk like other men, head down, thinking, praying. He walked like a man who already knew everything he needed to know, didn't need to think about anything, pray about anything. When he got to the window, he turned around, the brooch at his shoulder glinting in the light, eyes cold and white. I wondered if, someday, I would be as tall as he.

"Have they told you how you came by your name?"

I was embarrassed. I knew it was a funny name, that no one had a name like mine, but I didn't want to talk about that now.

"Well, have they?"

I shook my head. "Father Prior says there's a river with the same...."

Ceolwulf smiled.

For a moment I wasn't sure I understood, and then....

He nodded. "It was the Winwæd that rose that day at Gaius Field."

I smiled.

"At Yeavering, men raise their cups at the mention of your name."

Ceolwulf was showing me his sword when the bell rang. I started to get up but he stopped me.

"Terce," I said. "It's Terce. I have to go now."

Ceolwulf just looked at me.

"You know, the office? When we chant?"

Ceolwulf shook his head. "But you don't have to go, you're not a monk. You're a....an...."

"An oblate."

Ceolwulf looked at me as if I'd said something wrong.

"I have to go too, oblates have to go too." I started to get up again but Ceolwulf's hand was still on my shoulder. Outside the bell had stopped ringing.

"You don't really want to go, do you?"

I glanced toward the door. I didn't want to go, he was right, but I had to, it was Terce. If I didn't hurry I was going to be late.

"What difference does it make if you miss this...this Terce? I mean just once?"

I looked at Ceolwulf. Was he serious?

"I mean how important can Terce be?"

Father Prior said that it was very important. He said the office was the way the abbey breathed.

"It's not as if it were a Mass or something."

"Father Prior says it's like breathing. He says…."

"Prior Dagan won't mind if you miss it once, just this once."

I wasn't so sure.

"Besides, I don't want you to go."

Again I just looked at him.

"Really, I'm enjoying this."

He did seem to be. Ceolwulf, the companion of kings, the man who was my father, seemed honestly to be enjoying my company.

"You are my son. I may not ever get to see you again. Don't leave me for something you get to do every day."

I may not ever get to see you again.

"I am asking you to stay."

"I will," I said, wishing I could stand up to say it. I didn't care if Father punished me. I didn't care if I had to beg for my food. I didn't care if the lord abbot made me kneel before Faults and confess my sin. Ceolwulf was my father and a guest at our abbey: *I would not disappoint him.*

Ceolwulf smiled. "That's my boy, that's my boy!" He rubbed his hands on his knees as he had when I first came in. "Now where was I?"

"You were telling me about your sword, about how it got its name."

Ceolwulf glanced at the sword lying on the bed beside him. "That, yes that. Well, that will have to wait. Right now it is important that you learn about us, about our family."

Our family.

Ceolwulf got up and walked over to the window. He placed both hands on the sill and leaned out. He looked to his left, toward the village, and to his right, toward the reredorter and the mountain. He pulled his head back in, reached out, pulled the shutters to behind him. For a moment there was just a place where the light leaking around the edges of the shutters struck something dark; then, slowly,

I began to see my father again, the face, the eyes. He was doing something with his hand, maybe tapping at his lips, maybe rubbing his nose. He said something.

"Sir?"

He shook his head and walked back toward me, firelight glancing off belt and brooch. He squatted down next to me. He smiled. He put a finger to his lips like a monk signalling silence and then he said something.

Again I couldn't hear him.

"Your bishop. I want you to tell me about your bishop."

The bishop?

"Tell me about Wilfrid."

I shook my head. "He's our bishop, our father. He built the abbey and the terrace, he built the bridge."

Ceolwulf said something but he spoke so low I had to lean toward him to hear him. "He's Northumbrian," I said, thinking that was what he'd asked, "Deiran, I think." I thought it would please Ceolwulf to think our bishop Deiran.

"No, not *where* does he come from, *which way* does he come from?"

"I'm sorry?"

"When he visits I mean."

"Here you mean? When he visits here?"

"Yes," Ceolwulf glanced toward the door as if he'd forgotten everyone was at Terce. "Does he come from the east like most people, up the valley, or does he use some other route?"

"I don't know," I said, never having thought about it before.

"You don't know which direction he comes from?" Ceolwulf looked surprised. "You've never noticed when the bishop arrives?"

I was embarrassed. "No," I said. "I mean, no, I've never seen which way he comes because he doesn't come here. The bishop doesn't ever come here."

"Um-hmm."

I had to admit it didn't make sense. If the bishop built the bridge, he had to have been here to do it. I had always pictured him standing in the water, a little man wearing a crown and vestments, lifting the stones into place one by one. But now that I thought about it, it seemed unlikely that one man, no matter how important, could have done that, built the bridge all by himself. To say nothing of the other things he was given credit for, the church, our furnace, the terrace, the mill. He must have had help. But he must also have been here. I mean why else would they say he built the bridge if he couldn't have, if he'd never even been here to build it?

"You know, there aren't many of us left."

"Sir?"

Ceolwulf stood up again and his knees made a noise. I was always surprised when that happened, when grown-ups' knees spoke, but I didn't say anything. Ceolwulf didn't say anything either. He turned around and began to warm his backsides before the fire. He looked up into the roof. I didn't think he could see anything up there. After a while he spoke again. "There's an old man," he said, "lives on my place. Everyone calls him 'Old Wighard' now but I remember him when he was just 'Wighard'. Anyway, he's an old man now, and he spends most of his days sitting in the shade outside my door. I suppose he's entertained there. People come and go. Sometimes he talks with them, passes the time of day, sometimes he just sits there. His wife died years ago. Childbirth I think, but he still has the boys, men really, Eanred and Lyfing. Their place is on the high ground." Ceolwulf glanced down at me. "Not far from here, I must have passed it on my way in. Anyhow, it's a little distance from the hall so, every morning, one of the boys brings him down, Wighard I mean. I don't know, they must have a lantern or something because it's usually before sunrise."

Ceolwulf looked at me again. "You know I helped daub their house when I was a boy. Beornwine must have been away—Mercians, land clearing, I don't know—but I was there when he put up his house." Ceolwulf shook his head. "Probably time for a new one now. But it's some distance anyway, for an old man to walk I mean. So every evening, just before sunset, one of the boys comes back again for his father. From down where I sit I can't hear what they say, how they greet one another, but I can see it. The hall faces south, our hall faces south, and I can see it, the last of the light coming in at an angle like that. Old Man Wighard doesn't have many teeth left but he shows what he has when the boy arrives. You'd think it was something marvellous he was bringing him, some kind of message the way he smiles. But the boy's still serious, been in the fields all day, working in the fields. He picks up his father's staff, helps his father to his feet, business-like, intent on the work-at-hand. You can tell Wighard understands this—the fieldwork, the pride his son takes in it. For his sake he tries to look serious himself, checking the ground around the door, making sure he hasn't left anything behind. But when his son hands him his staff he has to look at him again and then of course he can't help himself, he smiles. It's as if he were looking at him for the first time again, as if he had the little toes again, the perfect little fingers."

Ceolwulf looked away, seemed to think about something. After a moment or two, he looked back at me. "Sooner or later of course the boy notices this, the grin, his father's idiot grin. It embarrasses him I suppose—I don't know, but he's a good boy, polite, he smiles back. Usually he says something too, to the father I mean, probably something funny, something to break the mood, remind his father that people are watching. But it doesn't matter. I mean the father says something back, replies, but you can tell his heart's not in it. It's the boy he's interested in, the wonder of the boy, this big, grown-up son. He shakes his head, he smiles his toothless smile. He…I don't know… he delights in the boy."

Ceolwulf turned back toward the fire. "You know there's only the two of you left now." He indicated the door with his head but kept his eyes on the fire. "Only Oisc and you. Of course I never get to see you, and Oisc…. Well, Oisc's Oisc. The rest of my boys are gone."

For a while after that Ceolwulf was silent. He had his good side toward me. I sat on the floor and looked up at him. He was, I decided, the handsomest man I had ever seen. And quite likely the saddest. It was obvious that he loved his family very much. I had never realized how hard it must have been for him to give me up.

"How about when he comes for the iron?"

I looked at him.

"Wilfrid I mean. How about when he comes for the iron, which way does he come then?"

I had to think for a moment. "He doesn't come for the iron," I said finally. "I mean he doesn't come himself. He sends someone, a man, he sends a man for the iron."

"Is it always the same man?"

"Yes," I thought so. "Yes, I'm pretty sure it's always the same man."

"Do you know who he is?"

I shook my head. Oblates weren't permitted to speak with guests.

"Is he a priest?"

"I don't know."

"A monk I mean, does he chant like you?"

I smiled and nodded, pleased to be compared with a grown-up.

"Does he come alone?"

"Yes sir, but there are plenty of us here to help him load his wagon."

That we helped the bishop's man in this way seemed to please Ceolwulf. He looked back at the fire. He brought his hand up in front of his eyes, looked at his rings. "Of course the priests would have said it was all your fault. Did say it was all your fault, or your mother's. Whole thing started when she refused to give you up. Everyone dated it from the ox, from the day when the ox fell, broke its leg, but everyone knew what they were really talking about, what the real starting point was. It's a very public place you know, the hall, everyone thinks it's so grand but it's not, not really. Just a bit of wool separating us from everyone else, no real door, just a thickness of sheep's wool. You can hear everything. Of course nobody says anything but they heard. You can always tell when they have, the woman yelling like that. So we didn't give you up and the ox broke its leg. And then the harvest wasn't so good that year, the woman still saying next year, and then that harvest really wasn't any good either. Oh, and we lost part of the roof to fire too. You should have heard the grumbling then, everyone looking at your mother, at me, cutting thatch when they should have been working in their own fields, bloodying their fingers on our work when they had plenty of their own to do. But she was a stubborn woman, no one can deny that, and we repaired the roof and we ate what we harvested and we went on raids and ate what others had harvested and nobody said anything, at least not aloud. And then the next year the rain came, too much rain really, too wet, and then the sickness on its heels. Not the same one you had here but a really bad one, much worse, animals dying, people dying, two of your brothers dying, your mother, and still she's refusing to give you up, making me promise I'll keep you, take care of you after she's gone. Of course I didn't, couldn't really. By then I think my own people would have…." Ceolwulf stopped, looked at me. "Well it was impossible really. I had to give you up whether I wanted to or not. But I don't blame you. I don't think it was your fault, not really. I don't care what the priests say. Because it didn't really stop then. The bad times I mean. Oh the sickness went away. The harvests improved. The cattle were fertile again. Everyone else thought that was it, that it was over, that God had relented, but not me. Because I knew what was going on elsewhere. I knew how bad things really were."

Ceolwulf walked back over to the window, opened one of the shutters a little. He bent down, looked out. When he looked to the left the sun painted a white line down the middle of his face. "How long does this last?" he asked. "Terce, I mean. How long does this Terce last?"

Too long? It had always just seemed too long to me. "A little while longer," I guessed. "I'm not sure. Maybe as long again as it's been since the bell."

My opinion was good enough for Ceolwulf. He nodded, pulled the shutter back into place. He returned to the fire, squatted down, held out his hands. "It's like a sickness, isn't it?" Ceolwulf asked the fire. "When you know a sickness is coming? You can see it, you've heard about it, you know it's coming but there's nothing you can do about it. That was what it was like at first, Streoneshalh. Everything was fine, everybody going on about their work, planting crops, tilling fields, and all the time I knew it was out there, Streoneshalh. I knew Streoneshalh was coming and it was going to get us." Ceolwulf looked over at me, studied my face. "You haven't any idea what I'm talking about, have you?"

I shook my head.

"They've never mentioned that name to you? They've never told you about Streoneshalh, about Folian, about what happened there?"

"I know about Folian," I said, proud of the knowledge. "Father Folian was abbot here. I mean he was abbot here before Father Abbot was abbot here."

"Uh-huh, and what happened to Father Folian? Where do you think the good father is now?"

I shrugged. He wasn't among the graves.

"I'll tell you what happened to Father Folian. Streoneshalh happened to him. Streoneshalh came and took this monastery, stole it from him." Ceolwulf glanced once around Father's room. "Not that he'd want it now anyway. Liked to sleep rough, caves, under the stars, that sort of thing. 'God's roof' he called it. But Folian loved this place, these people. And someone came and took it away from him, someone who hadn't worked for it, earned it the way he had." Ceolwulf nodded at the door. "They ever tell you what's out there? What's buried out there, under your cloister?"

"Hadulac who came from east of here, Ælfstan son of Eadbert, Oslac who was an old man, Fursa who was cellarer in this place...."

Ceolwulf smiled. "No, not them. Under them. Under the whole place."

The ridge? Was he talking about the ridge?

"There's a ridge out there, all rock where it sticks out from the mountain, big long chunk of solid rock. Can't see much of it now, buried under your terrace, but there was a time when you could see it, when everyone knew it was there. People used to come from far and wide to see that rock. Long and dark it was, and where it stuck out from the mountain it looked just like a.... Well, it turned dark when it rained, did I tell you that? Purplish. And they liked that, when it changed I mean, they liked things that changed. Probably still do for all I know." Ceolwulf hesitated, looked at me. "You ever find anything out there?" he nodded toward the door. "You know, lying around the church or anything? Pieces of holly? Maybe something painted on the door?"

I thought about the wagon, but shook my head, *No*. There wouldn't be anything like that around the church.

Ceolwulf nodded. "Well you never know. Still a lot of them out there, up in the hills I mean. And I guarantee you, if one of them saw that ridge out there, even just that little bit still sticks out beneath the church…. Well, they'd know what it is. Right away they'd know. They have a gift for that sort of thing, telling about things, how things came to be. But not anymore, I mean not anymore since Folian. He changed all that. Came in here in rags, hair down to here, skinnier than you, and damned if he didn't talk them out of it, talked them out of everything they'd ever believed in. Out there." Ceolwulf indicated the door with his chin. "Your church. Father Folian built his church right on top of…on top of their holiest site."

Ceolwulf got up, walked around behind me to the door. I was about to get up myself when he stopped, asked me to wait for him. "I'll be back," he said. "You can look at my sword if you want." Then he went out into the front room. I heard the outside door open and, after that, voices, but I couldn't hear what they were saying. I guessed that Ceolwulf was talking to the man who was my brother, Oisc, but I couldn't hear what they were saying. I got up and walked around, working the stiffness out of my legs. I tried not to look at Father's things. I did look at Ceolwulf's sword because he had said I could, and I thought about what he had told me. Also I thought about the garth, what was buried out there under the garth. No one else knew about that. Only Ceolwulf and me. I wondered if I would be brave enough to tell Waldhere about it.

When Ceolwulf came back into the room he seemed surprised to find me by the bed.

"How do you keep it so clean?" I asked to remind him I'd been given permission.

"Looking for blood?"

I was embarrassed.

Ceolwulf smiled. "When I was your age, I used to do the same thing. Beornwine's sword."

I smiled.

"It's goose-fat," he said. "You rub it down with goose-fat. You take care of it and it will take care of you, know what I mean?"

I nodded, for a moment imagining myself someone who would someday take care of a sword, would know about goose-fat and such things.

Ceolwulf picked up the sword and hung it from a hook on Father's wall. He sat down on the bed and patted the place beside him. He looked at me and I looked at him and then he patted the empty place again. I could feel the blood in my cheeks. I didn't say anything. I sat down next to my father.

"Now where was I?" asked Ceolwulf, smiling to himself.

"Streoneshalh," I whispered. "You were going to tell me about Streoneshalh, what Streoneshalh is."

Ceolwulf nodded. "Was. What Streoneshalh was. I mean it's still there, the abbey, but when people talk about it, when they use the word, usually they're talking about something else, about the assembly that was held there, the decision." Ceolwulf frowned. "They really haven't told you about this?"

I shook my head.

He shook his. "Well, Streoneshalh was how they did it, how they stole this place, Redestone I mean. In the old days, before you were born, there weren't any places like this, any big churches and monasteries the way there are now. It was dangerous here, Deira was dangerous, and people stayed away from it, priests stayed away from it. Especially the hill country. So, for a long time, no one here heard about the Christ. Then a few monks, mostly northern monks, began to wander in. You know what I mean, northern monks? Foreign monks, from Hii." Ceolwulf laughed. "You should have heard the way they talked. Even Folian, when I knew him, even Folian couldn't speak properly. Oh he'd learned the language by then, could say most of the words, but he never put them together right. Half the time he ended up saying the opposite of what he meant." Ceolwulf looked at me. "Not that the other monks sounded any better. I mean there were other monks too, monks who came from the south, Roman monks. Not as many but some. You've probably heard of Paulinus."

I nodded.

Ceolwulf studied the fire. "You could tell them apart. I mean even before they spoke you could tell a Roman from a northern monk, because of the way they cut their hair. And other things too, not important things, just differences, little things. Not that it mattered. I mean who cared how they cut their hair? But then everything changed. Fate, I suppose. What's good turns bad, what's bad good. Even Beornwine knew that. And once that's started.... Well, there's no point in trying to make the sun run backward. Things only get worse." Ceolwulf looked at me. "Same with priests as anybody else. I mean they can say they're different—refuse women, meat, cut their hair funny—but underneath we're all the same. We all want something someone else has. It's only natural. And that's what happened. Especially once the kings got into it. That's how Streoneshalh happened."

Ceolwulf nudged a log with his foot, pushed it back toward the center of the fire. "Alcfrith held Deira in those days, and he didn't like his father." Ceolwulf laughed, eyes still on the log. "What under-king does? But he can't come right out and say that, can he? I mean he can't just march up there with his army and lay siege to Bamburgh. For one thing he hasn't got an army, not really. I mean half the men he had weren't really his. I mean we only stayed with him because of his father. So he can't fight Oswiu honestly, not in open battle, and he can't just be obedient because that would go against his nature, so, instead, he tries to undercut him, slip the sword between the sheets so to speak. And there was no better way to do it than with the new religion. You have to understand that Oswiu had encouraged the new religion, supported it. It was the perfect way to bring people together against the Mercians. I mean, because Penda followed the old ways, didn't he? Thought the Christ a bit of a joke.

"But Penda's dead now, his son, a Christer if ever there was one, holds Mercia in his place, has made all his subjects obedient to the new ways. But Oswiu's still confident enough to place Alcfrith in charge of Deira. And Alcfrith of course, being the son of a good man, wants to make trouble, good things going, as they do, bad. So he finds himself a Roman priest, a bit of a fanatic, and he gives him a monastery at In-Hrypum. Doesn't matter that he's earlier given it to a group of northern monks because that's the point isn't it, to upset things, make things happen? And he certainly does that, I mean he certainly upset things. The new priest hardly arrives before he's telling all the monks, all the monks already living at In-Hrypum, that they have to change, have to let their hair grow out, start all over again, shave it in the new way, shave it like his. From now on they have to act the way he does, follow his rules, or he's going to throw them out, take everything they have and put them out in the cold. Now you have to remember they've already worked this place, they've cleared the land—forty hides—built the buildings, worked the fields, and they consider it theirs. I know they're not supposed to but you can't help it—I mean you work a place, turn the earth, cut the trees, even a monk, sooner or later even a monk is going to think a place is his. And here's this priest, this man they've never even heard of, coming in uninvited, and he's going to throw them out. Because of their hair! And he does, did. Well over half of them anyway. Some stayed, some decided to change, but most left, most left rather than submit to...submit to this new abbot. Their beds, their tools, their work, everything they'd ever owned, gone, because of this one priest, because of...." Ceolwulf stopped, looked at me. "You don't have any idea who I'm talking about, do you? No idea who would do such a thing, steal forty hides of land and call himself holy for doing it?"

I shook my head, I could not imagine.

Ceolwulf studied me for a moment. "Do you like me, son? Do you like your father?"

Of course I liked my father. I liked how big he was. I liked how he sat and how he walked. I liked the sound of his voice. He wore pretty things, manly things, the brooch at his shoulder, the belt on his waist, the sword. Father Gwynedd smelled like wood smoke and Father Prior like the front of the refectory when it rained, but Ceolwulf smelled like the oil he wore in his hair, the goose-fat he used to clean his sword. He smelled rich, he smelled like feast days and harvest-time, he smelled good. Of course I liked my father—I nodded, I loved my father.

Ceolwulf looked at me, looked back at the fire. "It was Wilfrid," he said. "Your Bishop Wilfrid was the new abbot, the man who stole In-Hrypum."

The man who was my brother had come to the door. Ceolwulf was with him now and the two men were talking, the man who was my brother leaning in to hear what the man who was my father was saying. I wasn't listening. I was looking at them but I wasn't listening. I was thinking about the bishop, about Bishop Wilfrid whom we prayed for every day, Bishop Wilfrid who built the bridge and gave us everything we had, Bishop Wilfrid who was my father and Father Abbot's father and everyone's father. Bishop Wilfrid who was a thief.

My brother did something that made a noise and Ceolwulf shook his head. He brought a finger to his lips, shook his head, glanced over at me. I was looking at them. Ceolwulf began to talk once more with my brother.

We never saw the bishop but I loved him. It was easy to love him. Whenever a feast was announced, it was announced in the name of the bishop who gave it to us. When the whole abbey had to fast and pray for some wrong, some problem somewhere I didn't understand, it was the bishop who lifted the fast, declared himself (through the mouth of his servant Father Abbot) happy with our sacrifice, pleased. The bishop was our shepherd, he watched over us, took care of us, protected us from our enemies. I knew this. Had known it all my life. Father Prior said so. The bishop was the shepherd and we were the flock. But the bishop had done something wrong. My father said so. The bishop had taken a monastery from its rightful owners, turned the monks out into the cold. A shepherd wouldn't do that, would he, not to the sheep he loved?

"It's over."

It was Ceolwulf. He was standing by the bed.

"It's over. The thing, what do you call it? The hour? It's over. They'll be coming soon."

Terce was over.

"Are you all right?"

I thought about that. I didn't feel well. It had been a long time since I had eaten and maybe that was it, maybe I just didn't feel well, the fasting, maybe if I sat still for a while this would pass, I would feel better. I looked up at Ceolwulf and the room tilted to the left. When I opened my eyes again, the room tilted to the right.

Something large and heavy, a hand, forced my head down between my legs. For a moment I felt sick and then I felt better. A pair of sandals was resting under Father's bed. You could see where his toes had rubbed the leather shiny.

"Are you better now?"

I nodded and my hair moved against my father's hand.

The pressure at the back of my head relaxed and was gone. I sat up, looked around. Everything looked the same. Father's chest still rested against the far wall, light still leaked in around the shutters, the fire still smoked and smoldered. But everything looked different too, as if I'd just woken up and everything that had happened before had been a dream. I looked at my father. He nodded and then, taking both my hands in his, pulled me to my feet and led me over to the window. He opened the shutters.

It was not as bright as I had expected but it was bright. I blinked and then looked again. The sun was well up now, mid-morning, and it looked as if it would be a nice day. It had rained during the night and the air was sweet and fragrant. I placed my hands on the windowsill and leaned out. A breeze moved over the surface of the outer wall and the perspiration on my forehead began to dry, the skin there suddenly feeling cool and fresh. I smelled the air. I looked around. Below me a small group of monks was making its way down the abbey path, hoods up, hoes on their shoulders. The two in the back were signing to each other. Someone had left a ladder leaning against one of the pollards and I wondered if I would hear about it at Faults. I thought about Waldhere and Ealhmund. I wondered what they were doing. I wished I was with them.

"So after In-Hrypum things got worse. You know what I'm saying? Worse, bad."

I looked at Ceolwulf. He was standing back a little from the window, talking, his face in shadow.

"I mean Wilfrid wouldn't sit still. The man was born angry. He liked to…." Ceolwulf hesitated. He moved into the light, studied my face. "Are you all right?"

I looked at my father. He had a scar down one side of his face. His hair was shiny with oil. He wore a brooch. I didn't know what to say.

Ceolwulf joined me in the window. "See that dark place in the trees?" He pointed toward the Far Wood. "Down there, where your path enters the wood?" He moved back to give me a clearer view.

Where the abbey path entered the forest there was a sort of dark place in the trees. It reminded me of the fox's tunnel.

"All right. Now, look at the top of the forest, the upper part of the trees. Can you see how there's a break in the tops of the trees there, above the path? It's darker, a sort of shadow. Are you tall enough? Can you see that?"

I nodded. I was tall enough.

"Good. Now can you see how that dark place continues on across the top of the trees? See? See how it bends to the right there?"

From the point where the abbey path joined the Far Wood a faint shadow ran out across the roof of the forest. It travelled a short distance and then, as Ceolwulf had indicated, turned to the right.

"That's the path, the shadow marks the path, the break in the trees. That's where it meets the river, that bend there? The track follows the river after that. See that. Now, can you see where it goes from there?"

After turning right, the break in the trees continued out across the roof of the wood, then, with distance, became indistinct. I couldn't see where it went.

"Well you can't really see it but that's where our land is, down there, at the far end of that track." Ceolwulf shook his head, still looking at the forest. "It's beautiful, Winwæd, beautiful. I wish you could see it." He looked at me. "Do you remember it at all? Do you remember the spring? Do you remember the watercress?"

I didn't remember the spring. I remembered a warm place with blankets. I remembered a woman.

"Well it doesn't matter, it's there. It's still there. Can you see the track—the break in the trees that marks the track—can you see that from your building, from the place where you sleep?"

I thought about it. I should be able to see it from the dortoir, especially if I stood on the bed and leaned out. I nodded. I probably would be able to see it even better from the crag.

"Good, that's good, because I want you to do that from time to time. I mean I want you to look at that place and think about me, think about your brother and sisters, the buildings we've put up, the fields we've…. What? What is it?"

I was stunned.

"Your sisters? I haven't mentioned your sisters?"

Sisters. I had sisters.

"Æbbe and Hildegyth." Ceolwulf smiled. He looked back at the forest. He shook his head. "They're a handful. Well, Æbbe is. Climbing trees, hiding food, you know what I'm talking about. But Hildegyth's different, more like her mother." Ceolwulf looked at the back of his hand. He rubbed it like a man smoothing something into place. "Sometimes I don't even know she's there and then she hands me something, a beaker of milk, a bowl of pudding, I don't know. It's nice. Looks like Gytha too, the hair, the way she tips her head like that." Ceolwulf thought about it. "I'm going to give her the brooches. I am. Next year. I'm going to give her your mother's brooches."

Gytha. My mother's name was Gytha. And her daughter looked like her. Hildegyth.

"Of course I'm going to have to be putting things away for her soon. Won't be long now." Ceolwulf looked at me. "You know what I'm talking about don't you? I want to give her everything, pots, woolens, you know, everything. Maybe even a new loom. I don't know, I want to see her smiling. When they carry her out I mean, I want to see her smiling, hair up for the first time, draped in linens and beads. That's the way it should be. All of Deira will know she's my daughter, my daughter and she can have anything she wants. And she'll be quiet and she'll smile that smile of hers and…." Ceolwulf looked back toward the wood for a moment so I could only see part of his face. The side of his throat was moving as if he were trying to swallow something. "When she does that, when she smiles like that, well…I don't know. I'll probably think about your mother." He shook his head. "I never thought about it before but I guess that's what'll happen, I'll think about your mother." He looked at me. "You ever do that? You ever think about your mother, remember her?"

I nodded, the face, the smell.

Ceolwulf looked back toward the wood. "She was beautiful you know. She was the most beautiful woman in the world and I built that place for her. Built it up from what Beornwine gave me. And now I will hand it on to her, to her daughters and her son. That's what she'd want, don't you think?" Ceolwulf looked at me. "Don't you think she'd want that? Would want your brother and sisters to carry on there in the home she made for them, the place where she nursed them, tended them?"

It was a nice thought. I smiled. Yes. Yes, the lady whose face I recalled (who had loved me), her children, her daughter who was like her, would live on, lived on even now, in the place she had made for them, in the place that had been my home. Yes. Yes, I liked that. I liked the idea of that.

Ceolwulf knelt down in front of me. He looked at me and, for a moment, two dim reflections of my own face stared back at me from his eyes. "Good," he said. "That's good, because that's why I came here. That's what I came for, to stop him. To try to stop Wilfrid from stealing your mother's home."

I shook my head.

Ceolwulf held my shoulders. "No. No, you have to listen, it's your duty. You have to listen. You have to be very brave now. You have to be a warrior. You have to stand up for us. For all of us. For your mother and me."

My mother. For my mother.

"That's my boy!" He squeezed my shoulders. "That's my boy, that's my boy!" He stood up. He glanced toward the door then back at me again. "We have to hurry now," he said. "Is there anyone here who can teach you to pray better, someone you can trust? You know what I'm talking about, is there anyone here who can teach you how to do it better, to pray better?"

I looked at Ceolwulf.

"Better I mean. You know what I mean, better than you pray now. Is there someone here who could do that, someone, I don't know, a priest, an adept, whatever they call them nowadays, someone whose prayers really work."

"There's a hermit. He lives up on the mountain."

"Gwynedd?"

My father knew everything.

"Bad name but he's good isn't he? I mean he's good, has the touch. But doesn't he live up on the mountain? I mean I know you just said that but I thought he never comes down. I mean I thought he never comes down, that that was where his power comes from, the mountain. He has to stay up there, doesn't he? How could you get to him, learn anything from him up on the mountain?"

I straightened my shoulders. "I am Father's servant. I visit him often."

"Often?"

I swallowed.

Ceolwulf looked at me.

"I mean whenever Father Abbot wants. Sometimes I go twice a week, but most times just once. I bring him food and things, tabula."

"You do."

I nodded, a little more sure of myself now.

"Good. Well that's good. But will this Gwynedd teach you? I mean it's a secret thing isn't it, that sort of prayer? I mean they don't teach it to just anyone, do they?"

I shrugged. I didn't know.

Ceolwulf nodded. "Well you work on him. You work on him, get him to teach you that. Because you're not so good at it you know, I mean prayer. You're not so good at this praying."

I hadn't died during the pestilence.

"You know what I'm talking about don't you? Your prayer I mean?"

I didn't know what he was talking about.

"The prayer I taught you? The one I had old Edgils compose. How did it go? 'Give him a strong right arm. Make his animals fertile, his fields....' I don't know, 'fertile' or something."

"Fecund."

"What?"

"Fecund. 'Make his animals fecund, his fields fertile.'" It had been a hard word for me too.

Ceolwulf frowned. "Oh. Fecund. So what happened? Did you quit saying it or what?"

Ceolwulf had taught me the prayer. All these years I had thought it was Father Abbot and it was Ceolwulf instead.

"Because it didn't work. I mean there was another part, wasn't there, something about Oswiu, something about long life?"

I thought to myself, *Fill his hall with drink, good food, happiness; let the sounds of harp and laughter ring in that place. Give him long life....* "'Give him long life, God'" I said, "'for his followers would miss his voice as they do those of the great heroes long gone.'"

"Exactly. Exactly. And it didn't work, did it? I mean your prayer didn't work."

I looked at my father.

"Oswiu's dead, isn't he? Wilfrid killed him, as good as killed him, last winter, didn't he?"

"Sir?"

"Oswiu's dead, don't they tell you anything up here? Ecgfrith's king now, been king over a year, though Wilfrid might as well be."

Oswiu was dead. The man I had prayed for at Mass this morning was dead.

Ceolwulf frowned. "You're not going to faint again, are you?"

I held onto the windowsill. I wasn't going to faint.

"Good, good boy. It's not your fault, not really. I mean you can't blame yourself, a powerful priest like that. Hell, Wilfrid's got hundreds of people praying for him, thousands. What are the prayers of a single ab…. You know what I mean, a single boy against all that? I mean you didn't stand much of a chance, did you?"

I didn't?

"Oswiu died didn't he? Perfectly healthy, not much older than I am, and he takes sick and dies. What does that tell you? I mean the man had been out to get him since the beginning."

"Father Bishop?"

"He's not your father! You've never even met him!"

I blinked.

"No, it's all right." Ceolwulf smiled. "I mean it's all right. I know they teach you to call him that, but he's not. I mean he's not your father, *I'm* your father. He's a thief. I told you about In-Hrypum, didn't I?"

I nodded.

"Well, things got worse after In-Hrypum. Wilfrid wasn't satisfied. Never is satisfied. He kept after them, the northerners, the hair, how they did everything wrong, how bad they were. Got to the point he refused to talk with them, eat food they'd prayed over, sing their songs, that sort of thing. It was embarrassing. But it worked. People began to worry, talk. Some said if you'd had water sprinkled on you by the wrong side, you hadn't really been saved, and everyone knew what that meant. I mean it was the one thing both sides agreed on. So if priests with the wrong style of hair buried your father, where was he now? And if the wrong type blessed your bread at Mass, who had you eaten? I mean I know it's all absurd but people really care about such things. Soon enough they were calling each other names, heathen, drawing lines, forming alliances. You can't imagine how bad it was, the fear, the accusations. You could see how it was going to end. Poor Oswiu, everything he'd ever worked for, the unity, Northumbria, the peace, everything falling apart. There could have been a war you know. Can you believe that? I mean can you imagine people fighting over something like that?"

I tried to imagine Bishop Wilfrid in a shield and helmet, the little man I had pictured building our bridge.

Ceolwulf shook his head. "So Oswiu did it. I mean he had to, Alcfrith left him no room. Of course he thought Streoneshalh was going to work for him, because of Hilda, because she was abbess at Streoneshalh. But it didn't, couldn't really when you think about it. Called the northerners stupid. Can you imagine that? Wilfrid I mean. Stands up there in front of the entire assembly and calls the northerners stupid. His hostess was northern, his king!" Ceolwulf looked at me. "Is that what you call courteous? Is that what you call proper?"

Waldhere had been made to kneel before Faults for calling Ealhmund stupid.

Ceolwulf made a face and the whiskers between his lip and chin stuck out at an angle. "They should have strung him up, that's what they should have done. I mean that's what I would have done, from the nearest drying rack. But I guess they couldn't anymore. I mean all the Colmans and Hildas in the world couldn't make any difference now, could they? Not against Rome. Someone tells you the Empire's dead, you ask them about the Church, what they think the Church is they think the Empire's dead. All Wilfrid had to do was point south, remind everyone who was behind him, that all the lands from Rome to Mercia followed his rule, and that was that. Mercia was a nice touch, don't you think, mentioning Mercia? So what could Oswiu do? St. Peter holds the key, doesn't he? Everyone knows that. So Rome wins. The great assembly at Streoneshalh is adjourned, Colman sent into exile, and the upstart Wilfrid made bishop in his place."

Ceolwulf looked down at something on his hand, brushed it off. "Of course after that, everything went to hell. Wilfrid begins interfering with the monasteries, insulting monks, throwing them off their land. Bishops weren't supposed to do that in those days. I mean monasteries were special places then, safe, respected. Even the king had to ask permission to enter a monastery. But not Wilfrid. What did he care if an abbot's hat was the same as his? If one of them didn't abide by Streoneshalh, follow the Roman ways, he was out on his ear. And of course Folian wouldn't, crazy old man. He loved Redestone." Ceolwulf looked at me. "You know what he used to say? He'd pour some water out on the ground and, well, you know how the earth around here turns color when you do that, pour water on it? Well Folian loved that! He'd preach about it, said the place was suffused with God's blood. *Suffused.* Used to use words like that, *suffused!* Crazy old man. But not Wilfrid. I mean it certainly wasn't the blood of Christ he saw. First thing he did, he kicked Folian out and built himself a furnace."

Ceolwulf paused, looked at me as if expecting me to say something. When I didn't, he shook his head. "The people were outraged of course. The idea of a holy man touching iron…well it wasn't done. 'Neither sword nor scythe.' And the northern priests had always respected that, except for tools of course. But not Wilfrid. No, his hands were never so clean he couldn't grab a little metal. And they missed the monks too. The people I mean. I mean they missed the northern monks. Monasteries weren't monasteries anymore. A pestilence comes now, famine, first thing the monasteries do is close their gates. Redestone didn't even have gates in Folian's day. Hell, didn't even have buildings except for the church!"

I looked out at the Far Wood, remembered the beggars.

"Of course Oswiu tried to fix things. When he saw how bad it'd gotten, how upset people were, he tried to reverse his decision, make Northumbria part of the northern Church again. Wilfrid must have been out of the country, a pilgrimage or something, because I remember for a while it worked. I don't know whether Oswiu actually forswore Streoneshalh but he might as well have done. Named Chad bishop, didn't he? Acted as if he'd never heard of anyone named Wilfrid, reverted to the old ways, the original feast days. Not that it worked. Couldn't really I suppose. Like trying to push back the sea, fighting Rome. Wherever Wilfrid was, he came back. Joined forces with the Mercians and before you know it, Roman monks are showing up all over the place crying out against Oswiu, calling his bishop a fraud. You just can't beat him. Cut off an arm and Wilfrid sprouts two more. So Chad's sent off in disgrace, the country's in an uproar, and Wilfrid is a power to contend with, Rome and Mercia at his back. Poor Oswiu, all he'd ever worked for, all he'd tried to accomplish, undone by a man doesn't even carry a sword."

Ceolwulf looked out toward the Far Wood, became silent. I looked out that way too. It made sense in a way, when you thought about it. Why else did we always have to eat so little, even when we weren't fasting? Why else was the work so hard? Why else was there always so much porridge, never any honey? Why else the canes that cut my hands, the cold in church, the bad smell by the ditch? Why else Baldwin? In a place that was so good and kind and loving, where did all these evils come from? Unless there was someone out there, someone bad, someone whose prayers worked against us, someone who turned fresh to sour, made Father cranky, rain cold, the ox mad. I looked at the fish ponds and thought about that. It made you wonder.

"Of course Oswiu died after that." Ceolwulf was still looking at the Far Wood. "Probably the disappointment that killed him. All his plans, all his dreams." He shook his head. "And then, as if that weren't enough, this." Ceolwulf made a vague gesture toward the orchard. He frowned, looked back at me. "You know they're going to tell you he gave it to him, don't you? I mean if they find out. Don't tell them. You mustn't tell them, Winwæd, it's our little secret, all right? What we've talked about today? Is our secret, father and son. If you tell them, if your prior or abbot finds out anything about what I've said, it will hurt me. Do you understand what I'm saying?"

I nodded, terrified to think that something I knew could hurt my father.

"It will hurt me, it will hurt your family. And they'd only lie anyway. I mean they'd have to, wouldn't they? I mean they have to do whatever Bishop Wilfrid tells them to do, don't they?"

Lie?

"Of course they would. Because that's what he claims, what Wilfrid claims, that Oswiu gave it to him on his death bed." Ceolwulf chuckled. "Claims he gave it to him in return for Wilfrid's promise to take him to Rome. Can you imagine? Oswiu's dying and suddenly he wants more than anything in the world to go to the one place in the world he hated more than Mercia. Certainly! And of course he wants to go in the company of the only man in the world he ever hated more than Penda. Of course! And in return for this promise, what does Wilfrid expect us to believe Oswiu gave him? My land. Why not? I mean it is only the last bulwark between him and Mercia, what better property to give your sworn enemy and Mercia's favorite ally. Of course Wilfrid, we believe you, with his dying breath Oswiu made you a gift of my land! Trees can talk, pigs can fly!"

I looked away. I was unaccustomed to seeing someone so visibly angry, so I looked away. Besides, I didn't need to look at Ceolwulf anymore, it was obvious what he wanted. I mean it should have been all along but I hadn't seen it up until now. I wasn't used to this. I wasn't used to grown-ups wanting something from me, trying to talk me into something. Usually they just told me what I was to do. I looked away. I could feel Ceolwulf looking at me but I looked away, I looked out the window. Below me Brother Wictbert was doing something in the pollards but I didn't look at him. I looked at the orchard. Though it was too far away to actually see them, you could tell that the buds had swollen during the night because of the haze. Father Cuthwine had taught me about this. If you looked at a single tree you saw nothing, but if you looked at all the trees together, a sort of reddish haze became visible among the limbs. It meant that spring was coming, that the buds would soon open, flower. But still it seemed funny. I mean it seemed funny that there was something you could see and could not see at the same time.

"I'll do it," I said.

"You'll do it?"

"I will pray for you. I'll learn how from Father Gwynedd and then I'll pray that you keep the land and Bishop Wilfrid loses it. I'll do that. I will pray that you win and our bishop loses."

Ceolwulf smiled. "Thank you," he said. "I knew you'd say that. The moment I saw you I knew you'd say that, that you were my son, you wouldn't desert us." For the second time that day my father reached out, touched my head. "But of course that's not enough, is it? You're a warrior's son so you must know that. I mean a part of you must know already that's not enough, that it isn't as easy as that. You don't just push your enemy back, win a little breathing room, push him back some more. Deep down inside I think you must already know that. I mean I think you must already know what you have to do. I am asking you to pray for our enemy's death, Winwæd. I am asking you to ask God to kill him, to kill Bishop Wilfrid."

I am fairly certain I never actually replied to Ceolwulf's demand. I remember him telling me what he wanted me to do (I remember the way his face looked as he said the words), and then I remember Father Prior rejoining us. I don't remember anything else in between. Father Prior bundled me off to work or lessons, what-have-you. The man who was my father completed whatever business he had with the abbey, packed his things and rode off as he had come in, my brother walking behind him. Perhaps he hadn't really expected me to say anything, would have thought a response unnecessary, redundant, my compliance understood. Honor thy father and thy mother. Or perhaps he saw something in my face that made him think an answer unlikely, that I was too stunned by what he asked to say anything. I have no idea what he saw in my face. Or, perhaps, he just thought that it was best not to push it. That he was more likely to get what he wanted if he gave me time, time to think it over, time to miss him, to remember him fondly, to come to think of him as a true father, as a man I knew instead of a man I had merely met. Possibly that is it. Possibly he was smart enough to know that, inevitably, a time would come when I would do anything in my power to defeat the fathers I knew in favor of the father I only thought I knew. I don't know. All I know for sure is that, except in my dreams, I never saw Ceolwulf again.

XVI

hough my memory is not now what it once was and I sometimes confuse one year with another, I have no reason to
believe that spring was any different from those that came
before or after it. There would have been days when the air was light
and fresh and it was a joy to be alive, and there would have been days
when the air was cold and damp and our fingers cracked and bled. I'm
sure we dug seed beds, pulled weeds, planted and hoed. Doubtless we
thought the world was starting over again, that life was good, fresh,
new. We think that every spring.

I do remember the trouble I got into. We feed on stories, don't we,
we monks? The woes of Abraham, the exploits of David, Daniel in
the Lion's Den—these are our daily bread. Small wonder then that, at
least at first, the tales I had learned in the abbot's lodge brought me
a sort of following among the younger members of our community,
postulants and novices for the most part, to say nothing of my fellow oblates. But fame may be more than fleeting, it may be perilous
as well. Overnight I went from fair-haired boy to pariah, brothers
turning away from me on the garth, looking down their noses at me.
It was Waldhere of all people who saved me, warned me of the fate
I risked. Though no one had yet dared report my stories to Chapter,
word of their subject-matter, the scent of profanity, a whiff of our
impious past, had drifted up to the abbot's chair. And Father was
not pleased. Indeed, he was so displeased he had threatened anyone
found repeating such tales—attempting, as he put it, to resurrect the
thing buried at such cost beneath our garth—with separation from
the Body of Christ.

So I shoved my stories down inside me, buried them next to Ceolwulf's commission in the place I now constructed for such things. And it was in this, I think, that this spring differed from all others. There were no comets that year, no new stars. The sun rose and set as it always had. But, for the first time in my life, there were secrets. And isn't it with secrets, the keeping of secrets (and by this I mean true secrets, secrets that carry weight, have the potential to harm, to cure) that childhood comes to an end? Before there are secrets, before we hold a portion of ourselves aloof, separate from the community, then, by definition, we simply are what we are. Food is food, Father Father, and God resides not in Heaven but all around us. But when we begin to keep secrets, we begin also, I think, to step away from Him. Not entirely. Only Hell can separate us entirely from the Kingdom. But with secrets It is placed at a remove. A sort of sundering occurs between our selves and our souls. Where before He was ever-present, now there is this thing, this bad place we carry around inside us like a wall, a bit of rough masonry that stands between us and Creation. Looking back on it now, that spring was different. From that time forward my actions could no longer be trusted—not by me or anyone else. I was my father's son, I was my bishop's. And what that meant, I had not a clue.

Not that I didn't try to work it out. I went about my daily round as before. I worked in the fields, I visited the hermit, I sang the office. But I thought about Ceolwulf almost constantly. I thought about his visit. I thought about the request he had made of me. I wondered what I would do about it. That he was my father I could not deny. Prior Dagan himself had called him so, and now I too found myself emphasizing the relationship, reminding myself again and again of his kindness, how he had cared for me when I felt faint, how he had touched my head, how he had loved my mother. At night I would lie in bed and remember the story he had told of the old man who waited each day by the door for the return of his son, how my father had liked that story, how he had liked the man, liked to watch him, to see the way he greeted his son when he came to take him home. Sometimes, as I drifted off to sleep, unaware of the shift from thought to dream, Ceolwulf would become the man, eyes catching the last of the day's light, happy, contented, delighted by the return of his son.

But then, sometimes, I would wake up terrified, sweaty, certain I had already done it, that I had prayed as my father wished and it had worked, he was dead, the bishop was dead, and I had killed him. I always woke up just after it had happened, just after I had dropped the bishop from Dacca's crag, fed him some sort of poisonous stone, driven a hoe into his chest. Once—I must admit it here—I had even eaten a portion of him. I had killed the bishop—I can't remember how now—and then, in my hunger, I had sliced off a piece of his side (which, in the way of dreams, immediately became like a serving of fish) and eaten it. For three days after that I could keep no food down. Father Prior thought it was the porridge, that I had stolen and eaten some of the porridge Botulf had thrown out, but I hadn't. Everything tasted of flesh—everything was rotten, corrupt, my fault, the evil *in me* as surely as, in my dream, the bishop had been *in me*.

But he was my father. I was supposed to love him just as I was supposed to love the bishop. Indeed I found it easier to love Ceolwulf. I knew him, he was flesh and blood; I had touched him, smelled him, sat by his fire. What could I say of this bishop that was causing me so much trouble, who haunted my sleep with his screams and his blood and his grasping fingers? Nothing. He was as distant and removed from my experience as Oswiu or this new king, Ecgfrith. I could no more conjure up an image of him than I could of God. Indeed, when I thought about it, I realized that even in my dreams it wasn't the bishop I killed, not really. I had no idea what the bishop looked like. The man I killed was his man, the brother he sent each year for the iron. I hadn't realized I even remembered what he looked like but I did. I could see him now, staring up at me as he fell toward the Meolch, fingers outstretched, mouth open, screaming. Even he, even this stranger, this foreigner whose name I did not know, was more real to me than the man my father wanted dead. How hard could it be to do something like that, to pray for the death of a man you had never seen for the good of a man you had? How hard to honor your father at the expense of your father?

And then again the reality of what I was contemplating would set in. This was no story I was telling myself, this was real. I was actually thinking of killing someone. If I had left some of the innocence of childhood behind, I remained as yet close enough to its certainties to have no doubt about this. Our Lord teaches that with faith you can cast a mountain into the sea; how much easier it must be then to kill a man. How much easier and how much more awful. Though I had always liked to pretend to manhood, to think myself the son of a great warrior, I was ashamed to discover that, in reality, the idea of actually doing physical damage to someone, hurting him badly, repelled me. Just the thought of saying the words, the actual prayer that would send Bishop Wilfrid to his death, terrified me.

So this was my predicament. On the one hand I could not disobey my father and, on the other, to obey him required an act of disobedience so monstrous as to be unimaginable. Faced with this imponderable, I would like to say I turned to Father Prior or Father Gwynedd for guidance, but I did not. Instead, like the equivocating adult so many of us eventually become, I arrived at a sort of vague and nearly unconscious compromise. In keeping with my father's wishes, I would ask the hermit to teach me to pray; but (and I liked this part immensely) I wouldn't have to actually start praying for anybody's death until—*as my father wished*—I had really gotten good at what it was the hermit was teaching me. The beauty of this plan was that it allowed me to tell myself I was following my father's wishes even as, in reality, I was doing something all my other fathers would find perfectly acceptable, even praiseworthy. Moreover, should the time ever come when I did feel comfortable with Ceolwulf's objective (I imagined a distant future in which squeamishness would be shed like baby fat), I would then—thanks to my course of preparation—be equipped to carry it out.

There was another reason, too, that I was happy with this plan, a reason completely unrelated to Ceolwulf or the bishop or anything having to do with the power struggle then going on in Northumbria. For two years now I had served the hermit. I had brought him food, maintained his fire, shaved his head, mended his cloak, carried his messages, watched him pray. Mostly I had watched him pray. There were times when it had bored me, times when it had fascinated me, and times when I had thought myself indifferent. But I was not indifferent. What servant ever is? Whether I watched him, ignored him, or went off by myself to track deer, a part of me always envied my master. Even in the middle of the week, my eye would stray from the weeds or the peas or whatever I was supposed to be doing to look up at Dacca's crag. Even when I was in church I would sometimes look up through the walls at him, picture him there, sitting by his little stream, body perfectly still, settled, soul afloat. How nice it would be to be away from all this I would think, to escape the work, the endless chanting, the hunger. How nice to leave whenever you wanted, visit Paradise at a moment's notice, sing to the Blessed Mother, find rest with the Father, salvation through the Son. That my father had asked me to do this, learn the hermit's craft, made it all the nicer—I was merely being a good son, dutiful, obedient—but it was something I had longed to do ever since the hermit had first bowed before me, ever since first he had asked my name.

XVII

I am fairly certain it was that year, during the haying, that I met the woman.

I loved the haying—all the men working together, woolens kilted up around their thighs, big arms swinging back and forth. In those days we used to practice as we worked and our chant would pick up the rhythm of the scythes, back and forth, to and fro, deep and happy. The smell of the fresh-cut grass always brought back memories of previous years, previous hayings; it made you feel as if summer would go on forever, that there would always be plenty of food, plenty of sunlight, that no one would ever go hungry again. By the end of the day, when the corncrakes began to call, everyone would be covered with dust and chaff. Sometimes someone would laugh. Once or twice even Father Abbot laughed. I always liked it when that happened.

One of our jobs was helping Brother Tunbert with the sheaves. I liked the haying, but putting up sheaves was miserable work. By midday the flesh along the inside of your arms was always covered with thin scratches that burned in the humid air. On one occasion I remember Ealhmund's arms swelled up so badly Father Prior thought something had bitten him. And Tunbert wasn't much help. I'm sure he was a good man but what I remember most about him was the way, when he checked your work, he would lean in too close and make disgusting noises in the back of his throat. All of which helps to explain why I think it was the sheaves I was working on when Brother Osric excused me to go get more water. Of course I always enjoyed the river—the coolness of the air down there, the shade, the smell of rushing water—but when I recall that day, I remember something more than that, a sort of guilty glee, which makes me think that even before I met the woman something out of the ordinary had happened, that by fulfilling my obligation to Brother Cellarer I had somehow escaped something more onerous. And so it is my guess that I had been helping Brother Tunbert with the sheaves.

The river at that time of year would have been running smooth and clear. Which, no doubt, interested me. The hermit had told me rivers mirrored the sky above—cloudy and full at spring, smooth and clear in summer—but I wasn't entirely sure I believed him. The hermit had also told me everyone had a river inside him and who could believe that? Did he really think Father Abbot had a river in him, Father Prior?

I placed one of the buckets in the water, held its lip under, forced it to sink.

Of course I had to admit the hermit's proof had been a good one. He had asked me to close my eyes and picture a river and then, when I did so, he'd divined as if it were nothing at all that the river I pictured flowed from left to right. Of course I'd been astonished but the hermit had only laughed. He'd guessed correctly he said because he knew which river was in me: the Meolch. Having grown up on its south bank, my inner river would forever flow—as did the Meolch when viewed from that side—from left to right. Or something like that. I remembered for sure that a person acquired his river at birth, that the river we see when we close our eyes resembles the river we knew as a child because it is that river—no other can match it, no other run so pure or taste so sweet. Which made sense. But then he'd said the thing about his own river that made no sense at all. Father claimed his river also ran from left to right because—and I was sure I'd heard this right—*because he too had grown up on the abbey side of the Meolch.*

A Cumbrogi child east of Modra nect. A Cumbrogi child on our side of the mountain. Even if it was Father Gwynedd, I didn't like the idea. Cumbrogi children didn't always grow up to be Cumbrogi hermits.

I pulled the first bucket from the water, placed it on the rock beside me, set the other in, forced it under. What was almost as strange, when you thought about it, was that my river should be the Meolch. I mean it wasn't as if I'd been born at Redestone.

I thought about the old memories, pulled them up one by one: the blankets, the flickering shadows, a beautiful woman. Had she carried me with her when she went for water? Had I walked with her beside some unknown stream? I could picture such an excursion, the child slapping at puddles with its hands, the woman wringing out her laundry, pausing now and then to watch me at play. But was such a picture true? I had no idea. In fact I couldn't even be sure the woman I remembered was my mother. For all I knew I'd had a nurse and the image I held so dear was actually that of a slave. Though I couldn't really let myself believe that. It had to be my mother I saw when I closed my eyes (I had only the one memory), just as, I was forced to admit, it was the Meolch I saw when I thought about a river. How odd that a child named for one river and doubtless born beside another should find them all supplanted by this unremarkable Meolch, this commonplace stream that lulled me at Vigil, cleansed me at the lavabo, fed me at collation, and carried off my leavings at the end of the day. I should have preferred something a little less prosaic. Still, a part of me liked that the hermit and I had the same river in us. And he was teaching me to pray like him too.

The bucket stared up at me from the bottom of the river. I jerked on the rope and the thing moved a little. I wondered what it would be like to live down there—the constant thrum of the water, the occasional knock of stone against stone. Out in the middle of the river you couldn't see the bottom, but up close here I could make out every stone and, occasionally, the flash of tiny fish. A large rock protruded from the water not far from me, its upper parts dry, reddish brown, flecked with mica. Below the waterline, on the side of the rock in shadow, I could see several snails grazing its surface, the track they left behind them surprisingly straight, obvious, the animals trusting, I supposed, in the security of their shells. Farther out, as the water gained depth, its current began to smear the colors of the riverbed until, eventually, they disappeared entirely and all you could see was the undifferentiated green of flowing surface. The hermit had told me to concentrate on such a place. He said it would help me pray.

I pulled my bucket up, saw there wasn't enough room for it next to its mate, set it down between my legs. I glanced over my shoulder, listened carefully. Nothing. They hadn't missed me yet. I looked back out at the center of the river. There was nothing to focus on, nothing to see. I picked a spot at random and stared at it. Like the bottom colors, my mind tried to race off downstream but I brought it back, concentrated. I thought about the spot itself, the fast water, the color—a grayish green that seemed to grow lighter as I watched it. I thought about how wet it was, how cold and wet. I wondered if the water tasted better out there. I thought about the sun. I thought about the Vigil, how it had droned on the previous night. I looked back up, found the spot again. Once more I concentrated, thinking about the river, about this single spot of water running constantly from left to right, every day the same thing: left to right, left to right....

When I opened my eyes again I found I had leaned so far over I had to catch my bucket to keep it from spilling into the Meolch. As it was, righting the thing, I emptied half its contents into my lap. But that didn't bother me, I ignored the cold, for there had been something else, hadn't there, a noise?

As if my noticing it caused the animal some displeasure, the sound repeated itself, a sort of slithering rustling sound that seemed to emanate from the largest of the bushes on the bank behind me. I picked up a stick and, advancing bravely upon the bush, began to poke at its base. I was about a third of the way around the thing—feet well back, expecting at any moment the raised head, the seamless glide—when it happened: the far end of my stick rose of its own accord and what I took at first to be the coils of a snake changed before my eyes into fingers, an old and scaly hand wrapped around the end of my stick.

I was halfway up the bank running full tilt, skirts in my hand—all thoughts of water, yoke, buckets, gone—when the demon spoke.

A woman?

I hesitated, took another few steps, stopped again.

"Boy," said the voice. "Boy!"

It was a woman!

I turned around slowly. No one seemed to have noticed what had happened. Monks weren't pouring through the trees, Brother Osric wasn't shouting orders, a cloud hadn't passed before the sun. Was I the only one who knew there was a woman down here?

The stick I'd abandoned began to move again, forcing branches aside, revealing the bush's shadowy interior. A pair of eyes appeared. A hand was produced. For a moment nothing happened (pig's teeth did not sprout from the knuckles, vipers' tongues did not flicker from the ends of digits), then—trembling slightly as if bothered by the sun—a finger was slowly unfurled, slowly retracted. The process repeated itself. I was being called. The woman was beckoning to me: she wanted me to join her beneath the bush.

I wouldn't have crawled under that bush for all of Solomon's treasure. But I didn't run either. I stood where I was, thinking about what was hidden in the shrubbery, how close it squatted.

"Come here!" said the voice. "I won't bite."

I crossed myself. The bottoms of my feet grew cold. I did not move. I was beginning to be able to see the woman's face now and I thought there was the suggestion of a change upon it. "Well," she said, "it's like that then." There was a whistle in her voice when she spoke and she held the hand with the stick in it up to her mouth as if she were ashamed of her teeth. "I suppose I must come to you," she said.

I didn't think she need come to me at all, but I didn't run when she began to work her way out from under the bush. There was something about the way she had hidden her teeth as she spoke that made me less afraid of her. I didn't think a witch would be so courteous.

Or so quick. Once she was out in the open, the woman moved with surprising alacrity, walking toward me boldly, hands outstretched as if she intended to take hold of me, maybe do me some harm.

I took a step backward.

The woman stopped, cocked her head, regarded me suspiciously. I was surprised by her size. I knew older monks tended to be smaller than young ones, but the characteristic was apparently more pronounced in women. Finding myself even moderately taller than a grown-up was a new experience for me; it restored some of my confidence.

"I have a daughter who is nearly as big as you." The woman's face grew serious. "She is dying."

I tried to look appropriately mournful.

"The men won't help me and I have no one else to turn to."

I nodded. Life was full of woe.

The face softened and again she brought her fingers to her mouth. "Will you help me?"

I drew back a step. Will *I* help you?

"No, it's all right." The wrinkles deepened now with concern. "I need your help."

I glanced back at the trees. She didn't need my help, she needed someone else's help. *I* needed someone else's help.

"No, they can't help."

I looked back at the woman. They can't help? *Monks* can't help!

Again the smile; this time I thought it was meant to be reassuring. "I need *your* help. I need...I need a boy."

A boy...?

"Yes, that's it, a boy. *He* was a boy wasn't he, the holy one?"

So that was what she was after, though I still didn't see why she needed me. The monks administered the stuff all the time. Father Eadric even had a special bag for it he carried when he went to visit the sick.

The woman could tell I doubted her. "A boy is better," she said, "more potent. He still has his whole life inside him."

To this I could give no response. I had no idea what she was talking about.

The woman stared at me. Realizing she must not find such behavior discourteous, I stared back. It was the hair that really bothered me. The face was not unlike that of some of the older monks. It was smaller, true, and there were dark spots sunk in it like bits of coal, but, otherwise, it was not that different from Brother Alhred's. The hair though was another matter. Dark, streaked with white, it hung about her head in lank dirty-looking cords that both repelled and fascinated me. I wondered what it would feel like, such a great amount of hair, if its weight bowed her down, if that perhaps explained her height. The string of beads that hung across her chest was old and gap-toothed. I wondered who had given her that, who the brooches from which it was suspended. Why hadn't he helped her?

While I thought about these things a change came over the woman. One finger began to kick at a thumb. A strand of hair was played with, rejected, played with again. I was too young to understand the effect our silence can have on people, but I couldn't help noticing the unrestrained behavior. It made me nervous. I wanted to get away, back to the fields, back where I belonged, but I had no idea how to go about it. Having reached this point in a conversation, how did one turn and walk away without appearing impolite? I had no idea how to say no to an adult and, in my whole life, I had never once turned my back on one. And besides, the woman was, in a sense, a guest. I had a duty to the abbey to be hospitable.

The woman leaned to one side, checked the trees behind me, looked at me again. This was bad; she was waiting for me to say something, do something. I had only recently been admitted to Chapter and I didn't like it, the endless palaver, the sense of options, choices, the possibility of dissent, all made me uncomfortable sitting down at the end of the bench where I was expected to remain quiet and still. And now here I was party to such a discussion. I looked around. There was no help. I said a prayer; there was no reply. Finally, forced by my own indecisiveness to be decisive, I did the one thing I knew would—however momentarily—make everyone happy: I thrust out my arms and, trying to look like Father Prior when he did it, showed her the palms of my hands.

As if granting *my* request, the woman repeated the gesture. "What's *that* supposed to mean?" she said.

"Yes," I said. "It means yes, I will help you." My voice didn't sound at all like the voice of someone taller than the person he was speaking to.

The woman nodded as though my acceptance had been taken for granted. "Take this," she said, pulling a small pouch from her girdle, "and put some of the holy one's...." She paused, looked at me in a way that reminded me of Brother Baldwin. "*Fill it*," she demanded, head cocked forward as if looking down at me. "Fill it with the holy one's earth and then leave the pouch under this bush. I'll come for it when I can."

For some reason I felt a sudden urge to be difficult. "I may not be able to do it right away."

The woman brightened as if she found my uncertainty pleasing. "That's all right. I'll check each day. You put it there and I'll find it." Behind her hand I could tell she was smiling. She didn't really look anything at all like Brother Alhred. Even as old as she was she looked, in a way, pretty.

I took the pouch, shoved it up a sleeve, bowed, turned and strode manfully toward the trees, suddenly feeling very good about myself, certain I was doing the right thing.

"Don't forget your water."

My cheeks burned.

I didn't look at the woman. I turned and walked back down to the river. I picked up my yoke—which suddenly seemed larger than I remembered—and, trying to look natural, trying to look as if I did this every day, placed a bucket loop over each of its ends. Then, as gracefully as I could, I shouldered my load.

Of course the bucket that was full immediately counterbalanced that which was not and it was only with a great deal of difficulty that I kept the whole arrangement from cartwheeling off my back.

The woman made a noise behind her hand.

Again my cheeks burned.

I did not say anything. Carefully, I lowered the full bucket to the ground and, in turn, its lighter mate. I unhooked the half-empty bucket. Still not looking at the woman, I knelt by the river and placed the bucket in the water, for the first time noticing how my backsides rose into the air when I did this. The bucket sat there. It did not sink. I smacked at it and the thing rocked back and forth mockingly. I took hold of it with both hands and forced it under, enjoying the rush of cold clear water down its unprotesting throat. Behind me, a rustling sound, the woman had started to walk off downriver. All joy left me. I wanted to say something, do something, to make this all seem better, end better, but what did I know of the rules of parting? All I could do was stare at my stupid bucket sitting on the bottom of this stupid stream.

The rustling sounds stopped.

I didn't do anything. I didn't look up to see if she was coming back. I didn't say anything. I waited.

The voice, when it came, wasn't soft or delicate, sweet or appreciative. It was a harsh voice, forced, a whisper meant to carry some distance. "I will thank your God for this!" it said.

Still I didn't move or look around. I knelt where I was and listened to the sounds the woman made as, once more, she began to work her way down the riverbank. When I could hear her no longer, I looked up and—though I had expected it—I was still a little disappointed to see how quickly she had disappeared. I waited a short while, and then I went over to the place where we had stood. The woman had small feet, flat like Brother Botulf's. Where a track had registered clearly, the toes looked like little beads pressed neatly into the mud.

Of course I knew that what I had done was wrong. Then as now the rules of contact were not always explained to oblates, but still I knew it was wrong. From the moment I first realized it was a woman, I had known I should get away from there, turn and run as fast as my legs would carry me. But I did not. Looking back on it now I find myself thinking about Ceolwulf, about his visit and the effect it must have had on me. Had his commission so undermined my natural loyalties that a second transgression now seemed minor by comparison? Are fathers even more powerful than we think? Did mine wittingly plant the seed that led eventually (inevitably?) to my estrangement from Redestone? Who knows? A part of me doubts the man capable of such guile, and yet…. And yet I did not tell Father Prior about the woman. Not even in confession. I knew I should. I worried over it, prayed over it, lost sleep. But I think not much sleep. After all this was no longer the first thing I had kept from him. How easy the second betrayal after the first. And how easy the excuses we make for ourselves. I told myself I was doing a good deed. I told myself the girl was sick, she needed my help. I told myself the Christ Himself would approve.

Still, there were doubts. The woman had explained her request by saying the men of the village wouldn't help her. Why wouldn't they help her? Was there something wrong with the woman? How bad must a woman be before she can no longer rely on the men of her village?

And how about Father Eadric? Now that Cuthwine was dead, he was supposed to be responsible for the village. How come he hadn't helped her? Or asked for prayers for her daughter for that matter? No mention had been made in Chapter of anyone being sick, and certainly not a girl. I would have remembered if there'd been talk of a girl.

Which led to a new and even more frightening possibility. What if the woman was not of our village? That she could be from elsewhere would never have crossed my mind had it not explained so much. Of course the men of our village hadn't helped her: she was a stranger. Of course Father Eadric hadn't mentioned her in Chapter: he probably didn't even know she existed. And, finally, that most vexing of problems…. Of course her parting words had been "I will praise your God for this!"—qualifying the phrase thus for the simple reason that (and the thought sent chills down my spine) *my* God was not necessarily hers.

But against these concerns I continued to hold up the image of a little girl on her sickbed. Her mother had told her about me, had sat by her side, fanning her, feeding her a little soup and telling her stories of the boy she had met by the river, the little monk who was going to save her, who had promised—*promised*—he would deliver her. That little girl was waiting for me. She lay on her bed as once I had lain on mine, too ill to get up, too ill to do anything other than count roof beams, try to remember what it was like to be happy, healthy, able to run and play. I had no choice. I had to do it.

As it happened, the next night was the new moon. As if planning to keep the long watch, I hung back after the Vigil, and then—once those monks that remained with me had become engrossed in their prayers—I slipped out of the church and into the cool air of the garth. There wasn't much to direct one to the pit in those days—no wall, no dressed stone, none of the sad little offerings left by pilgrims. Father Abbot had ordered a covering of thatch (which had seen previous service on a hayrick), but aside from that there was nothing to mark the spot as exceptional or different from any other on the garth. I can still remember the shock I received when I removed that covering, the breath of warm air that rose to greet me, the scent of raw earth, recent excavation. Of course I knew what this was, that the thatch had captured and retained some of the heat of the day, that it was this and only this that exhaled upon me—but, still, I did not care for the sensation.

It was Brother Baldwin that had seen to it I witnessed the washing. At the time I had still been too weak to walk on my own, so he and Tatwine had linked arms and carried me to the door. Of course they didn't bother to explain why they were doing this, where they were taking me, and so it had come as something of a relief to see the body lying there on the garth, the vessels set out on the turf around it: clearly some familiar if taxing rite was about to take place, clearly nothing else was going to happen, this wasn't what I had feared it was, Baldwin and Tatwine weren't delivering me to some final awful reckoning.

But of course, in reality, something else *was* going to happen, something which, in time, would cause a woman to hide beneath a bush, would draw me out on the garth like this in service to her, in service to her and—I had to admit it—decidedly not in service to the Rule.

Which made me remember the look he'd given us. Was it possible that, wise as he was, Father Abbot had known, had expected us to mark and recall this spot? For that was surely what had happened. Whenever the miracles were mentioned, the cures alluded to, each of us in our own way pictured that last moment, our lord abbot pouring the final drops over Oftfor's unflinching flesh, the way the water had run down his arm, disappeared into the earth around Father's knees. A moment's silence, thought, then the eyes raised again to look at us. *You saw it too*, they seemed to say, *you saw where it went, the ground into which it drained.* He didn't nod but he didn't have to. It is how we communicate, we monks, with looks, expressions. It was as if he knew.

But what did he know? I scooped up a handful of earth and thought about it, pressing the stuff between my fingers. A pinch of this dissolved in water and sipped while saying an "Our Father" was said to cure any ill. Brother Osric used it on Sinistra's knees; Baldwin had smeared it on his head during Lent. But what had any of this achieved? Sinistra was still too old for the plow; Baldwin remained a stern and heartless monk. No one's sight had been restored, no one's hearing recovered; the lame did not rise from their pallets and walk. I wondered what good it would have done as an antidote to the pestilence. I would have liked to have seen Oftfor try to cure that!

Oftfor. The little face that day in the reredorter, woolens hiked up, death tacked across his flesh, the smell of decay.

But I didn't want to think about that, didn't want to be reminded of that, of what had happened, of what still could happen.

Though it hadn't. It hadn't happened. I was alive. I was alive and well and the more I thought about it the easier it became to convince myself God wouldn't have done that, wouldn't have spared me like that, unless He wanted me alive, wanted me alive perhaps for a very long time. Who knew, maybe He even had some plans for me, wished to impart some task to me as Ceolwulf had, some secret mission that was as yet entirely unheard-of, unthought-of, something having nothing to do with things like this pit, its odor of earth, the grave, rank and unfortunate memory.

Unfortunate memory.

I looked back down at the hole, thought again about Oftfor, wondered why he had been chosen. Surely there must have been someone else who could have done it better, someone bigger, wiser, someone who didn't stutter as Oftfor often had. Despite myself, I remembered the time I'd pinched him, the time I'd held him down and wouldn't let him go, all the times I'd pushed him around, taken out some minor grievance or frustration on the one oblate who never out-grew the hunger in which he'd been delivered to Redestone. Could that be it? Could it be that God, like me, picked Oftfor, singled him out for such attention for the simple reason he was a weakling, a starveling easily dominated, easily ruled?

But that was of course ridiculous. God didn't need to find someone weak to dominate, He could dominate whomever He pleased. And besides, He loved children. Father Prior said so. He preferred children. Which, of course, might also explain it. Perhaps God had chosen Oftfor *because* he was a child, *because* he was small and delicate; perhaps it was precisely his weakness that had made him so attractive.

I squeezed the pouch, felt its load of earth, and it was as if I squeezed some portion of Oftfor, felt again the bone beneath that meager shoulder. It was funny how I felt about him, at one and the same time despising him for his unwarranted fame (Hadn't I suffered? Hadn't others died? Hadn't we all risked such a death?) while pitying him for the end that earned him that fame. I wondered what it had been like for him, those last moments before they carried him to the grave, put him (forever) underground. Did the dead feel their washing? I tried to imagine a body without feeling, the cold water pooling upon one's stomach, trickling down the back of one's legs, the gentle chafing of the abbot's hands. It seemed impossible. Skin without feeling wouldn't be skin anymore.

But of course Oftfor wasn't there too, he was in heaven. And perhaps this was the way a body could be so utterly immune to sensation; it would be like a dream, a dream in which you see yourself but are not yourself: you can't feel or see what your body feels and sees. I liked this idea, it made sense to me. When you died you went to heaven. And in heaven there would have to be a sense of distance, of detachment. You couldn't be expected to feel everything anymore. Which meant, it now occurred to me, you wouldn't even be able to feel fear anymore, not even the sort of fear that had given rise to this line of thought. What a relief that would be, to no longer fear death! No wonder the monks claimed to look forward to it. To be done with that, to have that over and done with, to never again have to worry about *that*.

I leaned back and looked up at the stars. For the first time in a while I thought about Oftfor—the real Oftfor, not the one everyone talked about, not the saint. I missed him in a way. I felt bad about the times I had abused him, and I missed him. But now at least I could tell myself he was all right. It was nice how much better this made me feel. I glanced over at the buildings standing along the terrace's southern edge. Earlier, when I had first come out of the church, the refectory and dortoir had seemed somehow overlarge and threatening—perched there before all that empty space—but now they resumed their proper dimensions, became again the warm, welcoming places I knew and trusted. I understood that my eyes had grown accustomed to the dark, that it was this and only this that made the buildings seem normal again, right and true, but I couldn't help thinking there was something more to it as well, that the change in perception marked a similar, if more subtle, change in discernment, that I had seen something more clearly this night, and that (as if I had been meant to) I recognized something familiar in its form. The more I thought about this, the more convinced I became that it was true. I told myself such insights would become more common now that I was growing up, that, inevitably, as I grew older, wiser, there would be fewer and fewer things that frightened me and more and more like this that I would understand.

I delivered the woman's pouch the next day and, true to her word, it had disappeared by the time I checked the bush later that afternoon. The prints were quick; she had come, found the thing, departed. But I knew she was thankful. And soon she would deliver her prize to the little girl, to her daughter, to the child who in such a short time had become so dear to me. It was strange really, how much I had come to care for this girl whose name I did not know. I prayed for her every day, pictured her in bed as I worked in the fields, ate in the refectory, chanted in choir. I had even picked out the house I thought she lived in (For it was of course ridiculous to have thought she had come from elsewhere. How could she? She was a good little girl, and, like all good little girls, she was Christian and lived in our village.): hers was the last house on the left, the one that, during the springtime floods, sometimes stood ankle-deep in water. It looked hungry and ill-kept even in summer, bare rafters showing through the thatch, wattle through the daub. Something, a broken shutter or something, lay at the base of the back wall waiting for someone to come along and repair it. But no one would. There was no man in that house, or so I had decided. The man had died and now no one would help the little girl. Except me. Except Oftfor and me. For Oftfor too had assumed a new place in my thoughts. He appeared less and less as the boy I'd known and more and more as the saint everyone talked about. Which, now that I needed him to play that role, made eminent sense to me. Who was I to doubt the convictions of my superiors? Father Abbot believed in Oftfor, Father Prior. The bishop himself had sent for the famous soil! I pushed aside Sinistra and her knees and focused instead on the stories of the miracles (for even then there were already many of these). Baldwin had appointed himself keeper of the tales and he must have been surprised by the interest I now showed in them. I learned of the rheumatism that had been eased, the rash that had receded, the flux that had been checked completely. I could list them all. I can still. And with their telling and re-telling I grew daily more certain of Oftfor's powers, of his ability to effect a cure; and, by extension, of the importance of what I had done. For—though I told myself I mustn't think about it too much—I did take pleasure in my accomplishment. I might not have fulfilled my father's charge, not yet, but I had the woman's. I had done something. At some risk to myself, I had done something and, as a result, the world had changed: a little girl would live. The air tasted sweet when I thought of this; God smiled. At least once each day (and sometimes two or three times) I checked the bush by the river where once a woman had hidden. Sooner or later I knew there would be something there, a sign—a bit of biscuit perhaps, a small cake—something to let me know that we had succeeded, that they were thankful, that the little girl and her mother appreciated the cure I had obtained for them. I looked forward to finding this offering happily, hopefully. I wondered if it would be wrapped in something she had made, wrapped in something made by the hands of my little girl.

It must have been about a week later that the wind changed. Have you ever wondered what a stranger would think of us, a stranger who happened upon our abbey on one of those rare days when the wind blows out of the east? Wouldn't he find this a strange place, an odd and undisciplined place where monks wander about like empty spirits without regard for order or decorum? But we know, don't we, we know what we're about? Though we never speak of it, even among ourselves, we know that such an event does not go unnoticed in the otherwise routine world of a monastery. After Vespers you will find a few more monks than usual upon the garth. The silence is maintained, but there is that tendency to stand in loose clusters: two here, three or four there, each with eyes hooded, faces oddly intent, as if listening for something, trying to hear something somewhere off in the distance, some lazy lilting air. What we are really doing of course is fairly simple. We are smelling the wind, sifting it, hoping to scent something new upon this fresh and unexpected breeze.

I was up by the church, looking out over the fields toward the village. It was a warm night, still very light. People were standing or sitting in front of their houses. Every now and then a word or laugh, somebody's name, would be carried up to us on the wind like the fragrance of something cooking. A few children were playing behind one of the houses. I think it was hide-'n-seek. As I stood there, watching the distant villagers, each of them sitting with their houses at their backs, shelters within which they could withdraw at will, it came to me why the woman had yet to leave me some gift, some offering to let me know that her daughter was well, that all had gone as hoped for. It would not occur to her to do so. The fields which separated her world from mine were more than just wheat and peas, they were a boundary as pure and perfect as that between heaven and earth (I had known without asking that I had sinned by even talking to her). Of course she wouldn't report to me on her daughter. I would never know the answers to my questions about her and her identity. The life of the village was as cut off from me, as much a mystery to me—and would remain so always—as I had to assume our life up here at the monastery was to them. That the woman had possessed the courage to approach one of the shades that haunted Redestone's terrace—albeit a boy—was miracle enough. To expect her to try again, and that only to inform me of the outcome of our trespass, was to expect a man to fly or a tree to talk—such things did not happen.

It was haying time. I was still very young. The next day I would work and play again with Waldhere and Ealhmund. But that night, as I stood on our terrace, the breeze just tickling the skin of my face, it was as if summer had come to an end.

XVIII

The sun must not have been fully up yet for the hermit's cheeks and eyes have a reddish cast in my memory, the light from the fire still barely perceptible. Probably it was the interval after Prime as I don't remember feeling particularly rushed or hurried. By Terce there was always a sense of urgency to the day, the feeling that my time on the mountain was running out. It would have been cold too. The mornings on Modra nect were always cold. As I remember it the hermit sits opposite me, the small fire burning between us, one or two tabula lying forgotten on the ground at his feet. Despite the chill, he doesn't have his hood up or a blanket around him. The patch over his right knee has worked free and, as he speaks, he picks at it absently. He was probably already talking about prayer. Ever since I'd asked him to teach me to pray, it seemed that was all he wanted to do, talk about it, not really showing me how to pray so much as explaining its existence, trying to get me to understand how such a thing as prayer came to be. I would have quit listening when he got to the part about obscurity, how, despite the free will He'd given us, God could still reach out to us, *however obscurely*. Father could prattle on about "obscurity" forever, citing examples from everyday life, things that we know but cannot see—hunger, love, yesterday, tomorrow—and generally making me wish I could go back to bed. But I wasn't thinking about bed that morning. For some reason Father himself had my attention, not what he was saying so much as what he was doing, his physical self, the shape and perfection of his hands, the way he sometimes winked when making a point. I was studying his feet, noticing the way his toes lined up in order from smallest to largest, when I realized it had gotten very quiet. I looked at the hermit. He looked at me.

"Sir?"

"I asked how you've been getting along with the river."

The river?

"The river? You were to concentrate on the river, on a spot in the middle of the river?"

"Oh, that." It was bad enough that he'd caught me not paying attention, but to be reminded of the woman…. "I don't see why I have to do that."

The eyebrows shot up. "It was difficult?"

"It's not that, it's just that…I mean what has all this got to do with prayer anyway, staring at the Meolch, talking about free will and obscurity. What's it got to do with learning how to pray?"

The hermit frowned, looked away, seemed to think about it. "You know you're probably right," he said, beginning to smile, "I mean you're probably right, nothing, it has nothing to do with prayer."

I looked at my feet. I never knew what to do when he agreed with me.

"Do you know what the word 'oblate' means, Winwæd, an *oblation*?"

"It's a sort of gift," I said.

The hermit nodded, not really looking at me, looking at something else, something out among the trees. "Yes," he said, closing his eyes. "Yes, a sort of gift."

A bird called somewhere off to our right, called again, was quiet. I waited.

"Woodpecker," said the hermit, thinking about something else. He opened his eyes, looked at me, frowned again. "Look," he said, big hands pulling the woolens taut over his knees, "if I'm going to show you how to pray, teach you to pray, I must show you, teach you, how to find God first, mustn't I?" He looked at me as if uncertain. "I mean that comes first, doesn't it? You can't pray to someone unless you know where he is, can you?"

"God's in heaven."

The hermit nodded. "Yes, yes He is, but He's here too, isn't He? I mean God's everywhere."

I looked around the campsite—dirty pots, broken bits of firewood, twigs, kindling, unswept leaves, a pile of roots—it seemed an unlikely spot for the Lord of Hosts.

The hermit laughed. "'And they found Him in a stable,'" he said. "Come on Winwæd…."

"I can't see Him."

The laugh became a smile, serious. "No. No you can't, can you?"

He didn't want an answer.

"So how can you pray to someone, commune with someone, if you can't see him? I mean if you're going to talk with someone, speak with him, you have to know where he is first, don't you?"

I nodded, *Yes?*

"Well, in a way, that's what the river is about. It's a sort of exercise, a first step, to prepare you for prayer. What happened when you looked at the river, when you stared at just the one spot?"

I shrugged. "It isn't easy."

"Yes?"

"Well, you know, I'd be watching it, watching the spot, and then I'd notice something else, a stick or something floating by, and before I knew it, I'd be watching that instead."

"So you had trouble keeping your attention on the one spot."

"Yes."

"And where do you think God is?"

I just looked at him.

"No, seriously, where do you think He is?"

"Everywhere? You said He's everywhere."

"Well, not quite everywhere, I mean not somewhere you won't let him in."

"Free will."

"Don't look like that. It's a powerful force."

"'Free will is God's greatest gift and pride the ring man places on his own finger in thanksgiving.'"

The hermit smiled. "It's nice to know you're listening. But it is you know, it's true. One could say free will is the most powerful force in Creation for it even walls out God."

I raised my feet to the fire, wiggled my toes. "I thought God could do anything."

"I know," the hermit said, thinking about it. He picked up a small stick, looked at it. "It doesn't make sense does it, I mean that something can wall God out? It doesn't seem right." The hermit bent the stick in two but it wouldn't break, was too green. He straightened it back out, bent it again, but still it wouldn't break. The hermit pitched the stick onto the fire. "In this sort of work," he said, eyes still on the place where the stick had landed, "and praying is work like any other, you will find many things that don't seem right, don't make sense. Such things are called contradictions, paradoxes. You will have to get used to contradictions, Winwæd, if you want to succeed at prayer." The stick, having nearly straightened out again in the heat, now began to turn black. It did not catch fire. "I could tell you it's not so much that we wall Him out as that He *permits* us to wall Him out, but it still doesn't seem right, does it, more like the answer to a clever riddle than the truth? But it is the truth somehow; I mean we can hold Him at a distance if we're not careful."

"How?"

The hermit looked at me, looked back at the fire. He rubbed his hands on his knees, noticed the patch, pulled it back to look at the skin of his knee. A few hairs sprang out and I was reminded of the hairs on Brother Botulf's head. "Well, I don't know how," he said, "not exactly. But I do know the form it takes." He looked at me, pointed at the side of his head. "Thoughts. God grants you the freedom of your thoughts, your ideas, independent of Him. He doesn't intrude upon them. It's the one place He doesn't go unless He's invited. And even then it's not really Him. I mean when you think about Him you're not really experiencing Him, you're think-ing *about* Him, that's all."

"Sir?"

"It's similar to what we were talking about earlier, what you pointed out. Thinking about God is as different from experiencing God as talking about prayer is from actually praying."

The first wind of the day passed through the trees overhead on its way down the mountain. A smaller, reverse breeze slipped back up the mountain beneath it, moving over the ground at our feet. I moved a little to my right to keep the smoke out of my eyes.

"Thoughts aren't real, are they? I mean you can't touch a thought, can't feed it, cut it in two, set it upon a table? Thoughts are just thoughts, Winwæd, phantoms. We invent them, we create them, and, no matter how great they are, they are still only thoughts, ideas, puffs of smoke."

"So?"

"So God is real, isn't He? I mean He's as real as that tree or this rock. He exists. And, like the tree or rock, if you want to experience Him, know Him, you don't close your eyes and think about Him. No, you get up, walk over there, touch Him, look at Him, smell His bark, chip at His edges."

"God doesn't have bark."

"Exactly!" The hermit smiled as if I'd said something clever. "You can't see God that way, you can't smell Him, can you? But, just like the tree and the rock, to have contact with Him you must know where He is. I mean you wouldn't walk over to this rock to experience the tree, or to the tree to touch this rock, would you?"

"No...?"

"Well then, that's what the Meolch's all about."

"Sir?"

"The Meolch? I had you concentrating on a spot on the river?"

"I know but I mean I don't see how it's...."

"Look, we know God doesn't exist in thoughts, right? Created can't contain Creator?"

"Yes...." I didn't really understand that but I didn't want him to explain it again.

"And if you want to experience God, like the tree or the rock, you have to go where He is?"

I nodded.

"So you have to go someplace where thoughts aren't."

"Sir?"

"In order to experience God you have to go someplace where thoughts aren't. You have to stop thinking because, when you're thinking, the best you can hope for is to think *about* God, your image of God. And while your image of God may be very nice, it isn't God. Right?"

I felt as though I'd been tricked. A part of me could see where we were and the track the hermit had followed to get us there, but I didn't see how it could possibly be true. How could you go where there weren't any thoughts? You would have to leave your head behind. And once you got there, how could you experience God without thinking about Him?

"Do you find that contradictory, Winwæd, paradoxical?"

That he had an answer to my objection didn't make me feel any better about it.

"Remember the river you have inside you?"

"The one that flows from left to right?"

The hermit blinked. "Yes, yes, in your case it does. But that doesn't matter. What matters, left to right or right to left, is that the river is you, I mean in the sort of work I'm teaching you, the river is you— your life, your mind, your soul—it is you."

"The river is me."

"I know, I know, but bear with me." The hermit stopped, thought about it. When he began to speak again it was in a different voice, as if we were now talking about something else, an entirely new subject. "Have you ever seen something," he asked, "have you ever seen something or heard something that so surprised you, so startled you that, for a moment or two, your mind went blank? In the world they talk of being rendered speechless by something and this is what they mean. They are not really speechless, though they cannot speak, it is that, however momentarily, they have been rendered thoughtless, empty, their minds deaf and dumb, pure. Do you know what I'm talking about Winwæd, have you ever experienced anything like that?"

I nodded. Brother Eadnoth covered with spots, humming to the moon.

The hermit smiled. "Good. That's good. But, as I'm sure you know, such moments are rare. Most of the time, most of the time whether you are awake or asleep, your river is like a river at flood, all sorts of things bobbing along on the surface—sticks, logs, leaves, maybe even bits of houses, fences, somebody's hat. These things are your thoughts, the thoughts that constitute the daily activity of your mind, the thoughts that *are*—in a sense—your mind, the thoughts that many people take to be their complete and utter selves."

"My thoughts are me."

"No, no they're not! That's what other people think, not you, not a monk. Thoughts are just thoughts, remember, phantoms."

"Thoughts are just thoughts."

"What you want is to not think, to be able to leave your thoughts behind, let them pass by without bothering you."

Why did it have to be so hard? All I wanted was to learn how to pray like Father Hermit, maybe save a few lives, work a few miracles.

"That's what the river is all about. If you can let its current, its load of debris, flow by without distraction, you will find you can do the same thing with your thoughts, with…. What? What is it?"

I didn't say anything.

The hermit watched me, waited.

I shook my head, looked away, looked back. "It doesn't look so difficult when you do it; I mean you don't make it look so difficult."

"It isn't…."

"I thought God loved us. I thought He was reaching out to us, *however obscurely*, all the time. Why's He make it so difficult if He loves us, why's it have to be so complicated?"

The hermit smiled, apparently pleased with my problem. "It isn't difficult, Winwæd, it just seems that way. We're unaccustomed to it, that's all, unaccustomed to emptying ourselves, humbling ourselves…."

"Right."

The hermit frowned. He looked around the campsite absently, noticed the tabula lying at his feet, picked one up. "Look, what must I do if I want to write on this?"

I glanced at the thing—it was covered with writing, someone's prayer request. I shrugged. "Remove the old writing?"

"Exactly. There isn't enough room for more words, is there? Not as it is now. But if...." Father swept the tabulum back and forth over the fire. He looked at it, passed it over the fire once more, examined it again, showed it to me—eyes asking what I thought of his work. The surface of the wax was smooth now, only a few swirls remaining to mark the spots where, before, there had been letters, entire words. I had to smile. It had been neatly done.

The hermit didn't smile but you could tell he was pleased with himself. He shook his head. "Our minds are not unlike tabula," he said, "covered day and night with thoughts: old thoughts, new thoughts, thoughts about work and people. Sometimes there are even mistaken thoughts, strange scrambled things full of misplaced words, errant ideas, ancient worries lording it over new." The hermit paused, looked at his tabulum. "It's a complicated block of wax, the mind. And on top of all that, we expect God to write something." He looked at me. "That's what prayer's all about, that's what the center of the river's all about, asking God to write something on our tabulum. And of course He *wants* to write something, has been dying to write something ever since the beginning of time; and, now that we've asked Him to, asked Him of our own free will, He finally can. But how can He?" The hermit looked at me as if expecting an answer. "How can He write something on your mind if it's so cluttered, so confused with your own thoughts and messages that anything He placed there would be misunderstood, misread, mistaken for something else, part of another thought, something about yesterday's supper or the color of that bruise?" He pointed at the place where Waldhere had pinched me. "What then, Winwæd, what then?"

I shook my head. I hadn't the slightest idea.

Father smiled. "We must clear our tabula. When you pray—when you pray as I am teaching you to pray—you must warm the wax of your mind, allow the heat to erase your thoughts, allow it to erase your thoughts one by one. And then you must wait. You must wait quietly, absently, while God writes what He will. And what He wills, of course, is Himself. What you will read, encounter, is God." Father shook his head. "You mustn't worry about the thoughts, they'll come back. They may even try to come back before you're ready for them, while you're still at prayer. But when this happens you must erase them again. With a simple sweep of the will you must soften the wax of your mind, keep your tabulum clear and empty so as to leave it open to God."

"Absently?"

"Absently?"

"You said I have to wait 'absently' for God. To write on my mind or whatever. What do you mean…'absently'?"

The hermit looked up at the trees. "I said that, 'absently'? Well, that's all right. That's good." He looked at me. "You do wait on Him *absently*, or you should, *absent* will, *absent* thoughts, *absent* everything but Him. You empty yourself of all but Him, no thoughts, no sounds, so you can hear Him."

"I thought He was going to write something."

The hermit frowned. "Write something, say something, these are metaphors, Winwæd, metaphors. You understand the word?"

I nodded quickly. The last thing I wanted was another definition.

"We say He speaks or writes because it is the only way we have to describe the Father. The Christ Himself is a sort of metaphor for God, or His story is. But it is not a metaphor when I say we must wait upon Him *absently*. That is real. That is true humility, to empty one's self of one's self—of one's thoughts and feelings—before God. We humble ourselves before Him, which is to say we present our selves before Him without excuse or embellishment. We are quiet. We let Him take us as we are." The hermit shook his head, looked off down the mountain. "We let Him take us as we are."

Father said no more after that. Though I waited respectfully, did not fidget or prod, he remained quiet, withdrawn. Over time I would learn this was typical of the hermit. About plants or track he could go on at great length, but when the subject was prayer, the *how* of prayer, our lessons were often truncated, abrupt. Sometimes it made me wonder about him. When he did talk of prayer, he often did so hurriedly, as if, having thought of something, he wanted to spit it out quickly before the idea got away from him, before that particular well ran dry. The silences that followed these proclamations I found worrisome. I had seen such behavior before, grown-ups who, when questioned directly by an oblate too innocent to know better, would abruptly lose their taste for instruction, begin a fluttering and inconsequential display of sign language—protestations of fatigue, overwork, of being pestered by foundlings. Father Hermit never complained like that but, as I have said, he often grew quiet and—it seemed to me—a little sad. "They call me a 'master'," he once said, "but I think that is only because I am old. I am not a master. Far from it. Every day I'm struck by how little I know. From one morning to the next I am uncertain even where to begin. I start each day like a novice, a desperate frightened novice: 'God,' I cry out, 'where are You? Speak to me, I beg you, give me a sign!' There are no masters but *the* Master. The only wise men I know are those who know nothing. Nothing. We are fools, all of us fools, calling into the night."

Funny how much I miss him now. And how wrong that assessment of his seems after all these years. I have told this story as stories must be told—with a beginning, a middle, and an end—but that is not how I think of it, that is not how I remember it. In my memory there is no talk of the meaning of prayer, there is no reticence, no uncertainty; there is only the image of Father sitting there by his fire, waving his tabulum back and forth; and then that final graceful display of smooth wax. It seemed a perfect movement, elegant, sublime, and remembering it, remembering the way he looked as he did it, I find myself once more charmed—charmed and bereft—for he *was* a master (his own doubts and those of lesser men notwithstanding), and I miss him so very much.

XIX

ow old was I when I was given to the furnace master? At the time I remember thinking I was young, too young for such work, but looking back on it now I find myself doubting that. Surely Father Abbot wouldn't have assigned me to the yard if I was unequal to the demands of the place. It's a pity Osric's gone, he would know for sure, and there is no other record to consult. Vellum, as they say, requires a death. So I must admit to being uncertain, though I would guess I was fairly young. Most work in those days began fairly young.

I was envious. I remember that well. In some ways I suppose Ealhmund received the best assignment. He was given to Botulf, which, as it turned out, meant all the food he could eat and no one to beat him for the offense, as Brother Kitchens took an unusual liking to the boy. Still it was Waldhere's assignment that bothered me most. Father Abbot had given him to Brother Sacristan. Now normally the abuse Waldhere could expect from that quarter would have pleased me no end, but in this case there was, of course, the obvious difference: sacristy, Baldwin, and church meant Father intended Waldhere for the priesthood; while I was left to endlessly grab and pump, grab and pump, Victricius's mindless bellows.

Victricius. What an odd monk he was. While most of the brothers went to some lengths to appear serene and detached, Brother Victricius was the exact opposite, always moving, always intent upon doing something, fixing something, making something work better. In Faults he used to excuse such conduct by claiming it to be a sort of discipline, *age quod agis*, but everyone knew he just liked to be busy.

Brother could fiddle with a broken piece of harness or a loose ax handle from dawn to dusk and never notice the day had passed him by. And who knows, there may have been a spiritual dimension to it. Certainly I never saw the man unhappy or discouraged, at least not until the end. No matter how difficult the task, how many times he jammed a finger, barked his shin, Brother remained the same monk he had been when he commenced his labors, determined, self-assured, ready for whatever duty God or Father Abbot placed before him. And he was very good at it. The other monks may not have cared for him but they knew his worth. Afterwards, after he was gone, we all felt his absence, things lying about broken, no one to repair them, the furnace in ruins.

A part of me feels sorry for him now, looking back on it. When the brothers used to draw together after collation, forming small knots upon the garth, Victricius's lone figure inevitably marked the spot from which they had withdrawn. I suppose it was his manner that made him appear so unattractive, the way he had of standing there by himself, a small smile on his face, patting his foot as if keeping time with some other, some unknown and probably better, choir. He didn't seem to need us, behaved as if he found all of us, in a way, vaguely ridiculous. And so we pretended to not need him, made jokes at his expense, shunned him as if possessed of a like and possibly even superior knowledge.

Needless to say, I wholeheartedly concurred in my community's opinion of the man, and deeply resented being assigned to him. I was the hermit's boy, the one everyone was supposed to turn to when they needed Gwynedd's prayers, yet here I was bowing and scraping before this outcast, this foreigner who couldn't even speak properly, the unwitting clown who never seemed to realize how silly he looked, face streaked with soot, eyes and nose sometimes running black with the stuff.

Still, in a way, that soot was a mark of Victricius's importance. As you can well imagine, any other monk appearing for Vespers in such a state would have been sent immediately to the lavabo, a curt abbatial warning ringing in his ears. But not Victricius. Despite the contempt they felt for the man, the monks of Redestone took great pride in his work; and the absurd face that occasionally stared out from our choir's otherwise pristine ranks seemed a small price to pay for the prestige that work brought our abbey.

But not all the soot adorning that countenance was the result of a monk's legitimate labors. I—and I alone—knew Victricius had a secret, a dark and awful secret he kept buried at the yard.

I may be uncertain of my age at the time I was given to the furnace master, but I know it cannot have been *before* I was admitted to Chapter. I know this for I remember well the shock I received when first I saw Victricius's fire-pits, first realized the extent of his offense, the horrible punishment he risked. For I had been present when Brother asked if he might build a kiln, had heard Father Abbot tell him—all of Chapter had heard Father Abbot tell him—that under no circumstances was he to begin such a project, that he was to focus all his energies (as our lord bishop had ordered) upon the making of iron.

To be separated from the community, shunned, made to crawl from table to table, bowl in hand, begging for your food—this was the fate Victricius courted, this the power his secret, and my knowledge of that secret, gave me over him, a power that at once both tempted and terrified me. I could not imagine denouncing the man (for separation from the community exemplified the worst of my oblate fears); I could not imagine not denouncing him (for by failing to report him, I knew I risked the very thing I most dreaded). So—as was fast becoming my practice when faced with such imponderables—I did nothing, all the while telling myself I was biding my time. Then came a day late one cold and windy spring.

The upper part of the valley receives little sun in the morning, shielded as it is by a shoulder of the ridge that, further down, undergirds our garth. We would have arrived at the yard, as we did most days, to a work-place still sunk in the light of pre-dawn, all surfaces damp, all sounds muted, the air an odd mix of stale and fresh—burnt earth, burnt shell, wet pine, falling water. Brother would have been in even more of a hurry than usual, though I wouldn't have known why. Still he would have found time to check his pits. The man was inordinately proud of his fire-pits, though I wasn't that impressed. They were just holes in the ground, little more than postholes really, each just wide enough and deep enough to hold one of Victricius's modest pots. The furnace master would have made four or five of these fresh the day before—as he did every day—would have placed one in each pit, packed the space around it with whatever fuel he was then experimenting with (I saw him use everything from wet leaves to dry manure), then sealed the pit with a thick layer of mud. A small hole—like the smoke hole in a roof—was always left at the center of this layer of mud so that, at the end of the day, a single hot coal could be introduced into the otherwise airtight chamber. The pits were then left to burn through the night.

On that morning, as I remember it, we arrived to find two of the pits still burning. This was not that unusual. On one occasion I remember we arrived to find them all still burning, the ground around the furnace smoking alarmingly and, every now and then, emitting uncarthly pops and groans. But even the pits that seemed to have burned out could still hurt you. Brother would have made me stand back, would have squatted by each, a gardener inspecting his plants, running the palm of his hand over the ground, testing for warmth. Doubtless I stood and watched as I did most mornings, wondering why the man still bothered. Burning or not, the results were always the same—broken pottery, dust, ashes.

Victricius stood back up. Pursing his lips in a way I always found mildly repellent, he indicated the pit he wanted me to extinguish, then picked up his shovel and went to work on the other one. We only had the one shovel; I got the hoe.

It made sense to smother quickly those pits still burning: inevitably their contents had long since been reduced by the heat to fragments and you might as well rid yourself of the smoke. Of course none of the pits ever produced a whole pot. But Victricius kept trying. He was nothing if not patient. And it didn't seem to worry him that I had discovered what he was up to. Probably he told himself that digging pits wasn't the same as building a kiln, that strictly speaking he wasn't in violation of the abbot's ruling. But he never bothered to explain that to me. The monks were like that. They did things in front of us oblates they would never have done in front of a grown-up. But they shouldn't have. I was admitted to Chapter now, Faults, I could stand up as easily as anyone.

I scraped a little more dust into the fire-pit, making a sort of game of it, seeing how much I could work into the vent before it quit smoking; and I thought about the similar game Victricius was playing: obeying the abbot, not obeying him, a little dust goes in, a little smoke comes out. Then—as if he'd divined what I was thinking and wished to put an immediate stop to it—Victricius was suddenly beside me, slinging great banners of earth across my pit and, incidentally, my feet as well. Of course I should have been used to such discourtesy by now (if you came between the furnace master and something he wished to do, he could shove you aside as easily as a farmer might his most obstinate cow), but I wasn't. I stepped back and watched Brother work, thinking about what I could do to him if he wasn't careful, what I very well *might* do to him.

Not surprisingly, given the strength of Victricius's assault, my pit quickly gave up the ghost. I expected the furnace master to turn next to one of those that had burned out during the night (Brother being forever anxious to examine their contents), but on this occasion Victricius surprised me, beginning instead to clear a spot of ground next to the rock-pile. A small thrill ran through me: *a visit from the charcoaler!* I picked up my hoe, began to help Victricius rake the place clean. I always liked it when Stuf showed up.

In the old days, before the pestilence, the monks had made their own charcoal. I had witnessed this, could still remember the gangs of men marching off into the Great North Wood with their sharpened axes, their sledges, the lowing oxen. But it had been a long time now since the abbey could spare such numbers and we had come to depend upon men like Stuf to supply our furnace with fuel. Which, when you think about it, says a great deal about our circumstances, for normally we would never have employed a pagan, not even for work as miserable as charcoaling. Of course no one had actually come right out and told me Stuf was a pagan—then as now people seldom spoke of such things openly—but like all oblates I knew how to read the signs; and with a man like Stuf such signs were legion. Here was a fellow who never bothered to cross himself or bow his head when the Name was mentioned, a filthy inhabitant of the hills who nevertheless refused to show Victricius the respect due a solemnly-professed monk. Why Stuf had even been known to wink at me when the furnace master mispronounced a word! Yet despite this, despite the fact the man was so obvious a cur, a part of me always looked forward to his visits, looked forward to seeing someone behave so outrageously.

Brother set his shovel aside, straightened up, placed his hands on the backs of his hips and, stretching his back, surveyed the space we had cleared. An uninformed observer might have been excused for thinking there was a reason for such attentiveness, that Victricius wanted to make sure this section of yard was swept clear so he could better appreciate the size of the load Stuf would dump there; but in this such an observer would have been wrong. Stuf's payment was based solely on the *number* of loads he delivered, their size having been predetermined by that of the dosser we gave him to transport them in. Victricius wasn't worried about measuring anything, he was simply vain of the appearance of his yard, didn't like to think of even a pagan finding fault with it.

As if to emphasize this, Brother now nodded at a small drift of dust and pine needles, mimed raking it up with a hoe.

Contemptuously, I swept the stuff away.

When I looked back to see if there was anything else the good brother wanted me to do, the expression on my master's face gave me pause and I assumed custody of the eyes. After a moment or two, Victricius's feet moved out of my field of vision and, looking back up, I was pleased to see the danger passed, Brother already intent upon something else, kneeling by one of his pits, beginning to break apart the outer covering. Watching him, I found myself thinking (as I had before) how different the furnace master was from Father Abbot. Here were two men who both came from the same country, both spoke with the same accent, used the same peculiar gestures, yet

Father's ways always struck me as worldly, a sign of broad experience and sophistication, while in Victricius the same manners seemed proof of the opposite, that this was a man out of his depth, a foreigner unequal to the noble culture in which he found himself. And what was more, Father Abbot was considerably taller than Brother Victricius. Of course I knew I should attach no importance to this, but I could see no reason why I shouldn't someday be tall myself; after all, Ceolwulf was.

It was as I was thinking these thoughts that Victricius's back straightened suddenly. He cocked his head, seemed to study something in the pit before him, then bent once more to his work. With little else to do, I stepped closer, wondering what had caught the fool's attention this time.

The ground around my master's knees was littered with broken bits of fired earth—the remains of the pit's covering. Looking over his shoulder, I could see that, in removing this, he had exposed an uncommonly fine layer of dark gray ash. Like a man clearing the water before he drinks, Brother was now brushing at this ash with his fingertips. At first I thought the care with which he did this just another of my master's pointless preoccupations, but then I noticed—at the very center of the ash—a fiery slip of color. As Victricius brushed at this, the pinkish color grew, blossomed grotesquely outward, became the dome of a child's head; of course I knew what it really was—the furnace master always placed his pots upside down like this to conserve heat—but, still, this was the first one I had ever seen come out perfectly whole.

Taking care not to injure what he had made, Victricius pulled his pot from its bed of ashes, singing a little piece of psalmody to himself as he did so, "'You will give me life again, you will pull me up again from the depths of the earth....'"

Instinctively, I sang the antiphon: "'I will thank you on the lyre, my ever-faithful God, I will play the harp in your honor, Holy One of Israel.'"

Victricius's head spun around, eyes wide, blinking. For a moment he looked at me as if surprised to find himself unalone, then, tentatively, he sang back: "'My lips shall sing for joy as I play to you, and this soul of mine which....'"

A loud noise and a horribly painted man stood at the edge of the yard, arms back, ready to hurl a....

Stuf?

I opened my eyes again.

And it was Stuf. Stuf the charcoal-maker was standing at the edge of the yard, eyes closed, fingers massaging his forehead thoughtfully. On the ground behind him lay the dosser, a telltale cloud of dust still hanging in the air around it.

I looked back at my master, hoping to find him ready to berate the filthy pagan for scaring us so. But, typically, Victricius's mind had already moved on to the day's next order of business; the man climbing awkwardly to his feet, the pot still cradled in his arms.

"Why don't you set that down first?" said Stuf. He looked at me, rolled his eyes.

I looked down, embarrassed for everyone.

When I looked back up, Victricius's pot was nestled among the canes of the shed's roof and Brother was once more sweeping the place he and I had already swept earlier. The charcoal-maker seemed amused by this, the smile on his face making it clear what he thought of a man who swept clean a spot soon to be dirtied by charcoal. I liked the shells. Stuf had sewn a number of snail shells onto the front of his jerkin, their colors alternating between brown and white. The man often decorated his person in this way with things he'd found in the wood. Once he'd even shown up wearing a hat made entirely of mud and leaves. As if remembering this himself, the charcoal-maker now rubbed his forehead, looked at his hand, rubbed it again. Even relieved of his dosser, the man stood in a sort of crouch, head back, arms hanging down in front of him as if still countering the weight. I wondered what it would be like to carry such a load suspended like that across your forehead. Waldhere said it made your eyes pop out, that that was why Brother Egric's bulged so, because he'd carried such heavy loads before coming to the monastery, but I wasn't entirely sure I believed Waldhere about this. Still I had to admit such a weight must constrict your thoughts...which probably explained why Stuf remained so stubbornly heathen.

Apparently satisfied with the spot he had cleared for it, Victricius now indicated the charcoal-maker might empty his dosser. With some difficulty—muscles straining as he lifted the basket before his chest—Stuf did so, charcoal clattering out in a great cloud of sparkling black dust. When the dust had settled, the resulting pile appeared, as it always did, smaller than I had expected. The two men looked at each other as if they too were disappointed. Brother picked up the now-empty dosser, raised it easily above his head, shook it out over the pile. One or two stray pieces of charcoal slid out along with a final spray of dust. Brother righted the thing, stuck his head in its mouth, looked around, then tossed it aside, a smudge of soot now decorating his nose. The charcoal-maker didn't remark upon the soot; he watched the furnace master closely. Victricius squatted down, picked up a piece of charcoal, broke it in two. Inspecting each half, he noticed something on the larger of the two and showed it to Stuf. Stuf looked at it, didn't say anything. The furnace master waited for a moment and then, when it became clear Stuf wasn't going to say anything, he looked again at the piece, shrugged, tossed both halves back onto the pile. He stood up, dusted off his hands.

The charcoal-maker remained silent, eyes locked upon the furnace master.

Victricius noticed Stuf looking at him, returned the look, didn't say anything.

"Well?"

The furnace master raised his shoulders, stuck out his lower lip. "I want to examine it more closely when Winwæd puts it away."

"What about my board?" Stuf was supposed to receive a tabulum specifying the amount to be paid for his charcoal out of the abbey stores.

"I said I want to examine it more closely as Winwæd stacks it in the shed."

The charcoal-maker's eyebrows rose imploringly.

Brother Victricius didn't say anything.

"Master, please, this is good charcoal. You know it is good charcoal."

"How can I know that until I've had time to examine it properly?"

"Master felt it with his hands, looked at it with his eyes; he is a wizard when it comes to charcoal, a sage!"

Brother smiled. "In the meantime you can bring down another load. This isn't nearly enough."

"But what if I have nothing to eat!"

The smile became indulgent. "Is that so?"

The charcoal-maker looked at his waist, undid the knot in his belt, tied it tight again.

"Well I'm sure Brother Almoner could find you...."

Stuf spit, his phlegm as black as his charcoal.

The furnace master didn't say anything. He looked at the place where the charcoal-maker had spit, but he didn't say anything. Stuf stood with his hands on his hips, a great lord disgusted with his servant, glowering at him. It always went like this, Victricius quietly standing his ground, refusing to issue a tabulum, Stuf dancing around him, petulant and imperious one moment, fretful and obsequious the next. Of course I knew the charcoal-maker was in the wrong, that—were he a monk—he would be chastised for such immoderation, but, still, I couldn't help being fascinated by the behavior. I wondered if it was typical of pagans, if, perhaps, having turned their backs on Christ, they had escaped other responsibilities as well, even, it seemed (if the charcoal-maker was any guide), the need to act like a grown-up, to be forever quiet, humble, self-restrained.

Stuf spit again, turned away, stared off indignantly up-river. I recognized the look. Victricius held the key, the mysterious runes he scratched upon his "board," and Stuf had finally faced the fact he could not force said key—or anything else for that matter—from the master of Redstone's furnace. But he wouldn't go yet. He never did. Though he had admitted defeat, Stuf would put off leaving as long as possible. I had seen other men, other visitors to the abbey, tarry like this as well. Never the villagers. They knew better. But the people who came from beyond the valley—pilgrims, beggars, the occasional traveler—seemed always to expect more of us, could never quite bring themselves to believe in our indifference to news. And so Stuf daw-dled. He scratched behind a knee, toyed with his snail shells, picked up Victricius's shovel, examined it closely. Already breaking open another pit, the furnace master ignored him. I knew he wanted me to start putting the charcoal away, but I was equally sure he wouldn't say anything about it in front of Stuf. He was hoping the man would go away, didn't want to give him anything else to comment upon, another excuse to linger.

Stuf finished his inspection of the shovel, set it aside, worked his shoulders as if trying to ease a stiff muscle. The snail shells made a sound. When the furnace master didn't look up, Stuf pretended not to care. He let his eyes pass proprietorially over the yard, approving of our charcoal, questioning our ore, studying the bellows, affecting an immense knowledge of furnaces and their design. Then, as if he'd just remembered something that needed attending to, the charcoal-maker glanced back at the shed. "I've seen children make better pots than that," he declared.

Victricius couldn't help himself: he tossed a quick glance at the pot he had so carefully placed on the shed roof.

Stuf smiled, a hit. "Yes, at Verbanum they don't even use kilns. Clay fires itself! A day in the sun and they're ready for hot oil."

"I doubt even the Verbana are as stupid as that."

Stuf pretended surprise but was clearly pleased to have gotten a response. "Well I don't know," he said, shaking his head doubtfully, "perhaps I did get that wrong. But they're good pots, you must admit. I think both my pots came from Verbanum."

Victricius smiled but didn't say anything. We both knew Stuf's pots came from Gaul. All the abbey's ceramics did.

Stuf saw the furnace master smile, glanced in my direction and caught me smiling as well. He frowned, looked back at Victricius who was once again calmly digging out his pit. "Well, anyway, I don't think they cure them in the ground like that. I don't think anyone does that. They know you do that down at Redestone?"

Stuf was perfectly capable of blabbing about the fire-pits to Brother Cellarer, but the furnace master seemed unconcerned. Using index fingers only, he was teasing a sliver of pottery from the ashes, bending a little to the left as he did so.

The charcoal-maker snorted derisively. "Osric always claiming everything belongs to God, so stingy with his seed, and here you are breaking up perfectly good pots, sticking them in the ground like so many onions! I don't understand this silly Rule of yours."

The furnace master looked up at that, eyes flashing.

Stuf became immediately interested in something on the ground by his feet.

Victricius pursed his lips, shook his head, then seemed to lose interest. He looked back down at the bits and pieces of pottery on the ground before him, began to rearrange them as if curious to see what sort of pot they would have made. When the charcoal-maker saw this, he tossed an impish grin in my direction, picked up his dosser and announced it was time for him to go.

The furnace master nodded perfunctorily.

Stuf moved to the far side of the yard, looked up the path before him, seemed to think about it, then, as if delivering himself of some final piece of wisdom, addressed the furnace master. "Of course I really shouldn't speak on matters such as this," he said, nodding toward Victricius's shards, "woman's work after all. But, then again, you wouldn't know about that, would you? Women I mean." A big smile, a final shift of the basket, and the charcoal-maker turned and was gone.

Later that day, for some reason I can only guess at, I found myself asking Victricius what I had never asked before: why he risked so much just to make a rather poor pot. His answer surprised me. "Oh I'll be punished," he said, "I know that. But won't Father Abbot be proud of me!"

XX

Those of you who remember Agatho's abbacy may perceive the occasional knot in this record, as if the year had looped back on itself and winter followed spring, summer autumn. But I fear that's the way my mind works these days, the stories falling from me like leaves from a tree, one after the other, with little regard for order or precedence. Of course I could go back and rearrange things, try to place these chapters in some sort of proper sequence, but at my age I find little interest in doing so. I make the usual excuses for this of course, telling myself it is God's will, that such disorder may, in fact, follow some higher order known only to Him; but, truth be told, I am probably just being lazy. These days I feel less and less inclined to anything like real work.

Yet even so indulgent an approach can cause its author problems. For what am I to do with Eanflæd, where am I to place her story? Hers is hardly some feeble phantom rising unexpectedly from memory. Indeed—may God forgive me—had I recorded Eanflæd's name every time it occurred to me naturally, by now I fear I should long since have copied it out many more times than I have His. Yet surely it does belong here, this being by way of a confession. And so I choose to write it now (and even after all these years—may God forgive me yet again—I must admit, take pleasure in the act).

Of course Waldhere will appreciate the fact I was on a ladder when I met her, that I was—as he will doubtless someday preach—caught thus between heaven and earth, the sacred and the profane. Similarly, Father Cellarer will point out the occasion found me gathering wool instead of cherries, that it was through idleness that the Devil ensnared me. And of course they would both be right. But I should like to note I was ordered onto that ladder, that my being there was a result of obedience, and which of us—when it comes to it—finding himself looking out over the top of the orchard like that, the abbey seeming to float upon a green and leafy sea, which of us has not fallen prey to daydream? Of course I have no idea what I was really thinking about, where my thoughts had wandered that particular late summer day, but, for the sake of chronicle, let us say they went to Rome. It makes sense. Father Abbot was only recently returned therefrom, and, staring absently across the treetops at Redestone, my mind may well have made the leap from its rosy walls to those of the holy see—the crowded streets, the narrow alleyways, buildings stacked one behind another (or so Father claimed) like so many sheaves at harvest.

"Would you like some water?"

I grasped the ladder, clung to it as in a high wind. The girl again.

"It's good, cold."

What did she want? Why did she keep coming back?

"Sir?"

I looked out across the tops of the trees, saw nothing, tried to appear interested in nothing. Sir. No one had ever called me "sir" before.

"Brother?"

I looked down.

"Water," she said, holding the bucket up as if uncertain I knew the word.

Again I looked out over the treetops, tried to imagine what I should do, what Father Gwynedd would do, Father Prior. Nothing? Perhaps nothing? If I ignored the girl, would she go away? She had the day before.

I began to pick cherries. Slowly at first, and then with more confidence, I picked cherries. I heard movement but I did not look down. I worked. I tried not to fall. The day had acquired an unwonted breeziness, the top of my ladder rising and settling against its branch like a ship at sea.

After a while the sounds of movement ceased below me and I told myself I was glad she was gone, that at least that was taken care of. I continued to pick cherries. I did not look at Redestone. I did not stare off across the top of the orchard. I was a good boy. I picked cherries. When the time came to move the ladder, I thought it would be all right to take one last look at her, to make sure she really was leaving, that she had indeed quit the orchard, was now making her way back down the abbey path toward the village. Awkwardly, hooking an arm through the ladder, I turned halfway around, looked out toward the ditch, hoping to catch a glimpse of blue, the dark head bobbing along, receding into afternoon light. But there was nothing, no one, the path empty, the emptiness itself somehow threatening, vertiginous. I reached back with my free hand, felt nothing, felt the world fall away from me, reached once more and caught a desperate purchase. Twisted now—back to ladder, feet still facing it—I took a deep breath, looked down.

And the world spun.

Or seemed to. The girl was still there—as I had feared she must be—sitting now on the ground by my ladder, but between us, impossibly, the air turned, revolved, gray spots wheeling round a dark and pretty crown. Then, as if sensing my fear, the dark head shifted, looked up...and suddenly I understood everything, saw the weed in her hand, the tufts of seed, realized what this was, what all this was that turned in the air between us, clung to her hair, the various parts of her costume. I frowned, looked back out at the ditch. Silliness. It was all just a silly girlish game!

I turned back around.

Carefully, like a man who has regained his faith in up and down, like a man at the top of a very tall ladder, I turned back around, faced once more the ladder's rungs. I took a big breath. The limbs in my vicinity seemed to remonstrate with me, their outer branches clearly empty of cherries. I thought about this, studied the near flank of Modra nect (blue now with shadow), looked up at Dacca's crag. No answers came to me.

I began to pick cherries, or pretended to, turning leaves over I'd already inspected, finding nothing, knowing there was nothing to find. Soon it would be Vespers and they would come looking for me, might come looking even before Vespers. I had to do something, must do something soon, the feeling of this growing in me, an itch that had to be looked to, soothed, before it became too nettlesome to ignore. The afternoon grew still more windy, my ladder rising and falling against its branch like something alive, breathing. The rung I stood on hardened beneath me, turned to iron, set the soles of my feet a-tingling. My hands grew damp, slippery. An image of myself tumbling from the tree rose before me, began to taunt me, the sight of myself lying on the ground in front of the girl, all elbows and knees, skirts hiked up indecently.

When, finally, I gave up and climbed down, I was surprised to discover I no longer knew how to descend a ladder, my knees getting in the way, my rump swaying unnaturally.

"May I talk to you?"

She had spread her shawl on the ground beneath her, bucket placed to one side like someone intending to eat their supper in the field. Already I regretted having set my basket down, the impression it gave of a meal about to be shared. The girl had looked at the cherries and smiled. She had not made room for me on the shawl. I stood before her, uncertain of what to do with my hands, where to place my feet, achingly aware of the figure I presented, both to her and to anyone who might happen into the orchard.

The girl nodded as if I had said something. She smiled. "I understand about the not talking," she said, "the silence."

I could have cried. I could have gotten down on my hands and knees and paid her homage. *She understood!* I wouldn't have to use any of the silly hand gestures, try to explain everything—the wonderful creature understood!

"You can speak only to God."

Well, that of course wasn't precisely true…. But I liked the sound of it. On her lips it sounded somehow better, finer, almost heroic. I stood a little taller.

"Oh! The water!" The girl rose to her knees, wrapping her skirts about her expertly. I didn't really want any water, was suddenly surprisingly uncertain how one went about drinking water (Do you bend over? Do you take the ladle directly from her hand? Should I close my eyes?), but what could I do?

From her knees, the girl lifted the ladle to me so that I had a sudden vision of Brother Sighere and the time he had had to beg for his food. Taking the ladle from her, I spilled most of the water. The girl seemed not to notice. She looked down, waited while I drank. I have no idea what that water tasted like. It could have been full of mud for all I knew or cared.

When I was done, the girl took the ladle from me, returned it to the bucket, thankfully offered me no more. With a simple movement of hand and skirt, she settled herself once more on the ground. Her hair was dark and long and moved as she moved, back and forth. Her arms were uncovered. For some reason my mind kept returning to the way she had slipped her skirts beneath her as she sat down, the movement practiced, graceful, arresting.

"Don't you want to sit?"

Didn't I want to sit?

The girl glanced at the ground before me as if giving me a hint.

I looked around, peopled the orchard with a hundred monks, remembered again my hands, was again uncertain what to do with my hands. I looked at the girl, tried to smile, found myself incapable of smiling, and, not knowing what else to do, desperate for something to do, sat down, collapsed onto the ground, knees sticking out like donkey's ears.

The girl smiled. I smiled. I thought my cheeks would crack from the effort, but I did it, I smiled.

"I am Eanflæd, Ealdgyth's daughter."

Still I smiled, the grin now apparently a permanent fixture on my face.

The girl nodded, the suggestion of a doubt hovering at her brow.

"You may call me Eanflæd," she said. "I mean if you…. I mean if you could…" and then she laughed. I had never heard a girl laugh before, have, I suppose, never heard a girl laugh since. It is different from our laughter, lighter, fresher, a small brook descending a gentle slope, birch leaves in the wind. I couldn't help myself, hearing it, I laughed too.

The girl stopped, a look of surprise animating her face. She put a finger to her lips, smiled, shook her head. I was reminded of something, someone. My mother? Had my mother hushed me like this?

"I will call you 'Brother'," she said, whispering for some reason. "If that's all right."

I nodded. Of course it wasn't. I mean I knew she mistook the situation, my status, but I could not have corrected her had I wanted to; so I nodded, the smile on my face feeling better now, more relaxed, almost natural.

The girl became sober, serious. "You are so thin," she said, shaking her head, "all of you, so very thin."

Of course I had noticed the difference between us already, how full she looked, brimming, but I hadn't really thought about how I must look by comparison. I wanted to assume custody of the eyes, knew I should have earlier, but found myself too embarrassed to display even so simple a courtesy. I did try to pull my woolens down, the cloth suddenly shorter than I remembered, my knees sticking out in a way I'd never noticed before, obtrusive, embarrassing.

As if she understood all this, knew exactly what I was thinking, the girl nodded. "You do it for us," she said.

I glanced out at the orchard, adopted an expression I hoped looked wise, understanding. In my mind Brother Baldwin signed angrily, *Deny the flesh that the soul might live!* I had no idea what the girl was talking about.

When I looked back at her, she was smiling again, her cheeks flushed, rosy. She glanced down at my basket, back up at me. "May I have one of your cherries?" she asked.

I blinked, felt myself blink again. They weren't *my* cherries, not really my cherries at all. I swallowed, fought the urge to look around, see if anyone was watching. I looked at her. She looked at me, the question blooming in her eyes, doubt returning. I didn't say anything. I didn't nod or say anything outright but, staring at her as if, together, we crossed some inconceivable threshold, I offered her the basket.

Eanflæd ate slowly. She made a sort of game of it. Instead of tossing her stems away as I would have, she stacked them neatly in the grass at her side, each vine-red length lined up perfectly with its neighbor. While a part of me was hardly there, floating along like a man in a dream, another began to think, function, ponder. Was this perhaps a characteristic of girls, this neatness, this attention to order? I noticed how, instead of trying for distance, Eanflæd spit her stones carefully into her hand, concealing the action with a slight tilt of her head. When, later, her fingers relaxed, un-cupped, the additional pit was revealed as something new and unexpected, a little miracle in the palm of her hand.

Eanflæd smiled, touched her lips as if indicating how good the cherries had been. Carefully she deposited the stones on the grass at her side, stones on the right, stems on the left. Girls were becoming less of a mystery to me.

She sat up, looked at me, her skin suddenly different, pale, freckles and hair contrastingly darker. "I have something to say," she said, though of course I already knew that, could see it in her eyebrows, the way her lips bunched as if holding something back. Stuf couldn't conceal such things either.

She shook her head, closed her eyes as if visualizing what she wished to say, opened her eyes again. "I have had a dream," she said.

I nodded, thinking about the eyes, thinking about how dark they were, the lips, the hair, like water in shadow.

"I said I had a dream."

I sat up, nodded again, tried to appear attentive.

Eanflæd hesitated for a moment, then began again. "I mean," she said, "I want to tell you about it, tell a monk."

This was what came of deception. It was a hard world that made you face such things so young, but I told myself I could do it, *would* do it, for her, for Eanflæd. I straightened my back, stuck out my chin, broke the silence. "I am not a priest," I said.

Immediately I knew how wrong I'd been, the girl's hand going to her lips, trying to hide the amusement she so obviously felt. I looked away, cheeks burning.

"No it's my fault,"—fingers on my knee (the big embarrassing knee), apologizing, touching me. "I didn't mean a confession. At least not that kind of confession."

I looked at her, the hand already gone, the feel of the fingers still there. She was smiling, wanting to see me smile, wanting it badly. I looked at her. I was an oblate, a member of the community at Redstone, I knew how to hide my feelings.

The girl looked down. Like a brother assuming custody of the eyes, Eanflæd looked down, hesitated, and immediately I regretted what I had done, the resentment that had caused it, the wounded pride. I smiled but it was too late. Eanflæd wasn't looking at me anymore, she was looking at the ground.

"It was really more of a nightmare than a dream," she said. "I was a little girl. In the dream I mean, I was a little girl. Maybe eight or nine, and Acca and Deor were still alive." She looked at me. "Acca and Deor?" I smiled but I didn't know the names. "They were friends of mine, little girls I used to play with?" I nodded, still smiling. Eanflæd shrugged. She closed her eyes. I felt bad about not knowing the names.

"We were jumping rope. First Acca and I would hold the rope and Deor would jump, and then Deor and I would hold the rope and Acca would jump. For some reason I remember I was afraid it was going to get dark before it would be my turn. Actually it was still very light, but for some reason I remember being afraid it was going to get dark before they let me jump. I kept begging and begging them to let me take my turn but they wouldn't. They'd laugh and say, 'You're next! You're next!' but they never let me jump. And then a cloud must have passed in front of the sun because it got dark." Eanflæd paused and, as if a cloud really had passed before the sun, she rubbed her arms. I looked around. No one was coming.

"Well," she continued, "I began to gather up the rope, thinking how unfair everything was, how unfair Acca and Deor had been. And then one of them said, 'Look!' and I looked and, instead of being in the field back of our house, we were deep in the wood." Eanflæd shut her eyes and I remembered the first time I went into the forest, how close I had kept to Brother Tatwine's heels. As if she remembered this too, Eanflæd shuddered, opened her eyes, looked at me. "So, anyway, we started to hunt about, tried to find our way home. But of course we couldn't. I mean we had no idea where we were, what wood this was, and for a long time we just wandered. Sometimes there seemed to be a path and then sometimes there wasn't. Most of the time we simply pulled our way through the forest, everything clinging to us, messing our clothes. I lost my father's rope. And it got darker and darker but it never seemed to become full night.

"Eventually we came to a sort of clearing. There was a house in it, all shuttered, bolted up, and it looked different from the houses in our village. Acca and Deor wanted to try to get inside the house before it got too dark, but I didn't. Even with night coming on, there was something about the place that frightened me. I didn't want to go in.

"And then a funny thing happened. I was wishing I could see into the house, wishing I was up on the roof, you know so I could look down through the smoke-hole, see if there really was anything inside the house to be frightened of, when, suddenly, for no apparent reason, I was on the roof. Acca and Deor were still down on the ground, calling up to me, begging me to come down and enter the house with them, but I was way up on the roof." Eanflæd looked at me. "You know how dreams are. It's only later, when you wake up, that you realize how strange everything was, that you wanted to be on a roof and then, suddenly, you were. But in the dream it all seems perfectly natural. And so I didn't think about it. I began to crawl along the roof-line, thinking that now I would be able to look down through the smoke-hole. But, as it happened, for the longest time I couldn't seem to get there. I kept crawling and crawling but the smoke-hole never got any closer. Below me, down on the ground where I had left Acca and Deor, I heard the door open and, at the same moment, a lot of noise coming from inside the house. It sounded as if they were having some sort of feast in there. I remember I heard Acca laugh, then the door closed and it was immediately quiet again, the noise gone, the house and its clearing still, not even a bird calling.

"By the time I finally reached the smoke-hole I no longer wanted to look in. I knew what I was going to see. Dead people. I don't know how, but I just knew...*I was on top of the dead people's house.*" Eanflæd hesitated, looked away. "Still I had to see." She looked back at me. "Have you ever found something dead?" she asked. "Not a person I mean but an animal, something, I don't know, furry. You know what I mean?"

I shrugged, recalled Oftfor's tiny corpses.

The girl nodded, her mouth turned up in an odd mix of excitement and revulsion. "Then you know how it is, how they look stiff, the hair all stiff and dusty and dry. And then you turn them over and underneath, on their undersides? It's just the opposite, isn't it? Wet, soft, and the worms? How everything's crawling with those little worms?"

I just looked at her.

"That's how it was!" The hand touched me again, touched my knee. "That's how the house was, on the outside fine, normal, all right, but when I turned it over, I mean when I looked down through the thatch...." Eanflæd closed her eyes, shook her head. "It was full of them." She opened her eyes but still didn't look at me. "Bodies. More bodies than I'd ever seen—naked, pale, crawling over each other, bumping into each other, faces touching things, knees, backsides— not seeing, not caring—mouths touching.... I thought I was going to be sick.

"And then I was sick." Eanflæd smiled. "I vomited and my mother was there, holding the pot. 'It's all right,' she said, 'it's all right. Evil in, evil out.'" Eanflæd gave a little laugh. "Mother always knows what to say. She wiped my forehead and kissed me and I guess I believed her. I mean I felt better. God forgive me, Acca and Deor were dead, but I wasn't, and I felt better. Wonderful. I was going to live and they were dead. I felt like singing."

Eanflæd held herself quiet for a time, staring out through the orchard. When she spoke again it was in a different, abstracted voice. "It was only the summer wobbles," she said. "I was helping with the carding the next day. But it stayed with me, the dream I mean. All those bodies." Eanflæd closed her eyes. "It's death," she said, her voice soft now, resigned. "I, Eanflæd, Ealdgyth's daughter…I am afraid of death."

A breeze moved suddenly through the trees around us, leaves whispering to one another, branches rustling. I looked away. "All those people will rise again," I said, not wanting to think about it, not really sure I wanted them to.

"Yes," I heard her say, "yes, I suppose so." I didn't look at her, didn't have to look at her to know she wasn't pleased with this, was probably studying her hands, maybe looking off through the trees.

"But it's not them I'm thinking about, it's me."

I looked at her and I had been wrong, she was looking at me. "Doesn't it ever scare you?" she asked, wanting it to, wanting me to be as scared as she. "Being sewn up in a sheet? Being dumped in a hole, buried?"

I didn't say anything, didn't know what to say.

"You can't breathe down there you know. You can't see anything or feel anything, except, maybe…." She hugged herself, looked away, bit her lip. I thought about Oftfor, poor little Oftfor, lying up there beneath the cloister garth.

Eanflæd shook her head, thought about something, changed her mind. She looked at me. "But at least we have you."

You have me?

She nodded. "That's why I wanted to talk to you, why I had to talk to you, to a monk?"

I didn't say anything.

Eanflæd smiled and, as if I had said something, had said something beautiful, her eyes filled suddenly with tears. "You know they call it Redestone? The village I mean. Outside the valley they don't call it 'the village', or 'Wilfrid's village'. They call it 'Redestone'."

I nodded uncertainly, never having thought about it before, not seeing why it should matter what people outside the valley called the village.

Eanflæd closed her eyes, lashes dark and wet against her cheek. "Redestone," she said, as if the word itself were something special, sacred. She opened her eyes, looked at me. "We're part of the monastery, as much a part of the monastery as your fields or this orchard. You look after us, take care of us. You have to. It's what you're here for."

Not according to my father.

But I didn't say that. I just looked at her and smiled, an uneasy feeling taking root in the pit of my stomach.

Eanflæd looked away, stared off through the trees, holding herself tight, upper body bobbing in apparent agreement with something. "You're heroes," she said, nodding to herself, "heroes." She looked back at me, cocked an appraising eyebrow. "Of course you don't look like it. I mean you don't look like heroes, but that makes it even better, doesn't it, grander somehow, more heroic?" She smiled. "I mean you stand up there unarmed don't you?" She indicated the abbey with a tilt of her chin, looked back at me. "That's what Mother says. She says all you have is your prayer, and your chanting and fasting. I mean those are all the weapons you have. But it's enough. Just enough. You stand up there and hold Him off, you hold off God. You keep Him from getting us, keep Him from coming too close." The girl looked at me as if expecting something, as if expecting me to say something, and when I didn't, couldn't, had no idea what to say, she began to cry, the tears spilling from her like something she was giving me, something she wanted me to have, an offering, a gift. "That's what I wanted to say," she said. "That's what I came for. To tell you thank you. I want to thank you. I Eanflæd, Ealdgyth's daughter, thank you for your prayers, for your sacrifice."

I cannot say with any certainty what I did then. Probably I blinked, looked away, tried to appear once more wise and understanding. It is the way of children. But in truth, of course, the only wisdom I possessed was a certainty that this girl was wrong, deluding herself. Not that we didn't pray for them. We did, then as now. In Chapter Father would tell us of their woes, the weeping wound, the torn palate, and we would pray for them. And in church too, when we offered up prayers for the work, the harvest, we prayed for the village as well, the people who lived in the village. But it wasn't the same. I mean I knew that. We prayed for Dextra too, during her final illness, and for the sheep. But that wasn't why we were here. We were here for us. To save us. It wasn't the same. But I couldn't say that—the girl so clearly wanting to believe otherwise, wanting to think herself and her family a part of the monastery, that, in some way, we were there *for them*, that we held God at bay *for them*. How could I contradict her? Have you ever looked a young girl in the eye? When they want something, when they want something badly, their eyes have a considerable power. And so I did the easy thing, telling myself it was the right thing, that even Father Abbot would have approved in the face of so tenuous a faith, I nodded. I looked at the girl as if she had said something profound, and I nodded.

The girl smiled. I remember that. As if she knew, as if at some level she knew how unlikely her view of things was, how great an effort she had required of me, she smiled, seemed relieved, bowed her head. I think she might have wanted to kiss me. Or at least my hand. I remember I had that impression. I don't know what I would have done if she had, don't know how I should have responded, turned her from such a course, but, as it happened, she did not. The moment passed.

And then a strange fancy came over me. Father Gwynedd had told me about it, the way the monasteries used to be, the way he said some of them still were, mixed, men and women living together—chastely of course but together—and a sudden vision of us as old religious, Eanflæd and me, came over me, our hands worn with the work, knees swollen from praying, the two of us sitting side by side in Chapter, not saying anything, not needing to say anything, just sitting there, quiet, together. I looked at Eanflæd and, outlandish as it was, found the idea suddenly reasonable, apt, and, fool that I was, I acted upon it, I ventured a suggestion. "You should think about entering a monastery," I said, "a community like ours."

The look again, the same look as before, so that, for a moment, I thought I might never speak again, might never be so stupid as to give voice to my thoughts again. "Oh no," she said, smiling as if it were the most obvious thing in the world, as if I had missed the fact she had dark hair instead of light, was a girl and not a boy. "No," she said, "I want to have babies." She laughed a little. "You know, lots and lots of babies."

I assumed custody of the eyes.

"No, really, I'm sorry," the hand on my knee again, the weight of it, the warmth. "It's just..." she leaned forward so she could look up into my face. "It's just that I want to have...well...children." She smiled, the hand already gone, no longer touching me. "You understand. I want to have children."

I nodded, trying not to look at her, trying to avoid her eyes, those intense, those demanding, eyes.

"I just...." Eanflæd sat back up, withdrew. "When Mother told me about you, I don't know. I thought about it. I did. And the more I thought about it, the more I realized how fortunate I was, we are, to have you praying for us, protecting us."

I looked up, but Eanflæd wasn't looking at me anymore. She was looking at the sky, had leaned back, braced herself, hands flat out on the ground behind her, so that she could look directly up into the sky. "I wanted to thank you," she said, "thank someone, for all you do for us." She closed her eyes, opened them again, pupils white with light from the sky. "You really are wonderful you know, just...wonderful!"

It was two or three days later, standing once more at the top of a ladder in a cherry tree, that I had my vision regarding Ealhmund. I was thinking about Eanflæd when it happened. Truth be told, I was, in those first days, almost always thinking about Eanflæd. Of course I knew this was wrong, that I should be ashamed of this, but there was something about our encounter, something about having sat with her, been so close to her, that I could not put out of my mind, could not force myself to forget. I pictured her. I pictured her face, the way the freckles lay upon it, the way her lips changed when she smiled, grew thin, dark, the way she cocked her head when she laughed at me. I wondered about her hair, why she didn't wear her hair up like the other women. I thought about her dress, how nice it was, how soft, the effort someone had put into making it, making something so nice, so soft. I thought about her arms. Of course they had been covered. Before I mean, before she took her shawl off, her arms had been covered. But they weren't when I sat with her. They had been uncovered, and I thought about that.

And then, because I couldn't help it, because it came to me as it always did when I thought about Eanflæd, when I pictured her, thought about the way we had sat together, I found myself remembering the other thing, the embarrassing thing, the part that made me feel so ashamed for her. For there was no denying she had said it. I could still see the way she had looked at me when she said it, the brazenness of her announcement, the utter lack of self-respect. I want to have babies, she had declared, lots and lots of babies.

The first of the day's breezes moved through the orchard, caused the branches around me to rise and fall, entered the trees at my back, passed on off down the valley. I supposed I too should be moving on, shifting the ladder to another part of the tree, but I didn't want to. The sun was warm on my head, my hands, the surrounding leaves; I felt no urge to go.

And what if she was a bad girl? What if she did want to have babies, what was wrong with that? I mean I knew what was wrong with that but, at the same time, a part of me sympathized with her, felt what I told myself was a Christian's necessary compassion for the sinner. After all, she *wasn't* part of Redestone, not really, didn't live in a monastery, hadn't grown up in a monastery as I had. How could you expect her to be different from what she was? I blushed to think about it but it was true, they all did it, all of them, all the way back to Eve. I had even seen a woman big with child myself once, down by the river, so I knew this to be true. I supposed, living together the way they did, it was bound to happen, the poor wretches prey to the most disgusting of passions.

Of course the thought itself was lascivious, and even as I thought it I knew I had sinned, could feel the power of the sin swell within me as the tree that day had seemed to swell beneath me in the wind. Which made me feel bad even as, at the same time, it also made me feel good, as if by being bad—by being bad like Eanflæd—I had somehow moved closer to her, had, in fact, stepped between her and something, protected her as she had dreamt I would protect her, dreamt all monks would protect her.

And it was at that moment—as I was feeling this, thinking this— that I saw my fellow oblate, saw Ealhmund. The boy was standing in the very top of a tree way over on the other side of the orchard; and it seemed he was looking at me. Was he looking at me? I squinted my eyes but couldn't tell, he was too far away. Still, a part of me felt like laughing. Ealhmund never had been well coordinated and now that he was working for Brother Kitchens he'd grown fat as well, far too fat to try to stand like this in the top of a tree. And then suddenly I had the notion, the idea, that it wasn't Ealhmund. That what I was looking at was not Ealhmund, not Ealhmund standing in the top of a tree, but a vision of such a thing. And with this thought came another, a warning, a presentiment. He isn't going to make it. With a certainty that frightened me I suddenly knew, *knew*, that Ealhmund wasn't going to make it, that he was going to die or be expelled or some- thing but—surely and irrefutably—there was no way the comical thing standing in the tree over there would ever, could ever, become a monk. It was impossible. Ealhmund didn't stand a chance.

The two of us stood like that for some time—Ealhmund occasion- ally throwing an arm out for balance, I wondering if he could really see me at such a distance, if, in fact, he was even looking at me. Then, quite unexpectedly, the boy waved. In apparent defiance of awkward- ness and propriety alike, Ealhmund released whatever branch he was holding, raised his arm high over his head, and waved.

A few days later I went back to the place where Eanflæd and I had spoken. I remember there was something rather sad about the spot. Only a very good tracker could have told that anyone had ever sat there, the one person apparently facing the tree, the other turned slightly as if distracted by something, perhaps the abbey. Like all sign, Eanflæd's mark retained a suggestion of the creature that had made it, her order, her softness, the way the grass lay not flat but rounded, full. Of course I didn't allow myself to get too close, but I did get down on my hands and knees to study the spot, noticing the curve, the suggestion of a shape, the pressure that had formed it. It was as I knelt like this that I first saw the bit of color. I removed a fallen leaf, parted the grasses, and there they were…the stones…the stones Eanflæd had so carefully deposited at her side.

Of course I had been bound to find them. I think a part of me had been expecting to find them all along, had known they would be there, had been looking for them without ever consciously knowing that I was looking for them. Still I was shocked. Like a man coming upon another making water, I thought I should turn my head, avoid looking upon something so private, so exposed.

But I did not look away. I did not replace the fallen leaf, fold back the grasses, leave the stones as Eanflæd had left them. God forgive me, I picked them up; I picked them up and held them in the palm of my hand.

They were a pale color, I remember that well, pale as if washed with blood, and they were light, lighter than I had expected. How could something so light, so negligible, carry the weight of so much that was vile, forbidden, impossible? For the idea was there already, complete and inescapable. How could I do such a thing? How could I not?

I put the stones in my mouth.

Before I could change my mind, I put the stones that had been in Eanflæd's mouth in my mouth. I began to suck on them.

XXI

hen I think of Father now and the gifts he gave me, my mind rises of its own not to tracking or prayer, or even love, but to the crag, to that lone bit of rock sticking like the finger of God out over the valley of Redestone. When things got bad, when I was tired or hungry, frustrated or feeling alone, the crag was always there. I could look at it, dream of it, know that soon, tomorrow or the next day, I would climb there, rise above Redestone and its small concerns, look out upon a wider world.

Have you ever noticed how, even at a distance, you can identify someone by his gait, his posture, the way he holds his head? If you are like me (and as I grow older I realize that it is in such things that, like true brothers, we are so very much alike), no matter how poor your eyesight, you can still identify the one who dips as he walks as Brother James, the one with the bad hand as Deacon Hæmgils, and that shuffling form at the far end of the field, the yoke balanced so carelessly across his shoulders, as the new boy, what is his name?, Eafa, bringing you cold water on a hot day. If we who are old and diminished can so easily distinguish those who may otherwise hold little interest for us, how much more easily did I, then young and possessed of the powers of youth, find it to pick out Eanflæd's form among the many that moved in those days about Wilfrid's village.

And the crag was so much better for this. There was a place behind the church, just inside the angle created by the outer wall of the apse, that allowed me the occasional furtive privacy, the opportunity to stare out over the fields unseen, imagine the life of the village, its inhabitants, their world. But it was an uncomfortable spot, the threat of discovery real, close at hand. No such fears intruded upon the crag. There the day proceeded at its own pace, my mind left to wander where it would, with Ceolwulf on some distant march, with Eanflæd in some other, some wholly unowned and unpeopled orchard. I would sit and dream of these things and, whenever I descried movement in the village (two women making their way, laughingly, down to the river, a basket of wash slung between them; a man carrying materials out to repair a fence), I would lock upon it, search it for those features I now recognized as Eanflæd's, the loose hair, the blue dress, the way she seemed always ready to spin, turn, as if, inside her, music played.

I was sitting thus one day, dreaming of who knows what, when, quite unexpectedly, I heard something on the mountain behind me. I did not move. As desperately as I wanted to, I did not turn my head, look. The exposed animal's only covert Father called it—stillness, immobility. Second only to silence.

Another noise reached my ear, then another, drawing closer. I felt myself grow irritated. Whoever it was, they were certainly going out of their way to make themselves heard.

"It's all right, it's all right. It's just me."

I turned around, looked back down the length of the crag. The hermit was standing by the last tree, one hand on his chest, trying to smile even as he caught his breath. "I thought I might find you here," he said.

I didn't say anything.

"May I join you?"

I shrugged, looked back at Redestone. The place seemed suddenly different, paler, as if the day had grown cloudy. Behind me the careful tread of bare feet on bare rock. I would have loved to turn around, watch that creeping progress (an old man doing something he could not have done for a very long time now), but I was afraid he would smile, mistake my disdain for concern. When he finally did sit down I made no room for him and instantly regretted it as he gave me the kiss of peace. I looked away, embarrassed, angry.

"Are you all right?"

Nothing. A slight shrug of one shoulder. Would they never learn?

"Well," the hands on the knees now, fingers drumming, "I suppose this isn't a good time to talk about prayer."

For a moment I looked at the hermit, my eyes telling him everything he needed to know about *that* subject.

Father didn't say anything, eyebrows alone affecting surprise.

I looked away. Down in the village there was movement, someone beating out a bolster. She stood downwind of the last house, legs well apart, taking long swatting strikes at the thing. Too big, too old. Someone else was mucking out the stalls. A boy, I thought, maybe a girl. I looked at the house I had decided was Eanflæd's, willed it to breathe, move, give evidence of life, habitation. But there was nothing, the churn stood idle by the door, the window remained dark, uninteresting, the garden untended. "You never say anything about praying for people," I said, still looking at the house. "I mean about praying for other people."

"I beg your pardon?"

I looked at the hermit. He seemed genuinely surprised. "I mean that's what you're supposed to be so good at, isn't it? I mean isn't that why I have to carry all these tabula up here, so you can pray for people, other people?"

The hermit blinked, thought about it for a moment, looked down at Redestone as if seeking guidance. "Yes," he said, eyes still on the abbey, "yes…well, yes, of course it is."

"Then why don't you ever teach me about that? All we ever do is talk about ourselves. That's all this really is, isn't it?" I looked out at Redestone but included Modra nect in my complaint. "I mean all we're really interested in is us, isn't it, in saving ourselves?"

"Is something wrong, Winwæd? Has something happened?"

Why did everything always have to be something else, why couldn't it just be what you said it was?

"Are you all right?"

I looked back at the village. "I'm all right." For a while I didn't say anything. I thought about it but I didn't know what I could say, what would be right. I noticed I was pulling on my sleeves again and stopped. It was bad for the cloth. "Did you know they call this

place 'Redstone'? I mean outside the valley, they call it 'Redstone'."
I looked at Father but had to look away, his face so mournful, so concerned. I looked out at the sky, noticed the clouds, four long streamers stretching from west to east, the weather about to turn. "Not just the monastery," I said, still watching the sky, trying to appear casual, indifferent, "but the village too. I mean they don't know any better, do they? They call the village 'Redstone,' and the fields I guess, and... who knows...." I looked at Father again. "Maybe even the mountain. I mean maybe they even call the mountain 'Redstone,' the people outside the valley."

The hermit didn't say anything. He looked at me as if thinking about something else and then he seemed to remember what I had said. "I doubt it," he said, eyes still studying me, "not the mountain. The mountain's been 'Modra nect' for a long time now. A long time."

I didn't say anything. They were all like that, the way things had been were the way they'd always be. But I wasn't so sure anymore. I'd been thinking about it a lot lately. "But it makes sense, doesn't it? I mean when you think about it. I mean there really isn't anything else is there, just trees." I braced myself on the rock and leaned out as far as I could. There was always a breeze at the crag, sometimes moving from right to left and sometimes rising straight up out of the valley below. Today the air moved from right to left and you could smell the rain in it, the clouds. It made a shiver run up my back. "I mean it's all a waste isn't it?" I indicated the South Wood with my chin. "I mean as far as you can see there's nothing, is there, forest, trees? And then there's this one place, this one little place everybody calls 'Redstone'. We're all here, I don't know..."—for some reason I shivered again—"...together."

The hermit didn't say anything. I looked over at the Far Wood, my eyes tracing the dark space through the trees, not even thinking about it anymore, not even conscious of what I was doing.

"You *have* been praying, haven't you?"

I looked back at the hermit, the bottoms of my feet suddenly cold. It had nothing to do with prayer yet the question bothered me, frightened me, as if somehow it did.

The hermit nodded though I hadn't said anything. "You've been trying again, haven't you?"

I looked away, didn't want to think about it, didn't want to think about how frustrating it was.

"At the river?"

You could stare at the thing all day, God didn't care.

"With me it was forgiveness."

I'm sorry?

"Forgiveness." He shook his head, looked around as if noticing for the first time where he sat, the crag, the valley below. "I had hardened my heart."

"You had hardened your heart?"

The hermit looked at me, the smile thin, rueful. "But that's the way it is, isn't it, prayer?"

"Against what?"

"You think it's not working, empty, dry, and then one day you notice it's gone, resentment, envy, some sin that's stuck in your side for years." He shook his head, apparently still amazed. "You don't even feel it, do you?" He looked at me as if expecting confirmation. "At first I mean, you don't even feel it, realize it's happened. One day it's just gone, sloughed off like an old skin, like a cloak you need no more and—now that it's summer—can't imagine ever being cold enough to need again."

"Against what? You hardened your heart against what?"

But the hermit was ignoring me now, looking down at the abbey, amused, thoughtful. "And then of course there's the final temptation. You want to believe *you*'ve done it, that all the denial and sacrifice has paid off, that, somehow, you've *earned* this." He shook his head, smiled, looked at me. "But of course we know better, don't we?"

We do?

The hermit nodded. "It's the secret writing. The quiet messages God has placed in our souls during those moments when, somehow, impossibly, we've kept our tabula clean."

Oh, that. "But you still haven't told me what you hardened your heart against."

The hermit looked out at the valley, the South Wood. "You know I've never been out here before."

"I'm sorry?"

"The crag?" He nodded as if approving of its placement. "I've never been out here before."

"But you…?"

The hermit smiled, still studying the view. "I know, but I never came out here. I mean, I've never walked out here, sat on the crag before. It's nice, isn't it?"

He was changing subjects too quickly for me, I couldn't keep up.

"So you want to learn how to pray for other people."

It was like throwing a rope to a drowning man. I nodded.

"Tell me about your prayer now, how does it proceed?"

How does it proceed? It doesn't *proceed* at all. I could sit for entire intervals by the river and nothing happened. Or everything did. Eanflæd, cherries, food, Ceolwulf, my mother, Baldwin, the bishop—all of them, all of them and everything came floating down that river, barges full of them, but never God. God was the only one who seemed uninterested in my stream. How I missed those days when He had been everywhere, when I was little and He had seemed always to hold my hand as I walked across the garth, to wrap me beneath His wing at night. But things had changed. I wasn't sure how or why, or even when, but they had. He wasn't there. Or, worse, He had left, departed, abandoned me. My prayer was, as Father said, empty, dry. At the very time I needed Him most, God wasn't there.

"It doesn't go well?"

I looked at him and for a moment all the frustration, all the failure, hopelessness, welled up in me, rose to the surface as if somehow, in some way I could not understand, Father could actually fix this, would actually be able to help me, change all this, make everything better. But that, of course, was the thinking of a child. I shook my head, looked away. "I have trouble," I said. "I have trouble…keeping my tabulum clean."—this last contemptuous, derisive, the very idea of a tabulum!

The hermit ignored the sarcasm. "You mustn't fight it," he said, "the river I mean."

I looked at him. He was leaning out, hands braced on his knees, an old man perched on a high rock. "I mean it's natural," he said. "We are creatures of the world, however much we may wish we weren't."

Somehow the care, the obvious concern, made me even more unhappy.

Father nodded as if I'd spoken. "You must let the distractions float by, Winwæd, but it's even more important that you not blame yourself for them when they appear. They are only natural. We are a river at flood."

"Of course."

"I know, sometimes it's hard."

"I am trying to not think! You told me to not think, if I wanted to pray I had to empty my mind! But it's impossible! No one can do it!"

"They're just thoughts Winwæd, puffs of smoke, empty breezes. They don't exist."

"They're maddening, I can't stop them!"

"No, sometimes you can't, can you? You can't control them." The hermit looked pleased with himself.

"It's maddening!" I'd said that before.

Father nodded. "And the more upset you get, the more of them there are."

I looked away, not pleased that he knew that, not pleased that my problems were so obvious, my person so transparent.

"Or at least that's the way it is with me."

I looked at him and the hermit laughed. "The trick is to not let them bother you, to just let them float by. If you blame yourself for the thoughts, get angry at them, angry at yourself, it just makes matters worse. Who can settle down, be still, when moment by moment they're getting angrier and angrier?"

I didn't say anything.

"And the beauty of it is that, by not blaming yourself, not bothering with that but returning to what is important, you are, in a sense, *forgiving* yourself." Father thought about this. "It's God-like, isn't it, forgiveness, letting things go? Holy in and of itself. I mean.... I mean you become more like Him when you forgive yourself, don't you, forgive someone? You move closer to Him." The eyes came back into focus, looked at me. "Do you understand what I'm saying, 'closer to Him'? The act itself is a sort of communion."

"I don't know." I looked away, looked back at him. "It makes me…I don't know."

The hermit nodded. "To persevere," he said, "that's the important thing. When all else fails, when the thoughts pass down your river like great warships one after another, you must not give up, you must persevere. Onslaught is prelude. Folian used to say that, 'The onslaught is prelude.' Satan doesn't give up easily. But if you persevere, God will come to you. Eventually, after who knows how long, He will wrap a divine weariness around you, cover you with a fatigue the devil cannot penetrate. And within that fatigue, that tiredness, you will find peace. You will Winwæd, I promise, the most wonderful peace, the most perfect stillness."

I didn't say anything.

Father watched me for a moment, closed his eyes, opened them again. "Do you remember the fox's cave, the sort of tunnel we found?"

Of course I remembered.

"Father told me a story about a similar passageway once, long ago. There was a boy, a little boy who got lost in the forest. It was dark and, no matter which way the boy went, he ended up in thick trees and brush. Finally, at some distance, he began to see a light far off through the wood. He ran toward the light and, as he got closer to it, it grew in size until he could see that it was a large open field, separated from the forest by a fence. He was excited. Surely when he got to this field he would be able to see where he was, determine his way home. But when the boy finally reached the fence he discovered the forest had grown so close against it he could not break through. Desperately he pulled himself along through the tangle but to no avail—the light of the field remaining forever just beyond his reach. Finally, exhausted, he collapsed onto the forest floor. He had been lying there for a little time, too tired to breathe, too tired to move, when a bit of light attracted his attention. It was down low, near the ground. He rolled over, put his face close to the earth, saw that there was a place at the foot of the fence where a fox or badger had dug out a passage between the forest and the field. It was just large enough for him. The boy slipped through this passage, under the fence, and into the brilliant sunlight of his family's own field.

"This is the way of prayer, Winwæd. Most of the time we feel like the little boy in the wood, our minds racing back and forth, trying to find God, trying to do it all on our own, finding nothing, only more forest, more meaningless thought. Eventually, more out of dumb luck than anything else, we catch a glimpse of light, something perceived only dimly, flickering in and out of existence just beyond the furthest trees. But the harder we try to reach that light, concentrate on it, the further it slips away. Finally, if we are fortunate, we wear ourselves out, collapse in a heap. And it is then that—exhausted, empty, incapable of doing anything more on our own—we discover the fox's tunnel right beside us. Without even thinking, without even trying, we've slipped through and come up blinking in the light."

It had been a long time since Father had done that, said just the right thing. When I was a child he had managed the trick often, answers and explanations bubbling from him like spring-water, but, as I had grown older, he had seemed to lose the ability. Or so I had thought.

Father picked up a small rock, flipped it out into the air over the valley. "So who is it you wish to pray for?"

My mind drew a sudden and awful blank.

The hermit didn't say anything, watched his rock fall, looked back at me.

I glanced at the village, immediately away.

"Forgive me, I assumed you had someone in mind."

"No, it's all right. Ealhmund!"—the name having popped into my head like answered prayer. "Ealhmund. I want to pray for Ealhmund."

"The oblate?"

"Yes." I looked at Father, suddenly more sure of myself, liking the idea of myself as defender of the downtrodden. "Yes, Ealhmund. Anything wrong with that?"

The hermit shrugged. "Nothing, just surprised. I hadn't expected it."

That I could surprise the hermit did not surprise me.

"Well that's good." The eyebrows rose, fell, Father reconciling himself to the protector of the weak and innocent who now sat beside him. "You know he needs your prayers. I mean we all do, but…. Tell me, how bad is his face?"

"His face?"

Father nodded, looked at me. "The spots? The white pox?"

I had forgotten. When we were little, all four of us had come down with an illness that had caused a sort of pox. I had no real memory of this but had been told about it by one of the novices (who had himself fallen victim subsequently to the pestilence). According to this Dudda, Brother Baldwin had taken advantage of our illness to frighten half the monastery into believing we carried the red plague. If it hadn't been for Father Prior, we would have been expelled. Dudda also claimed the pitting on Ealhmund's back and face was a result of this pox, but that never made any sense to me. None of the rest of us had been scarred. Of course by now I was so accustomed to the marks on Ealhmund's face I gave them no more thought than I would have his mouth or nose. I shrugged. "I don't know, they're around his mouth mostly. Why?"

The hermit didn't say anything.

"I mean I don't think they hurt him or anything."

Still the hermit remained silent, just looked at me, and I had to accept the fact that somehow, incredibly, he knew. About a year or two earlier, in the teasing sort of way he had, Waldhere had begun calling Ealhmund "Catfish." He didn't really look like a catfish, I mean the pox were concave, they didn't protrude or anything, but there was something about their placement around his mouth that made the name seem funny, apt. Sometimes, when I was angry or tired of listening to his complaints, I called Ealhmund "Catfish" too.

I shrugged, tried to change the subject, "How do you know about his face?"

The hermit just looked at me which made the answer obvious. He never spoke about the tabula, what was in them, but that had to be it.

Someone had decided the situation warranted recourse to the hermit. I felt myself blush.

"You know they used to call me 'Foreigner', 'Cumbrogi Dirt Boy', when I was little. My mother too."

His mother.

"Can you imagine how that made me feel?"

I looked away—forgetting for a moment the incredible discovery that Father had had a mother—feeling bad, guilty, as if I had been the one to call him "Dirt Boy."

Father straightened up, fingered his lower back, glanced over at Modra nect's southern peak. It was his way of letting me know the subject had changed, that we need speak of this no more.

"Who looks after the sluice-gate now?"

"The sluice-gate?"

Father looked at me, cocked an eye.

"Brother Victricius."

He nodded, "The furnace master." He looked up toward the head of the valley as if hoping to see the man, shook his head. "I hear it smells bad. I mean the works, his place? I hear it smells bad."

"It does. It smells like something burning, something…you know, something that shouldn't burn."

Father nodded. "I can't smell it up here." He looked back at me. "So, anyway, when this Victricius opens his sluice-gate, what happens?"

"The water runs through it?"

Father gave me a look. "And after that? After the water runs through the gate?"

I looked up the valley, thought about it. "Well, first, Victricius uses it." I pointed. "Up at the furnace? Then, further down, it turns the mill and then…." My finger traced the water's course as it turned before the church, burrowed beneath the western edge of the garth. "It fills the lavabo, clears Botulf's drains, and then it…." I stopped, my finger hesitating at the far edge of the kitchens. "And then it goes on out and waters our fields and fills our ponds!"

Father looked at me, his expression amused, mildly interrogative. "And the little house…? What about the little house?"

"And it carries off…you know." I looked away. He loved to tease me about the reredorter.

The hermit laughed. I looked back at him. He smiled. "Praying for someone is a lot like the work of Brother Victricius." He hesitated. "It is *Brother*?"

"Yes, Brother."

"Good. What do you suppose it is like when Brother Victricius opens his gate?"

I had never thought about it before, one moment the ditch was dry and the next the water ran through it like the Red Sea. And even that didn't happen often, once in the spring when we cleared the ditch and otherwise only if something hung up in the mill or in one of Brother Kitchens' drains.

"Have you ever opened one of the dikes at the head of a row?"

"Yes." Brother Cellarer sometimes let us do that.

The hermit looked at me.

I thought about it, looked down at the fields, remembered what they looked like in the summer, the parched and dusty-looking plants, the grayish earth. You got to stand in the ditch when you did it, skirts up, water cold around your legs, feet unseen, hidden from you, underwater, toes doing things by feel, touch. It wasn't hard. You pulled out the broken piece of crockery or whatever had been used to create the dike and then the water did most of the work—the first break, rupture, and the water did most of the work, spilled through, poured through, the sun-baked clay dissolving quickly, like sand, becoming mud again, silt, the water pouring through, pouring through so fast it went from muddy to clear again in an instant, tumbling out, racing off down the row, home, back home to the river at the far end of the field. And you had done it. You stood there in the cold water and watched that tiny stream run straight and true, dark, down to the line of trees that marked the boundary between our fields and the Meolch, and you had done it. You did that. You stood up, straightened your back, watched it run. And then Father Abbot or Brother Osric or someone signed for you to move on, burst the next one, and you did, happy, resplendent, breaker of dams, creator of river-courses.

"And now think about what it's like for Brother Victricius."

Of course it wasn't fair. Father didn't know the furnace master, didn't know what he was like. I had never actually seen Brother open the gate but I knew how he'd do it, properly, efficiently, taking pleasure perhaps in the works, checking their operation, visually measuring the flow, and then moving on, skipping ahead, already thinking about the next task, already considering that, what he would do next. For Brother there would be no dark trip beneath the furnace path, he would not bend with the water as it entered the monastery proper, turned before the church, would not hear the subterranean rumblings, feel the pulse beneath his feet.

"There is a measure of fear I should imagine, the Meolch at his back, roaring, the spray." The hermit was staring out at the South Wood, eyes glazed, seeing something he could not see. "And this one small gate, fragile, unassuming, holding it back, holding everything back. Before him, what? Nothing. Only the dark fall of the valley, alone, empty, the furnace master himself alone, perhaps a little afraid. It is cool up there as I remember it, the mosses, the pines, maybe he trembles a little as he stands there in the spray, the shadow. But then he does it, doesn't he? He thinks about the mill and the fields, the kitchen and the drains, and he does it, sound or no sound, he bends over, pulls the board free, and the mighty Meolch goes rushing through."

Actually there was a sort of lever arrangement—Victricius had constructed it, part wood, part iron—but I liked the way the hermit saw it, the image of it, a man standing there all by himself, straddling the race, releasing its force with a single upward sweep of his arms.

The hermit thought about it, shook his head, looked at me. "That's the way I do it, when I pray I mean, that's the way I do it."

"You pull up a gate?"

The hermit smiled. "In a sense."

I just looked at him.

Father sighed. "When you pray for your friend, when you pray for Ealhmund, you must stand like Victricius with the river at your back, only this time, this time the river is not the Meolch but God, the love of God pouring down from on high like a torrent, like a mighty torrent."

I swallowed.

"Yes. Yes I know. Frightening. Extravagant. Of course it's around us always when you think about it, here, there, but when you perform this sort of prayer you must imagine its source, the great cataract at its beginning, and you must imagine yourself the only thing holding that back, the only thing restraining the flood, keeping it from roaring down, from washing over Ealhmund and his fields, making everything turn green, flourish." The hermit blinked, looked at me. "And then you must open your gate. Just as, with a single sweep of the will, you cleared your tabulum, now you must open your gate, allow God's love to pour through you, race down toward what you cannot see, the fields, the mill, Ealhmund's face, his hands, the fear he feels when people abuse him, call him names."

I smiled, for a moment forgetting the person I intended to pray for, seeing instead Ealhmund's face, the spots receding, the boy thankful, happy, new. The hermit watched me, nodded as if seeing what I saw, looked away. I thought some more about Ealhmund, remembered Eanflæd, thought about her, saw myself on my knees, praying, darkness all around me, Eanflæd in darkness also, asleep, unaware, my prayers settling around her like blankets, like dreams, keeping her warm. I liked the image, liked the idea of it, the hardness of the stones I knelt upon, the softness of Eanflæd's sleep, my prayers unsought, unasked-for, their devising utterly selfless, unknown and unseen. Of course the changes would be slow at first (a less colorful dress perhaps, fewer ornaments, the hair a little more chaste, a little less wild), but it would work, of that I was certain. I had absolute faith in the hermit. Indeed, at that moment, with his help, an entire range of possibilities, hopes, opened up before me. "Is it true," I asked, wanting it to be true, wanting the hermit and his prayer to be omnipotent, capable of anything, "I mean is it true what they say Father, that if Ælfhelm had made it, if he'd made it up here before he died, you would have been able to save him. I mean none of it would have happened—Oftfor, Father Cellarer—they'd all still be alive?"

Of course the mention of Ælfhelm's name had been a mistake, I knew that as soon as it came out of my mouth. Father looked at me as if stricken, looked down at the slope of the mountain beneath us, imagined, I suppose, the path, Ælfhelm climbing. "I don't know," he said, a small smile, apologetic, embarrassed. "Possibly."

For a while after that neither of us said anything. I was used to this, the quiet. Father always became quiet at the mention of Ælfhelm's name. Overhead, God's shuttle continued its work, back and forth, warp and woof, the day turning cold, gray, a storm in the offing. Brother Botulf appeared from somewhere back of the sinks, tied down his beloved drying racks. Brother Osric sent someone to carry the unfinished hurtles in. When the lowing reached us, the deep notes only, Sinistra's knees bothering her again, it was as if I'd heard it all a thousand times before, as if I could have predicted it, could predict what would happen next, the office, the long walk down the mountain, the rain, the wet, the work. I looked out at the Far Wood and thought about my father, the life I might have had, the life that could have been. "What about against?" I asked, not really thinking about it, thinking about something else, the dark place, the empty place in the trees that marked the way, the road away from here, away from Redestone, away from this place.

"Against?"

I looked at the hermit, realized what I had said, done, saw Father Bishop's face, his hands, falling from me, away, dropping from the crag, down into the trees below. "You know, against?" A smile here to let him know I was still just a boy, curious, an oblate, nothing more. "Against instead of for? Can you pray *against* someone in the same way you can *for* them? I mean could you, an enemy or something?"

The hermit didn't say anything, looked at me.

I looked away.

Still the hermit did not speak. I could feel him looking at me.

I affected anger, started to get up. "If you don't want to tell me...."
The hermit placed a hand on my knee.

"An interesting question." He meant why do you ask such a question, where does it come from?

I sat back down, shrugged.

The hermit didn't say anything. From somewhere below us a raven left its roost, sailed out over the Meolch, drifted down toward the village. I looked over at Father but he was looking up the valley now, his nearest hand still stretched toward me, fingers just touching the rock. I noticed the scar, found myself angry once more with the man for having such a scar, for the guilt it caused me—the obvious naïveté, the stupidity, of the boy that had done that. I looked away. The raven had reached the village gardens but it did not descend. Instead, it turned and, pumping hard, began to beat its way back up toward the abbey, head working back and forth, beak shiny, black.

"It affects you you know, the love." The hermit gestured vaguely toward the mountain's upper slopes. "You can't feel it. I mean when it's happening, when it's happening you don't know it's happening and afterwards, afterwards you can't remember but, you know, you know something's happened." A small smile here, still looking up the valley, embarrassed to find himself stammering. "I mean you feel better, don't you, different? It's…it's like…." He looked around, looked at me. "It's like the sluice-gate! That's what I said. It's like water, like holy water pouring through you." A big smile now, pleased with himself for having remembered this, pleased to be remembering it. "Cleansed, you feel cleansed, washed clean, better, good."

If he'd forgotten, if that was what this was, if he'd just forgotten, wandered off, I wasn't going to remind him. I would let it go, forget for now about *against*, about Ceolwulf and his wishes, the bishop, death.

Father had become interested in his feet. He raised them into the air before him, turned them first right and then left, flexed his toes. He shook his head. "That's what it's like." He lowered the feet, looked back at me. "That's what it's like when you pray *for* someone."

And suddenly I knew where he was going, where this was all leading, what he was talking about, had to be talking about, and the thought, the idea, sent a shiver through me that had nothing to do with rain or cliff-side breezes.

"But when you pray against someone...." Father turned and his shoulders seemed to sag as he looked once more away from me, up the valley. "Well...."

"It's not love.... It's not love that pours through you then, is it?"

He looked back at me, shook his head, eyes full open now, clear, watching me.

XXII

The cold weather arrived early that year and with it there was much rain. The plowing went poorly. Toward the end of the season a bad cough got in among us and carried off old Brother Hygbald. When the first frost came, the ground grew glassy and slick, yesterday's footprints rising and breaking open like flowers. We lit the big fire in the center of the dortoir and Father Abbot began to spend more time with his monks.

Throughout the bad weather I prayed as Father had taught me. I knelt in church each night, the sound of the river just audible through the stones, and I would think about the power at my back, think about it building there, piling up, only me holding it back, and I would think about Eanflæd down in the village below, waiting, asleep, the fingertips of one hand just brushing her lips. And then, with a single sweep of my will, I would open my gate, open it wide, and God's love would come pouring through, spilling through me as Father had said it would, like a flood, a cataract, obliterating everything in its path, me, the church, everything, in its mad dash to get to Eanflæd, fill her up, fill her out. And then afterwards, sometimes afterwards when I opened my eyes, I would find everyone was looking at me, the old monks, the serious monks who stayed for the long watch, would all have turned and looked at me as if I'd said something, done something, maybe groaned, in the midst of their prayers. It made me want to laugh they knew so little, it made me feel sorry for them, almost pity them, they seemed so small, so unimportant compared to what I knew, compared to what I knew that the hermit was teaching me.

I also prayed for Ealhmund. I hadn't expected to. Ealhmund had just been a ruse, an excuse, a stand-in for Eanflæd in my discussions with Father Hermit. I didn't really care about Ealhmund. But, having told Father I would pray for him, I felt I should. And there was time. The weather was so bad we often spent entire days inside, weaving hurtles, copying text.

The Bishop's man came for his iron and, as it always did, his presence made me feel guilty, reminded me of my duty to my father, his request, my failure to fulfill it. I would stand by the window in the dortoir and look out at the Far Wood, the path less obvious now with the leaves gone, and I would think about Legacestir, the battle which Father Hermit insisted upon calling Carlegion. The story was old even then but it was still told, most frequently when we were worried, when there were rumors of movement on the Mercian border, councils of war among the Cumbrogi. It was comforting at such times to think of our warriors as this tale depicted them—savage, unstoppable—they were, after all, our only defense. And besides, the whole thing had happened long ago, to other monks, Cumbrogi monks.

I tried to imagine what it must have been like for them. According to Waldhere our people hung human arms from their wheels in those days, impaled infants on spears, wore paint on their faces, dyed their hair. I didn't know if any of this was true but I could imagine what the monks must have thought. Though no one ever said so, they had to have been worried about their holy places. After all, we were heathen ourselves then. No one will ever tell you what we did to churches, altars, but it can't have been good. I mean, think about what we do nowadays to pagan sites. So the Cumbrogi brothers must have felt they were doing God's will when they marched out that day, set up at their army's side, began to pray for their pagan enemy's destruction. When our warriors charged in among them, charged their ranks first, it must have seemed as if God had misunderstood, as if the wrath they had called down upon the heathen had descended instead upon their own heads. Everyone's heard the stories of course, the slit throats, the decapitations, how our warriors strolled among them like men with scythes, bemused at first by the lack of resistance, then growing bored, tired, working quickly, wanting to get it over with, on with the real work, the real fighting. But can you imagine how the monks would have felt? Father Hermit had no illusions. "God killed them," he said. "In answer to their prayers, the God they loved picked them up in His teeth and shook them till they were dead."

I looked out at the Far Wood and thought about my father and I did not pray for the death of our bishop.

But I did attempt again to pray in the other way, the special way Father was trying to teach me. The story he had told of the boy and the hole he'd found beneath the fence, the field full of light, was so good, so perfect, I felt certain it would work for me. All I had to do was sit and wait, *persevere* as he put it, and, eventually, I would grow tired, slump forward, collapse, into God.

As it happened of course, it wasn't as easy as that. Nothing ever is. Which is not to say that it isn't simple. As Father said, God is there, everywhere, waiting on us. All we need do is let Him in. But our minds get in the way of such simplicity don't they, rush ahead of it, dance around it like dogs yapping at the feet of a noble horse? And that is, of course, exactly what happened to me. Now, in addition to the distractions, there was the idea of perseverance to distract me. Again and again I would tell myself, as I sat by the river, in church, wherever, that my thoughts were just thoughts, puffs of smoke, that I must let them float by, give them no more thought than I would a passing cloud, a falling star. And I would. And I would congratulate myself on the success of my disinterest. And I would wonder what this meant, that I was becoming so good at prayer, see myself some-day becoming a hermit, a holy man like Father, maybe even a saint, pilgrims visiting me, bishops, abbots. I would be called upon to teach, found a monastery, accept the mitre, and all of these I would refuse, my humility not suffering such a thing, wanting to remain here, in these woods, like Father Gwynedd, where I could be poor, humble, and at peace with God. And then I would realize what I had been doing, remember where I was, what I was supposed to be attempting. And, anxious now, maddened despite myself by the profusion of my thoughts and their unrelenting pride, I would hurry ahead, tell myself that now, surely, I had persevered long enough, that I had grown tired, exhausted, and now, reliably, I could rest in God. And of course nothing of the sort would happen. My mind was just as alert and active as ever, had indeed been made more so by the feverish pace of my speculations, and, within moments, I would be off on another course, inventing visions, telling myself I was seeing lights where there were none, burning bushes, shimmering halos.

It has been said that failure is a condition of success, that without failure we would not know where failure ends, success begins. It has also been said that God uses failure, that it is a kind of communion, that He prefers to see us beaten, worn down, weary, dejected, for it brings us that much closer to Him, His own experience of life. But I don't know. Such a view of things…well, it seems to me there could be problems with such a view of things. Still I must admit I failed many times when I attempted this sort of prayer, have failed many times. I sat by the river and failed. I knelt in church and failed. I lay in my bed and failed. And then, one day, like a gift, Brother Victricius sent me home early.

Being sent home early was not a common thing. I can remember it happening on only one other occasion, and that was the day Victricius died. Normally, even if there had been nothing for me to do, I would have been expected to wait on the furnace master, follow him around as he performed his various chores, be ready to help him should he need me. And yet, for some reason I can no longer remember, on that day he sent me home early. Indeed it must have been very early because I can remember thinking, when I stopped and sat down, that there were absolutely no demands upon me, that, for once, I had no place to be soon, no office to sing, no lessons to be learned. It was as if, in the middle of the week, I had been sent to the hermit.

I do remember the place I stopped. There was nothing particularly remarkable about it. It was a place like any other along that path, the ground high at my back, falling away before me. I sat on the edge of the path and looked down at the river. The water is swift there but no longer as fast and loud as it is up by the furnace. Large flat slabs of rock occupy the far bank. Where the rocks enter the water, they are

washed by the current and their reddish color becomes dark, almost
purple. The hill people believe them the broken shoulder blades of a
dead giant. Between the breaks in the rocks, sycamores have grown
and, in some places, spread their bellies out over the surrounding
stone. At that time of year there would have been dead leaves plas-
tered to the rocks like yellow handprints.

My guess is that it was the interval after None, certainly a long
interval, either None or Terce, for, as I have said, there was no feeling of urgency, hurry to the day. Indeed, the idea of the interval, a
significant block of time stretching out before me without plan or
requirement is an important part of the memory. Interestingly, I also
remember feeling a certain sense of futility as I began the exercise,
the idea that, having failed so many times, it really didn't matter if
I failed again, now, here, this time. I sat down, closed my eyes, the
smells of autumn and the river filling my nostrils, and almost immediately a blessed sort of darkness enveloped me, doused my mind.
This of course was exactly what you might expect the hermit's emptiness to look like, feel like, but I wasn't fooled. It was always like this
when you first began, first closed your eyes, and, sure enough, once
I recognized this darkness for the false dawn it was, the recognition
itself became my first distraction.

I took a big breath, eyes still resolutely closed, and imagined the
distraction, the idea of a false dawn, bobbing up against the rocks
on the opposite shore, catching once, then floating off downstream.
I sat, waited, not pressing it, not hurrying, just empty, the river, my
river, empty before me. It is always at this point, after the first distraction has penetrated your consciousness, that, as if it had pierced some
heretofore impenetrable wall, a great flotilla of distractions breaks
through, sails down your river—the soup we had at last night's collation, the bread, Father Prior's beard, the gray in it, why he wouldn't
let me ride in the wagon, the new ox, her eyes, and did they see as we
do, oxen, do their great and luminous eyes see more than ours, better
than ours, being as large and luminous as they are? Each of these I
let float by me, willing my mind to ignore them, think no more of
them than I would a log or stick, some piece of flotsam floating by,

and, eventually, as if my mind itself had grown tired of such foolishness, a sort of peace settled over me, a sort of absence. It is comforting, not thinking, as if thinking itself were an exercise which, when relinquished, leaves a person as tired and enervated as if he had been weeding or hoeing or doing something hard. And so, not thinking, empty of thoughts, I settled into a sort of rest, the murmur of water before me, water flowing from left to right, left to right as God's waters flowed, left to right through me, through me and over the lip of our terrace, spilling down over the terrace, across the fields and into the village, into Eanflæd, the thought of this comforting, settling, lulling as sunshine lulls, my head inching forward, eyes closed, relaxed, Eanflæd now visible before me, Eanflæd as she would someday be, hair up, cheeks exposed, sweet, temperate, kneeling before the altar, fresh, virginal, maybe myself behind her, praying, the two of us belonging to the same monastery now, our monastery, Redestone, the whole thing coming together naturally like this, perfectly, God having created man and woman so that, naturally enough, in the great scheme of things, they would come together like this, it being God's plan, Eanflæd there, kneeling, I behind her.

I sat up as if kicked, looked around. There was nothing, no one, the flags stretching off up-river and down, mossy, silent, empty. I was horrified and at the same time elated. It was always like this when it happened, the mix of feelings, the confusion, the sense of having come very close to something very wicked. You felt at once both happy to have escaped and mortified at having allowed yourself to get so close. That such things could coexist was what was most frightening, that the world's extremes survived in such proximity, prayer and profanity, good and evil, heaven and hell. That it was so easy to slip from one to the other, that prayer apparently left you open to this, opened you up, let Whatever in. The hermit didn't talk much about it but Waldhere did. When he had found out about the sort of prayer Father was teaching me, he had said that I was playing with fire, that when you closed your eyes and emptied your mind like that, lowered all your defenses, anything could get in. I had never seen Waldhere so exercised. Of course by then he had begun his studies for the priesthood and so I knew he knew more than I about such things, but I also knew that a part of it might be envy, that Waldhere envied me the hermit, envied my relationship with him, the trips I got to make each week to the mountain. Still I listened to him when it came to the devil. I listened because, though Waldhere couldn't know it, he was describing something I had already experienced. Sometimes, even when I wasn't trying to pray, when I was just kneeling quietly in church, I would find myself thinking thoughts utterly alien to my own, images of Eanflæd and myself engaged in activities which I had never imagined, could not have imagined, activities which, clearly, must be coming from somewhere, Something, else.

I crossed myself, looked out at the stones the hill people believe belonged to a giant and said, "In Christ's name I abjure you, Satan. Depart and be gone." It made me feel better. Waldhere had suggested the formulation and I liked it, especially the word "abjure." Then, because it seemed to flow naturally from one to the other, I added a bit of the prayer the hermit had taught me, "Christ with me, Christ before me, Christ behind me, Christ in me, Christ beneath me, Christ above me, Christ on my right, Christ on my left, Christ when I lie down, Christ when I sit down, Christ when I arise, Christ in the heart of everyone who thinks of me, Christ in the mouth of everyone who speaks of me, Christ in the eye that sees me, Christ in the ear that hears me." Something about the rhythm of the words as I said them, the repetition of the Name, relaxed me, comforted me. I remembered something the hermit had said when he was talking about God's love, that it was around us always, here, there, everywhere, and again I closed my eyes and relaxed in that image, not really caring anymore whether I succeeded or not, the interval stretching out before me like summer, endless, eternal, nothing to do, no place to be, nothing to worry about, sitting, eyes closed, the river flowing past, my thoughts, my cares, flowing past, one by one, slowly, and, slowly, blessedly, I sunk into silence.

When next I opened my eyes the far bank looked different, flat, a picture of itself rather than the reality. I blinked, opened my eyes, blinked again. Sound returned, the drone of the river, the whisper of air; trees resumed their proper dimensions, moved again in the breeze. Had it all stopped? While I was gone, absent, whatever, had everything stopped, the water frozen in place, the trees, sound, clouds, been arrested in time? I did not know. The sun seemed to stand in roughly the same position, and yet you could have told me an entire interval had passed and I would have believed you, an entire day and I would have been forced to believe you. I had no idea how much time had passed. I hadn't been here. Or, rather, I'd been here but the here I had occupied was different from the here before me—a different here, a better here, the real here. I shook my head, looked around, laughed out loud, the laugh itself sounding different now, a bell of an entirely different character. I was happy. It had happened, I could tell, and I was very happy.

XXIII

That was the winter of the famous storm when I was trapped by a great snowfall at the furnace and had to spend two nights alone with Brother Victricius. Victricius was funny about weather. For such a vigorous man, he was surprisingly susceptible to damp. I can still see him standing in the back of choir, sneezing and sniffling, one hand held out as if to say, *A moment, a moment please and this will pass.* Yet, despite his weakness, he behaved like someone inured to the elements. If it rained, the furnace master worked on. If it poured, still he worked on. I remember one time he caught a chill so bad he had to lean on me to get back to the monastery, sweat dripping from him like candle-wax, yet even that did not stop him. A night's rest and he was back at the furnace, ignoring once more whatever ill wind the Lord chose to send his way.

After such a cold and wet autumn, that was actually not a particularly bad winter. Indeed, many were already looking forward to spring when the storm struck. There was even a story told of a man who had chosen that day to begin his plowing, how they found him in the middle of his field, goad frozen in place over his head, only the horns of his ox protruding from the snow before him. But I don't know if that is true. The weather may have been mild, but I doubt anyone had really begun their plowing, at least not in our part of the country. But there is no denying it had been an easy winter and, in my memory, the day of the storm itself began agreeably enough. I remember coming out of Chapter, hurrying to catch up with Victricius who was always well ahead of me, and being surprised to find him still on the garth, head turned to the south, eyes closed, sniffing at the breeze that blew out of that quarter.

The weather held through the interval. In my memory there may have been a few pale clouds overhead but I am not sure. I remember only that it was nice, that we had no need of a fire. We sang Sext and None at the furnace and, after each, resumed our work. I think Victricius was breaking rocks when the wind changed. I'm not sure, but that is the sort of thing he would have been doing at that time of year. I know I was working on the bellows, I remember that because I remember seeing the first of the snow flakes falling and melting on its brown and stippled surface. But that was later. The first change was the wind. Up there in the steep part of the valley the wind is a funny thing. A south wind such as we had that morning, because of the deflection of the valley wall, can feel as if it is coming from the north, and, likewise, a north wind out of the south. But there was no mistaking the sudden chill. One moment the skin of the bellows was soft and supple and, the next, it had become stiff and hard and there was a coldness around my ankles. I looked up. The sky overhead remained clear but there was a change in the quality of the light, as if it were no longer midday but sunset or sunrise, the light made bright by proximity to something large and dark. I shivered, dipped my finger in the oil (warm now compared to the surrounding air), applied another daub to the hide. I worked on for a while, the skin continuing to pucker and tighten beneath my fingers like something alive, like something retreating before the cold. Then the light went away. I looked up, saw something I could not believe, looked down again. Out of the clear blue air a dusting of snowflakes blew through the yard. One or two fell on the hide before me and I can remember still the way they looked, the damp shadows they left as they melted. Again I looked up, looked at the thing I had seen over Modra nect, the black curtain of cloud that had risen there like a new mountain, like a new mountain threatening to tumble down on us. I looked over at Victricius, pounded on the bellows to gain his attention. Though the wind was not yet strong, there was already something in the air that, in my memory, deadened the sound, as if even the cloud's silence were louder than any noise I could produce. But I was heard. Victricius looked up, looked where I was pointing, blinked, looked again. He stood up, straightened his back, studied the dark thing hanging in the air over Modra nect. He shook his head, squinted as if doubting his eyesight, looked at his pile of unbroken rock, looked back up at the long sloping mass of cloud. Before he began again to swing his hammer, he signaled for me to build a fire.

At the western edge of the furnace yard there stood a small structure we called the "woodshed," though even such an unassuming name seems a little grand for a building that stood open to the elements on three of its four sides. It was in front of this structure that I built my fire, using its one wall and the firewood and charcoal stacked against it to shield me from the wind that now began to pour down the valley like a second river. Before me, Victricius continued to work. Woolens blown tight against him, tonsure flickering madly, he swung his hammer, swung his hammer, but the wind was so loud I could not hear the blows.

I had just thrown the first sizeable piece of wood on when the storm struck. I remember that because I can remember staring at it as it flew past my little fire, thinking maybe I had thrown it too hard, that maybe that could explain such a marvel. And then, with a shock that threatened to knock me into the fire, the wind became solid, filled with snow, and the tops of the trees behind me dangled before me like little upside-down toy trees.

I closed my eyes, opened them again, and the far side of the yard had vanished, tool shed, path, furnace, everything gone, buried behind a swirling curtain of snow. Victricius himself, though only a few steps from me, was like a figure seen through an ocean wave, watery, vague, indistinct. I started to get up, go to him, and, as I did so, I realized the fire was blowing away, individual pieces of kindling rolling away still alight, still burning, their smoke just another part of the wind, the snow. I yelled something, could not hear my own voice, reached back, grabbed something heavy from the shed, threw it on the fire. The log landed, fell to one side, began to roll away. I bent over, tried to protect the fire with my body, will it to stay in place. I prayed. Then, like something rising from the sea, Victricius was beside me, grabbing burning faggots with his bare hands, throwing them heedlessly into the shed, working faster than I'd ever seen him work before.

After that there is a period of time I don't remember so well. Though I don't remember his doing so, Victricius must have gotten the fire going again because I remember that, can remember looking at it, noticing the fire, thinking how funny it was that it should be there, I next to it, and, despite this nearness, that I should be so cold, so dangerously cold, fingers like ice, the wind sucking everything—heat, smoke, even light—away from us, away down the valley, down into what had become a twisting howling gyre.

Of course I have heard the stories, how everyone says the snow, instead of falling from above, blew that day from side to side, how looking across the garth was like looking through the woof of a loom, how all the windows in the dortoir seemed curtained with lace. But it was not like that for us. Where we were the snow did not blow from side to side but from behind you to in front of you. With the shed at our backs, it was like sitting behind a rock in the middle of a flood. You could snap your fingers and the roar of the storm would deafen you to their snap. Surely the logs popped from time to time, but we heard neither hiss nor crackle. Looking back on it now I suppose I shouldn't be so surprised by the vagueness of my memories. Loud sound, no noise; big fire, no warmth—it was a strange world we occupied that day. Only the wind and the snow remained constant, and that maddening, inexact, nothing to hear, nothing to focus on, just the gray and swirling vortex of snow that seemed always to pour away from us down the valley. It was an odd property of that storm that the center of that vortex, always receding, always flowing away from you, seemed at the same time (regardless of where you sat or how you turned your head) to be always directly before you, creating an endless vexing center for your vision so that, sometimes, it was as if you were moving and it was holding still, as if, instead of sitting there in that cramped and freezing shed, you were actually rising rapidly, flying up out of the depths of some gray and murky well. Eventually it seemed as if everything had been sucked down that hole—sound, warmth, even time itself—the light growing dim, dimmer, as what we assumed was afternoon passed slowly into what we assumed was evening, only the snow itself providing any clues, the swirling spots becoming gradually grayer, darker, coalescing, until finally they merged into a single black and moving night.

And still the wind howled, still the snow blew across our floor, still God tried to bury us.

I don't remember falling asleep but I do remember being awakened. It was Brother Victricius and he was shaking me roughly. For a moment I was confused, uncertain why he should be there, if this was the Vigil, and then I remembered, became aware again of the roar, realized it had been no dream, that the wind still blew, the snow still fell, we were still trapped. Victricius shook me again, pointed at the roof. A section of thatch had given way and a portion of the charcoal was now covered with a white and glistening snow. Through the opening I could see more snow, a great blanket of moving snow that made me fear for the roof. Victricius held up two sturdy pieces of kindling, mimed their placement in the rafters, tipped his head up at the opening. I saw what he wanted, placed my hands under the sagging section of thatch, pushed upwards. Above me I could feel the weight of the snow give and, peripherally, I saw something fall from the top of the shed, turn white in the firelight, blow immediately away. Victricius slipped the two pieces of wood into the open space I had created above the rafters. He picked up four smaller pieces, slipped them through crosswise. He looked at me, nodded, looked back up at the roof. Carefully, ever so carefully, I lowered my hands. A small dusting of snow fell onto my shoulders but nothing more. The roof held. Victricius did not smile. He sat back down, tossed another piece of wood onto the fire, watched the roof. I sat down too, then lay back, anxious to return to the comfort of my dreams. As I drifted off I can remember a part of me thinking about Victricius, pleased that he was there, pleased that someone was watching over me.

When I woke up the furnace master had not moved and the shed was full of light. I turned over, looked out, had to cover my eyes. Before me a wall of snow, blue with shadow, rose nearly to the roof of the shed. In the crack between the roof and the uppermost layer of snow, light poured through so bright it hurt my eyes. The wind had stopped. Everything was silent. I sat up, looked at Victricius, surprised that he had let the fire burn down. The good brother looked at me as if I'd done something wrong, as if the fire was maybe my fault. His eyes were red and, as I looked at him, he sniffed and rubbed at his nose with the back of his hand. He looked at his hand, wiped the back of it down the inside of his sleeve, looked back at me. He put one finger in the air, crossed it with another, then opened his fingers like a mouth singing. So that was the sort of morning it was to be. I nodded, held one finger up to indicate Matins could wait, then began to rebuild the fire. By the time I had it going again, Brother seemed to have forgotten about the office and was bent over staring morosely out through the crack between roof and snow, light draped over the upper part of his face like a mask, eyes empty, white.

I moved over next to him, looked out. You couldn't really see anything. The snow had piled up so high in front of the shed that the only view between its crest and the roof was straight up. The sky was clear and blue and looking at it made your eyes water. I looked over at Victricius but he wasn't looking at me, was for some reason studying his hand, thinking about something. I looked back out and noticed that the snow seemed to slope down toward the corner of the shed. Shielding my eyes from the glare, I took a step in that direction and the view improved. From the corner post itself I found I was able to see some distance across the yard. It was like looking up a narrow valley or trough. I moved around Victricius to the opposite corner and saw that here too a small valley shot out through the snow, following exactly the line taken by the previous day's wind. Still there was little to look at. I told myself I was seeing the ridge where the furnace sat and the first of the trees by the path but I wasn't at all sure. The snow had changed everything, made everything look different, strange, and it was very hard to look at. Still it was nice to be able to look out at all. The air in the shed was close and cold and stank of smoke and fresh-cut oak. Standing at one of the corners like this, at least you could breathe a little.

The furnace master touched my shoulder, indicated the yard with rheumy eyes, pointed at my chest, the side of his head, then made a sign I did not recognize. I repeated it for him, something with the tips of one's fingers, shook my head. He shook his, tried again. Still no good. "Rust," he said, irritated by the state of my schooling. "Do you think it will *rust?*" I held out my hands, dumbfounded. The eyebrows flew up and Brother made a swinging motion with his arms, looked out longingly at the yard, back at me. The hammer. He was worried about his hammer. He'd left it out in the snow.

We did sing Matins as it turned out, and Prime and Terce in their turn, though we would hear no bells that day and had to guess at each hour by the position of the sun. Looking back on it now, it seems a little odd we didn't try to dig our way out. Of course it wouldn't have been easy. The snow stood level with the chest of a tall man and our only shovel lay buried along with the rest of our tools in the shed on the far side of the yard. But such a predicament normally would have served only as a goad to the furnace master's sense of purpose. He would have devised a shovel from a piece of firewood, dug with his bare hands, maybe placed the fire closer to the snow itself. But not that day. That day, for some reason, he was content to sit and wait for the rescue he assured me was coming. Maybe it was the catarrh that made him behave so strangely. I can still remember the uncharacteristically extravagant gestures he used to describe our situation, how *fortunate* we were that we had *so much* firewood, the *wind* had stopped blowing, and the coming fast was going to be *so* good for us…. I don't think I'd ever seen Brother use the sign for "fast" before.

The day wore on and, though the sun continued to shine, the walls of snow that hemmed us in were in no way that I could see diminished. Of course it was very cold. Even the snow that stood nearest the fire, instead of melting, seemed to become merely glassy as if, like clay, the heat of the flames served only to harden it, make it more firm. Victricius seldom strayed from his post by the fire, blowing his nose often and loudly and looking at me yearningly, like a man who wants to talk. I stayed as far away from him as I could, spending most of my time at one of the corners where I could see out, staring up the little valleys, dreaming of the world beyond. For a while I remember worrying about the hermit. I felt little concern for the abbey or village, they could take care of themselves, but the idea of the old man up there on the mountain by himself worried me. Then I thought about other bad weather I'd seen him in, how he would sometimes wander out into a thunderstorm like a man wandering out into a field full of flowers, enjoying himself, and I worried less. He was probably already digging his way out, looking for prints, taking advantage of the snow-fall to see what types of animal had visited during the night. Which got me thinking about the prints that might be in the snow around us. I covered my eyes, looked out. A breeze blew across the yard, raised a tiny whirlwind of snow, sent it sparkling up and out of the trough before me. Father and I had tracked in snow like this. Prints tended to fill quickly but they filled with a snow that was finer than the snow the print was created in. The finer snow reflected light differently and, as a result, filled prints showed up as slightly grayer stains upon the surrounding whiteness. It wasn't easy track to follow but, if you paid attention, you could…just. Which, in turn, got me to thinking about the trough in the snow before me. Why hadn't it filled too? As if in answer to this, another tiny storm of flakes rose from the floor of the trough, extended its arms and, sparkling in the sun, danced up and out onto the main surface of the snow. Was there something about this place that repelled snow, kept it from accumulating? I tried to visualize the shed and its attendant troughs from above and was immediately struck by the similarity of what I saw to a deer print. The mound of snow on the roof of the shed was like the turf pushed up before a hoof as it penetrates the earth, the pile of snow between the two troughs corresponded to the v-shaped cup of mud left in the cen-ter of a print by the hollow of the hoof, and the troughs themselves were the marks made by the two halves of the hoof as they struck the ground, even showing by their length and depth—shallowest on the far side of the yard, deeper here at the woodshed's corner posts—the speed and direction in which the animal had travelled. What sort of beast would leave a print like that? As if time could move backward, I heard again the wind, felt the snow at my back, watched from above as it blew through our yard, blew over and around the shed, piling up downwind of the shed as flowing water will sometimes pile up in a plume behind a rock, troughs defining the boundaries of the plume at each of the rock's downstream edges. I blinked, thought about it. What looked like the track of a giant deer travelling in one direction, was, it seemed, the print left by a great wind travelling in the other. I smiled. Father's methods worked even with snowstorms. I wondered if I should tell Victricius. That this might only be a drift... that, beyond the contours of this great sparkling hump-backed pile, the snow might be only knee-deep.... Wouldn't they laugh at us if we hadn't dug out of that!

It took a while for my eyes to become accustomed to the darkness of the shed. When they did, I saw that the furnace master was still sitting by the fire, eyes red, vacant, lips moving as if speaking to the flames. I shivered, looked back out, was immediately blinded by the glittering surfaces beyond the shed. I closed my eyes, waited. This would pass, it had before. I opened my eyes, forced myself to look, ignore the glare. Where before the light on the snow had glistened and sparkled, now it pricked and stabbed, a thousand needles pierced my eyes, grew into rocky cores, shards of broken glass, pressed against the soft parts of my brain. I couldn't stand it. I closed my eyes, almost said something, turned back to look at Victricius, was blinded again, even the interior of the shed now too bright for me, too hard, sharp, brilliant, to look at. I closed my eyes, panicked (*I cannot see!*), took a step toward Victricius, remembered the fire, stepped to one side, tripped over something, fell. And then the hands were on me, my shoulders, forehead, the sides of my face, fluttering.

It's funny how people talk of the furnace master now. If a novice or postulant asks about the old days, what it was like when we were rich and our abbey well known, the answers they receive invariably make mention of a strange monk who came from across the water, an odd-looking man, often as not covered with soot, who spoke poorly if at all and was possessed of an uncanny ability to mend things, to turn broken bits of rock into fine steel, worthless clay into creamy ceramic. And if they listen closely, if the novice or postulant is as alert to the nuances of speech and gesture as most young men are, they cannot help but detect a note of disapproval, the suggestion that there was something not quite right with this man, this foreigner, that, perhaps, it would be best if we did not speak of him again. We are, after all, a fallen race. We must justify ourselves, our histories, excuse whatever slights we may once have bestowed, come to terms with our current decline. I have been, I suppose, as guilty as the next.

But Victricius deserves better than that. He may have been a hard master, he may have worked me in all weathers, been short with me when I erred, shown little gratitude for my efforts, but he never asked more of me than he did of himself. He never once struck me. He was strange, it is true. He was a foreigner. Contrary to the Rule, he sometimes spoke of things—the charcoal, the hammer, even the yard—as though they were his. He was proud. His behavior in the matter of the fire-pits is, of course, inexcusable. But he was not without good qualities. If he sometimes moved too quickly, focused too closely on the temporal, how can we be sure he did not believe, in so doing, he best served both abbot and Church? And on that day, that strange snow-blind day when I lay in the midst of so much light and could see nothing at all, Victricius was a true brother to me. He watched over me. He tore a strip of cloth from his own woolens, laid it across my eyes. He fretted over his inability to give me something to drink, trying even to melt snow in his bare hands. As the day wore on and I sensed my eyesight returning, he refused to let me open my eyes, endanger them at a time when he judged them still feeble, susceptible to influence. And he spoke to me. That is the thing I remember best from that day, lying there, eyes closed, the unfamiliar sound of Brother's voice filling the spaces in my head with pictures, images of a place where vineyards draped the hillsides, herbs grew underfoot, and every step scented the air with rosemary and thyme.

His father had been a potter, I remember him telling me that, and though I can't remember now why, there was something about this that was both good and bad. Good, I suppose, because it must have been good to be the son of a craftsman, someone with a trade, but bad too in some way I am no longer sure of. Did they shun him perhaps, the other boys, shun him as our monks did now, because he was different, aloof, the potter's son? There were sighs too, long pauses, when he spoke of the agricultural work, the fields, the vineyards. Unlike Deira, the wells in Victricius's homeland were, it seemed, unreliable. As a boy he was sometimes sent by his father to take water from the village to the men in the fields. He spoke of those trips as you or I might a still-remembered teacher, a long-dead friend, how the men would crowd around him, clapping him on the head and sipping loudly from his ladle, how the earth had smelled, the grapes, how the sky had been blue, the sun had shined. I lay with my eyes closed and in my mind I saw the places he spoke of, the long days, the cool shade, and I dreamt that I was the furnace master, that it was I who had a father that made things, lived in a village, sent me with water from the well.

My mind must have sailed along like that for some time, catching whatever breezes pleased it, ignoring those that did not, because I can remember being surprised when I realized the wind had shifted, that Brother Victricius was talking about something else now, some holy man that had wandered into his village one morning when he was still little more than a boy. I smiled to let him know I was still listening but beneath my bandage I wondered what Brother was so excited about. Holy men might be rare in his part of the world but they certainly weren't in ours, wandering in whenever the weather turned cold, often as not hungry and unkempt, clothes stinking of leaf mold and pitch. But then Brother referred to the fellow as *Father* and there was something in the way he said it, something familiar in the way his voice dipped as he pronounced the title, that I recognized. With a shudder I realized who this was that Victricius was talking about, that this was not some holy vagabond wandered in from the wood but our own Father Abbot, that I was being vouchsafed an image of Father Abbot as he looked when Victricius first saw him, as he looked when he was not yet Father Abbot but merely Father Agatho, young, virile, a priest, a missionary, just like anyone else.

I sat up a little, thought about this, wished I could look at Victricius, see the expression on his face. But there was little need. From the tone of his voice I could tell how happy he was, how even the mention of Father's name in this context—a personal remembrance, his alone—pleased him. For some reason I found myself thinking about the way he had looked when that first pot came out of the ground without crack or blemish. There were, I realized, memories, experiences, that only the furnace master and Father Abbot knew, stories they could share with no one else in all of Northumbria.

A small crowd gathered. I remember him telling me that, that despite the fact most of the men had already left for the fields, there had been enough women and children remaining in the village that morning to create something of a crowd. They offered the priest food and water. They brought him a beaker of wine, a garland of flowers. They vied with one another for the honor of having him sleep beneath their roof. Such was their isolation and the respect accorded holy men in that country that they would have done anything to make him feel welcome, at home. But Agatho was unmoved. Victricius said he stood in their midst like a great stone and said nothing. And, finally, the people grew still, hushed. And it was then that he began to speak.

He began, appropriately enough, at the beginning, how our Lord's advent had been predicted, how the stars and prophets had foreseen His coming. By mid-morning he had reached the annunciation and, by mid-day, the Sermon on the Mount. He quoted it word for word, as if giving it himself, and Victricius told me he had lain on the ground and listened, chin on his arm, and felt neither ground nor arm. It was so clear, he said, so obvious. After the Sermon on the Mount, the miracles—the lepers touched, the sinners spared—by nightfall Jerusalem. As the last of the men streamed in from the fields, so Jesus and His disciples entered the holy city, anthems rising from every corner, all Heaven singing. By the time of the betrayal, they had all moved into one of the farmer's houses, everyone gathered around the fire, Father foremost, seeming to talk to each singly and all at once, eyes red in the firelight, the enormity of what they had done becoming real, the pain Christ had suffered for them. And then, finally, the end.

Father must have arranged it all beforehand because, when he said the words and the temple curtain was torn, a way was made clear for him and he disappeared into the rear of the house. One moment he was there, and the next he was gone. The people of the village had expected a feast, it apparently being the custom on such occasions, but there was to be none that night. The holy man was gone. The story was over. They all made their way home in the dark, hungry and, as Victricius remembered it, a little afraid.

The next morning Father Agatho was up before everyone else. I remember a note of pride in Brother's voice here, some pleasure he still took in the fact that his abbot, his holy man, had risen before everyone else, been up before all those farmers and their women. But the farmers and their women did get up. Victricius said they stumbled from their homes that morning like people walking in their sleep, bleary-eyed, confused, trying to understand what the noise was, what it was that had awakened them, whether it was dangerous, and what it might mean for their world. Brother stopped here, paused, and I remember the urgency in his voice when he started up again, asked, demanded, if I remembered the first time, the very first time I had heard the chant. And before I could answer, before I could remember or think of anything, he was off again, remembering himself. It was, he said, like nothing he'd ever heard before, and, at the same time, it was like something natural, something so perfectly natural and proper he had wondered if it might *be* natural, might be some everyday part of the dawn he'd simply never been up early enough to hear before. And the people had been drawn to it. Mysteriously, ineluctably, it had pulled them from their beds, pulled them from the safety of their village and out into the darkness at the edge of the fields.

The holy man was there of course, they could tell that by the singing, but they could not see him. At first at least, it was so dark, they could see him only by not seeing him, the darkness that blocked out the stars, the standing singing figure that moved between them and the stars like something wild, like something that had crept in out of the forest during the night and now stood before them singing and wild at the edge of their fields. Then, slowly, long after they had taken their seats on the ground around him, long after their bottoms had turned cold and hard against the hard and freezing ground, the silhouette slowly began to change, gain substance, form, the sky to lighten, sky and field still one in the predawn darkness, trees floating in the mist like dreams. And, finally, Father began to speak. As if no time had intervened between the previous night and this, as if he had paused only to catch his breath, the holy man opened his mouth and out came the rest of the story, the next chapter, Christ's burial, the posting of the guards.

The women came and, in the stillness of morning, found nothing, the tomb empty, their Lord taken away. A man approached and asked Mary of Magdala why she was crying. Thinking Him the gardener, she wondered if He had removed the body, asked Him to show her where He had placed it. And then, as if on command, the sun rose.

Victricius said it was like no sunrise he had seen before. He said the earth itself seemed to sigh with relief, the hills to tremble at that first touch of light. And as if he too had waited for this moment, as if the sun itself imparted some necessary strength, it was then that the holy man first quoted the risen Christ. "Mary," He said, and she recognized Him. "Master," she replied in the language of that day. *Master*.

Brother Victricius became quiet after that. I remember him speculating about Mary of Magdala, wondering if she might have been confused by the sun, if it might have been the sun coming up behind our Lord (as it had behind Father Agatho) that explained her failure to recognize Him at first. But, aside from that, he was silent. As was I. I lay in my darkness, comfortable and warm now, and I reveled in the story he had told. It was perfect. It always was. No matter how many times I heard the tale, no matter how many times it was drummed into me, I liked it. It made me happy.

After a while Brother began speaking again, something about the rest of that day, the Mass Father had celebrated, his homily. I found Agatho's choice of text, the story of Elijah and Elisha, annoying. I often had trouble with those names when reciting. But Victricius didn't. As he told the tale his foreigner's tongue curved around those like-sounding syllables with an oily dexterity I found disagreeable. Once again I allowed myself to dislike the man a little, blaming him for the story Father had chosen to tell and wishing we could just be quiet now, rest in the peacefulness created by the earlier tale. Still, a part of me had always enjoyed the idea of a boy's adoption by a great prophet and, in particular, the story's remarkable conclusion. You remember the lines…. "Leaving there, he came to Elisha son of Shaphat as he was plowing behind twelve yoke of oxen, he himself being with the twelfth. Elijah passed near to him and threw his cloak over him. Elisha left his oxen and ran after Elijah. 'Let me kiss my father and mother, then I will follow you,' he said. Elijah answered, 'Go, go back; for have I done anything to you?' Elisha turned away, took the pair of oxen and slaughtered them. He used the plow for cooking the oxen, then gave to his men, who ate. He then rose, and followed Elijah and became his servant." There was something about that ending with its suggestion of filial disobedience and the ease with which a child might turn his back on family and obligation that had always secretly appealed to me.

But Victricius was blind to such notions, the temptations he might be causing me. Indeed, the way he told it, the destruction of the plow became the point of Father's sermon. "We must burn our tools," he said, in an accent identical to Father Abbot's, "all of our possessions, and follow Him. When the Master places His cloak upon us, when He casts it over our shoulders and calls us His own, what right have we to a past, a livelihood, to anything at all? We are His; whatever we own, His by default. To cling to anything—mother, father, plow, past—is to deny Him, to say that there is some part of us that is not His, not wholly given, that a part of us belongs not to Christ but to things corruptible, empty of worth." How perfectly the furnace master remembered that speech! How perfectly, after all those years, he recalled our lord abbot's theme! "I see how you shudder," he declaimed, speaking not to me but to the crowd that had sat on the ground that morning, the boy in its midst. "The sun has risen, you cannot hide. You draw back, you shrink from my words, but this is your servitude, your slavery. You own not your plow, your oxen, your plot of land; they own you. Think what a gift it is our Lord offers you. Freedom. Freedom from all that weighs you down, from all that daily grinds your teeth and wrinkles your brow. Freedom to be what you were meant to be from the beginning of time. Men. Men of God, men of understanding. Throw everything away, He said, and follow me. 'Anyone who prefers father or mother to me is not worthy of me. Anyone who prefers son or daughter to me is not worthy of me. Anyone who does not take his cross and follow in my footsteps is not worthy of me. Anyone who finds his life will lose it; anyone who loses his life for my sake will find it.'"

The speech was so grand, its delivery so faithful, that for a moment or two I lost myself in admiration of it and of the demand our lord abbot had placed upon those farmers. That they give up everything! That they turn their backs on all they valued, all they loved and cherished, and for what? To follow him! To wander off after what must have seemed a half-crazed priest into a life of certain hunger, hardship, self-denial. For the first time in my life I realized how mad we must seem to the world, how mad and how glorious! This was the life my father had given me, this impossibility, this obverse paradise. No wonder Eanflæd had been so impressed. How grand it suddenly seemed, how heroic, how fine!

Brother sat down. As if the speech itself had been the whole of his story, as if, having delivered himself of it, there was nothing left to say, nothing left to prop him up, bear him on, the furnace master sat down, gave a little sigh, became still. I noticed his quiet and, in my triumph, felt an unexpected compassion for him. I would reach out to Victricius. I who had given up everything to be here, had had everything—mother, father, family, home—stripped from me to live here, could give up this little more to make him happy too, make even someone as lowly and unimportant as the furnace master feel wanted, interesting, a person of consequence. "And so," I asked, pretending an interest I did not feel, "that was how you became a monk? You got up and went after him, you followed Father Abbot?"

"Yes. No." More silence. "No, not right away. I was too young, my parents wouldn't permit it, wouldn't let me go. Which of course made me unhappy. I must have moped around, sackcloth and ashes, because I remember my father yelling at me—a pot had been broken, some clay set up improperly, I'm not sure what, but apparently I hadn't been watching what I was doing." Victricius stopped for a moment, then added, "That was the last time he ever spoke to me." Another pause, longer this time. "Anyway. Anyway, it's clear what he was angry about, the impudence, the suggestion that I was holier than he. Or…. Or maybe not. Maybe he just felt sorry for me. I don't know. Whatever it was, he sent me away. I remember that, threw me out of his workshop, told me to take some water to the men in the fields, make myself useful." A small laugh here. "So I was walking down the hill when I saw him. It's funny I would have gone that way but I guess I was taking my time, wasting my time. And then I saw Father. He must have been talking to the brothers of Dalfinus because he was coming from their vineyard when I saw him, heading downhill, walking between the rows, working his way toward the village path.

"I'd known he was leaving of course, but I'd thought he was already gone. It was the purest of chances that I met him there." Victricius hesitated as if expecting me to argue this point. When I didn't, he continued. "So of course I ran to him. I mean what boy wouldn't? I hid my yoke in the grass alongside the road and ran after him. I had to. He was like no one I had ever seen before, no one I had ever imagined.

"He acted as if he knew me. Funny, I never thought about it before, but I doubt he did. I mean I doubt he really knew me, recognized me. There had been plenty of boys there that morning, plenty of adult faces to hold his attention. But he let me think he knew me, recognized me, and you cannot imagine what that did for me, how it made me feel. We walked along, me talking, him listening, smiling every now and then, probably wondering where this gangling boy got the idea he could someday be among his followers." Once again the little laugh. "I suppose I cut a fairly comical figure. But, anyway, after a while, we came to the bridge. I knew I had to go then, I mean to let him go. It wasn't permitted to cross the bridge. And besides it was late. But I lingered. I didn't want to say good-bye. I kept talking, trying to hold Father back, hold him back with my words, telling him everything about myself, my life, my dreams, the sort of potter I would be, the fields I would work, wishing with all my heart that this could go

on forever, that somehow I could be allowed to stand by this bridge
forever and talk with this man.

"But of course it couldn't. I mean it couldn't go on forever and
Father clearly knew that, looking at his feet, trying to let me know
as politely as he could that he had to be off. And it was getting on in
the day. The air had grown cold." For some reason Victricius ran his
hand over my arm as if fearful that day's cold might somehow reach
me. "Spring is like that where I come from. The days are warm but, by
late afternoon, there is a freshness to the air, a chill. So, anyway, the
sun must have passed behind a cloud or something because I shivered and it was then that it happened, that Father placed his mantle
over me. Of course it was a perfectly natural gesture. I don't think
anyone can doubt that, that, by his nature, Father is a perfectly caring,
paternal man and, therefore, the gesture itself was natural, entirely
natural and spontaneous. I can still remember the way it felt, its heft,
the smell of Father's body in its wool, the roughness at my neck. And
then of course it dawned on me. On both of us I suppose. He had
placed his cloak on me."

Once again Brother became still and I found myself growing
annoyed with him, his apparent inability to get to the end of this tale.
So Father Abbot had placed his cloak over him, so Brother had gotten to play the role of Elisha in Scripture, had gotten to run away, follow Father Abbot, I didn't see that it mattered so very much. After all,
it wasn't as if he had been such a great catch. It wasn't as if the whole
village had risen up, followed Father Abbot, become his disciples.
Actually, when you thought about it, you could believe Father Abbot
would have been disappointed. To have preached to an entire village
and won but this single boy, this whelp, this potter's dog. Father must
have wondered what people would think of him, deliverer of children,
messiah to the small and insignificant. "So that was it?" I asked, feign-
ing even less interest now. "You crossed the bridge, went after him,
followed Father Abbot?"

Victricius must have thought the answer to my question obvious
because he went on as if he'd already given it. "You know," he said, "I
sometimes wonder about those buckets, if they're still there. I can still

see them, just as I placed them among the grasses, the water rocking a bit, reflecting the sky. I wonder if anyone ever found them."

For some reason I shivered and again Brother touched my arm. "I wish I had something to put over you," he said, "a cloak or something…." And then he stopped, laughed his little nervous laugh.

I didn't laugh. I turned my back to the furnace master and pressed the bandage he had given me tight against my eyes. It was an unnecessary cruelty. He had meant nothing by the comment—I am sure of that—and when he had realized what he had said, he had laughed at himself. Yet I turned from him, made it clear how such a notion repelled me. After a moment or two, Victricius started up again, changed the subject, began to tell me about In-Hrypum, what it was like in the monastery at In-Hrypum. You would never have known I had slighted him.

As it turned out I was wrong about the depth of that snowfall. That was no mere drift that stood before our shed: it took two full days for the brothers to get to us, the sounds of their shoveling reaching us first, the strange unnatural clamor of their hellos. Of course my eyesight returned as Brother had predicted it would. Only in recent years has it begun to fail me again so that now I must lean back from this work if I am to see it. Brother made no more mention of his early life that day or any other day for that matter. At least not within my hearing. And of course I never brought it up. I suppose all those stories are lost now except to God.

XXIV

They say that, even when the weather is fair, those who live on the coast can tell a storm is coming if there is a change in the size and intensity of the waves that beat upon their shore. Likewise, even when to all outward appearances our lives seem calm and clear, nightmares may roll suddenly in upon our sleeping selves so that, by day, we find ourselves like anxious watermen looking out to sea. So now was such a time in my life—the dreams fell one upon another as if driven by some awful storm and, pray as I might, God was disinclined to relieve me of them or give me any sign as to their source or purpose. Then, finally, there came a nightmare that seemed by its very nature so preposterous I felt I could relate it to Father Abbot without fear of repercussion. Still, I was no fool. What oblate is? I decided to tell Father Hermit about it first.

Those of you who know of Father Gwynedd only by the stories that have grown up around his name may wonder at this. Is it true then, you ask, what has been suggested, that he was less than strict in his attention to the Rule, that his faith lacked orthodoxy, precision? Even as I have recorded these remembrances, I have found myself asking similar questions, remembering again the apparent ease with which he faced his life, the humor, the fun. But I believe it is wrong to think that way about the man. It was a different time, a different place, Redestone in those days—we forget how recently we had escaped both temple and grove. And Father was one of those who had made that escape possible. Surely we must grant him and his contemporaries the pardon of their times, their age.

Still I must admit—as I record these stories and remember the man

I once knew and as yet so love—that I am beginning to see even at this stage in his life the first subtle signs of the entirely unsubtle change that would eventually come over him and so irrevocably transform our relationship. But of course at the time I was, in the arrogance of youth, blind to such subtleties. Indeed, in my pride, I think I must have thought Father's increasing failure to rise to the challenge of my transgressions, to condemn my failings as once he would have, an entirely appropriate, even long overdue, recognition of the fact that I was growing up, that it was long since past time for the bonds to be loosened, the strictures relaxed, that I was becoming an adult, a man, worthy not only of respect but of a certain latitude, freedom, the room necessary to move and venture out on my own. What indignities I must have heaped upon him in the name of emancipation!

But I stray from my subject. It is the dream I have set out to tell you about, the dream which, with only minor variations, occasionally visits me even now. The most important and initial sensation is always one of confusion, disaffection, the sense that, in some way I cannot understand, *I do not belong here.* Of course this is ridiculous. I mean if anyone belongs to a monastery, it is an oblate. But, in the dream, though I know I *must*, I also know *I do not belong here.* As if to prove this, as if to make it eminently clear, I no longer know my way around. I am in a room which ought to be the abbot's lodge but, instead, wrongly and impossibly, is full of people. Monks I have never seen before scurry back and forth, engaged in some business that makes no sense to me. I assume custody of the eyes and hurry toward a door which should not be there, trying to look busy.

I walk through the door, which, if such a door existed, would lead into the dortoir, and enter instead another room like the first. Here there are fewer monks but they too are busy. Most seem to be carrying something toward the door I have just exited, vague bundles which, in my desire to appear involved, knowledgeable, a part of this ceaseless activity, I ignore. No one says anything, no one smiles or offers a kiss of peace. At the far end of the room there is another door which I no longer expect to lead into the refectory. I cross to it quickly, afraid to hesitate and at the same time afraid to go forward.

I walk through the second door and this time find myself in an empty room. Though I recognize nothing, my mind tells me this is an older abandoned part of the monastery, that trespass here is forbidden, that continuing forward puts me in danger of grave sin. But despite this, I hurry on. I do not know what is going on in the rooms behind me and I'm afraid that if I return to them I will be found out.

Wanting to put as much distance as I can between myself and that possibility, I hurry through the next door and at last find myself in a place I recognize. This is the old stable I think, this must be where, once, they kept the abbey horses. I don't know why I think this because of course there have never been any abbey horses, never could be any abbey horses, but, for some reason, in my dream, I believe there have been, and the idea that I have found their stable, that I have at least heard of this place, comforts me, makes me feel a little less anxious, a little more at home. Also I think it unlikely I will be discovered here. No one would come back here: it is out-of-bounds, off-limits; I am safe here.

With nothing else to do, I begin to explore. The stalls are all open now and empty, a little straw still littering the floor. The place smells faintly of horse. At the far end of the stable, partially concealed behind a stack of old hurdles, there is yet another door. It is heavy and large and for some reason, when I try to open it, it catches at the bottom. By pulling with all my might and stepping it over the place where it catches, I am able to open it just wide enough for my body to squeeze through.

I have come to the end of the monastery. This chamber is so old and uncared-for, parts of the roof have fallen in. Small ineffectual beams of light leak through here and there, illuminating empty space, a dangling bit of spider web, movement. My eyes grow accustomed to the dark and I realize that the greater part of the room is fenced off, creating a single over-sized stall. Within this stall stands the largest horse I have ever seen. Waking I will realize the animal was actually bigger than it is possible for a horse to be, but in my dream I seem blind to this. It is just a very big horse, very big and very beautiful. I am afraid of it and, at the same time, I am attracted to it. Somehow

I know that this is Father Abbot's horse, that I am not supposed to be here, probably not even supposed to know that it exists (Why else should it be hidden away like this?), yet I cannot help myself, I like horses, have always liked horses. My father brought me here on a horse like this, a horse that, I now realize, I was equally afraid of, equally attracted to. I cannot help myself, I reach up, going way up on my toes: I try to pat the horse on its nose.

Faster than I would like, the great head swings down, bristly lips blunder against my hand, scour my palm. The animal has mistaken my intentions, has expected a treat. A blast of hot moist air signals its disgust. I want to say I'm sorry, pat its nose, but before I can do anything, say anything, the head has jerked away from me, risen screaming to the ceiling, eyes wild, mane flying, teeth exposed. I try to placate the beast—one hand up, reaching toward it, the other trying to close the door behind me, afraid lest someone hear. As if it knows I seek to contain it, the animal kicks up its heels, throws its massive body against the side wall. Timbers groan, a rafter breaks free of the roof, splits over the horse's back. Maddened further, the great beast rears, tosses its head, kicks out at the wall. A new crack appears, dust and bits of thatch floating suddenly in the new and sudden light.

And there is nothing I can do—they must hear this! How could anyone not hear this? I want to run, to hide, to be anywhere but here, but there is no way out (behind me the monastery, before the horse), and it's all my fault. He was contained before, hidden, but now I've roused him there's no stopping him. He will break free, will wreck the place, the entire monastery, maybe even kill people, Eanflæd, Father Abbot, maybe even me!

And then of course I wake up, the fear retreating once more, unexpressed, to my heart. The dream, as I have said, returns occasionally even now. Sometimes the horse is a bull, sometimes its stall stands not at the rear of the monastery but in the middle of Chapter (or even, once, scandalously, in the church), but the story is always the same: the interest and the trepidation, the incitement, the resulting horror. I awaken to a sense of my own guilt and the danger I have brought upon the community. And all of it so familiar, so personal, so mine (I have done this before, been guilty of this before)—and, lying there in my bed, hardly daring to look up, look around me, lest someone see, know, what I have done, I remember, as I am remembering now, the first time I dreamt of the horse, the first time I spoke of its existence, told people about the beast that inhabited my dreams, dwelt in the hidden parts of an unknown yet disturbingly familiar place—my abbey, my cloister.

Nose pressed flat against the refectory floor, the ancient smell of meals past welling up from its surface, the silence, the waiting—it was Faults I think, not Chapter. Yes, yes of course it was Faults. How sly we are even when we wish to appear most forthcoming, how clever, how calculating! To bring this night-dream before them as if I knew nothing of its meaning, as if confessing a flaw, expecting rebuke, penance, that the resulting adulation, the resulting praise, might by the comparison seem all the greater, all the more resounding. For Father Hermit had already told me what the dream meant, what the horse represented. That it was a gift, the gift of my youth, my essence, my energy and enthusiasm, which I and not the abbot restrained, which, indeed, for the good of the abbey, I must release. Next time, Father had said, next time (and I now see that, for all his diminished powers, Father knew then, knew even then, that I would have this dream again, that it would recur), next time he told me, you must throw open that door, release the animal: it is beautiful and it is terrifying but it is you and you must release it for your sake and the sake of the abbey. And so I had braved Faults, repeated the story of my dream for Father Abbot (placing particular emphasis upon the beauty of the horse, its strength, its majesty, wanting these qualities to be remembered when all was said and done, when, finally, its true identity had been revealed), and now I lay on the floor, smelling the smells of rancid butter, spilled porridge, picturing Father Abbot's face in my mind, the smile of recognition, enlightenment, that must, even now, be spreading across his face.

"Prior Dagan!" It was not the tone I had expected.

"Father."

"Perhaps the good prior recalls a matter which has been often on our lips of late?"

"I do Father."

"And that this represented a confidence? That Father was privy to it in his capacity as servant only and had no right to it, no right to display or declare it as he might some possession of his own?"

Silence.

"Father?"

"I have told no one."

Empty silence—Faults now fully awake, alert, something new in the air, something different and unexpected.

"Perhaps the boy is merely ill."

Ill? I wasn't ill. What was Father Abbot talking about? Why had he changed the subject?

"A miasma of the air, some foul exhalation of the earth. The child must be prayed over, made to fast, perform mortifications." A hesitation here, Father apparently considering his options, who to oversee this task now that Father Prior, the usual choice, was, however temporarily, out of favor.

A bench creaked and I allowed myself to hope. Surely someone would rise to my defense, point out the real meaning of the dream.

"Does someone wish to comment upon this, this delirium?"

Another sound, the clearing of an old man's throat. "Father?"

All hope exited my chest. There would be no salvation from this quarter.

"Brother Sacristan."

"Could not the boy's dream betoken change, some disturbance in the life of our community?"

Another sound of movement, bodies leaning forward, shifting position, attention, from Brother Baldwin back to Father Abbot. Would such a question—suggesting, as it did, dissension—be allowed? Would Father silence Brother, silence one of the oldest members of the community, one of the few men as yet alive from the time before his time?

A small uncharacteristic laugh. "Surely Brother Sacristan does not mean to imply that his father is wrong."

The uneasy stirring of brothers unaccustomed to dispute and then a sudden and startling whiff of sour breath, the sound of old bones bending beside me.

I was no longer alone.

Brother Baldwin had prostrated himself!

My heart filled with admiration for the man. He might be cruel, he might smell bad and possibly even be bad, but at least he was with me. I was no longer alone. Brother Baldwin had lain down beside me.

"If my question has dishonored Father Abbot, I ask only that my punishment be certain and severe."

Again the sounds of monks shifting in place as brothers turned toward their father, change in the air now, the sense that such a gesture required a similar grace of their lord.

"Yes.... Yes, but as I think further on this I can see how you could believe such a thing. And while brothers should 'not presume stubbornly to defend what seemeth right to them, for it must depend rather on the Abbot's will, so that all obey him in what he considereth best.' Still, when 'weighty matters are to be transacted in the monastery, let the Abbot call together the whole community... that all should be called for counsel.'"

A collective sigh of relief as Faults savored Father's triumph: the perfect reference, the perfect resolution. All was forgiven, the Rule, as it was meant to, having saved us once more.

"But if this is so, if the dream is in some sense valid, possibly even visionary, is not the fact of the buildings, I mean their age, relevant? The boy seemed to think he was in a part of the monastery that was old, didn't he, no longer used, no longer necessary?"

I had not considered this aspect of the dream. Nor had Father Gwynedd so far as I could recall.

"And is not the nature of the horse of some importance? I mean the boy was at some pains to impress upon us the animal's comeliness, its nobility, despite the apparent willfullness of its character."

Now we were getting somewhere.

"Father?"

"Prior Dagan."

"Perhaps you are right. Perhaps this is the best way to view the…. view such a change."

"That it is good?" Brother Baldwin clearly thought otherwise.

"Why not good?" Father Prior pleased with himself now, pleased to find himself once again on the side of his abbot. "If the buildings were old, if there are parts of our life here, structures, methods, that have outlived their usefulness, outlasted their need, what better than to remove them from our path, kick them down, let in the light? If the tree is barren, it must be cast into the sea; the Master Himself teaches this."

"But the boy was frightened. He thought the horse dangerous."

Father had explained all that, that the animal's violence, its potential for violence, was emblematic of something else, my essence or something, my manhood.

"Yes but the boy is just a boy, isn't he?" Father Abbot picking up Father Prior's theme now, the two men once more in accord, master and servant, father and son. "I mean how can we expect a child to understand such a vision. He is just the vessel, isn't he, the messenger, the errand boy? We do not expect the ox to understand the row it plows, the tabula the words they transmit."

But I was the point of it, wasn't I? I was the one who got to kick out the slats, cast Father Prior's tree into the ocean.

"Father?" Shock falling upon shock now, people who never spoke in Faults joining the fray.

"Brother."

"Nothing. Nothing, I didn't mean to speak. Forgive me Father."

"Brother Furnace, if you have something to say, say it. You have my permission."

"Well, it is just that…. The boy thought the horse might harm you. He did! That it might *kill* you."

"Your concern for my person is, as always, dear Victricius, commendable, but really there must be some limit. The boy had a dream. Authority tells us that dreams are communications sent via appetite rather than reason. They are things smelled not tasted, felt not seen, heard not thought. This, this intimation of danger, was at best the garbled utterance of something trying desperately, using the tools at hand, to be understood. I am this boy's father, his priest, his lord. What better way to indicate change, profound change, than to suggest a threat to me?"

Silence, the import of Father's words spreading down the benches like contagion. The pestilence? Some lesser or greater calamity? What else could "profound change" mean?

Another laugh, Father Abbot certainly feeling cheerful this morning. "The buildings were old, weren't they, decrepit? The horse beautiful, grand? Why the gloomy faces? What are you afraid of? Is this what we have come to? Are we so set in our ways that we fear all change, all transformation? Is that wise? Is it monastic? We are called to be different, are we not, renewed, reborn? Does not the bread change, the wine? Are we not asked to do likewise?"

A slight stirring along the benches, monks doubtless looking at one another, trying to reconcile a life of utter routine with that suggested by their father.

"Brothers, we must greet change with open arms. The Rule frees us for this. It is why we became monks, that we might the more readily accept whatever change God sends our way. And change will come. It is the one certainty, the one inevitability. He is Change."

Quiet now, the entire community attentive, wondering.

"So please, please, whatever this dream's meaning, it is safe to assume our Lord has something in store for us. He always does. Let us pray for it. Let us pray that it will come swiftly and that God will grant us the grace to submit to it, whatever form it takes, humbly and in compliance with our vows of obedience and stability."

A sound which, after a moment's consideration, I recognized as that made by monks when, as a body, they cross themselves.

"Good, that is good. And now.... Father Prior? You have something you would like to add Father Prior?"

"My Lord Abbot I.... No. No, thy will be done."

"Yes. Yes, Father reminds us of the approved response. And now it is, I believe, time for the office. Brother Tatwine?"

As I remember it, Father Abbot left us to lie there till they'd all filed out, Tatwine giving the bell his usual methodical best. I remember the swishing of the robes as the monks performed their obeisances, and I remember the air that spilled in over us when the door was opened, Baldwin's bones doubtless aching with the cold, my own thinking of days outside and the coming spring, the smells, the food. I remember too the moment when Father Abbot himself arose, no one left to bow to him, no one left to watch his departure, the sounds almost perfunctory, banal, as, slowly, one foot after another, he crossed the floor, exited the hall, the cold air still pouring in over us, the door left open, signalling his forgiveness, that we too might rise, follow him, join the community at prayer. I'm not sure how much longer we lay there. I suppose I would have let Baldwin take the lead. At any rate, at some point we rose, I remember that, and, feeling rather foolish, bowed to the empty chair, made our own silent and somehow niggardly departure.

That meeting of the chapter would provide a model for those to come, the feeling that some unnatural break had taken place in the relationship between our abbot and his prior, the growing suspicion that our community faced a similar disruption, that something hung over our heads, something terrible, and the certainty that (Father Abbot's arguments to the contrary notwithstanding) change was not always welcome: change could be bad too, threatening, obscure, demeaning. Of course it all seems obvious now, clear. Hindsight is, after all, a wonderful thing. But at the time I couldn't help believing it might all go away, that Father Abbot might have been wrong, Father Hermit right, that Father Abbot might merely have appropriated my dream for his own purposes, ridden my cart to his farm. Of course I know that's not true. I mean I know now, have experienced, what happened next. But at the time this uncertainty produced within me not a little anxiety, even fear. And, to a degree, I suppose it does still. I mean, if Father Abbot's interpretation was right, if my dream merely foretold the coming of Godwin, then why, pray, does it persist? Why do I have it still? Godwin is long dead now, Maban too, but the horse lives on, the horse still visits me, still beats at the walls of my sleep. And every now and then I still wonder, should I open that stall door, should I set it free?

XXV

Those last days before the bad times began seem, in the light of memory, to have a special quality, a different texture, as if at some level the air itself knew what was coming, was readying itself, growing sharper, more focused, prepared. Yet when I think about this difference, when I try to illustrate for my own mind the quality that set those days apart, I find myself recalling an event it is difficult to date or even place in context. The three of us—Waldhere, Ealhmund, and I—are sitting on the ground in Botulf's kitchen, our backs to the oven's south wall, trying to keep warm, repeating our lessons for Father Prior. And now that I think about it, that's interesting, isn't it? I mean the location itself may tell us something. Normally we took our lessons in the refectory, the adults using the dortoir for their scriptorium, but on this occasion both buildings were, I believe, under repair—a new roof, fresh plaster, who knows—but it is the fact of these repairs, the need for our removal to the kitchens, that is suggestive, that makes me wonder if my mind has, for once, proffered a memory that is not just fitting but also pertinent. There were many such repairs that last spring, finishing touches that were, I suppose, meant to please, impress. Not that I was impressed. For me the additional work seemed just another example of the endless folly of grown-ups, another in the long and unbroken line of tasks they seemed pleased to set themselves especially during this, the busiest of seasons.

In my memory, though the sun was out and it was spring, it was one of those days in spring when winter takes a last stab at the season that supplants it, the air unexpectedly cold and clear and tasting slightly of ice. In those days oblates received an oversized set of woolens for the cold months and, as a result, the three of us would have sat that day bundled up before the stove like three young chickens trussed and ready for the fire, our faces alone peeking from beneath our cowls. There is a sort of reverie that comes over you when you are warm like that, the oven warm at your back, the air cold before you. It is as if your mind as well as your flesh withdraws before the cold into its own snug recesses and is justifiably loath to venture out. Not that Father Prior wasn't doing everything in his power to draw our minds from their cozy retreats. He was, as I remember him, a good teacher, knowledgeable in the ways of attracting and holding the attention of boys. Indeed, it seems likely he had placed himself before the drying racks with this in mind, thinking their contents would block any view of the orchard and its distractions. But it happened that, on this particular morning, there was a spot on one of the drying racks that had been left bare. From where I sat, through this gap, I had a view of a cherry tree as it came into bloom.

There was nothing special about the tree as I remember it. It isn't there anymore. I've just looked, hoping to be reminded of that long ago time, the three of us sitting there, young and cold, Father Prior before us, still in his prime, still so much to teach, and instead of the tree there is nothing, the place my memory as yet fills with blossom, empty now, devoid of life. They don't live long, do they, the fruiting trees? But it was there once, and, now that I think about it, its placement was a little out of the ordinary, for it stood at the far end of the orchard all by itself. I wonder, did someone place a seedling there by mistake? Was another row envisioned and then voted down, the earth becoming too rocky that high up, too liable to erosion, acid leaching from the pines? Whatever, a cherry tree once stood at the far end of our orchard and, as a result of this placement and the occasion of a gap in the contents of Brother Botulf's drying racks, I, on a particular day in spring, had a view of it as it came into bloom.

And it was beautiful.

I don't know, maybe it was the novelty of its location, or the novelty of mine, maybe it was just that I was a boy and would have welcomed any distraction, but I remember being astonished by that tree. I looked at it as if I had never seen a cherry tree before, as if the very idea of a tree ornamenting itself with flower, especially on a day as cold as this, was unheard-of, outlandish, mad and impossible. I remember thinking this is the most beautiful tree I have ever seen, and, in the same instant, that it was identical to every other tree I had ever seen. And that this was good. That the fact that this beauty had been there all along and I had failed to see it, had been blind to it, was in point of fact what made this tree special. That I saw its beauty now, knew it now, *recognized* it now. And, however empty that hillside today, I recognize it still. I close my eyes and there (framed by a gap in Brother Botulf's drying racks) it stands, God's idea of a cherry tree, perfect, gem-like, a frail pink flame burning before a pale spring landscape.

Of course one can find many explanations for such a vision, and the strength of the memory it created. I suppose there comes a time in every boy's life when he falls under the spell of his own faculties, his ability to think as swiftly as he does, run as fast, see so well. Images adhere when accompanied by such a glue. And of course there is the all-important fact of my prayer life. Many will have recognized in my description of this tree their own experience with the sort of prayer Father Gwynedd was then teaching me. When going well (and, as if taking formal leave of me, my prayer went very well in those days), such prayer lends itself to visions, can make anything, the grass, the river, the back of one's hand, seem suddenly splendid, miraculous. But, whatever the reason (and doubtless there are many), it is this memory that returns to me when I try to remember those times, those long ago times when things seemed so good, before the bad times began. I see myself sitting there in my little cocoon of warmth, safe and sure, the familiar hectoring figure of Father Prior before me, and I see the cherry tree that bloomed that day at the far end of our orchard, how perfect it was, how perfect and beautiful everything was.

XXVI

Of course, as with so many things in life, I missed the event itself. How many times have I had to explain that I was not present on the day Godwin arrived, that I did not see the horse itself, hear the words that were exchanged, the explanations given? How many times have I watched the light recede from some novice's eye, watched him bow respectfully, only to turn and hurry off after someone else, to seek out some other ancient who might claim to have been there, to have been there on that fateful day? But that is the way of life, isn't it, and of old age? Brother Cedric may protest we are valued only for our memories, for our knowledge of what is dead, past, extinct, but I'm not so sure I mind. I like my memories. I like the respect that accrues to me for possession of them. But I cannot claim to have been here on the day Godwin arrived. I was away on Modra nect with the hermit. And I think I must have been away some time, that Father must have been ill or something (he was often ill in those days), for my memory of the Redestone I encountered upon my return is of a world that, however new it might have seemed to me, had already grown accustomed to itself, the need to explain, to equivocate, long since discarded, worn away.

I don't really remember the walk down the mountain that day, though I have tried to resurrect it often enough. It was, after all, the last of those long lazy walks that I would ever take. But who knows how I actually spent that afternoon, who knows what I dreamt of, how many times I stopped along the way, unknowingly drew out the period of my ignorance, the time in which, for me and me alone, Redestone remained Redestone, unchanged and unchangeable, life proceeding as it always had, as I must have thought it always would. There were favorite stopping points along the way, I remember that, can see them even now though I have not visited them in years. One of these of course was Ælfhelm's shrine, the chestnut grown taller by then, the brush around it denuded by those seeking relics. But there were other springs too, one of which, for a very good prayer I received there when I was younger, I called after the Mother of God, and another, for less holy reasons, after Eanflæd. Probably I stopped at each of these, telling myself I was going to pray, practice the sort of prayer Gwynedd was teaching me, or that I was thirsty, tired, that I needed rest. But the real reason of course was always the same, the need to prolong the journey, prolong my stay on Modra nect, the freedom I felt while I was on Modra nect. I had dawdled like this a hundred times before, doubtless thought I would dawdle so again a hundred times more.

I have often wondered what Maban was doing out there on the bridge that day. Do you suppose he was surveying our holdings, measuring the extent of our demesne, imagining the possibilities? Or is that unfair? He was, after all, a great servant of the office. Everyone says so. When they speak kindly of him, and they do, they speak of the office, what he did for the office, and especially the chant. But still it is odd, don't you think, that he should have been there that day, the interval between None and Vespers, waiting on Wilfrid's bridge like some sort of sentinel, when of course he should have been in the sacristy preparing for the hour, making sure everything was in its proper place, the candles lit, Father Abbot's crozier ready? I don't think I ever saw him on the bridge again, either at that time or any other. And he certainly can't have been set there to watch for me. He was clearly just as startled by my appearance as I was by his.

"Here! You there! What do you think you're doing?!"

It was a monk, a brother, face turning red now as he realized it was just a boy, the shaved area of his tonsure becoming nearly as dark as the surrounding hair. He stepped back out from behind the railing. "Well? Devil got your tongue?"

He had forgotten and, whoever he was, I took pleasure in reminding him: assuming custody of the eyes, smiling to myself.

"Oh for Heaven's sake! You have permission to speak; speak you little idiot!"

Now it was my turn to blush. Brothers did not use such language in those days.

"Forgive me, Father, I am Winwæd, an oblate of this monastery."

"It is 'Brother'," the monk said, though something about the way he said it made me think the mistake had not gone unappreciated. "How come you not to know this?"

I didn't say anything. It seemed a stupid question.

Brother didn't say anything either, eyeballs growing large, jaw tight, skin ruddy, rigid.

"I am sorry Father, Brother, but I do not believe I have seen you before, heard of you before. Your visit here must have begun in my absence."

For some reason the man laughed and there was something about the way he laughed, standing there on our bridge, blocking my way, that made me uneasy. I glanced up at Redestone, wishing someone would come to my assistance.

The man noticed my glance, smiled as if reading my thoughts. "And where have you been," he asked, "that you have remained unaware of me?" He glanced up the way I'd come, became suddenly serious. "You're not a runaway, are you? You're not.... You're not a little oblate apostate?" He chuckled.

"I was with Father Gwynedd. I am servant to Father Gwynedd."

The man didn't say anything.

"The hermit?" I cocked my head back at the mountain, trying not to reveal any surprise at this shocking lack of knowledge. "The holy man who lives on Modra nect?"

Again the man looked up the path behind me. He smiled as if remembering something. "Oh," he said, "that one."

Still I revealed nothing.

The man waited a moment or two, then added, "Another dusty renegade."

"Sir?"

The man smiled, looked away. "A mistake I think, letting a child have such contacts."

"Father's a holy man! Father's…Father's a holy man!"

The man's eyebrows rose as if both surprised and pleased by my response. "Oh, I see. There is a…*relationship*." He made a sort of clicking sound with his mouth, tapping his tongue against the back of his teeth.

"Father Abbot knows I go there. Father Prior knows I go there; he sends me there!"

The man nodded, eyebrows raised inquisitively now, "Oh really… *Father Prior*? I don't believe I know this 'Father Prior'."

All the wind went out of me. The monk was mad, had to be. How could you visit Redestone and not know Father Prior? I smiled, nodding as if agreeing with him about something, all the while studying the ground between us, estimating the distance, trying to remember what stood behind me. Were there any impediments, anything that might block my escape? The trail rose steeply here but I knew it well, and I was younger than he, possibly faster. I told myself I could make it.

And, probably, I could have. Probably, if I'd turned then, turned quickly enough, I could have outrun Maban. But of course I never could have outrun his message. Interestingly, in my memory, he doesn't look at me when he says it. He stands with his face tilted in that way he had, a man scenting something only mildly disagreeable, and, thus placed, relaxed and at ease, beyond the reach of the world, he delivers himself of the end of mine. "No," he said, "no I do not believe there is a 'Father Prior'. There is only a '*Brother* Prior'. And I, of course, am he."

XXVII

ddly enough, as I remember it, it was Ealhmund who told me the story of Godwin's arrival. Normally of course it would have been Waldhere. I mean I would have turned to Waldhere for such information. But for some reason, in this case, I did not. I wonder, had he already begun to change? Was it at this time that Waldhere began to grow cold, aloof, trying, it seemed, to turn himself into a grown-up before his time? For that did happen. I remember that well, the sudden distance, the way he could look down his nose at you (Maban himself) when you suggested a game or some other mischief, something which, only a year before, he would have suggested himself. Though my mind has never made the connection before—Waldhere's change, Redestone's change—it does make sense. And would go a long way toward explaining why I should have turned to Ealhmund of all people for the story of Godwin's arrival. But I can't really know for sure. I want to be fair about this, honest. I mustn't blame everything on Godwin. So I will leave it that, for whatever reason, and entirely out of keeping with past practice, I turned to Ealhmund for enlightenment.

Poor Ealhmund. As Waldhere and I grew up, he seemed to grow in the opposite direction. Not that he wasn't big. No, as a matter of fact, for an oblate, a member of a monastic community, Ealhmund had by this time become embarrassingly large, almost obese. But even as his body swelled, his mind seemed to contract, becoming ever more childlike, ever more infantile. He began to walk in his sleep again for the first time in years and, every now and then, he wet his bed. His powers of concentration had never been good but by this time he couldn't even look at you as he spoke, eyes flitting hither and thither, attention likewise, so that getting a story out of the boy could be a real trial. And of course it was about this same time that Ealhmund came under Brother Prior's watchful eye, and if that didn't distract you, nothing would. But despite these obstacles, Ealhmund did eventually tell me what had happened.

Of course at first all I got was the horse, how big a horse it was and how pretty. From the way Ealhmund's cheeks flushed as he described the animal and the priest on its back you could tell he had been impressed by the vision, though I doubt anyone else was. Father Dagan would have been scandalized and Brother Baldwin doubtless signed something disrespectful. It seems hard to believe that Father Abbot had given his monks no warning, yet Ealhmund remembered none. According to him, the brothers were as surprised that morning as he by the appearance of two men on the abbey path, one mounted, the other walking close behind. There must have been a great to-do. I can imagine Father Prior running around, giving orders for their welcome, Father Abbot hovering in the background, doubtless excited himself, trying not to show it. In the confusion the horse was placed in the care of Brother Ida; who, of course, had not the slightest idea what to do with it and consequently turned it over to one of the villagers. Apparently there was quite a stir the next morning when Father Godwin asked after the animal and—at least at first—no one was certain where it could be found.

In keeping with tradition, the new arrivals were ushered directly into the refectory (probably still set for Chapter at that time of day), where Father Abbot welcomed them according to the Rule, washing first Maban's feet, then Godwin's. But at the end of the ceremony Father turned to the community and, as if everyone present hadn't just heard the newcomer pronounce his name, introduced the priest again, this time adding, as if it were a matter of little consequence, that hereafter Father Godwin would also be known by the name "Lord Abbot of Redestone."

Can you imagine the shock that passed down the hall at that moment? And what a way to spring it on them! Who could have the temerity to protest, to point out the obvious, with their new lord and master sitting right there? Still, our Redestone monks are not without backbone. Questions were asked. And though Ealhmund remembered little of their substance, you can gather their gist from what he did recall, that Father Abbot (Agatho) had gone on "interminably" about bishops, how important bishops were, that they were our true fathers, our true abbots, and that, when you came right down to it, he and Godwin served only at Wilfrid's pleasure, rather more as sub-priors than actual lords. But such a view of things, however subtle, did little to answer the obvious objection. And Father must have known as much. Was not Chapter itself so-called for our daily reading of a section of the Rule? I will not embarrass my brothers by copying down here the whole of a chapter I'm sure they can recite as well or better than I, but (for the sake of those who come after us, that they might know we followed the same Rule as they) will record only its most pertinent (and opening) lines:

> In the election of an Abbot let this always be observed
> as a rule, that he be placed in the position whom the
> whole community with one consent, in the fear of
> God, or even a small part, with sounder judgment,
> shall elect. But let him who is to be elected be chosen
> for the merit of his life and the wisdom of his doctrine,
> though he be the last in the community.

By placing a stranger at our head in lieu of a proper election, Bishop Wilfrid had contravened the commanding instrument of our lives. Holy Rule is unequivocal: only in cases in which a community elects someone "who agreeth to connive in their evil ways" do grounds exist for a bishop to step in and "appoint a worthy" alternative. Allow me to assure those who read this at some future time that this most fundamental of rights was as jealously guarded in our day as I am sure it is in yours.

Still we had all sworn (or had sworn for us) vows of stability and obedience, and I suppose such an appointment, however irregular, might have been accepted with little grumbling had it not been for the fact that Godwin's relationship with Irminberga, Ecgfrith's new wife, was well known. Now in these unsettled times when comets appear to dance around the sun and Saracens march through Andalusia, a brother might be forgiven for forgetting that our day had its own share of disorder and calamity. History alone must judge whether Wilfrid was victim or agent of the difficulties that beset his episcopate, I can only attest to the fact that, under his rule, the Church in Northumbria suffered a series of setbacks and dislocations from which it is only now recovering. Among the most severe of these of course were the hardships accompanying Irminberga's assumption of the title "Queen."

For the sake of those too young to remember, I must point out here that Irminberga was not King Ecgfrith's first wife. That honor belonged to Æthelthryth, a daughter of the king of the East Angles. Now it happened that, before she was given in marriage to Ecgfrith, this Æthelthryth had been married to a prince of the South Gyrwas who died before their marriage could be consummated. So it was that, when her betrothal to Ecgfrith was announced, Æthelthryth, though a widow, remained as yet in possession of her virginity. And did not care to lose it. So she told Ecgfrith, before they married, that under no circumstances, including marriage, would she surrender that which God had gone to such lengths to preserve. But, strangely enough, and despite the fact she was several years his senior, this declaration of Æthelthryth's served only to increase Ecgfrith's ardor. Not only did he marry her in spite of her stated intentions but, as the years passed and she persisted in them, refusing every inducement to enter his bed, the king's desire for her is said to have grown ever stronger. In the midst of his torment, he turned for help to a man from whom he had every reason to expect loyalty and kindness. Bishop Wilfrid owed everything to Ecgfrith and his family. Oswiu, Ecgfrith's father, had declared for Wilfrid and the Roman Easter at Streoneshalh, thereby winning all Northumbria for the Church and, coincidentally, rendering suspect most of the monasteries in the land. Once he had become bishop (thanks again to the Northumbrian royal house), Wilfrid removed all those abbots who refused to swear loyalty to Rome and replaced them with men of his own choosing. For the first time in the history of the land a bishop now held power over not only his own priests but all the country's abbots as well. Wilfrid had become a man of substance. He travelled in great state and maintained a sizeable armed guard. People said he was the second most powerful man in the land and whispered he was the first. And all of this of course, all of this including Redestone and Redestone's steel, had been given Wilfrid by Ecgfrith and his family. The same Ecgfrith who now turned to him for help.

There are of course two ways of looking at the response Wilfrid gave his patron. His supporters claim that, in ignoring Ecgfrith's legitimate claims and encouraging instead Æthelthryth's desire to remain a virgin, Wilfrid showed himself a true follower of Christ, preferring, regardless of consequence, a straight and narrow path over that followed by the world. While his detractors would counter that the counsel he gave Æthelthryth (that she neglect the duty owed her rightful husband) showed Wilfrid willfull to the point of folly, providing his enemies, and the enemies of the true Church, with all they needed to bring him down. But, whichever camp one belongs to, surely no one can argue with the outcome. Æthelthryth showered Wilfrid with gifts of land and treasure, remained a virgin as he counselled, and, ultimately, was permitted to enter a convent; while Wilfrid and the flock he shepherded were thrown into a state of utter confusion and even tyranny. For Ecgfrith, while he may have consented to Æthelthryth's desire to live out her life a virgin, made no similar provision for himself. After she left him, the king took a second wife, this same Irminberga whom I mentioned at the beginning of this account. Now Irminberga, as is the way with women, resented any reminder of her predecessor, even to the point of hating the man who had been the first queen's counselor. So she turned the king against the bishop, filling his ear with tales of Wilfrid's temporal power, the extent of his lands, the size of his buildings, the magnificence of his retinue. There would have been no need to mention Redestone. That Wilfrid held Redestone and Redestone's steel (close by his border with Mercia) must have stuck in the king's craw like a great and pointed stone.

The result of course was inevitable. Wilfrid owned lands the king desired, he had cost Ecgfrith his first wife, and now his second detested the man. The bishop would have to go, his holdings, by default, reverting to the king. And this is of course what eventually happened. But it is important that the full story be told as well. Wilfrid did not give up without a fight. If Irminberga was the cause of his unpopularity with the king then that was the quarter in which he would attack. There was a cousin, wasn't there, one of his priests, a man not known for his wisdom but pliable surely, ambitious, more than willing to be used? Yes, of course, that is the way, I will show preferment to Irminberga's cousin. And what better way to allay the king's concerns than to place him, at least nominally, in charge of the one place Ecgfrith most covets. Yes, yes of course, I will give him Redestone. I will give Irminberga's cousin Godwin Redestone.

And that of course is what he did. And why the hall became so quiet when Father Agatho called upon his monks to swear allegiance to Godwin. You know how it must have been, brothers looking at one another to see who would go first, hoping that seniority would hold precedence here as it did in most situations, and then remembering Baldwin, realizing that in this case things would have to be different. And then Father Dagan of all people, still Father Prior then, surprising everyone by kneeling first, going down on his knees before a perfect stranger to swear vows of loyalty and obedience. How Maban must have enjoyed that, knowing what was to come, that no amount of obsequiousness could supplant him in Godwin's eye. But then Maban never did understand Dagan, couldn't really I suppose. As of course, neither did I. When Ealhmund told me it was Father Prior who was first to kneel, I was embarrassed for him, embarrassed and even a little ashamed. Not that it didn't work. I mean they all followed Dagan's example. If Father Prior accepted Godwin, who could deny him? Still they say Brother Baldwin was the last to submit and, though I cannot pretend to have cared for the man, I do admire him for that. Even today I sometimes picture the event in my mind, the way it would have been, Brother's meaning perfectly clear to an assembly used to communicating only by sign. He would have knelt slowly I think, I mean he always did that in those days, old bones, old joints, but in this case the slowness would have been intentional, Baldwin wanting to draw it out, prolong the act so that everyone could see what he was doing, see how the cords stood out on his neck, see how he held his head, eyes half-closed, face slightly averted, not really looking at Godwin as he spoke, not really looking at anyone, just saying the words, repeating the words, meaning them and not meaning them, swearing allegiance, but swearing allegiance to an idea, a chair, not the man.

According to Ealhmund, Father Agatho left the next day. No ceremony, no special Mass, just a brief farewell before Chapter and he was gone. I wonder what he thought of the horse, what he thought when Godwin gave him the horse, declared it a gift from Bishop Wilfrid in return for loyal service…what sort of struggle do you suppose he went through over that? For he did ride the thing, there can be no denying it. They say he climbed aboard the beast as if it were the most natural thing in the world, as if spreading his legs around a horse's back was something he did every day. But I wonder about that. Father was no fool, and though Victricius later told me things were different in his country, that priests in Father's country often rode out on horseback, Father Agatho had never done so in our presence. Yet he did that morning. Was it perhaps, like so much else in Father's life, intentional, a final message for his monks, a reminder that in this as in all things, like us, he was obliged to obey his bishop? And if that is the case, if Agatho, even in this, thought of his flock, had their interests in mind, what parting advice do you suppose he had for their new shepherd? That must have been an interesting conversation, the two of them sitting alone in the abbot's lodge that last night, the one coming from the cultured world of Roman Gaul, the other from the Northumbrian Church that so wished to ape it. Or did he instead save his breath and advise his successor, as he had Chapter, through example? For the story of what happened to the horse is of course still told. Doubtless Godwin himself heard it more times than he would have liked. For Father did not keep the beast. He travelled only a short distance before giving it away, handing it over to the first beggar he came upon along the road. Godwin must have been outraged, but what could he say? Father had shown himself the perfect monk, obedient to his Lord in heaven as well as the one that sat at In-Hrypum.

For my part, I have often wondered about the beggar. If Father truly hadn't travelled far, he may only have reached my father's land (they say you must pass through it on your way down the mountain). If this is the case, then the man Father gave his horse to could conceivably have belonged to Ceolwulf. He might even have been the one my father told me about, the old man who liked to spend his days sitting at the entrance to his hall. I think Father Agatho would have liked that, would have enjoyed the fact they shared such a bond. He too loved his sons.

It would be unfair of me to tell the beginning of Æthelthryth's story without making some mention of its end—for there have been those who have doubted her word, pointing out that it is rare for a woman twice married to die a virgin.

After leaving the king, Æthelthryth entered a convent and, eventually, became herself an abbess. In this capacity she led a life of exemplary virtue, wearing only the simplest of woolens and rarely eating more than one meal a day. Toward the end of her life she not only predicted a visitation by the pestilence but the names of those, including her own, that would die therein. All came to pass as she had said it would and the woman who had once been queen was buried, like any other nun, in the wooden coffin in which she had died.

Now it happened that, some sixteen years later, a stone sarcophagus having been found, Æthelthryth's successor as abbess decided to exhume the former queen and have her bones placed in this more fitting receptacle. Cynifrid, who had been Æthelthryth's physician in her last illness, happened to be present at the exhumation and, living still, can attest to what he saw. Not only was Æthelthryth's body found to be free of corruption but, to Cynifrid's amazement, a tumor under her jaw which he himself had lanced only moments before her death was discovered to have healed over completely, only a small gray scar showing where his blade had pierced the flesh. By such signs did God exalt his handmaiden and bring low those who had doubted her. Pieces of wood taken from the coffin in which the good abbess was first buried have been found to cure diseases of the eye.

XXVIII

Though at the time it seemed as if I and I alone suffered under Redestone's new rulers, I realize now this could not have been the case. One of the first things Maban did as prior was to institute a daily practice, which meant that, in addition to the work of the fields and the hourly commitment to the office, the community now had to spend an entire interval listening to Brother Prior ridicule its chant. You know what it is like during the intervals, the great and luminous silence that settles over our abbey like a glass. Imagine having that peace broken each day at exactly the time you need it most. The older monks must have felt their one and only pleasure had been taken from them.

As, of course, did I.

I can't really be sure now if it was the first time I saw Abbot Godwin preside over Chapter that he made the announcement or if it only seems that way in retrospect. All I know for sure is that, just as first impressions tend to color all our subsequent knowledge of a person, to this day I associate remembered expressions of Godwin's (the way his lower lip would droop when he finished speaking, the way his eyebrows could sink disarmingly if you questioned one of his ideas) with what my memory tells me was that first and most awful pronouncement. The production of iron at Redestone was to be increased. The production of iron at Redestone was to be increased significantly. Bishop Wilfrid, it was explained (a small smile here, the good abbot encouraging us to become part of a larger and more important world), required more iron of us if he was to negotiate with his friend and companion the king. Three monks would be removed from Brother

Cellarer's jurisdiction and placed at Victricius's disposal. They were to work exclusively in the quarry. The more ore, Father Abbot assured us (already an expert), the more iron. "Oh and something else, there was something else, wasn't there?" Maban bends forward here, Godwin's head turning to catch the whisper, eyes wide open, listening, agreeing. "Yes, yes, that's it, the boy!" A quick glance around the hall and, failing to find anything that looks like a boy, Godwin shakes his finger at Brother Ninian. "No more of these two-day jaunts up the mountain. From now on you will make yourself useful at the yard. Someone else can take care of that ridiculous old man, someone who can make the trip in a single day."

And so, at a stroke, I was separated from all that had seemed to make life bearable at Redestone. I remember wandering out onto the garth that night, gazing out at the village, the little house I believed to be Eanflæd's, and thinking how unfair it all was, how unfair and how unkind. And the worst of it of course was that I would not be able to tell Father myself, that Brother Edgar, a man completely unknown to him, would wander into the hermit's camp in a couple of days and deliver himself of the news that Father would never see me again. That I would never see him again.

For a while I stood like that at the edge of the terrace, my mind's eye picturing Father as he heard the news, the little circle his beard would make around his mouth, the disappointment, the sorrow. It was as if Father's face and the grief it held was, in some way I could not explain, my face, my grief. I stood there and thought about it, recalling other blows, other setbacks, and then slowly the image, if not the sorrow itself, faded from my mind. I found myself staring absently at the river, its moonlit surface, the dark mass of Wilfrid's bridge, thinking about all the times I had watched Ælfhelm cross that way, how angry it was going to make me to see Brother Edgar do likewise. And at the same time realizing, noticing, how appropriate such a thing was. For just as it was Wilfrid's bridge that would make it possible for Edgar to pass over the Meolch dry-shod, so it was Wilfrid's surrogate who had set him on that path in the first place, assigned him this journey that was, by all rights, mine. Just as—the one thought following easily upon the other—Wilfrid had set Godwin in Agatho's place, Maban in Dagan's. You can see where this was leading me. It would have been impossible, I think, for a boy my age to have lived through what I lived through, lost what I had just lost, to go unreminded of that first loss, that primal loss which had brought me here, the father to whom I had made a promise, the father who had warned me of all this, warned me that the bishop could not be trusted, was, indeed, treacherous, warned me and had now (How could I have judged otherwise?) been proven right, justified, almost omniscient. What child would not have harkened back to such things? What child, having remembered them, would not have been tempted?

As if God Himself had taken the bishop's side and sought now to mock any resistance I might offer, it was as I thought these thoughts that a girl appeared at the edge of the village garden, stepped out into the moonlight before the peas, began to dance. Of course it might not have been Eanflæd. At that distance, it could, I suppose, have been any of the younger women who lived that summer in our village. For that matter I sometimes wonder if the memory itself might be wrong. It does seem unlikely that two such events—Godwin's announcement and that clandestine dance—should have taken place on the same day. Life at Redestone is not known for its drama. Yet that is the way I remember it, have, I think, always remembered it. I am standing at the edge of the terrace, probably the interval after Compline, thoughts of betrayal, rebellion, running through my mind, and out of the grasses at the far edge of the village steps a dancer. That a dancer did appear to me one night as I stood on the terrace I do not doubt. I remember the image too well, the garment she wore, the light it gathered to itself as the girl turned and moved beneath the moon. Was she really dancing? Or was this just the elaborate play-acting of some dreamy-eyed adolescent? Looking back on it now, who can claim to know? But for me, as I stood there that night, the gentle breath of the fields rising to me still warm on the cool evening air, there could be no doubt that what I was seeing was a dance, that I was watching the elaboration of some heartfelt and complicated longing. That I was watching Eanflæd. I remember I stood and I watched that figure move soundlessly back and forth, arms thrown out as in prayer, and everything I had ever hoped for or wanted seemed to go out of me. All was vain, futile, lost. My life stretched out before me like a long and dreary road.

It can only have been about a week or two later that I began to pray in earnest for the destruction of Bishop Wilfrid.

XXIX

hose were hard days, dead days. We quit the abbey in darkness each morning and returned again in darkness each night. After only a few days of this it began to feel as if winter had come early that year, the sun already retreated from the sky. Of course I still tried to pray as Father had taught me but even there (as if Godwin's hand reached every sphere of my life) I now found difficulties I had not known before. The months leading up to our new abbot's arrival had been good ones for me, among, I now realize, the best of my life. Since my initial success by the Meolch, prayer had become as natural to me as eating or breathing. I had only to sit and close my eyes to feel the Presence, to know myself unalone. And, as Father had predicted it would, the practice itself had had its effect upon me. Even when I wasn't praying, a part of me, however unconscious, knew myself *attended*, felt and responded to the Spirit that is, of course, with us always. Everything became easier for me. Issues that had troubled or even defeated me, seemed now minor, unimportant. I found myself praying for Ealhmund again, not because I thought I ought to but naturally, fervently, with a devotion that approached true affection. And wherever I went, whatever I did, God seemed to take pleasure in surprising me with His goodness, His comeliness, the grace of His presence.

And then Godwin came, and Father Hermit and Modra nect were taken from me, and it was as if I had fallen into a deep dark pit from which even God's light could not pull me. I went from bed to furnace and back again and the soot and dust of the yard clung to me like the soot and dust of that pit. Morning and night, whenever time allowed,

I tried to pray as Father had taught me and all that passed before my eyes were images of Maban and Godwin and the evil Bishop Wilfrid had done me. I would shake my head, close my eyes, try again, and always, within moments, the anger, the unhappiness, came floating down my river like flotsam after a storm. Where before my prayers had been bothered by thoughts of food or sunlight or Eanflæd, now it was only Wilfrid, Wilfrid and his minions, that cluttered my waters. I could not believe I would never see Father Hermit again and I could not fool myself into believing I would see him again. Desire and reality had become irreconcilable. And when I prayed for help, asked God for a miracle, begged Him to change Godwin's mind, I prayed to an empty hall. God had abandoned me. Everything I had ever known, trusted, or loved had abandoned me.

Everything, that is, except Ceolwulf. For now, as he had not been for many years, my father was with me again. Ceolwulf and the promise I had made him rose up within me, rose up to fill and conquer the space left vacant by Agatho, Gwynedd, Dagan, God. I stood at the bellows and watched Victricius, the petty anger he gave in to so easily now, and I thought of Ceolwulf, his strength, the strength I had of him by birth, and I despised the furnace master, despised him for his weakness, his failure to run away, chase after Agatho if that was what he wanted, his failure to confront Godwin, confront his enemy, rout him as Ceolwulf would, as my father would. I knelt in church and stole glances at Dagan, still near the front but oh so reduced in stature, the little man down on his hands and knees before his own usurper, before the men who had stolen his title, his rights, our church; and I despised him, despised him for his acquiescence, his easy capitulation to treachery, and again I thought of Ceolwulf, his strength, his anger, and the secret I held deep within me grew warm and full, warming me like a bowl of warm soup on a cold day. And, finally, I sat in Chapter and watched as one monk after another scraped and bowed before Maban's little puppet, and I swore I would never submit, that, bow as I might, it would mean nothing, that the outward signs of obedience I gave would be like Godwin's signs of piety, a hide, a camouflage for true intent. Let Wilfrid's servant beware, a son of Ceolwulf stood in his hall.

One wonders how many such homunculi our cloister nurtured in those days. Pride begs me believe there would have been several but, many or few, I have only myself to answer for. Looking back on it now, and considering the state of my soul at the time, it can only have been thanks to the force of Father Gwynedd's warnings that it took as long as it did for me to act.

It was a day like any other as I remember it, late afternoon, warm, overcast, Vespers still a little way off. Probably everyone else was asleep, or in church, as it was the Sabbath. I remember that well, the fact that I had picked the Sabbath, my sense of the occasion demanding a little drama, the opportunity for withdrawal afforded by a day of rest, the holy day, the day set aside for communion. Though a part of me doubted anything would happen, doubted all prayer now, I had taken no chances. Father Beorhtfrith had heard my confession and, except for the Host, I had received no food since the night before. It was easy to slip away. If anyone had seen me entering the furnace path they would have thought nothing of it—I was, after all, Victricius's boy— but no one saw me. The garth was empty, the church door closed.

I will admit to having been a little uneasy when I got to the spot itself. Despite all my unhappiness, the place still held meaning for me. I could not look at it, or the slabs of rock along the opposite bank, without remembering what I had experienced there, the certainty I had felt. I glanced back down the way I had come, fearful lest anyone should have followed me, and a sudden chill ran down my back, made my flesh crawl. But there was no one there; I had not been followed. And I told myself I was a fool if I thought this place was different from any other. It was just a rather uninteresting bend in the path I walked every day to and from my work at the yard. The hill people thought the rocks on the far bank were part of the skeleton of a great giant, but everyone knew the hill people were nothing more than superstitious fools.

I sat down. Though I had not intended to, the place evoked such a strong desire in me to pray as Father Hermit prayed that, almost despite myself, I closed my eyes, crossed myself, tried to become calm, tried to replace the river that flowed before me with the one I hoped as yet flowed through me. For a moment, a certain expectancy came over me. Could it really work? Was the power of this place, its associations, so strong that God would visit me again, come to me as once He had, come to me as I so needed Him to now, to hold and comfort me, to set my worries aside, hold them at bay, protect and love me as only He could?

But of course there was nothing. Within moments the urgency of my need, coupled with the clamoring of the problems that occasioned it, swept down my river in wave upon wave of self-pity and disgust. Maban looked down his nose at me, called me a "little idiot," and Father Abbot and the entire chapter laughed and laughed, pointing at the little fool where he sat upon his river bank, eyes squeezed shut, trying desperately to keep out the light, ignore the obvious, his impotence, his lack of cunning, the utter absurdity of his plight.

When I opened my eyes I almost laughed. To think that I had expected it to work! Such prayers were a delusion, a delusion created by the needs of men like Father Dagan, Father Gwynedd, men obsequious and retiring, men incapable of action, of *doing* anything. I was no such man. I was Winwæd, son of Ceolwulf. The river I was named for, the river that ran through me, rolled over its enemies, rolled over its enemies and sucked them in, pulled them down. I closed my eyes, thought about the wrath of God, thought about its dwelling place high up on the mountain, the great lake of wrath glowing with heat, seething, and I thought about the wall that holds it there, the flimsy barrier erected by God Himself to keep us safe, safe from His fury, the legitimate fury that caused the bush to burn, blinded the Aramaeans, struck the pagans deaf and dumb. And I pulled it free. With my prayer I reached up, took hold of that flimsiest of barriers and, with all my might, I pulled it free, the barrier coming apart in my hands as easily as an old and derelict wall, God's wrath spilling out, pouring down the mountain in a white-hot flow, like the flow that sometimes poured from Victricius's furnace, like iron, like steel. And the molten steel of God's wrath poured down the valley and through my gate and, like a great and burning sword, it pierced Wilfrid's bridge, pierced his bridge and everything—bridge, boards, stones, bishop—burst into flame, burst into flame and as quickly burned away, burned away like grass cast into a hot and fiery oven.

When, finally, I opened my eyes again, it was with an obscure sense of relief that I saw that everything was as it had been. Nothing had burned away; the river ran as quietly as before, the trees still bending toward it, the rocks on its far side still dipping their lower parts in its shallows, still blushing at its touch. I stood up, feeling a little ashamed of myself, embarrassed by the strength of what I had felt. Lightning had not flashed, thunder did not sound. The sky remained intact, however overcast, the afternoon warm. And doubtless this was how it would always be. I would continue to pray for Wilfrid's downfall as my father had directed, but nothing would come of it. I would live out my life at Redestone in compliance with the Rule and the vows made for me, and probably nothing would come of that either. I might as well get used to the idea.

XXX

he world looks upon us as celibates, doesn't it? When someone from beyond the wall thinks of a monk (and I don't fool
myself that they do this often), they think first I believe of
chastity, and then, most likely, of poverty, thinking, as all men do, of
those things they hold most dear, those they cannot imagine giving
up, would least like to lose. But we know better, don't we? Chastity
and poverty are important of course, but what makes a monk a monk,
and—more important—a monastery a monastery, are the vows we
take of obedience and stability. Sins of the flesh, sins of avarice, these
can be easily forgiven, but what can be hoped for from a monastery where open rebellion rules, or, worse, apostasy unrules? Without monasticism's two great pillars, obedience and stability, the entire
edifice comes tumbling down.

Of course all of this is obvious, a recitation of truisms self-evi-
dent to any that could ever possibly read this work. Yet sometimes it
is necessary to remind ourselves of such things. For someday some
brother, wishing to think himself charitable, may try to make a case
for leniency, may argue that, however rebellious my prayer, it was at
least a prayer, that, disobedient as I was, the form of rebellion I chose
was at least a monastic one. From such reasoning it is but a small step
to turn the child I was into a sort of example for today's youth, the
oblate who, as wicked as his disobedience was, didn't compound his
sin by adding to it apostasy, didn't, in other words, at the first provo-
cation, think of climbing a wall. I too of course would like to think of
myself in this way, have, I suppose, up until now, always done just that.
But writing out this confession (as doubtless Father Abbot intended)

serves as a corrective to pride. For remembering is like a contagion, it spreads, memory giving birth to memory, until what had seemed an isolated recollection, unconnected to anything either before or after it, has become the mother of an entire season of memories. And such a brood of memories cannot help but produce the occasional monster.

Of course the thing has surfaced before. But in the past I have always been able to tell myself it was nothing but a dream, that I am remembering not an actual event but something I once imagined or experienced only in sleep. And in this I have been helped by the fact that the recollection itself rises from my memory very much like the memory of a dream, vague and insubstantial, its particulars changing, shifting, even as they are recalled. Yet there are some things I remember well, what Stuf said, what I said, how it felt to hear such things said. Yet even now I find it difficult to let go of the notion (certainly the hope) that it was only a dream. And it may have been, it could have been. Think about dreams, the sort of people you encounter, the sort of places you go. Things arc always *like* but not quite the *same as* what they seem, so that, when you awaken, your memories of what transpired as you slept are forever evolving, the mountain turning into a hill, Father Dagan into Brother Baldwin, the horse into a cow. And so it is with this memory, for while my waking mind tries to place it, like the memory that gave birth to it, on the upper Meolch where I used to pray, as in a dream remembered the landscape keeps sliding away from me, the river rising, myself falling, so that finally I must admit the obvious: I wasn't looking *down* at the water but *out* at the water, the upper Meolch is the lower.... And I realize that nothing is as it seems, that, however improbable, I must have been sitting down below the terrace, somewhere down among the trees that border our fields.

But just as I get my location fixed, time itself slips away. For though, as I recall it, the encounter took place in the afternoon, late afternoon, the clouds over Modra nect already touched by a westering sun, you must also remember that he found me sitting down, that Stuf came upon me *sitting* by the river, out where anyone might have seen me. You will explain away such idleness by making the day

a Sabbath, saying that, as on the previous occasion, I have recalled a
Sabbath memory. But once again we run up against the strangeness
of this recollection, for another part of my memory, another part of
its dreamlike character, is the sound I remember floating in and out
of that glade, rising upon the breeze and, as quickly, dissipating. It
was practice, one of Maban's daily practices, and so of course it could
not have been the Sabbath. Even under Godwin, God's day of rest
remained sacrosanct.

So, for some reason I cannot fathom, on a day in summer (it is
warm), I find myself sitting in the shade of the trees by our river.
Which, of course, would have made its own contribution to the
dreamlike quality of this memory. For you know how it is down there,
shadows the color of water, stones still warm to the touch, the air
humid yet fresh, smelling distantly of rapids; here and there the sun
breaks through, touches one last rock, a green swell of water, causes
the rotting husk of a tree on the opposite bank to glow amid the
shadows like something special, something almost remembered, just
beyond the reach of memory. And then of course there would have
been the surprise of seeing Stuf in such a setting, of seeing the black
and sooty figure of our charcoaler step into the quiet of that place like
(as of course he was) a spirit from another world. He had beetle shells
in his hair, I remember that. Somewhere he had found the carcasses
of a strange and heretofore unheard-of forest beetle and, apparently
liking their hue, had woven them like so many brightly colored beads
into his dark and greasy hair.

Had I been praying? Had I been sitting there in that strange half-
light cavalierly invoking the wrath of God? I don't know. Though it
would go a long way toward explaining the sense of surprise I recall,
the sense of being caught out, exposed, that I felt when I looked up
and saw him, saw our charcoaler rear up before me like a wild animal,
his face turned suddenly tawny in a stray shaft of light, leaf shadow
playing over it like spots, like the marks of some darker, even more
savage beast. But the surprise must not have lasted, or, lasting, must
immediately have been joined by another, even stronger sensation, for
I also remember the sudden excitement, the thrill I felt upon seeing

Stuf, as if his physical presence in and of itself conveyed the idea, placed it warm and glowing in my mind, as if, at some level, I already knew, even then, what was going to happen, what I would do.

I must have glanced out at the fields, checked to make sure no one could see us, for I have a memory of Stuf mocking me, spinning around as if trying to catch someone hiding behind him. I asked after the man then, demanded to know how he came to be there, what he thought he was doing down on that side of the terrace. But if I had hoped to put him in his place with these questions, remind him of the path I followed, the community I belonged to, I must have been disappointed for I remember no response. It would have been like Stuf to have said nothing, to have giggled maybe, looked at me as if a close study of *my* features might reveal an explanation, some clue, some reason, for the existence of something as silly and outrageous as Stuf the charcoal-maker. Surely such behavior would have caused me to question what I was feeling, where my thoughts were leading me, but all I remember doing is going on, changing direction, asking about the one subject I knew would catch and hold Stuf's attention.

"How goes it with the charcoal? Did you get your board?"

You would have thought I had asked after the man's dying mother. Stuf drew himself up tall, his expression immediately sober, sincere. "I make good charcoal," he said.

I assured Stuf I had never doubted it.

He nodded, paused. "But his excellency wants more."

"Abbot Godwin?"

Again Stuf nodded, apparently reluctant to use any names. "And the little one, the one with the nose."

"Brother Prior?"

"Just so." Stuf's face was long now, sorrowful, the face of a saint.

"But what will you do?" I asked, trying to sound neutral, calm, the way opening up before me like a road, like something God had placed there, a gift, a challenge, something He *wanted* me to do.

Stuf looked up at Modra nect, shook his head. "The little father says he will send his own monks into the mountain, build his own clamps, make his own charcoal."

"Would he still also use your charcoal?"

Stuf could not look at me, held his hands out to indicate the hope-lessness of his position. Of course it was like a hill person to milk a problem for all it was worth, but I knew Stuf had a legitimate cause for concern. Indeed, I was depending on it.

"But what if you had help?"

The man looked at me as if I'd said something in a foreign tongue.

"Help? Someone to assist you, help you make charcoal?"

Stuf blinked, frowned, the exertion required to grasp such a con-cept apparently taking its toll. "I had someone once," he said, pausing as if to remember, "but she went away."

A tide of anger and confusion swept over me.

Stuf just stood there. When he realized I wasn't going to say any-thing more, he leaned in close, his expression almost ludicrously con-cerned, a man studying a plow that has ceased to plow, a scythe that has lost its edge.

I leaned back and away from him, the stench of meat on his breath returning me to myself. "Well," I said, trying to sound calm, relaxed, unperturbed. "Was she, was it nice having someone up there with you? I mean didn't it help, didn't it help to have a, couldn't you accom-plish more with…. I mean wouldn't you agree, based upon your expe-rience, it would be nice to have someone up there with you, someone to help you make charcoal?" I could feel myself blush.

Stuf's eyes lit up with a sudden understanding. "Oh," he said. "Oh yes," nodding now, a monk conferring with another on a fine point of the Rule, "Well it *was* nice now, wasn't it? She wasn't afraid of work, that one, could walk a clamp like a man." He smiled. "And of course I never got lonely."

Images of Eanflæd, terrible images, images of shame and degradation.

The charcoal-maker laughed.

I gave him a look and immediately regretted it, the man cringing like a dog. I took a deep breath, told myself not to be taken in by this easy contrition, that hill people were like that, changeable, their senti-ments, like their allegiances, as fleeting as cloud shadow. "So," I began again, congratulating myself on how grown-up I had become, "it.... *she* was a big help. And therefore we can safely assume it would be helpful to have someone up there with you again, preferably someone who knew a little something about charcoal, had worked with it before. Yes?"

As if to confirm my opinion of him, all signs of remorse vanished from Stuf's face. He looked at me as if surprised by what I had said, as if it were only now dawning on him what we were talking about, that someone might be made to come up on the mountain and help him, that with such help he might produce more charcoal. Then he looked up toward Modra nect and, in apparent response to this suggestion, said, "Yes, a bad day." He shook his head thoughtfully. "I have been thinking this. The old one has had a bad day."

Of course I could have gotten angry. Victricius would have. The furnace master would have ranted and raved if Stuf had said something like that to him. He hated it when Stuf spoke to things as though they were alive, addressed the river as if he might reasonably expect a reply. But I was different. Or at least I was now. I had acquired a new attitude toward the charcoal-maker. From now on I was going to accept him as he was, respect (if not honor) his beliefs, indulge (if not engage in) his ways. Who knew what might be accomplished thereby? This might be the very thing God had in mind for me. A vision of myself as one of the great missionary monks rose up before me and I almost missed what Stuf said next.

"I'm sorry?"

Stuf looked at me. He looked back up at the mountain. "*I said* do you see those clouds? The way they're gathering?"

A scattering of clouds hung in the sky over Modra nect, small wispy things, dirty blue with just a touch of pink around the edges. Once, years before, when collecting water, I had seen where someone had broken a jar as they lifted it from the river. It was in one of the shallow places and the pieces had sunk together, their arrangement on the rocky bottom still suggesting the shape of a pot.

"It's like a broken pot," I said.

Stuf snorted, though you could tell he was pleased to have my attention. "More like a broken head," he said. "Those are his brains."

I didn't say anything, just looked at the man, wanting to get back to the subject of charcoal, how, with help, he might make more charcoal.

"Allfather did that," Stuf said, nodding to himself, eyes on the distant clouds. "He killed First One, then hung his brainpan up there for all to see. The roof of the world is the roof of the ice giant's skull." Stuf smiled, the image apparently pleasing to him.

I looked up at the pale dome of the sky. "A giant," I said, wondering if now maybe we could get back to the subject at hand.

Stuf turned on me. "You've seen brains before, haven't you? I mean I know they won't let you eat properly, but you've seen brains before haven't you, the way they look when they first come out? I mean they've let you watch when they butcher a pig, haven't they? Down at the village?"

I shook my head, the memory of Stuf's breath for some reason taking another stab at my senses.

"Oh they're beautiful when they're fresh, all pink and lumpy. But when they've drained, after they've set for a while?"

I tried not to think about it.

Stuf smiled. "Just like that." He indicated the clouds with a thrust of his chin. "And see how quiet they look now that the sun's going down. You know how storms happen in the heat of the day? I mean most storms, that's when most storms happen. Because of the sun? He doesn't like the sun. It bothers him, disturbs his sleep. First One's brains churn when they get hot, trying to remember what they're about, why it is they're so angry. If it weren't for the cool of the night, well, who knows?" Stuf stopped for a moment, straightened as if he'd seen a monk. I looked around but there was no one. When I looked back I was surprised to see that he had closed his eyes, cocked his head to the side like a man trying to remember something difficult. When the singing began it was almost as if it were someone other than Stuf singing, the voice high and quavering, bird-like. "But night comes," sang Stuf's mouth, "day fades, First One sleeps. He dreams…lunacy, nightmare, creeping death." The charcoal-maker's eyes popped open. He looked around, found me, smiled as if he'd done something funny. "Of course he *will* wake up again, someday. He must." Stuf shook his head, chuckled to himself. "And when that happens…well, when that happens, that will be the end."

A light sound, a sound scarcely recognizable as a sound, something just above the sound of the water, the whisper of the breeze, floated in upon us and, as quickly, disappeared. Stuf glanced up toward the abbey, no more disturbed by this reminder of holy office than he would have been by the chatter of a squirrel or the roll of distant thunder. I shuddered, thinking of what I was about to do, how, at one and the same time, it seemed both inconceivable and unavoidable.

"But what if you had help making the charcoal?" I asked again. "What if, well, what if I came up there to help you? What if you had me?"

Stuf looked at me and for the first time in my life I saw him as he really was, an older man, perhaps as many as thirty winters behind him, all the days he had lived through, all the afflictions, and in that instant I knew, knew as clearly as I knew his name, that Stuf was no fool, that, for all his childish antics, he would no more take me under his wing, risk the wrath of those he did business with, than he would knowingly build his clamp on bad ground, light it before a rain. Heathen or not, I was the child and he the adult, I the novice, he the solemnly-professed monk.

"The reason I came down here," he said, "was to find you."

A flicker of hope—the idea that he did want me, that this statement signalled deliverance—flared within me and was, as quickly, extinguished. "The hermit sent me," said Stuf, his voice calm, unhurried, an older man sharing a casual moment with a child. "I have a message for you."

I looked away, embarrassed. "Yes?"

"He asks," said Stuf, "that you pray for him."

XXXI

L ooking back on it now I sometimes wonder if the failure of the wheat didn't have something to do with it. It was bad enough that there was discontent, that the community had not failed to notice that its abbot did not eat with them, would not join with them in the work of the fields. But to have an oblate remain fat and oily despite their admonitions to the contrary must have seemed, in the face of impending famine, an affront to their authority that neither Maban nor Godwin could safely ignore. If one such nonentity could so blatantly flout convention, what might not the rest of the community contemplate?

And how easy it was, under such conditions, to direct attention away from their failing and onto Ealhmund. When everyone was hungry and grumbling about their hunger, how satisfying it must have been for Brother Prior to point out the fat boy at the end of the row, the one who, despite an otherwise universal shriveling, still managed to find enough to maintain his own bulk, in the process insinuating that, in keeping with the logic of want, it might be Ealhmund alone who, in his secret raids upon the larder, deprived the rest of us of our rightful share, and that therefore, both literally and figuratively, we all suffered for Ealhmund's sins.

Of course what this really meant was that Ealhmund suffered. He was made to beg for his food, crawling on his knees from table to table, his bowl held out before him, forbidden to speak, to sign, to do anything other than look up at us with those large uncomprehending eyes of his, those eyes that seemed to ask to be beaten even as they begged to be fed. I remember him lying on the floor before Faults.

He had never been allowed in Faults before, but Maban allowed him in for that. He was too fat to lie comfortably on the floor and, after a while, his belly would make strange noises. Maban used to laugh when that happened, ask, as if genuinely concerned, if Ealhmund were hungry, if there were anything he could get him, some honey-cakes perhaps? When this, as I suppose it was meant to, elicited still more sounds from the poor boy's abdomen, Maban would poke him with his shoe. Not hard. Never once did I see Maban actually kick Ealhmund. But he would poke him with the point of his shoe as one might poke a recalcitrant dog.

I would like to say that my fellow oblate drew comfort from his suffering, grew wise, accepting, detached. We are taught that, aren't we, that in suffering we become Christ-like, that through suffering we have the opportunity to redeem, if not the world, at least our selves? But what if suffering is just suffering? What if the one who suffers finds neither nobility nor reason in his pain? What if there is only confusion, hurt, loss? We do not expect a horse to learn from its suffering, a cow. Why then a boy like Ealhmund?

He began to prey upon his former master. Not viciously or vindictively but childishly, lashing out at him as a child lashes out at its playmate without thought or cause, knowing only that it wants something and hasn't got it. Of course there were those who said Botulf had only himself to blame. Botulf had been the first after all, in his capacity as Brother Kitchens, to encourage Ealhmund's gluttony, pouring treats down the boy as one pours scraps down a pig to ready it for slaughter. For some time before the arrival of Godwin this had been a minor, if constant, concern. Ealhmund had been whipped for his sin and Botulf required to explain himself before Faults. And the kitchen master had promised to mend his ways. But of course he hadn't. He seemed incapable of changing. Brother Botulf was in those days like a wren with a cuckoo's chick in its nest: standing on the foundling's massive head, cramming still more food down its throat, ignoring any appeal to common sense.

But, with the advent of Godwin, all this changed. There were no second chances under his leadership. Maban was not a man to tolerate backsliding. Brother Botulf and his servant Ealhmund were summarily removed from their posts and sent to work in the fields under Brother Cellarer. The quality of the food served in refectory declined markedly and, to the surprise of everyone, Ealhmund remained obstinately fat. Indeed, if anything, he grew larger still, his chest and shoulders swelling out under Brother Osric's regime to almost equal the size of his belly.

Of course, as there always is in a monastery sworn to silence, there was talk. Everyone had their theories as to how such a thing had come to pass. Some said a devil dwelt within the boy, others that it was a tumor and that soon it must burst. The only thing everyone agreed upon, Maban's accusations notwithstanding, was that, if it was pilfering that sustained Ealhmund's girth, he must have an accomplice, that no boy wearing such a look on his face could be capable of out-and-out thievery.

Then came the first of the attacks on Brother Botulf.

Oddly enough I vaguely recall having witnessed this attack. Or at least one of them. Of course I distrust the memory. I spent most of my days at the yard then, which makes it far more likely I only heard tell of the incident. Still I do remember something, one of those high clear perfect days in late autumn when the sky is so blue it hurts your eyes to look upon it. The day wasn't hot—I'm fairly sure of that—but it was dry, had, I believe, been dry for some time, for even now I can see the quiet bursts of dust that rose from Ealhmund's feet as he made his way across to Botulf's row, the pinkish haze that rose into the air behind him vaguely tinting, staining, a lower portion of that otherwise faultless sky. No one said anything. It had become a commonplace, the boy seeking out his former patron, the low mumbling that issued from that corner of the field accepted and consented to as though in corporate protest against the new regime. And then, as if our sins truly did cry out against us, a sudden cry from that part of the peas, Ealhmund's voice continuing out the other side, louder now, insistent, demanding, the two men starting up, Ealhmund towering over the man who had been his master, apparently doing something behind the screen of plants that has made Botulf bend like that, an expression of utter terror on the older man's face, eyes wide, beseeching, looking up at his former protégé as if at a stranger, as if he has found himself suddenly and irrevocably in the hands of an unknown and entirely hostile stranger.

I remember nothing more after that, the sudden cry, the two men locked in their strange embrace, the one looking down, the other up, and then nothing, my memory washed as clean and featureless as polished stone. Doubtless someone separated them. Doubtless someone else (Was it you Waldhere?) reported the incident to Faults. Doubtless there were punishments. There were always punishments. But they must have done little good for the one thing I am sure of, remember well, is that, from that time forward, Botulf lived in fear of his former charge. Whenever the two met, the smaller man would cringe and turn away, nature turned upside down, youth taking precedence over age, master bowing down before slave.

As it happened, an equally intense and only mildly less violent change took place in my relationship with Ealhmund. The boy had always liked me. Or at least since the days when I had begun to pray for him, he had liked me. But now, as if to counterbalance the disrespect he showed Botulf, Ealhmund's fondness for me grew out of all proportion to a proper fraternal regard. I never knew when his great moon face would rise up before me, looming over the partition in the reredorter, smiling down at me during Mass. Once, right in the middle of the garth, he hugged me from behind so tightly it took my breath away. I remember standing there, half bent over, little whooping sounds issuing from my chest, the cloister suddenly alive with gesticulating and wide-eyed monks, and Ealhmund just standing there, beaming down at me, the big shiny cheeks, that strange oily smell, utterly blind to the pain he has caused, the embarrassment, apparently waiting only for me to recover that he might the sooner hug me again.

And then there came that morning in the dortoir. Perhaps I would have reacted differently, perhaps I would have done something to save the boy, had it not been for the fact that this was not the first such morning. I had, on at least two previous occasions, been wrung from a deep sleep by just such a presentiment, just such a notion that something was wrong, perhaps terribly wrong. Each time I had been at first shocked and then infuriated to discover that it was only Ealhmund, that Ealhmund stood by my bed like some mad and overgrown child, grinning down at me, smelling of bedclothes. Which explains, I pray, why, on that particular morning, I did nothing, why I was able to convince myself that this was only one of those waking dreams, real mixing easily with unreal, that if I opened my eyes again I would find the boy stood not before the fire as it had seemed but by my bed as he had before, the same idiot grin on his face, the same confused excuses springing to his lips. It made me angry, even half asleep, and I held my eyes shut tight, refused to open them. Why should I wake up just because Ealhmund was lonely?

"Father!" It was Brother Baldwin calling out to someone.

"Father!" And it wasn't Brother Baldwin but Brother Egric, and he really was calling to someone. I blinked and the scene didn't change. I blinked again and Ealhmund still stood by the fire, still desperately tried to stop himself, to pull himself in. I looked away and the vision remained consistent, brothers coming awake, startled, looking at each other, looking toward the fire, Maban demanding, aloud, that Father Abbot be sent for, Brother Alhred hurrying on unsteady feet (as he did every morning, as he would, I was sure, on Judgment Day) toward the reredorter, and over all of this the other thing, that awful thing, scent of madness, scent of nightmare. Which meant I wasn't dreaming. Which meant that right now, right there—I couldn't help myself, I looked again—Ealhmund stood urinating into the fire.

Of course he was excommunicated. Completely. Godwin didn't even wait for Chapter. Clothes were brought, a sack filled with yesterday's bread, and Ealhmund given till first light to be off abbey lands. Father Dagan protested but it did little good. The incidents had been going on too long now—the assaults on Botulf, the strange laughing from the back of church—and of course, by that time, many had come round to Maban's way of thinking. They had seen what Ealhmund could do to a grown-up, had themselves grown wary of him, stepped aside when he approached on the garth, avoided his kiss of peace. Doubtless some even thought the hunger itself might be alleviated by the departure of one such as this. But still it was sad when it happened. You should have seen the look on Ealhmund's face when they set him before the gate, gave him that last little shove. You could tell he didn't know what was going on. I think he thought someone was having a sort of joke with him.

Within a week Brother Thruidred had reported seeing Ealhmund at the kitchen gate. Soon such reports were a regular feature at Faults and Maban began talking about posting a guard. Before they could run him off for good, I decided I would like to see the boy again myself one last time. You may wonder at this. You may ask yourself why I would risk such a thing, seek out an excommunicate, a being any proper monastic should shun. A good question, but a question asked, I think, by one whose life has been different from my own. Those of you who came of age prior to your entry into the monastery cannot imagine what it is like for one oblate to see another shown the door.

As it happened it wasn't that hard to find Ealhmund. I came across the first print almost immediately after stepping through the kitchen gate. Thanks to the wet winter we'd been having the ground was muddy and the print clear and expressive. I could tell at a glance that Ealhmund had lost weight. Yet he still walked like a fat man: short little steps, toes out, heels in, most of what weight he retained carried on the rear and outer edges of his feet. It was funny, when you thought about it, and sad too in a way. Ealhmund even walked wrong.

Whatever he'd been doing up by the kitchens, the boy hadn't lingered there, hurrying—I supposed at first light—from pollard to pollard down along the edge of the abbey path till he reached level ground. There he had abandoned the trees and climbed down into the ditch, walking for a little distance along its muddy banks. At about the point where the millet ends and the peas begin, he had hidden himself among the grasses that in those days grew along the ditch's far side. I wondered what he had done there. Had he sat and watched as we marched, sleepily, woolens pink with sunrise, from church to Chapter? Had he listened to the sounds of our washing up, smelled the last of the day's incense as it floated off to who knew where? I couldn't tell. There was only the flat place in the grass where his bottom had rested and the two sharper depressions in the mud behind it, Ealhmund having leaned back for a while, braced himself upon his elbows.

Whatever daydreams had occupied him there, the boy had grown tired of them, for he had gotten up once more and, this time, wandered out into the orchard. There the print became more difficult to follow. Again and again I had to stop to make sure that I followed the right track and not one of the many, also left by Ealhmund (yesterday, the day before?), that crossed and re-crossed this morning's path at odd angles. Anyone who has ever worked a trail as confused with print as this will know how strangely captivating the experience can be, forcing one, as it does, to concentrate all his attention on a narrow strip of ground to the exclusion of all else. When, finally, you straighten up again, give your eyes a rest, it is as if an immense obscuring wall has dropped away and the world appears suddenly overlarge and wide. Sometimes it is as if you saw with Adam's eyes. You think: *This is real. He made this.* And then, even as you reach out to hold the vision close, grasp it to your breast, familiarity's shabby net settles over Creation and everything becomes as it was, the ground just ground again, the trees trees, mountain mountain, and you find yourself wondering what you were so excited about. How could this old place—even for a moment—have seemed so grand?

It was, I believe, at such a point, as I cast about for something to distract me from the bleakness of our winter orchard, that I noticed what had, of course, been around me all along. Footprints. Ealhmund's footprints. Not just the ones I'd been following for the better part of an interval but the others, the ones I had been working so hard to ignore. They were everywhere. The muddy ground was so littered with Ealhmund's sign, both old and new, that to the untrained eye it might have seemed an entire herd of Ealhmunds had wandered here.

But why? It didn't make any sense. Why would he want to spend so much time in our orchard? I mean it wasn't as if there was anything to be found. The trees had been picked bare long ago and what fruit remained on the ground had long since ceased to be edible.

I walked through the orchard. With a growing sense of wonder, the feeling that I was in the presence of something exceedingly strange, I made my way across that vast sea of print. I no longer stopped to study the ground; I no longer needed to. As soon as I'd straightened up it had become obvious where Ealhmund's track was heading. The center of the orchard. The very oldest part. His trail led right into it, came to a stop, as I soon discovered, behind one of the largest of the trees. There Ealhmund had stood, standing sideways to avoid being seen from the abbey. Bits of bark and tree sap littered the ground, evidence, I supposed, of the boy's boredom. Or hunger.

For a while I stood, as Ealhmund had, behind the tree. It was cold. It was morning, the interval after Terce, and the day was cold, gray. It smelled of snow. I shivered. I stood behind the tree and I shivered, trying to imagine what it would be like to be Ealhmund, standing here with nothing to do, no place to go, the cold, the hunger, the smell of snow. Would he recognize that smell? Would he know what it meant? Did everyone know such things, or had Father taught me that? I worried about this, standing where Ealhmund had stood, my prints registering atop his, obscuring them as my mind attempted to obscure with this small concern the larger one raised by the track before me, the sign on the other side of the tree that declared, however mutely, Ealhmund's shock, the fear with which he had run from this place. The print was sloppy, abrupt. In making it, the boy had stepped from behind the tree, exposing himself to the abbey while still managing to keep the tree between himself and whatever it was that had surprised him.

I stepped from behind the tree, turned and looked as Ealhmund had. The view was unequivocal. Cherry trees in winter, the open ground between the orchard and the ditch, the ditch. I wondered at what point he had spotted me. As I studied his hiding place in the grasses? When I turned and, eyes intent upon his track, began to

walk toward his hiding place behind the tree? Whichever it was, it
hadn't taken him long to make up his mind. Ealhmund had turned,
taken one look at the South Wood and, without further hesitation, run headlong into it, great sloppy slirrups of mud marking his
passage.

The South Wood. Even as a child it had seemed a little less scary
to me than the others, a little less threatening. For one thing the
orchard was there, softening the forest's nearer approaches, giving
the place an almost civilized, cultivated appearance. And of course
in winter the sun took its daily stroll across the wood's far edge,
turning its hinterlands into something buttery and golden, a hazy
indeterminate place, distant, beckoning. But that, of course, was
the view from the abbey, the view from up on the terrace where
you could dream about such things secure in the knowledge you
would never have to go there, that the abbey and its monks would
keep you safe from ever having to act upon your dreams, test your
ability to make them come true. But that wasn't how it would have
looked from down here. That wouldn't have been how it had looked
to Ealhmund, to a boy who had lived all his life in the abbey, had
never climbed Modra nect, knew nothing of Father Hermit, this
wood, any wood, had never, so far as I knew, even ventured out
onto Bishop Wilfrid's bridge.

And suddenly I understood the track. Standing there as Ealhmund
had, air smelling of snow and cherry tree bark, looking at the South
Wood, thinking about the South Wood, I suddenly understood why
the ground was so littered with Ealhmund's sign. Of course the boy
had wandered here, of course the ground was trampled with his print.
Where else could he go? Redestone was his world, the wood the end
of that world. I knew what that was like, could still remember the first
time I had been forced to cross that border, had followed Tatwine
over Bishop Wilfrid's bridge. But Ealhmund had crossed no bridges.
For how many days now had he huddled behind these indifferent
trees? For how many nights had he wandered, aimlessly, back and
forth across our orchard? And yet something had finally driven him
into the wood. *I* had driven him into the wood.

As I crossed the open ground between the orchard and the forest, I caught a glimpse of something hurrying away from me among the nearer trees. I had forgotten they had given him a different set of clothes.

"Hello!"

Ealhmund stopped, looked around, his expression mildly distracted as though I had interrupted him in the middle of something important. "Oh, hello Winwæd."

I took a few steps toward him then stopped, surprised to find myself suddenly shy in the presence of someone I had known all my life.

Ealhmund did not move. He stood at the edge of the wood and watched me, bending over once to rub a knee.

"So, how are you?" I asked, thinking, even as I spoke, how stupid the question sounded.

"Fine," said Ealhmund, not really looking at me, looking off to the left as if expecting someone. "Fine."

"Really?"

No response, though there was the suggestion of a movement among the boy's fingers and he smiled as if apologizing for something.

"So, what are you doing?"

"Oh, you know." Ealhmund looked off doubtfully through the orchard.

I didn't say anything, took another step toward the boy, stopped when I saw that the movement seemed to frighten him. I looked around, thinking of all the things I had planned to say, how inadequate they suddenly seemed, how inadequate I suddenly seemed.

"You know," said Ealhmund, then faltered.

I looked at him, urged him to go on, wished him to feel as he once had in my presence, happy, big-hearted, secure.

"You know," Ealhmund began again, "I don't *have* to do anything."

I smiled, pleased that he had spoken. "No," I said, "no, I suppose not."

The boy frowned. "Really. I can hunt and fish and do anything I like. Live out here! In the forest!" Ealhmund threw a nervous glance into the darker part of the wood.

Again I smiled, tried to look encouraging.

Ealhmund didn't say anything. He looked at me as if expecting me to say something and then, when I didn't, he knelt down, pulled back his woolens, began to inspect a cut on his knee. Whatever the boy had fallen against, the violence of the blow had removed dirt as well as skin, leaving an abrasion that looked surprisingly pink and clean against what was an otherwise filthy knee. I found myself thinking about Oftfor, remembering the time he had pulled back his woolens like this, shown me the swelling on his groin. I wondered if Ealhmund had acquired his injury running away from me.

The boy noticed where I was looking, looked back down at the knee with renewed interest. "Could you bring me something?" he asked, head bent over the wound.

"What do you mean?"

Ealhmund looked up at me, back at the knee. "Oh, you know, some bread or something."

What would you have done? I mean I know, you would not even have been there. But if you had been there, if you had been there and this boy you had known all your life had asked for bread, had asked you to risk your life that his might be saved, what would you have done?

I did nothing. I stood where I was and, doing nothing, waited, my legs growing weak beneath me, hollow.

It was Ealhmund who finally broke the silence. "It's all right," he said, nodding to himself, picking something from the cut on his knee. "It doesn't matter. I was just wondering."

For a while after that neither of us said anything. A chough flew over I think, emitted its one lonely call. A child's voice rose in anger somewhere down by the village, was as quickly silenced by another, deeper voice. But otherwise there was nothing. The wind did not blow, the sun did not shine. I thought about Ealhmund. I thought about Ealhmund and I remembered him as he had once been, a little boy spinning round and round upon the garth, Waldhere beside him, the two boys laughing helplessly, eyes wild, expectant, waiting for the fall and laughing when it came, getting up only to fall again, still laughing, delighting in delirium. I had never been able to understand that, could find no pleasure in feeling dizzy, out of control. But they had. Waldhere and Ealhmund had. And now they had grown so far apart. Waldhere was fast becoming a little monk, his orbit bringing him every day closer and closer to the center of Holy Mother Rule; while Ealhmund, well it was obvious Ealhmund had finally spun himself out utterly beyond the reach of any rule. And where did that leave me? Somewhere in between? I could not fool myself, I who prayed daily for my bishop's death—no, mine was no happy mean. And what that meant I thought, standing there watching Ealhmund as he knelt at the edge of the wood, his once great body reduced to skin and bones, well, what that meant I would rather not know.

"I suppose I had better be going."

Ealhmund looked up at me, looked toward the abbey, lip protruding as if I had presented him with an interesting problem. "Sext," he surmised.

"Well, not yet. But I probably ought to be getting back."

A single nod here, abrupt, dismissive.

"You take care of yourself."

Ealhmund didn't say anything, seemed to have found something interesting to look at on the ground in front of him.

I raised my hand to wave, thought better of it, turned and began to walk back toward the orchard, embarrassed now by the sign that seemed to shout up from the ground all around me, glad Ealhmund hadn't noticed it, couldn't see how dumbly it proclaimed his fear, his hopelessness, for all the world to see.

When I reached the first of the cherry trees the urge to say something more, some last thing, came over me like a sort of hunger. I took one or two more steps and then, unable to stand it any longer, turned and, without thinking about what I was going to say, yelled, "So you'll know, just so you'll know? It really isn't as bad as they say it is. The forest I mean. It's not nearly as scary as they say it is!"

Ealhmund was looking at me. At the sound of my voice he had glanced quickly toward the abbey and then back at me. He didn't say anything. He didn't nod or shake his head. He looked at me. I looked at him. Then I nodded and, feeling for some reason better about myself, as though I'd done something helpful, generous, I turned and began to make my way back through the orchard toward the abbey path.

That was the last time I ever saw Ealhmund. He was sighted a few more times up by the kitchens, but even that stopped when Brother Wictbert began sleeping by the gate. After that the boy's print became rare around Redestone and, eventually, such sign disappeared altogether. I have no idea what became of him.

XXXII

That was the year our annual shipment to In-Hrypum was waylaid, the bishop's man brutally murdered, and an entire year's production of iron carried off. Most people, naturally enough, blamed the outrage on one of Northumbria's traditional enemies, and when an arrow fletched in the Mercian manner was found at the site such suspicions seemed confirmed. Still there were those who pointed out that Ecgfrith failed to mount any punitive raids in response to the attack, and that, almost simultaneously, his smiths ceased to clamor for iron.

The loss was a great one for Redestone. After the failure of our wheat Godwin had assured us we would not starve so long as we had Victricius's iron to offer. But now there was no iron. For the first time in the history of the abbey, Brother Cellarer was forced to barter among our neighbors against future harvests for our food. For a community with such a long tradition of self-sufficiency, this was a bitter blow. And, as it is said, when one is offered humility for his fare, one tends to blame the cook. So it was that everyone now spoke of the transfer of men from Brother Cellarer to Brother Furnace, how Godwin had ignored Osric's requests for additional help when the rust first got among the crop, how the new abbot had jested that, so long as we had Victricius, we could "eat iron." Well, we couldn't eat iron now. And the grumbling was become nearly universal. Even Maban was heard to blame Godwin for the decision, saying it was none of his affair, that he had cautioned against the transfer, had offered to help Osric himself but Godwin would hear none of it. Well Godwin would hear of it now. There would be no second failures.

That spring everyone from prior to oblate was commandeered for the planting. Tellingly, even Brother Victricius was sent into the fields. I remember watching him as he went about his assigned tasks, the smile that played over his face every now and then when he did something wrong, moved in some way that showed how unaccustomed he was to such labor. Though no one spoke to him, no one sought out his row to work in, his company, Brother seemed—for the first time since Agatho's departure—content, even happy. I wondered if, bent over our soggy Northumbrian soil, he saw something else, scented, perhaps, a drier, more fragrant air.

Upon being relieved of his responsibilities as a member of the hierarchy, Father Dagan had been placed under Brother Cellarer's authority, which meant that no special order was required to send him into the fields. But it was, I believe, Maban who saw to it he was assigned stone removal. Of course no one likes stone removal, but you cannot imagine how bad it was in those days. Back then, when many of our fields had only recently been cleared, the rocks seemed to rise from the ground each spring like mushrooms after a good rain. Dragon's eggs, the hill people called them, and, like all such superstitions, there was a grain of truth to it. For there was something perverse about those stones. No matter how many you carried off one day, a like number seemed always to greet your return upon the next, the gray-red piles of discarded rock growing big-bellied at the edge of our fields, slithering and cracking in the heat of the afternoon like big overfed adders.

None of which seemed to bother Father Dagan. Whatever task I had been assigned, setting stakes, digging seedbeds, I would glance every now and then toward his part of the field and always find him still at it, the man who had been prior down on all fours now, red with the red of our earth, Maban's dutiful servant, breaking his fingers upon yet another impossible stone. Oddly enough I think I wouldn't have minded so much had he shown a little more enthusiasm for the work, thrown himself into it as once he would have, intent, even in so menial a task, upon setting an example for those who labored alongside him. But Father showed no such inclination. He seemed content only to do as he was told, in all appearances so like the other workers, both lay and religious, that it was only with difficulty I could distinguish his sweat-stained back from among the many that clambered that spring over the rockier parts of our fields.

It was on a particularly wet and dreary day, as I remember it, that I was sent to assist our former prior. I don't know what I had done to deserve such an assignment, but I do remember that it was Brother Osric who ordered it, the good cellarer staring at me with eyes made dull by hunger, not even bothering to admonish me, just signalling *the rocks* with his hands, then returning doggedly to whatever task it was that then occupied that extraordinary mind. Though I have no memory of it, I would have walked slowly to where Dagan and the other men worked. I did everything slowly in those days. Likely too I noted with displeasure the build-up of mud on my feet, cast a disapproving eye over the blackened stumps as yet protruding from that part of the field. I was a difficult boy in those days, willfull, feckless, aggressively sullen.

Father didn't say anything when I walked up. Well, he wouldn't have, would he? Maban was there and, except in his own defense, Maban was always very strict about the silence. But he did smile. I remember the smile because I remember how stricken I was by it. That Father too (even Father!) should look at me like this, grin up at me as all the others did now, trying to conceal the dismay the thought of my company so clearly caused them with these insincere smiles, these wanton invitations to partake of whatever pleasure was then at hand—in this case, as it happened, stone removal.

I knelt down next to Father without looking at him, without signing anything. The stone he was working on didn't look like much to me. You could see that recent frosts had already had an effect upon it, heaving the thing up at night, lowering it again at sunrise, so that now the stone sat in its socket like a tooth loosened by much fingering. Surely it wouldn't take much to dislodge that.

I glanced over at Father, expecting to see a similar assessment on his face, and was surprised to find his brow furrowed, the eyes dark, uncertain. To think that I used to kneel before this man, this man who now kneeled—utterly stymied—before a lump of mindless stone.

I leaned forward, placed my fingers in the space between stone and earth, probed, gained some purchase, pulled. Nothing happened. Well, that was to be expected. I went forward on my knees, giving myself a better angle, dug my fingers deeper into the earth, not thinking about what might be there, thinking instead about how much I hated this work, Brother Cellarer for sending me here, Father Dagan for smiling at me like that. Again I pulled and this time, pulling very hard, I very nearly pulled myself off my knees, catching myself at the last moment before smashing face-first into the object of my efforts. I sat back, looked at the rock. Stupid thing. Mindless stupid thing, staring up at me with its mindless stupid face. Red. Red like all our rocks. Redestone. And angry now, inspired, I grabbed the thing again, pulled with all my might, pulled as if this *were* Redestone, as if, with one great effort, I might remove from this field, my life, this existence, all that I hated about this place: Maban, Godwin, the Rule, *everything*!

And of course managed only to strain my back, the stone still staring blandly up at me from its hole, unmoved, unthinking, ignorant even of the stupidity I attributed to it.

I glanced over at Father, anxious lest he laugh at me. But Father wasn't laughing. He was looking at the stone, hands resting cold and still on his knees. For the first time I noticed how tired he looked, the strain on his face, the place where, in wiping an eye, he'd left a track of reddish mud across his cheek, drying now to gray. I glanced down at the hands that had made that track and was surprised to see how old they looked—the skin cracked and dry, stained red with earth, the fingers bent, nails bloodless, pale, outlined in red.

Father felt my eyes on him, looked over at me, the head turning slowly, the neck apparently stiff.

I placed my hands at the sides of my head, index fingers pointed upward, raised my eyebrows.

Father shook his head, *No. No, we will not need the ox.* He smiled, brought a finger to his lips, signalled patience.

And tears sprang to my eyes. I don't know why. It doesn't make sense to me even now, but something about the gesture, the smile upon that chapped and broken face, brought everything back, the time before this time, before Maban, Godwin, before even Gwynedd, when Father was neither Dagan nor prior but just Father: the big man in the big clothes who smiled down at me, held a finger before his lips, played with me in the snow.

And I had to look away, swallow hard, the feelings coming fast and furious, sweet and painful. That once I had felt such things, known such things! I looked away. I looked away and I closed my eyes, shut them tight against this day, my tears, the difference between then and now. When I opened them again, the field before me appeared strange, bleary, gray figures walking upon a reddish sea. I sniffed, wiped my eyes, realized, vaguely, someone was looking at me, someone over by the wagon. I looked away, down toward the village, saw the house I thought Eanflæd's, had to close my eyes again, beat back the emotions, embarrassed now by the fatigue that seemed to be letting this happen, the strain which, once released, permitted such a display.

"Winwæd?"

Would it never end?—the sound of my name upon his lips suddenly enough to wring my heart, send it bleating off toward some distant heaven.

I held a hand out, begged a moment's patience, rubbing my eyes against the other arm, the familiar scratchiness of my sleeve for some reason helpful now, sobering.

"The season…" It was Father again, whispering. "It can do this, the season. The eyes I mean, make them water. Autumn can too."

I turned around—too abruptly—smiled at him, eyes doubtless red, brimming.

"They say it's the trees," he said, smiling uncertainly, clearly doubtful this had anything to do with trees.

I nodded, laughed, caught myself, looked away, looked back at him, my smile all the while growing, becoming large, too large, unsustainable.

Father's eyes narrowed like those of a man who notices something he has missed. He studied me a moment and then, almost imperceptibly, nodded to himself. Again he held a finger to his lips, but this time I did not cry. I was too tired to cry, too moved, too in thrall now to that gesture to do anything other than wonder at it. Father nodded. Finger at his lips, he nodded, stood up, walked away. When he returned, he carried some tree limbs and a small stone. He smiled, knelt down, placed his stone against the one I had been pulling on, stood back up, inserted the longest of the limbs between the two rocks, pressed down on it. As if bidden, the big stone rose from its seat, rocked back and forth upon the axis of the limb. Father looked at me, his face serious now, urgent, demanding. I grabbed one of the smaller limbs, placed it in the gap opened between earth and stone, blocking the one from falling back into the other. Father smiled, released the pressure on the limb he held, bent over, reset the stone in the gap next to mine, re-inserted the limb, began the process again. Once more the stone rose and, shoving, Father drove the limb beneath it, lifted again, this time using only the strength of his back. The stone rose a further hand's breadth, trembled upon the lip of its grave, fell out. I laughed. Of course I'd seen the thing done before—Brother Ælfric used a similar method to raise and lower the wagon when repairing its wheel—but today...today such a trick seemed exceptionally clever. I couldn't help myself, I laughed.

Someone coughed.

Father's face changed, looked over that way. He looked back at me, brought a finger to his lips, noticed the humor in the repetition of this gesture, laughed at himself soundlessly. He smiled, flicked a nod at the rock, held his hands out palms-up before him. I stood up, understanding what he wanted, faced him over the stone. Together we bent and, with difficulty, lifted the rock between us. Then almost dropped it when we each started moving in different directions. Father smiled, indicated the direction we should take with a movement of his shoulders. I nodded and, walking in unison now, however gracelessly, we transported our rock across the mud of that field to the nearer of the big piles.

You know it's interesting, isn't it, how you can remember something like that so clearly, can remember duck-walking a stone across a muddy field, what it was like when, arms tired from the carry, you heaved the thing onto the pile, the disappointment you felt as it landed lower than expected, slid miserably, unimportantly, to the bottom of the heap? But I suppose it's always that way with the conversations we value in our lives, the ones our memories serve up to us again and again. We remember what led up to them, the particulars of the event itself—the hall, the fire, the direction in which we faced—yet very little of the actual conversation, its ebb and flow, what came first, what second. Only the lessons learned, the secrets divulged, that is what we remember, and where we sat when we learned them, who was with us, whether or not the sun shone.

The sun did not shine that day. It was cloudy, overcast. And when Father suggested a break, led me around to the far side of the pile, stretched out upon it, I beside him, the two of us lying on our backs, heads resting on our hands, it was at a lowering sky that we looked. I remember that. And I remember the pile itself, that it was tall, nearly as tall as a man, the rocks we lay upon dusty, dirty, covered with a thin and flaking skin of dried mud. A sort of fly, tiny, black, was for some reason attracted to this mud, had perhaps been spontaneously generated by its drying. None flew, I remember that, but they crawled back and forth in their countless hundreds, scurrying now left, now right, avoiding us, the area around our bodies, but otherwise moving indiscriminately over the rocks, gathering in the declivities whenever the wind blew, all facing the same direction, all adhering to some secret order, some strange and entirely unknowable rule.

Doubtless for a while we said nothing. It makes sense, we would have done that, enjoying the quiet, the feel of lying on our backs, muscles relaxing, recovering. And then, possibly without preamble (for he was like that—though he was no longer permitted to teach, our former prior retained the habits of a pedant), Father began to talk. He didn't look at me as he spoke—I remember that well—looked instead at the sky, the dark and moving clouds, as if he spoke not to me but to the face of Heaven. His subject was, as of course it so often had been in the days when he was prior, monasticism, his calling, mine, but the way he spoke about it now struck me as different, unexpected. Before there had always been something strained about Father's lectures on the communal life, as if the man spoke not of something he knew but of something he wanted, something he hoped, through the force of his words, to coerce into being. But today, as I have said, things were different, the tone changed, as if, in some way I could not understand (I mean look at the man—the mud, the chapped hands, the unhealthy pallor), Father had achieved his dream, achieved the happiness he had always longed for. I remember he said it was the freedom that surprised him most, the freedom obedience gave a man from worry, anxiety, any and all forms of pride. Doubtless I remember this because I was so surprised by it, surprised to find Father surprised by it. After all it had been Father who had always preached so passionately on the subject, the supposed freedom conferred upon those willing to dispense with freedom, enter a monastery, submit their will to that of an abbot. But now he spoke of that freedom as if it were something he had never expected, as if, surprised by it, Father now took daily pleasure in its expression, as if even that day, even as he'd knelt in the mud, struggled with yet another crop of stone, his mind had risen free of care into the clouds, into Heaven, been permitted, finally, the peace and serenity it had so longed for. And none of this, he assured me, none of this would have been possible without obedience, without the God-given gift of obedience, the yoke which is no yoke, which is a taking-off of yokes, the yoke which places your body in harness to another that your mind might follow God, might be freed to follow God.

It began to rain, I remember that, a light rain at first, big drops falling wet and cold out of a dark gray sky. Behind us Brother Osric called everyone into the shelter of the trees, and I remember Father rising up on one elbow, the uncharacteristically mischievous grin that spread across his face as he peered over the top of the pile, checked to see if we had been missed. And I remember the way he lay back down too, lay back down as if this were all part of the same lecture, as if he'd done nothing wrong, had no need to explain why, having just praised obedience, he now played at its opposite, only laying a hand on mine to let me know that all was as it should be, that our absence had gone unnoticed, we might continue to speak.

I think it was then that I raised the issue of Ealhmund, reminded Father that he had not always felt this way, that he had fought his superior on that, disagreed with him about that. And not even in Chapter. In the dortoir! In the unseemly panic of the dortoir that morning, Father Dagan, lowly Father Dagan, had raised his voice, raised his voice to champion an oblate, to challenge and contradict his rightful superior, his abbot, over something as pitiful and insignificant as the expulsion of an oblate. But Dagan only smiled, patted the hand his rested upon, smiling as if he had not only foreseen this objection but hoped for it, sought it as one seeks the last step in his argument, the final proof, his coda. He turned his head toward me, the face close now, teeth visible, eyes red-rimmed, tired, smiling. "Yes," he said, "yes, I did do that, didn't I? But of course I did so openly." He looked away, looked back up at the sky, thought about it. "So long as you question your superior openly, in front of the entire community, there can be nothing wrong with it, nothing deceitful, for you submit your differences to his judgment, his review. You do so knowing full well he may punish you for challenging him and that such punishment would be right, proper, that you must live with it for it comes from your superior. And so, even in contradicting him, you are in a state of obedience, you submit to your superior, for you did not hide your differences from him." Father nodded to himself. He turned to me, fixed those eyes upon me. "You must remember, Winwæd, everyone has a superior. You cannot avoid it. The farmer is subject to his lord, the lord to his king. The only difference between them and us is that we have chosen to follow one who seeks for his men not earthly glory but heavenly, not material goods but spiritual. That is why the world finds us so strange, our lives so contradictory, both revolutionary *and* hidebound, poor *and* immensely wealthy. This is our station in life, our cross to bear, and, like any cross, it is both burden and glory." Dagan watched me for a moment. Then he looked back up at the sky, smiled. "But I did do that, didn't I?" He chuckled, shook his head, "I tried to keep Father Abbot from expelling Ealhmund."

After that the wind picked up and the rain began to pelt down on us in earnest, God Himself trying to drive us from the rocks, drive us back into the shelter of the trees where we belonged. I remember Father rising up on his elbows as if to support himself against the wind, still patting my hand absently, beard blown back flat against his throat, a damp spot, then a second, appearing on the gray streak of dried mud that decorated his cheek. I rose up on my elbows too, blinked into the rain, looked around.

The flies were gone, had disappeared so completely you could believe they'd never been there, had been nothing more than a dream, something brought on by hunger. Broken bits of last year's grass blew across the ground before us, hung up in the weeds at the edge of the ditch, pulled free, blew on. The rocks we sat upon were dappled now, a pattern of raindrops that grew and expanded even as we watched, spot linking up with spot, so that soon the pile would no longer be the gray and dusty thing it had been but something else entirely, something wet and shiny and dark. Father patted my hand again. I looked at him. He closed his eyes, nodded; it was time to go.

You know how it is after a rest: you stand up slowly, carefully, always surprised by the stiffness, to find yourself stiffer than you were when you lay down. And that is how I have always imagined the two of us, Father Dagan and I, getting up that day, the two of us climbing down carefully off the pile (fragrant now with the smell of wet earth, wet stone), two old men setting their feet cautiously amid the rocks, mindful of a fall. But I was not an old man; I was a boy, and being the sort of boy that I was, my mind would have already begun to worry about what lay ahead of us, the uncomfortable silence that awaited us under the trees, the turned heads, the embarrassed clearing of throats. Which would explain why I didn't see them at first, why Father had to nudge me, raise a hand, point. Even then I initially saw nothing, just a pile of damp reddish-looking rock, only one or two gray spots marring what had become an otherwise uniform surface of glistening wetness. And then there was a momentary sense of dislocation, even of fear, as the two dry areas resolved themselves into something else, something recognizable, however wrong, truant, impossible. For there, resting on the rocks where we had rested, lay two shadow figures exactly like us, the upper torsos only slightly foreshortened, the one on the right stretching out an arm (touchingly thin, child-like) to the other. This must be what it is like when we die and look back on our deathbeds, the empty husks of our selves. It takes a moment's getting used to. I am me, you think, I am he—and there is a bad feeling in the pit of your stomach.

It continued to rain. Even as I thought these thoughts—even as perhaps Dagan thought these thoughts—it continued to rain, the two quiet figures acquiring their own pattern of drops, the spots multiplying unhurriedly, dried mud going from gray to dark gray until, nearly saturated and decidedly reddish now, the two images began to lose definition, became almost indistinguishable from the rock they lay upon, the one on the right, Father's rain-shadow, for some reason lingering longer than the other, yet still dissolving, disintegrating, until, finally, there remained only a meaningless alphabet of dry places, a broken and fractured script that, even as we watched, faded, continued to suffer strike after strike, faded and, eventually, disappeared altogether.

Father turned, smiled at me, pulled his hood up, squinting into the rain, smiled a last time, then turned and began to walk toward the field, the shelter of the trees. I watched him go. I stood where I was and I watched his thin gray figure walk away from me, recede into the rain. When he was at such a distance I feared he must notice my absence, turn and signal for me to follow, I threw one last glance at the place where we had lain. The rain had rendered the entire rock pile wet now, shiny, its reddish-brown hues relieved only here and there by a faint slip of ochre-colored clay. And for some reason this made me sad. Doubtless it was my age but, for some reason, looking at those rocks, I felt sad, lonely, as if something had gone out of me with the disappearance of those two figures, as if some part of my childhood, recondite, irretrievable, had gone with them, slipped away, departed never to return. I studied the rock for some proof they had been there, some sign of their passing, but there was nothing. It was just a pile of rock now—wet, shiny, unimportant. I turned and, slowly, cautiously, I made my way back across the field.

XXXIII

Of course looking back on it now, it's easy to see why Father Dagan spoke to me of obedience that day. He had just watched a boy, a boy he no doubt loved, walk unhappily toward him across a field, a boy who had been like this for some time now, brooding, peevish, resolutely forlorn. And he guessed, as anyone would have guessed, that it was the usual problem—authority, a young man's reluctance to submit to authority—exacerbated in this case perhaps by the arrival of Godwin, but otherwise no different from any other. And now the boy had done something to earn himself stone removal, an assignment anyone might resent. So Father had lectured me on obedience, the joys accruing to those who lead a life of unquestioning obedience. Granted it had been a rather new speech, one made fresh by experience, but there was nothing truly extraordinary about it, certainly nothing clairvoyant. Yet how could I have seen it otherwise—I who then prayed daily for the destruction of my bishop? The young live life at a fever-pitch, don't they, wear their hearts upon their sleeves, see angels behind every kindness, the devil beneath every ill? And who's to say they're wrong? Scripture teaches kindness to strangers "for some have entertained angels unawares." Is it not possible that, on occasion, we entertain angels even absent the presence of strangers, that some thoughts, arising as they so often seem to out of thin air, may be just that: the issue of heavenly hosts? Who is to say then that Father, however unwittingly, did not give voice that day to Something long frustrated, Something yearning, groaning, to speak, Something which, up until that moment, had awaited only the proper vessel? Certainly not I. For if God Himself had come down and paid me a visit, His face afire, the effect could not have been greater.

And yet, when I think about it, it wasn't really Father's lecture so much as the manner of its delivery that affected me. Again and again, in the days that followed, my mind's eye pictured our former prior as he lay on those rocks, the little smile that played over his face when he spoke, the way his eyes had brightened as if, even as he made his points, he saw the logic of his argument unfold before him, as if God Himself supplied the text, revealed for him, moment by moment, the beauty of our Rule. And that he told me these things, said these things, not out of self-interest, not out of any hope that my acceptance of the Rule could make a difference to his station (for it could not), but because he so clearly wanted what was best for me, so clearly and unambiguously cared for me. And, finally, that he could do this without pretense. That this man who was assigned stone removal, who spent the better part of every day on his knees in the mud, could so unhesitatingly advise me to do the same thing, could lie there on the rock pile to which his Rule had led him and so humbly, so unselfconsciously, and yet so forthrightly, recommend the selfsame path…. This was what hurt. This was what cut to the bone. For I too had once been as sure as that. I too had once received the Body of Christ without thought or reservation. I too had seen God's bow in the sky, been saved by His grace, witnessed His presence in the flowering of a cherry tree, the kindness of the men who watched over me. But now I was no longer worthy of those men, that God: I was become different, soiled, impure: I carried my prayer within me like a contagion—noxious, lethal, malign. I was amazed no one noticed. As I walked about the cloister, I felt the evil within me as a sort of stain, a heat that bloomed upon my face, stole up on me from out of my loins. I needed a clapper, a bell, something to warn these good men away, turn them from the devil in their midst. And how I envied them their innocence, how I regretted that prayer, that prayer which now I could not undo, that prayer which set me apart, placed me at odds with my community, indeed, with the world!

Children revel in such predicaments, don't they, preferring always that which is unresolved, a middle course between two alternatives, over any decision that might set them finally and irrevocably upon what must seem to them a thankless path? Which is not to say I did nothing as a result of my conversation with Father Dagan. I did amend my behavior. From the moment Father and I arose from that rock pile, Bishop Wilfrid became safe from any further harm I might do him. But of course he was not safe from the harm already done. I *had* prayed for the man's downfall, and, though I now expressly unprayed those prayers, I was not so foolish as to blithely believe their effect undone. I was after all a child of the monastery, from my earliest days I had known only the familiar cycle of sin followed by confession, followed by sin and confession again. That my offense against the Rule could only be righted according to the Rule was as much a part of me as my hands or my feet. I could no more believe myself forgiven without recourse to Faults than I could believe myself fed without recourse to food. And unforgiven, my prayers might mean nothing. Yet I feared confession. I had seen what had happened to Ealhmund. To be expelled from the monastery at a time when winter stocks had been reduced to scraps and famine was abroad upon the land…it did not bear contemplation. Still, I *wanted* to confess. I wanted to be pure again. I wanted to be like Dagan, like Osric; I wanted to be as I believed I once had been: blameless, chaste, happy, free. And so, like many before me, I bargained with God. I would follow His Way, become a slave to His Rule, if He (I prayed) would overlook the sin that gave birth to my devotion, the broken vow that played both midwife and fool to it all.

I began again to keep the Vigil. For the first time in my life I threw myself into the monastic round. I fasted regularly, spent entire holy days lying prostrate on the floor of the church, the deep sounds of the river rising to me through the flags, thrumming the bones of my chest. The only thing that I did not do was pray as the hermit had taught me to pray. For I feared that form of prayer now, feared opening myself up like that, exposing myself like that before God because…well, who knew what God might do with someone who had asked what I had asked? But always excepting this, I otherwise became the very image of a good oblate: silent, devout, unstinting in his attention to the office, uncomplaining in his acceptance of fate. Of course very little of this was real, sincere, though it did provide some diversion. Fasting for instance made the general hunger (common, degrading, banal) seem somehow private and unique, while lack of sleep kept what bad thoughts did arise vague, fleeting, immaterial. Which is not to say that, just because my devotions lacked depth, they did not *appear* genuine. Indeed, it sometimes seems it is exactly those devotions that are the most vain, the most superficial, that attract the most attention. And in this, my case was no different from any other. I became an object of speculation in the monastery. The suddenness of my conversion of manners was commented upon favorably in Faults. Brothers began to point me out to one another upon the garth, their fingers a blur of breathless approval. Why once even Maban mentioned me in Chapter, setting me up as an example to be followed, and I had to swallow back the bile, assume custody of the eyes, pretend I was only embarrassed when in truth I felt an almost physical revulsion. Oddly enough it was Baldwin, grown deaf and half-blind with age now, who saw through this duplicity. I'll never forget the day he stood up in Faults and pointed at me across the hall, his face long and pale beneath his hood, arm stretched out before him like the arm of God, voice filling the space between us, rising into the rafters. "I know you," he said, "I know your secret. I know what goes on when you think no one is looking, how vile it is, how disgusting. I know what true innocence looks like!" And then, voice cracking, eyes filling suddenly with tears, he began to speak of Oftfor, little Oftfor, that name so seldom heard in Chapter now, so nearly unremembered, the earth where his body received its final ablutions long since grown untidy with weeds, neglected, forgotten. But of course the tears didn't help. Baldwin was old now, cried easily now, and so it was a simple matter to overlook what he said, the monks shouldering one another good-naturedly, pointing with their chins at the old has-been, chuckling silently. I'll never forget the way Prior Maban—tossing me a glance of understanding that froze my blood—walked across to the old obedientiary, patted him on the shoulder, whispered something in his ear; how Baldwin started up, glanced down at himself, back at the man before him, the man he probably only vaguely recognized, looked at him as if he were some sort of savior; and, finally, I'll never forget what it felt like to watch Baldwin—Baldwin who for so long had held such power over our lives—bow gratefully to that small man, bow and, holding himself like a little boy desperate for the reredorter, turn and hurry across the room, out the door. There were one or two snickers, silenced by a look from Maban, and then a general sigh of relief, the brothers settling back into the real business at hand, shaking their heads, congratulating themselves on the wisdom of their prior, the way in which he had so tactfully relieved them of this tiresome old man. And only I, only I, still felt the force of what had been said, still saw Baldwin standing there, arm raised, finger pointing, the name that he had spoken still hanging on the air—Oftfor, holy little Oftfor, he whose sandals I was not fit to untie.

But, as I have said, Baldwin was the only one who recognized my deceit. For the others I became, I think, a sort of ornament, the shiny bauble they held up to each other as proof of our monastery's precision: that such a place could turn a child so obdurate and pigheaded into one so humble and devout showed we must be headed in the right direction, proved that the Rule could be depended upon to deliver its charges safely and unerringly into the hands of God. What was for me a remedy, a salve, a penance for sin so grave as to be unmentionable, became likewise a balm for their doubts. When things went poorly, when the rains came and we couldn't plant or the drains clogged and the whole place smelled for days on end of fish, they nudged each other and smiled as I passed them on the garth, confident that, despite such minor setbacks, the monastery must be headed in the right direction...for look at Winwæd, how else to explain Winwæd?

When whimsy supplants wisdom as ruler of a man's thoughts, it's said he must give said whimsy a proper throne, place a laurel upon its brow, crown it with gold and precious stones, for how else can he see it, how else perceive such a formless nothing amid the hard cold realities of his world? And so it was with me and the role I now came to play in our monastery. Surely, it was said (upon the garth, at the lavabo, down among the peas), such a boy is destined for greatness—the priesthood, an abbacy, who knew, maybe even a bishopric? And, needless to say, I was not so lost in my devotion to the Rule as to be deaf to such opinions. Indeed, I even began to allow myself to consider them, to tell myself that maybe, maybe if I did all the wonderful things that were predicted for me, threw myself into a life of service, then maybe, maybe God would overlook the other, maybe, in some heavenly balance, such achievements would make expiation for my sin, outweigh the secret evil I had done. But God is a loving God. He will not permit such self-deception to go long unchecked. And, for One who was not above humbling Himself upon a cross, it must have seemed a minor thing to lower Himself that night to the dortoir.

For some reason Waldhere and I were being led around the village in a wagon. I knew we must have done something good because everyone was standing outside their houses clapping and cheering, but I had no idea what it was that we had done. And Eanflæd was there. Eanflæd and another girl were dancing in front of us, dancing in front of us as the great wagon (I now recognize it as the one we found upon the mountain) made its ponderous way around the village. The two girls had filled their aprons with cherry blossoms and, as they danced, they tossed great handfuls of these into the air. When Eanflæd threw to her right, a dark cloud burst suddenly into bright pink snow; but when she threw to her left, across her body, it was as if she were sowing seed.

After we had made several circuits of the village, the wagon turned away from the houses and entered the abbey path. The crowd moved with the wagon, side-stepping to avoid the oxen (which, rather alarmingly, I now saw to be without a driver). The people lined the path

ahead of us, clapping and shouting. Several held sheaves of wheat
and these they raised above their heads as the wagon drew even with
them, the sheaves golden against a pale blue sky. Eanflæd and the
other girl continued to dance. Once, apparently as part of the rite, the
two girls turned and bowed to us. When they straightened up again
our eyes met. The girl I did not know blushed and looked away, but
Eanflæd's gaze held mine for a moment, communicated something.
Then she too looked away.

It was now, as we began to approach the monastery, that I grew
apprehensive. What was going on? What was everyone so excited
about? Why were they hurrying us up toward the abbey? What were
they going to do to us up there? I looked over at Waldhere, hoping
he might have an answer to these questions, and was surprised to discover it wasn't Waldhere who rode beside me but someone else, some
oblate I had never seen before. Whoever this boy was, he now looked
at me, smiled. He had no teeth.

As if the world itself were shocked by this discovery, everything
became immediately quiet, still, the villagers staring wide-eyed up at
the monastery. I looked up that way and at first could find nothing
to explain their wonder, the abbey sitting as it always had, silent and
serene atop its terrace. Still, trying to think about it from their point
of view, I could see how the place might seem a little intimidating,
at least to a villager. And it was then, as if thoughts could call themselves into being, that before my eyes the abbey changed, grew overlarge, charged with menace, and in an instant the place I had known
all my life stood revealed as something else, a place I did not want
to go to, an assemblage of buildings that stared down at me from its
perch like something alive, something awful, an animal biding its
time, licking its chops.

Our wagon continued its slow progress up the path. One by one,
the villagers began to turn, fall away. They looked embarrassed as they
did so, shamefaced, as if they only now realized what they were doing,
sheaves hanging forgotten at their sides. Eanflæd and her friend had
stopped dancing. They walked solemnly before us now, heads down,
apparently afraid even to look at what sat upon the terrace. Somehow

I knew that they too would soon step aside, and then nothing would stand between us and the abbey.

The urge to say something, call a halt, demand an explanation, rose in my throat like something hot and cathartic. But when I tried to speak, nothing came out. It was as if a hand had been clamped over my mouth, stopping all my words. I looked over at the oblate who rode beside me, pointed at my mouth. He nodded, placed a similar finger to his lips: *Yes, we must be silent.*

I shook my head, desperate to be understood, trying as hard as I could to force the words through whatever it was that blocked them. And something gave. Though there was no sound, something gave, and far off in the distance I thought I heard something, something vague and tremulous, an echo, a distant reminder of what it felt like to speak, emote, proclaim. Again I pushed, excited now, heaving the thought before me like a battering ram, forcing it up and outward. And this time something definitely gave, something came out. But where I had expected a roar, a great torrent of exclamation and outrage, I heard instead only a small creaking sound, a voice so muffled and weak as to be scarcely recognizable as my own.

What?

I blinked.

Light.

There was light. Ceiling beams lay their long familiar lengths down across my world.

I closed my eyes, turned, opened my eyes, and there in the bed next to mine lay the stupid drooling face of old Brother Willibald. How many times had his countenance—foolish, senescent, benign—welcomed me back to the land of the living, signalled an end to some terrible dream, relief from the nameless horrors of night? But this morning I found it not so comforting. This morning, even old Brother Willibald looked unreliable. Of course I tried to reassure myself, remind myself that such things were to be expected, that it was in the nature of dreams that the world should be turned upside-down, the familiar seem alien, the alien familiar, right, commonplace. But the dream would not be so easily vanquished. The visions it had given birth to kept rising before me, clouding my mind, disturbing the natural peace of morning—that strange procession up the abbey path, my growing sense of apprehension, the feeling that I was being delivered into the clutches of something from which there would be no escape, and then the image of the monastery itself, my home, the place I had always run to when frightened, turned suddenly strange and forbidding, sentient, grotesque. Again I looked at Brother Willibald, again I tried to see him as I had seen him so many times before, old, friendly, harmless. But the vision would not hold. For the first time in my life I saw something unnatural in the life that lay on the bed before me, something cruel and inflexible, mindless and unrelenting. I swallowed. I swallowed and the muscles of my throat (against which I had struggled in my sleep) constricted painfully like the hinges of a door long since rusted into place.

XXXIV

s it happened, the sore throat lasted for the better part of a week. Brother Theodore was infirmarian in those days and a good one, but he could do nothing for me. When I swallowed it hurt, and when it hurt I saw again the monastery as I had seen it in my dream—smug and abiding, ravenous and self-assured. Because of my illness, I was excused from work which was probably not a good idea as it gave me time to dwell on my thoughts. Out of a vague sense of duty to my community and the expectations it held for me, I remained faithful to my devotions, though my silence was filled now not with prayer but visions. Again and again I rode that wagon up the abbey path, again and again I heard the crowd's roar, felt my pulse grow rapid, saw Eanflæd's look, the abbey waiting. It is in the nature of dreams that important aspects of their character should be revealed only upon reflection; over time we realize that the woman we spoke with was not a stranger but our mother, the ditch we tried to step across not a ditch but the Meolch. And so it was with this dream. The more I thought about it, the more certain I became that there had been something vaguely (and uncomfortably) familiar about the whole thing, a sense, almost a foreboding, that I had experienced it all before, been carried up the abbey path like that once before. Still, try as I might, I could not dredge up any memory of such an incident. Indeed, even as I became more and more convinced that a memory like this must exist, the very strength of that conviction seemed to drive any recollection of it from my mind. And then, just when I had given up all hope, had in fact turned in disgust from the problem, told myself I didn't care, didn't even want to know, the answer itself rose before me like an artifact of my capitulation. It wasn't me, it was Father. It wasn't my memory I'd dreamt that night but Father Hermit's.

As I remember it, Father told the story as a sort of cautionary tale, the sort of history one recounts to warn a child of the dangers of indiscriminate contact with other races; and thus I have always associated it with the time I caught him conversing with a shepherd in the tongue (harsh and vulgar) of the Cumbrogi. But now that I come to write the whole thing down, record it for the community, I realize such a conclusion doesn't bear scrutiny. The Cumbrogi are, after all—after a fashion—Christian, yet Father's story was a tale of pagan depravity, of the depths to which a life without Christ will lead a man. So I wonder now if it wasn't Stuf, if, perhaps, my introduction to Stuf might not have been the occasion for Father's revelation. The timing's right, and, though it seems hard to believe now, I suppose I might once have been drawn to the charcoal-maker, might once have found something to admire in a man who dressed so differently, spoke so wildly, held such a dim view of those his betters were required to respect. And, if that is the case, if such an infatuation did occur and was disclosed, then what better reason could Father have had for telling me about the old ones?

As is typical of dreams, the story that gave birth to mine would seem, at first glance, to bear little resemblance to its offspring. But it was, I believe, not so much the story Father told but the feeling that story evoked in me, the fear I must have felt as it developed, as I realized what I was hearing, what was about to happen, that inspired my nightmare, placed me in that wagon, sent it riding up the abbey path. But I get ahead of myself. First, if you are to understand any of this—Father's tale, my dream's connection to it—you must understand a little of the history of our valley. As unlikely as it seems now, it has not always been ours. There was a time when the Cumbrogi held this place, worked these fields, were baptized (after a fashion) in our stream. Then (thanks be to God) our people began their march from east to west across Northumbria, always driving the Cumbrogi before them, winning battle after glorious battle, until, finally, we pushed what remained of that people beyond the last of the mountains, pushed them until they held but a tiny remnant of their original land, testimony to the error of their faith and our Lord's contempt for such error. But here, as it so often does, history throws up a stumbling block for those foolish enough to trip over it. For it must be admitted that at this time our people were as yet unsaved. Paulinus had not then begun his ministry, and the beliefs we now ascribe to the hill people were, in those days, held by one and all. And so the fool, thinking himself the wiser for it, points out that a people who called themselves Christians had been defeated by one that openly practiced idolatry, leaping from this to the conclusion that the pagan gods must be the more powerful. Thus the unwary are caught in their own snares. For the fool cannot see (as God does) that, eventually, it would be our people who would show themselves open to the teachings of the missionary saint from Rome, while the Cumbrogi (to their unending shame) would turn their backs upon him, cling stubbornly to the Northern way long since proven unorthodox and wrong.

But no wave washes all before it; inevitably there will be a shell here, a stone there, left turned perhaps, up-ended, but otherwise in more or less the same position it held before. And so it is with people. We may have swept the Cumbrogi before us like a great tide but, here and there, individuals would have washed up in more or less the same place they occupied before. Which explains, we may assume, how Gwynedd and his mother—Cumbrogi both—came to rest in their native village (the one we now properly call Wilfrid's) even after the greater part of its inhabitants had been driven across Modra nect. Perhaps Gwynedd's father was killed in the fighting, perhaps he turned and ran—I do not know. All I know for sure is that, whatever became of the man, he left a wife and child behind him, left them to the mercy of those he must surely have thought incapable of mercy. But in this, of course, he was wrong. Our people (unlike his) do not slay the innocent; and so Gwynedd and his mother were permitted to live, kept as servants by a family that, even to this day, claims descendants among those that dwell in our village.

Now we of course cannot know what it is like to live as slaves— our people never having been reduced to such a state—but surely it cannot be pleasant. One thing I remember well from Father's story is the complaint he made of the changes effected in his mother by servitude. Apparently the woman (whose name, alas, I no longer recall) had been quite a beauty. Indeed, in the way of children, Gwynedd had believed her the most beautiful woman in the world. But in the course of her captivity the light went out of her beauty, her once supple skin become coarse and gray, her hair thin and tending, like a man's, toward baldness. I remember this because it was part of Father's story to remark upon the change that came over her when they began to feed her again, how she blossomed, seemed to regain her youth, became again the mother he had known, the beauty he had adored. Up until that time, Gwynedd and his mother had subsisted almost entirely upon what food they could pilfer from that set aside for their master's beasts. But suddenly, and without explanation, their status had changed. They were fed now upon sweetmeats and pie, butter and bread. Where before they had dwelt among the family's ducks in a lean-to affixed to the house, now they were permitted to move inside, take their meals with their master, sleep on the floor by his bed. Father told me he grew half a head taller during this period and that his mother's hair came back in, though he believed it a different shade after that, darker and less fine.

I have often wondered what it would be like to have something like that returned to you, to think your mother's beauty lost, that you would never see it again, and then to have her restored to you, to have her smile at you as she had before, laugh and share food with you as if nothing had happened, as if the two of you would live like this forever: healthy, happy, content and secure. Such a transformation must have seemed a miracle to Father, perhaps seemed so still, for I remember his eyes grew damp as he told me of it, his cheeks shiny with tears, glistening. I don't remember saying anything. I don't remember reaching out, touching his arm. I don't think I did anything at all. Doubtless I envied him. Doubtless I sat there and, fool that I was, thought him a fool for crying, thought him a fool for not appreciating what he had, the memories of his mother he as yet possessed, the time he had spent with her.

The day began, as Father remembered it, with a sudden and unexpected noise, an explosion of sound so loud and abrupt it brought him immediately awake, drew him so completely from sleep that, for the remainder of the day, Father said he experienced a sort of displacement, as if, in a sense, he slept still, lay as yet curled upon his bed, all that happened around him taking place as in a dream, a dream so vast and incomprehensible as to be someone else's, a dream dreamt not by him, the little boy Gwynedd, but by someone else, someone large and not altogether sane. When I asked about it, Father said he wasn't sure what had caused the noise—drums and cymbals certainly, a tambourine he thought, maybe a pipe or two, but what he was sure of, could still in a sense hear, was that, whatever the instruments employed, they had all been played at once, without regard for harmony or tone, as if every savage within two-days' walk of that place had been given a drum and told to beat on it as loudly as he could. And he had. And that, accompanying this cacophony, as if any noise so loud and fierce must generate its own heat, there had been a smell, the smell of something hot and disagreeable, as though the heathen had taken to burning not incense but hair, great long hanks of human hair.

And where was Gwynedd's mother during all of this? What did she do to allay her son's fears, soothe what must have been a growing sense of alarm? We do not know. Interestingly, Gwynedd remembered almost nothing of his mother from that day. Perhaps she had already been taken from him. Or, more likely, perhaps she kept him occupied with some childish game, pretended all was as it should be, the little boy becoming involved in her conceit, absorbed, lost, until, finally, he attends to her not at all. By such crafts mothers have always prevented the formation of unpleasant memories, in the process denying their children—it must be said—the consolation of a true good-bye.

What Gwynedd did remember was that night, what happened that evening after the sun went down. They had given him something to play with, a toy of some sort, something that belonged to the children of his master, and it was this, he told me, that first alerted him to the change in atmosphere, the feeling that somehow things were different, that maybe there was something about this day (the smell, the heat, the sound) that made people nice, friendly, for he had never been allowed to play with the toy before, had indeed been struck for so much as looking at it, and now, here, the selfsame woman who had dealt that blow gave it to him, leaned down and offered him the toy as if she were his mother herself, her hand not striking but stroking his head, her voice not raised in anger but soft, caressing, like a mother's, like his own dear mother's.

And then, just as the child Gwynedd lowers his defenses, begins to play with his toy, grow comfortable with the woman who has given it to him, perhaps even a little enamored of her, a familiar character enters our story to sound an alarm. For it is Folian, the same Folian who will someday found our monastery, become its first abbot, that now changes the tenor of the day, gives the first indication of the horrors it must contain, returns the boy, in an instant, from a growing sense of confidence to one of utter bewilderment. For why should the holy man cry out like that? Why should the stranger, the one everyone laughs at but his mother, the one his mother loves, respects, reveres, why should he cry out like that, why should his voice rise suddenly like that above the din, reach into this room as the smell does to distract him from his pleasure, draw his eyes from the toy to the women at the door, the women who, he now realizes, stand not like mothers but guards, their glances, however maternal, however caring, thrown at him over their shoulders, back at him over their shoulders, their real concern clearly elsewhere, outside, beyond this room, where whatever is happening is happening (the noise and confusion), outside where the holy man has just yelled? And why should he cry out like that? Why should the holy man yell *No!* like that?

And in an instant it is gone, the sense of security so carefully developed, so assiduously maintained, it is gone, vanished, the toy gone limp and unimportant in his hands, the women at the door no longer women but harpies, harridans, a troupe of witches set to guard him, keep him, who knew, fatten him for the fire, the terror he has suppressed all day unleashed, set loose, a terror so big he cannot contain it, a terror so big it spills from him like something alive, something crazed and alive that bounds about the room, howls and shrieks at him from the rafters, from beneath the bed, over the door, till it seems it must explode, the room, the house, must explode with the exigency of it all, the holy man yelling *No!* out there like that, and he has to get out of here, escape from this place, this room, these women, this living and uncontainable terror.

And the next thing he remembered was stars. A collision, someone's legs, the sound someone makes when their back strikes the ground, the wind driven from their lungs, and then he was out, free, the sky overhead dark and full of stars. And for a moment it was wonderful. When he told me about it all those years later that was one thing he remembered well, how good it had felt to be outside, how really fine, as if one actually could escape such terror, leave it behind, blind and shut-up in a room.

And then he saw the holy man.

The open area before the houses had at first seemed almost empty, surprisingly empty for all the noise it had generated, one or two old men beating on a drum, someone playing a pipe, but, otherwise, apparently, no one. Then he saw the priest, the one he had been taught to address as "Father." He hadn't noticed him at first because he hadn't expected to see him (anyone really) in such a position, the two of them, the priest and old man Baldred, not arguing with one another by the fire as might be expected after that *No!*, but lying on the ground, both of them dirty and disheveled, entangled in one another's arms like little boys tussling, like two little boys caught tussling. And they were looking at him. He remembered that well, Father did, the two faces almost comic in the firelight, open-mouthed, staring at him as if embarrassed to have been found in such a position, no one moving, no one saying a thing. And he almost laughed, the two grown-ups on the ground like that, their faces, his unexpected freedom, he almost laughed, but he didn't, because there was something about the faces he didn't like, something about the way they looked at him, the way they looked at him and then turned in unison, turned in unison as if part of the same pantomime, turned and looked from him up and out into the darkness over the fields.

And Gwynedd (the fear creeping back into him now, the fear seep-
ing from between the legs of the women in the doorway to creep
across the ground and back into him like something alive, something
alive and full of worms) looked that way as well. And saw lights. A
confusion of lights really. Torches. Most of them up on the rocky
place, Dacca's crag, but another, a single torch, down below the others, below the others and off to the left, above the fields. And for a
moment the little boy is very much afraid, terrified, his mind unable
to make the necessary connections, the lone torch seeming to float
ghost-like above the fields, a will o' the wisp, a fiery demon. But then,
thankfully, it all comes clear, his mind showing him the scene as it
would appear in daylight, the position of the light suddenly evident,
reasonable. Someone was up on the ridge. Someone was standing up
on the ridge (the one that rode the fields like a boat and sometimes
figured in his dreams), someone was standing up there and waving a
torch at the people up on the crag. Who, in turn, seemed to be waving
back. Or something.

But it was then that he heard the movement, all that had happened
since his escape taking but an instant—the collision, the firelight, the
priest and old Baldred, their look, the torches, his resolution of their
respective locations—all of this having taken but a moment, and then
the women were upon him and he was up and running, hands thrown
over his head, running out into the peas, the chard, hiding himself
among the plants of the field.

But it was here, as I remember it, that Father stopped for a moment
in the telling of his story, hesitated, cocked his head as if looking
at something he had not seen before. For though he knew he had
hidden among the peas, could as yet smell them, still, at the same
time, he also knew—or at least had always believed—that the rites
performed that night were undertaken by hill people only during the
short days, mid-winter, long before any crop would have come in. So
how could he have hidden among peas?

But there was no changing it. He remembered peas, the smell
of peas, their placid vegetable scent somehow reassuring after the
alarms of the night. And stars. He was sure of that, winter or summer

there had been stars, a great dark dome of sky struck through with stars—and beneath that silent turning beneficence, torches, the one upon the ridge waving and the others, those up on the mountain, waving back. Or something. Were they dancing? It seemed, as he watched them, that they were, and that there was one, a giant seemingly, taller than the others, much taller than the others, that danced with an abandon he could not credit, an improbable jangling that defied logic, the human form not meant to bend like that, the chest seeming to flex at mid-point so that, for a moment, his mind told him he watched not a man but a snake, a snake capable of bending where it willed. And then, again in an instant—the entire evening a collection of such moments, fragments of time clashing and colliding with one another—he realized his error, the dancer not taller but raised, suspended, the dancer not dancing but dangling, the dancer not a dancer but.... And again he was running, tearing through the fields mindless now of stake or stem, feeling neither obstacle nor blow, hurrying to her though it was of course impossible, too late, the fields great, the river deep, the mountain high between them, and yet he was already hurrying toward her, arms already raised as if to hold her, lift her above the noose's suffocating embrace, for what else could he do? What else could he do except pray, pray as he never had before, that the heathen would relent, relinquish their devilish plans for her, take his mother down, save her.

And it was that, he told me, that in the end he found the most cruel. For they did. Amazingly, incredibly, after he had taken not more than three or four running strides, as if in answer to his prayers, as if petitioning heaven with him, the heathen lifted their arms toward his mother, torches dancing, sparks rising into the sky, lifted their arms toward her and carefully, gently, took her down, removed his mother's head from the rope, deposed her, took her down from the tree. And she was still alive. You could see that—faint clearly, unable to walk on her own, men supporting her on either side, someone else holding their torches—yet alive, his prayers answered, fulfilled, the miracle, his first, performed, accomplished, confirmed.

But then they lifted her up again. At first it looked so gentle, so kind, the men locking arms, cradling her, each clearly taking his position with some pride, an awareness of the responsibility incumbent upon him, lifting in a single movement, all heads turned toward his mother's, gentle, caring, solicitous, but going the wrong way, the strange procession lit by torches held high as if to see her face, watch for any discomfort it might betray, but turning the wrong way, going not down but out, not down the mountain but out, out onto Dacca's crag.

And it was then that he knew what they were going to do. As if he controlled the men, as if it were his thoughts that determined their behavior, he knew what was going to happen next, how they would come to a stop at the end of the crag (his mother's feet suspended above the abyss), how they would stop, hesitate, look at one another, out at the lone torch floating above the fields, back at one other, and then, in accord with some signal he could not perceive (could not imagine), they would begin to move, begin to rock his mother, in unison, back and forth between them, rock her like a baby, arms swinging from side to side, first his mother's head, then her feet, protruding from their little huddle. And then they were doing it. As in a dream when our worst fears call forth exactly that which we most dread, they were doing it, rocking her, torches held high, the sacred bundle that was his mother rocking back and forth there upon the crag, upon the very tip of Dacca's crag.

When they threw her there was a moment in which Gwynedd's mother seemed to rise instead of fall. He told me that, remembered that, how she'd seemed to rise into the torchlight, arms thrown out as if enjoying herself, as if this were all just part of some wild and scary game; and then she'd vanished, disappeared into the vast and echoing darkness that hung, loomed, before the crag. She didn't say anything. He didn't hear her scream or anything. Just that one reflexive movement of the arms, a final attempt to grab something, save herself, and then the small bundle that was his mother had entered the night, his mind madly plotting the arc of her descent, making desperate calculations, contriving improbable outcomes, unlikely interventions.

There was a sound, he said, I remember him telling me that, that there was a noise. Branches breaking somewhere on the side of the mountain, the first of the trees being struck, and then, in quick succession, an awful sound, and a second. Gwynedd's mother had come to rest.

You know, even after all these years, even though I've had a lifetime to grow accustomed to the idea, it's still hard for me to believe that, child that I was, I was able to discern the link that exists between myself, that dream, and the disreputable doings of those old ones. And how much more difficult it must be for you, my brothers. Even now I can hear you complaining, reminding me (as we always do) that some things are best left unsaid, that some histories should not be recorded, are unworthy of the vellum. After all, you ask, what's the point? How could anyone, even in a dream, connect two such things, the pagan practices of our pagan past with a wagon ride up the abbey path? Yes. Yes indeed, how could one? Yet that is exactly what my mind did. And when, at last, my poor dim faculties recognized the connection, saw in it the genesis of my dream, the bolt slid quietly home. The door closed, the bolt slid home, and any other possibility was shut off from me. The fear the little boy Gwynedd felt when he realized the women who watched over him were not his guardians but his guards, this was my fear. The terror he felt, the terror that sprang from him at that moment, all the more ferocious for having been so long repressed, this was the terror I felt—had, I now realized, felt and repressed every day of my oblate life. For years now I had told myself I wanted nothing more than to grow up, could hardly wait to assume the responsibilities, the privileges, of a solemnly-professed monk. Yet now, now that the wagon had begun its climb, now that the monastery was within view, solemn profession an inevitable fact, I realized I knew nothing of this, had not an inkling of what it meant, where I was being led to, what I was going to do.

XXXV

The end, when it came, was, I suppose like most endings, anticlimactic. Godwin was not subsumed, bodily, into perdition; my father did not return to call me home, declare me his true and rightful heir; Eanflæd did not cover her hair, join us upon the terrace—my wishes, my dreams, remained, as I suppose they always had been, phantoms, nothing more. But Victricius did die. Oh yes, as we all know, Victricius died.

Of course people will tell you he sent everyone away, monks will tell you that, but it's not true. He didn't send me away. And if it really was intentional, if sin was involved, doesn't that strike you as odd? I mean, after all, he had no real affection for the helpers Godwin had given him, the ones he'd stolen from Brother Osric. Brothers Athelstan, Rufinianus, and Tilmon were good men, hard workers, but they were like everyone else. They didn't think much of Victricius, did little to hide their contempt for him. So why should he have gone to such lengths to save them, protect them from complicity in his supposed act? And what is more, why hold me close? Why risk the one person I honestly believe he still cared for? I know he should not have. It shames me now to remember how badly I treated him, but I believe Brother loved me still, cared for me, in his own peculiar way, as much as Gwynedd or even Dagan. Yet it was I he asked to remain behind that day, I he asked to take my place at the bellows, to pump as he fed, the two of us once again united in work if not in mind, our shoulders and backs in thrall to the furnace.

I can still see those bellows, can still feel the pole, solid, beneath my palms: the initial opposition as I bear down upon it, the anguished sigh when, reluctantly, it gives way, submits to the pressure of my weight, whistles—at my insistence and not its own—lewdly up the thighs of old brother furnace. All of which must seem strange to those of you whose only knowledge of such a thing is the pile of rotted hides and beams that now lies alongside what we still call the furnace path. Yes. Yes, that was the bellows. But when you imagine that moth-eaten collapse animated, breathing, you must not picture a simple bladder squeezed between two sticks such as Brother Kitchens might use at his oven or a smith at his forge. No, our bellows was a far grander affair than that. It took the lives of four full-grown deer to make the bag, their skins worked by a company of virgins that then lived upon the lower Meolch. When I was given in service to Brother Victricius that bag was already many years old, yet it remained soft, supple, like glove leather, its surface still bearing, here and there, the impress of tiny teeth. Ultimately the hides had been delivered (with much ceremony) to Redestone for sewing. Until just a few years ago there was a brother yet alive at our abbey who, when the weather changed, could point at a sliver of scar on the little finger of his right hand and, with a movement of that hand, remind you of the way in which he'd pulled those stitches tight. Once his (and how many others'?) work on the hides was done—the seams tarred, the chamber airtight—the resulting sack, looking now like a giant's stomach trussed and bound for market, was roped in place between linden poles and slung up at the base of the furnace. The whole thing—poles, bag, spout—nearly as big as an ox.

And this, I can hear you wondering, was driven by a boy? Well, yes and no. I did operate the bellows, but I would not have been able to do so long without the assistance of an ingenious device created by Brother Victricius. The way it worked was this: Pumping a blast of air into the furnace by forcing the top pole of the bellows down against the bottom had the simultaneous effect of raising a large stone into the air, the stone being connected to the upper pole by a length of cord strung over a beam. Once raised to the level of the beam—and left to its own devices—the stone naturally enough sank back to the earth whence it had come, its weight, in turn, pulling the cord after it over the top of the beam; which, in turn, pulled the bellows back open again. And here it was that I came in, for I weighed slightly more than the stone. Grabbing the upper pole and raising my feet, my weight alone was enough to pull the bar back down to earth, once more pumping air into the furnace and, at the same time, raising the stone back up to the wooden beam. Releasing the pole of course reversed the action, stone returning to earth and bellows reopening. A complete cycle took about as long as a Pater Noster said quickly, but over time I could, with the aid of Victricius's machine, deliver quite a bit of air into the furnace.

On that day, as I remember it, all was working as it should have been, the stone rising and falling monotonously, the furnace hissing and popping, so that, as was my habit, I had fallen into a sort of reverie, not really attending to the motions of the day but, instead, abstracted, the regular wheeze and sigh of the bellows providing a sort of rhythm for my thoughts.

And then it stopped. Suddenly and without warning, the bellows stopped, and for a moment I dangled beneath its upper pole, daydreams dissolving around me, thoughts in tatters, the bellows yawning wide-open before me, triumphant, leering, refusing to close. Then, thankfully, I noticed the hand, and was at once both furious and chagrined. It was Victricius. Victricius had crept up on me and, as was a habit of his, a trick he sometimes played, had stayed my stroke with the strength of one of his short but sturdy arms.

I lowered my feet to the ground. Feeling useless and small, impatient and annoyed, I lowered my feet to the ground, touched earth, stood up.

Victricius glanced at me, then back up at the sky, nodded in that direction. I looked where he indicated but could see nothing, the sun still below the tops of the trees, the light as yet liquid, fragile, cold. I shook my head, *No, no I don't think it's Terce yet.*

The furnace master's expression did not change. He lifted a hand, pointed, not at the sky but at the stack, the stack which…. But here my mind stuttered, stopped, went, for a moment, deaf and dumb. The stack was empty. The stack which sat atop the furnace, which sat atop the furnace I'd been stoking since before sunrise, the stack which sat atop the popping, hissing, broiling furnace was empty, not a whiff of smoke issuing from its throat, only a slow and sinuous wavering of the air around it to show it was even attached to, part of, the vent for, the hot and bulging shape beneath it.

"There's an obstruction," said Victricius. It was the first thing he'd said all day and—like so many things Victricius said—seemed unnecessarily brutal. "A pestilence is coming," he'd told the community, and so it had, and half the community had died. And now he said there was an obstruction and, by saying it, seemed to make it so, gave the situation all the gravity and alarm he had taught me to associate with the word *obstruction*. Yet even as I thought this, even as I felt myself annoyed with the furnace master, irritated, another part of me was secretly pleased with Victricius, glad to have him with me. For if anyone could deal with a problem like this, if anyone knew how to face down such a danger, defeat it, it was the furnace master. I looked at him. As a child looks to its mother when in danger, I looked at Victricius and, in my heart, I drew near.

I wondered what he would do. This had never happened before. He had talked about it of course, warned of such things, had even told me what must be done in the event of an obstruction, that the blast must be stopped, the furnace dismantled, the blockage, whatever it was, cleared; but I wondered if he would do that. Now that the crops were in the ground, Father Abbot was anxious again about his iron, had ordered Victricius to work unceasingly till he had made up all that had been lost to the Mercians in their raid. If Brother stopped now, all our charcoal would have been burned for naught, all the limestone ruined, to say nothing of the time required to rebuild the furnace, reëstablish a proper charge. Who knew what Godwin would say—Godwin who knew nothing of iron-making yet spoke as though he knew all?

Victricius didn't say anything. With one arm he forced me away from the bellows. Never taking his eyes off the stack, stepping between me and the furnace, he forced me firmly but not unkindly away from the bellows, shepherded me across the yard, moved me back down toward the path. When we reached the first of the trees, felt the crunch of pine needles underfoot, he stopped, began to speak, his back still toward me, arms spread wide, eyes upon the furnace. "I want you to go to the abbot," he said. "Go to Father Abbot, Brother Maban, tell them what's happened."

I was instantly disappointed. In the way of boys, I went from being terrified at the prospect of something happening to the furnace to being disappointed by the idea that, should something happen, I would miss it. "He isn't going to like this," I said, stalling for time, pointing out the obvious. "He isn't going to like it if you stop."

The back of Victricius's head moved. "It won't go out for a while. Hurry and we'll let him decide."

"But..."

"Go! Now! Run!"

And I was off and running, the smell of the river in my nostrils, trees flying by, the first broken beams of sunlight splintering the forest before me. Victricius had never yelled at me like that before. Truth be told, Victricius had never even raised his voice to me before. But, surprisingly, I wasn't angry with him. Indeed, as I ran along, I realized that for the first time in my life I was rather proud of my master, proud of the forcefulness with which he had spoken to me, sent me on this errand, proud of the importance it gave what I did, the speed with which I ran, the breathlessness with which I would deliver my message, wait upon Father's answer. I could see it all quite clearly, Chapter, the brothers sitting along the walls, heads turned, gaping, Prior Maban demanding an explanation, Father Abbot snorting, looking confused, standing on ceremony. And it would all be because of me. I would spill headlong through the door, throw myself on the ground before them, shout out my business, disrupt everything!

The sound, when it came, was like nothing I'd ever heard before. Have you ever had a bolt of lightning strike very near you? It was like that in a way and not like that too. For before this sound, before I could hear anything, I *felt* something, a sort of premonition, as if the earth itself moved, trembled, at the thought of what was going to happen. And then it was on me, the sound was on me, and, for a moment, I could hear nothing, the sound so loud it was a sort of silence, the sound so loud it flattened the air around me, rendered it dead, broken, incapable of bearing sound. And then it was by me. In a long instant the sound was by me, air and eardrums springing back to shape, the great boulder of sound rolling off down the valley, concussion falling upon concussion, meaning upon meaning, until, finally, the monstrous thing grew small with distance, attenuated, and slowly, slowly, faded and, eventually, disappeared.

I stopped. I remember that, the whole thing having taken so long and, at the same time, passed so quickly, that I still had to stop, had to consciously draw myself up, relinquish my errand to the abbey, before I could approach, understand, see, that which had preëmpted it. For a moment, nothing. For a moment I stood there without a thought in my head, stood like an idiot waiting for someone, some adult, Father Dagan maybe, to walk up and relieve me of this, take care of things, wash it all away. Then, gradually, a sort of sense returned to me. I remember thinking about safety. Shamefully, selfishly, my first thoughts were of safety, my own safety. If such a thing could happen, I thought, if such a thing could happen in a place as carefully run as the yard, then what about here, this wood, this path? How safe was I? How safe anyone? And then, oddly, idly, I thought about the hermit. For he must have heard it. And I wondered what he had thought, how an old man like that would have interpreted something like that, a sound as loud as that. And then, as if by introducing Father Gwynedd into my thoughts I could no longer avoid it, I thought about the thing itself. Carefully, gingerly, I walked up to the stone face that was the sound's meaning and, with the tip of my finger, I touched its surface. And was immediately off and running again, my mind full of terrible images, off and running back toward the yard, the furnace, back toward where I had last seen Brother Victricius.

Of course everyone makes a great deal of the bellows, the fact that the bellows were found closed. In all the discussions that took place afterwards, the endless Chapters, the pointless gossip, much was made of the fact that the bellows were found closed, that I had given testimony to the fact they were open when I left, that, indeed, Brother himself had stayed my final stroke, forced me to leave them open, full of air, ready to be discharged. But that doesn't really mean anything, does it? I mean, who's to say why they were closed? Maybe he thought the stack had cleared. Maybe he saw a puff of smoke escape from the stack and thought he could dislodge the obstruction, that a bit of vigorous pumping with the bellows might be all it would take. Brother never could resist the urge to fix something. Or, if we really want to be hard on him, we could go so far as to say he might have been impatient. He could have been. It happens sometimes, even to the best of us. Maybe Brother was impatient with the obstruction, irritated by this delay in his plans, his expectations for the day. You can see how that could have happened, how, not really thinking about it, he might have grabbed the bellows' upper pole, forced it down, driven a final blast into the furnace. *Take that!* he would have thought, maybe even picturing the source of his annoyance as he did so, the personage who had caused him all this anxiety, maybe even thinking about what it would look like to blow a great blast of heat up *his* skirts, cook *him* in the furnace. Anyone might have done that; *I* might have done that, probably had. But surely that is not sin, or at least not deadly sin. If thoughts and dreams, conceits and whimsy—not acted upon but merely imagined—can determine our fate, what chance have any of us? No. No, surely we will not suffer for the anger we feel when we stub a toe, crack a tooth. God cannot be as petty as that.

So the fact that the bellows were found closed can be shown to mean nothing. The fact that Victricius must have closed those bellows may very well mean nothing at all. Except that he died looking at the furnace. Except that he must have died bent over before the furnace like a supplicant before his master, the bellows thrust flat against the ground before him, no protection at all. Which means he died trying to make iron. Which means Victricius died trying to do exactly that which his abbot had ordered him to do.

But if even that is not enough, if even that does not quell the accusations, stay the tongues of those that would deny Brother heaven, have his body dug up, ripped, from consecrated ground, then I must point out one final—and I believe decisive—factor in his favor. He did not look at me. Think about that. When Victricius sent me off to the abbot, ordered me away from the yard, he did not look at me. Indeed, not only did he not look at me, but he stood with his back to me, eyes firmly locked upon the furnace. Now remember, after the departure of Agatho, I was as close to a companion as Brother had at Redestone. It was I who stood beside him when he pulled his illicit pots from the ashes, I who kept that secret safe. I was buried with him beneath the great snowfall, had been nursed by him, listened to his one and special tale. It was I, and I alone I believe, who understood what Brother lost when we lost Agatho, what that cost him, how unhappy he had become. And, finally, it was I who had shared the daily drudgery of his work. How often had the two of us, standing there cold and tired or hot and tired, dripping with rain or sweat, how often had we stood like that, the unpopular monk and his unhappy servant, how often had we stood like that in his small stinking yard and, however desultorily, however discordantly, sung the office? *Ora et labora*, the two poles of our existence, this is what we had shared, this what we had known. And he did not look at me. He stood between me and the furnace, blocked with his own body the dangerously primed furnace, but he did not look at me. How many of you, if you had made that decision, if you knew these to be the last moments of your life, would not steal a final glance at the one, that special brother with whom you had shared so much? Yes, yes I know it is sin. Yes, I know such attachments are wrong, against the Rule. But I am not a fool, and neither are you. The Rule was made because men require a rule, because, by our nature, we form attachments. And so, despite our better judgment, there is always the one. And how many of you, in your frailty, in your earthliness, would not cast a final glance, however surreptitious, however profane, at that one part of the world you have so loved? *But Victricius did not look at me.*

XXXVI

So it all came tumbling down—Victricius's works, Redestone's place in the land, Godwin's dreams of glory. In an instant we had once more become what I suppose Abbot Folian had always intended us to be: a collection of rather insignificant men pursuing otherworldly goals in a part of the country of no particular interest to anyone.

For several weeks, as I remember it, a peculiar silence prevailed at the abbey. This was a silence unlike that demanded by the Rule. The air did not tremble with repressed communication, eyes did not meet, fingers did not fly. The brothers went about their daily round like men walking in their sleep, heads down, shoulders rounded, hoods often as not up. I think there was little prayer at that time. The office suffered. Brother Prior's midday practice was discontinued but it made little difference. The community was uneasy, frightened, unsure. No one knew what was to become of us.

Of all people, it was Godwin who brought us back to ourselves, got us working again, thinking, planning ahead. Though there are those who will claim he did so for purely selfish reasons, no one can deny that the weeks following the destruction of the furnace were among his finest. While the rest of the community seemed willing to give up all hope and even Prior Maban appeared lost, Father Abbot went about the difficult task of rallying his troops. Shrewdly, he began by feeding our fears. The clever Gaul was dead, he told us, and without him there could be no more iron. Over night we had become an unimportant outpost set in rugged country on a contested and dangerous border. No longer could we hope for assistance from the outside world. Without iron, we mattered not to them. And so we must fend for ourselves. We must make food. If we were not to starve this winter, we must make a great deal of food indeed.

It was, as I remember it, about a week later, and a full three weeks sooner than was then customary, that Father Abbot turned over nominal control of the monastery to Brother Cellarer. All demands upon our work-force, all decisions concerning time and the allocation of resources, were now weighed against Osric's needs and the needs of the coming harvest. And it was into this new alignment, this accident of season and intent, that, like an angel from heaven, Brother Edgar now descended with his message from Modra nect. The hermit had grown feeble with age, he told Chapter, too feeble really to care for himself any longer. Someone was going to have to move up there with him. Someone was going to have to stay with him from now on, nurse him through what Edgar clearly believed to be Father's final days on earth.

There had of course been discussion. Prior Maban, not surprisingly, had been outraged. That we should lose an able-bodied man at such a time was absurd, he declared, preposterous. Anyone could see that it would be better for the old has-been to be carried down the mountain, in chains if need be, that here at least he could be cared for properly, and not at the expense of one of our workers. But for once Maban had not carried the day. I'll never forget the thrill I felt when Dagan rose to challenge him in Chapter, rose to remind the community in a voice not heard in that place for some time that the hermit's removal from the mountain was not an act to be taken lightly, that Father Gwynedd lived upon Modra nect, refused to descend from it, as the result of a vow, and if vows were now to be so easily dispensed with…. Well, where would any of us be?

It had, of course, been an argument that could not be countered. Maban had sputtered and fumed but there was little he could do. And so it was that I now found myself once again climbing Modra nect, once more wending my way up familiar paths, looking upon scenes I had not expected to see again in this life. That I had been chosen for this mission as a sop to Prior Maban's pride, that much had been made of the fact my loss would mean little to the harvest, that I had not yet achieved full stature, that I was, indeed, the small-est member of the community—these humiliations, these indignities, for once, mattered little, mattered not at all next to the fact that I was here, free, upon the mountain. And that I was here to stay. That tomorrow I would not have to climb down, nor the next day nor the next. That I was meant to remain, had been *ordered* to remain up here day after day, week after week, until such time as....

But I would not think about that. The hermit had always been old, and sometimes he had been ill. Doubtless Edgar exaggerated. He was known for that. Brother Prior had said as much in Chapter. And even if it was true, even if Gwynedd had experienced some sort of decline, he was still Father Hermit, would still, I knew—knew without even having to think about it—love me, love me when I needed him to and, more important still, leave me alone when I did not. I could not have asked for a better outcome. All my prayers, all my dreams, had come true. That Maban had been taken down a peg in the process only added to my delight. It was as if God Himself had joined forces with me against the world, returned Redestone in an instant to its proper state, reproved evildoers, vindicated saints. The days—the days of unrestricted freedom and liberty—stretched out before me like a great and endless feast. All seemed wonderful, perfect, grand.

Who knows why I turned from the path I was meant to follow that day, chose instead to delay my arrival at the hermit's camp, visit first the crag? It may have been nothing more than a childish desire to exercise my newfound freedom, put it to the test, watch it fly. Or, equally childlike, I may have wanted to look one final time upon the place I had just escaped, lord it over Maban from what was, after all, a fairly distant (and safe) height. I don't know, memory fails me here. All I know for sure is that I remember climbing—as I should have climbed, as I had been ordered to climb—up the path, toward the hermit, and the next thing I remember I am already seated on the crag, a gray and racing sky overhead, the world and all its trea-sure spread out at my feet. There must have been a deer somewhere on the mountain above me because I remember that too, have long associated the wild smell of deer with that day—the fresh smell of the sky, the pines, the rock, and the musky smell of deer. And of course the wind. I remember the wind, remember how surprised it seemed to find me there, the way it investigated my surfaces, a blind man trying to see, understand, with the tips of his fingers. Down in the valley nothing moved. Despite the wind that blew where I was, the world below remained hushed, still. The trees along the Meolch did not bend, the banner Brother Prior had placed over Godwin's lodgings did not fly. If it hadn't been for the river, the leaden glint of its waters, the suggestion of movement, sound, rising to me from its rapids, I might have thought all of Redestone an illusion, the picture of a monastery and its fields instead of the real and breathing place that it was.

I looked down toward the village, the house I had always believed to be Eanflæd's. On a ridge below me, a stand of pine had put out new growth which now partially blocked my view, but I could still see the door, the one window, the rather poorly kept garden. I wondered what Eanflæd was doing. Though there was little smoke rising from the roof, for some reason I pictured her cooking, body bent over a steaming array of pots, sleeves rolled up, cheeks moist and pink with effort. The vision pleased me. There seemed nothing wrong with it. From such a distance, how could my thoughts be anything other than pure? I wanted only what was best for her, that she might be happy and healthy, that she might have plenty of good food to eat.

Pleased with myself, I continued my survey: the ponds, the orchard, the South Wood. I found myself struck again by the size and extent of the latter. From the terrace you cannot help but feel if you were only a little taller, a little higher up, you might see to the far edge of the wood, perhaps even to that golden land the sun so likes to tarry over in winter. But from the crag such delusions fall away. Despite your vantage point, the wood marches on, vast, unending, indifferent. Everything—all that your precious world holds: church and cloister, terrace and fields—seems by comparison small and insignificant.

I looked back at the place made small by that comparison and found myself unexpectedly touched by its smallness. There was, after all, something endearing about such an enterprise, a world carved from the wilderness, sustaining itself upon the fruits of its labors, the strength of its devotions. I looked at the fields, the rows set off by long puddles reflecting gray sky, and I prayed that the rainy weather might cease, that the ground might dry, the harvest be brought in before the rot commence. From the crag, the sanctuary provided by the mountain, I found I could afford to be generous. Redestone looked a sweet place, however small, a benign place, however rigorous. I liked the way its buildings looked inward upon themselves, the doors and windows of dortoir and refectory opening onto the garth, the church returning their gaze, all of them safe and warm beneath their thatch, backs to the rest of the world, stones and daub faintly glowing. I remembered my dream, the rattle of the wagon, Eanflæd, the cherry blossoms. From the crag, I found it difficult to understand the apprehension that dream had caused me. How had I ever seen Redestone as malevolent? Surrounded on all sides by danger—opposing armies, devil worship, the wood—she nevertheless turned her eyes inward, kept watch not for evil but for God. You had to admire the audacity of such a place, the audacity of the men who built and sustained it. Those men had fed and clothed me. They cared for me. From up here it was easy to love them. Why I could almost love Father Abbot. Certainly I wished him well. I was, I suddenly realized, changed. The weeks of prayer and self-denial had had their inevitable effect. Almost despite myself, I had become a better person than I had been.

Absently, I let my eye wander on up the valley. At a little distance above the abbey mill, a spill of rock from the mountain's flank joins the river and the forest briefly changes character, becoming mostly sycamores. Here I lingered, regarding for a moment the spot where once I had been in the habit of praying, associating it in my mind with my present location, the lessons Father Hermit had taught me. A prickling, the suggestion of an anxiety, and I moved on. Still farther up-river I was able to pick out the break in the trees that marked the yard, and was relieved to see no evidence of the accident that had taken place there. I thought about Victricius, missed him. In an odd sort of way he and I had been very much alike—both of us sometimes awkward, uncomfortable in community, certainly different, set apart. True, his had been a difficult service, but he had never beaten me. I could have done worse. Indeed, I found myself thinking I would pray for Brother during my sojourn upon the mountain, that his cause would become mine. The thought cheered me. I rather liked the idea of myself as Victricius's champion. From now on people were going to have to answer to me if they wanted to say anything against the little man from Gaul.

Above the furnace, the wooded bank of the river is marked by an unnaturally straight line cut through the trees. This line marks the path our race follows as it rises to meet its source at the falls of the Meolch. Thinking about Victricius, I now directed my attention to this spot, remembering a time when, after a particularly bad flood, Brother and I had hiked up there to check on the gate. The thing I remembered best from that day was what it had felt like to stand at the top of the race and stare down its line of sight toward the yard. With the air around me full of vapor and the sound of the falls, it had been easy to imagine what had happened during the flood. Upon encountering the open sluice-gate, the swell of water had turned a portion of its fury upon the path thus exposed, roaring down the race toward our work-place. This secondary torrent had then ignored the way the race bends at the yard and, instead, plunged straight ahead, back down to the river, in the process ripping out flags, undermining the furnace, and carrying off the greater part of our charcoal. Eventually of course the waters had subsided, but not before they'd gouged out an entirely new channel back down to the Meolch, a channel down which our race continued to uselessly pour. At a time when all the world gave evidence of an excess of water, Redstone went without: the mill did not turn, the moss on the lavabo had grown dusty and dry, Brother Kitchen's drains did not drain, and the ditch had begun to smell. Victricius, I remembered, took one look at the sluice-gate— half-buried in silt and sand—and pronounced it salvageable. Without so much as a glance at the rest of the wonderful destruction wrought by the flood, he had turned and begun the march back down to the yard. "Come on," he'd called back to me, "we'll need shovels!"

Above the falls the river turns behind a long ridge and is no longer visible from the crag, though the valley that carries it can still be followed as it rises into the mountain. At a point hazy with distance, a pale ochre scar is just visible against the dark green of the valley's far wall. I can't remember what this really is—a cliff, the opening to a cave, I'm not sure—but I do remember Father Hermit telling me that it was a forbidden place, that the hill people still sometimes visited there, believing it to be the lair of a particularly strong demon. Above this, the valley continues to rise, narrowing as it winds up into the mountain until, having risen till it can rise no more, it buries its snout in the saddle that connects Modra nect's southern and northern peaks. Here it was that my praying self had once perceived a great and flimsy dam, had reached for it and, in my arrogance, pulled it down.

Perhaps it was my memory of the damage caused to the sluice-gate by the flood, or maybe it was just the opportunity provided by the crag to reconstruct something which, heretofore, I had only seen in my mind, but, for whatever reason, I now found myself absently retracing the route God's wrath would have taken as it poured down out of the mountain. I thought the high valleys would have filled first and, thinking it, watched as, one by one, they did, the red-hot vein of God's displeasure creeping slowly down Modra nect's brow. At the pagan site the livid stream flared momentarily as if undecided about its course, then, however reluctantly, moved on, great swaths of forest catching fire as it passed, rocky outcrops losing their grip upon the mountain, sliding off to join and swell the flood. A final turn and the leading edge of the flow swept into view; hot and roaring, voracious, engulfing rocks and rapids, it raced toward the falls.

And then I saw it. Sitting there on the crag, legs dangling beneath me, the wind still playing at my woolens, I saw it, saw what would have happened next, the pale thin line cut through the trees, the path provided, the easy slope, the yard, the furnace, Brother Victricius.

But that was absurd!

I looked away, down toward the village, refusing to see what I had seen and yet seeing it still, the sluice-gate, the sudden arrival of the flow, the inevitable diversion, the inevitable consequence. Was it possible? Could my prayer—unatoned for, unconfessed—have routed God's fury toward Victricius? No! No, I would not have it! I had prayed against Wilfrid, not the furnace master!

Still a part of me would not leave it alone. Who, I found myself thinking, who had stood the most to lose from Victricius's death? And silently, almost serenely, the answer rose before me like a dark unwanted sun. Wilfrid. Yes, Wilfrid surely. Without our furnace master, Redestone could produce no iron. And without Redestone's iron Wilfrid became, at least so far as Ecgfrith was concerned, next to nothing, powerless. The king could and had attacked him openly. There was even said to have been advantage in it. Many still remembered the forced expulsions, the shame of the Roman tonsure, the appropriations of land and title, the insults, the pride. Without iron, Wilfrid had few friends, many enemies. The latest reports had him in full retreat, hounded and harassed from country to country just as (and here I could no longer pretend otherwise) I had prayed he might be.

And if that were true, if it really had been my prayer that had brought all this about, then what might not be next? What else lay in the path of God's destruction—the terrace, our crops, Eanflæd, Father Dagan, Redestone itself?!

And I was up and running, up and running toward the hermit and his camp, toward the one priest, the one father I knew who—without threat of exposure or expulsion—could absolve me of all this, save me and the world from all that I had put in motion.

The camp that day, when I finally reached it, looked exactly as it had the first time I'd seen it. There was Father's hut, tumbledown and forlorn, Father's pots, Father's fire, and there, sitting by the stream like an old stump, like something that never moved, was Father himself. Of course I should have waited. If my life on the mountain had taught me anything it was this, that I should not disturb the hermit when he was at prayer. But I couldn't help myself. Forgetting everything in my relief at seeing him, forgetting even my prayer, the confession I had to make, I ran to him, ran to him and threw myself down on the ground beside him. "Father!" I shouted. "Father, it's me, Winwæd! I'm back!"

I'll never forget the look he threw me, eyes wide in astonishment, face pale, almost comically distraught. But he pulled himself together for my sake, visibly composed himself. "Yes," he said, as if it were the most natural thing in the world to discover me sitting on the ground beside him, "Yes, of course it is you." Then he looked away as if he'd heard something, a bird maybe.

I followed his gaze impatiently, saw nothing. "Father, I have to talk with you," I said. "You have to hear my confession."

Again the old man's head spun around, again he looked at me. For a moment he hesitated, frowning, then, in a voice full of suspicion and disapproval, he said, "You're not Edgar. Where's Brother Edgar with my biscuits and honey?"

ctually of course, he came and went. He was at his best in the morning. Sometimes, some mornings, I could almost believe him unchanged, that it was still the father I had known and loved that sat opposite me, smiled as I spoke, crunched into one of Brother Thruidred's biscuits. But then I would ask him something, something simple like How did this pot get broken? or Where is your belt?, and such a look of doubt and confusion would come over him that I would have to look away. For it was difficult for me to see the man who had taught me so much reduced to such a state.

At other times (I will admit it here), I could become quite impatient with Father. The hermit I had known seemed then gone, entirely absent, and, in his place, I found myself servant to a senile old man, a senile old man who required my constant attention, constant care. For Brother Edgar had been right, Father was now far too feeble to care for himself. If I had not been there to parcel out his food, I do not doubt he would have gone through his stores in a single week. If I had not mended his clothes...well...suffice it to say he would have brought shame upon himself. The office was of course utterly beyond him. Oh sometimes he would try to join in, climbing onto his feet as one would an unsteady table, teetering there, humming, so that I knew the old man planned to come in on the next antiphon. But he rarely managed more than a phrase or two, occasionally an entire verse, as if some ancient door had suddenly sprung wide, shed light upon some otherwise long-forgotten corner of Father's mind, only to close again as quickly, Father's eyes blinking in surprise, a small curious smile turning up the corners of his lips. And there were other things too of course. The usual problems associated with age. But, in Father's case, exacerbated by his lack of memory, the utter surprise with which he greeted each of his failings as if—to my consternation—this were the first time such a thing had ever happened to him.

Though that of course may have been as much a result of cunning as the forgetfulness of age. For the man who, to my way of thinking, had always been more than any other himself, unadorned and unaffected, became, in his dotage, something of a poseur, putting on whatever face his poor demented mind told him the present occasion called for. I'll never forget the time the pilgrim visited us, the last, as it happened, of the pilgrims I ever saw come to that place. Though I did not know the man, it was obvious from the way he greeted the hermit that this was not the first time he had been there, that he easily recognized Gwynedd, saw nothing in his appearance to suggest debility. It was hard for me to watch that exchange, the farmer at first happy, ebullient, the hermit dissembling outrageously, assuming an unnatural air (a hill person's idea of what a wise man might look like) in his bid to appear normal, still in command of his senses. For some reason (out of loyalty to the hermit, the holy man he once had been?) I found I could not bring myself to simply tell our visitor what the true situation was, pull the man aside and reveal Father's secret. Still, it was painful to watch him discover it for himself—Father's disingenuousness on display, the false conviviality, the clumsy attempts at conversation, the repetitions, the evasions, the speeches that began well only to trail off into unrelated remarks about the weather, the foliage, the taste of biscuits and honey.

Biscuits and honey. How Father could go on about biscuits and honey in those days. Weren't biscuits and honey delicious? Why didn't we have biscuits and honey more often? Do you suppose we could have some biscuits and honey now? Listening to the man you'd have thought the subject resolved some deep and powerful mystery for him, as if God Himself, the very nature of God, might depend upon a proper exegesis of biscuits and honey.

Which, truth be told, I rather liked. For—though I resented having to play cellarer to Father's hunger, having to tell him over and over again that he could not have that which he so clearly desired—still there was something about this obsession of his that reminded me of the man I had known, the way he had looked at life, the pleasure he had taken in it. Once, I remember, I even asked him why it was he went on so about biscuits and honey, what was it about biscuits and honey he liked so much, knowing full well such a question was beyond him but enjoying teasing him in this way, teasing him as once, when I was a child, he had teased me. But to my surprise Father took the question seriously, made a determined effort to answer it. Speaking slowly, his mind's cart bumping down a long-unused track, he said, "Well, you know…you know I've never…I've never had a *bad* biscuit and honey." That morning, for the first time in weeks, I laughed and laughed.

And so our lives progressed. Time passed slowly on the mountain, uneventfully. Once a week we received a visit from Brother Edgar: supplies were delivered, news of the abbey, but, nowadays, no tabula. Sometimes, when I could get away from the hermit for a moment or two, give him something to eat that I knew would keep him occupied for a while, I would run down to the crag, run down to the crag and watch as Brother wound his way back down the mountain away from us, away from me. And with each passing week it seemed the world Edgar returned to, the world of monks and order, Rule and discipline, became more and more distant, more and more removed, so that, in a way, it began to seem as though I watched not a brother walking away from me but Redestone itself, my life at Redestone, the boy I had been there, any obligations I might owe the place.

Which is not to say I didn't think about my prayer, worry about the fact that it might as yet be, in a very real sense, abroad upon the land. But I had been, I believe, shaken by what I had discovered on Modra nect, the profound change Father Hermit had undergone, so shaken that any decision, any course of action, seemed now beyond me, that just getting through this day and the next was the most I could hope for. Now some will say (some *have* said) that this was only a blind, that I took refuge in a pretended shock to avoid doing that which clearly I should have done: return to the abbey, confess my sin, suffer the consequences. And there may well be some truth to this. I was terrified of expulsion, had seen the pain it caused Ealhmund. Still, you must remember how close Father and I had been. This was the man whose Way I had followed. Did I now look upon the place to which it led me? What does it mean when the person you want to impress more than any other in the world can no longer remember your name, will never again be able to remember your name? When the man whose thoughts fill your tabulum has had his own effaced, what does anything matter at all?

Of course a great chorus of nameless monks rose from their graves to answer that question each time I asked it. "Faith!" they cried in the approved response, the word echoing across the centuries like an illustration of itself, empty of all but letters, affectionless, unsupported, emaciated, meaning absolutely everything or absolutely nothing at all. And this, I reminded myself, this was what Father himself had always wanted for me. "You must give up everything," he had said, "if you want to win anything at all." And now, surely, I had. All my hopes, all my dreams of becoming a holy man, my prayers, my devotions, all these seemed little more than self-indulgent fantasies before the fatherless reality I now faced. I told myself that this was true faith, that from this point forward I was on my own, whatever I accomplished, for good or ill, would be mine, that I would have no one to blame or praise but myself, that, indeed, by losing Father I now gained the solitude he had always wanted for me, that for the rest of my life I would know the true emptiness, the true reality: Creation bereft of all but Himself. But it was a lonely place I had come to. I suppose I had always known that it would be. And still I missed my Father Hermit.

These then were the thoughts, the worries, the concerns, that occupied my mind during that long wet summer's end. And then one day Brother Edgar failed to appear with our supplies. At first, of course, I assumed I had miscalculated, that tomorrow was the appointed day, or the next day or even the next. But then I walked once more through my fingers, remembered the days one by one and realized that, as incredible as it seemed, I was right, had to be right, that this was the Sabbath, that Edgar—no not Edgar but Redestone, mighty Redestone herself—*Redestone* had failed in her obligations to me!

It is sad but true that this realization brought me not a little cheer. You cannot imagine how difficult it is for an oblate, the unerring rectitude of his elders, the feeling that, surely, no one as unworthy as himself (we are, after all, reminded of it daily) could live up to such perfection. And then to discover them imperfect, flawed, pierced by the same weaknesses with which we are riddled…. Well, it was as if a great load had been lifted from my shoulders; I could hardly wait to get down to the crag, look upon the shameful miscreant, watch as she blushed and writhed. But even as I thought these thoughts, felt this perverse joy, another part of me hesitated. For nothing like this had ever happened before. Ever. Not that I was really worried about the supplies. We had plenty of food, at least enough to get us through the next week. But, still, it was a commonplace in my life that the commonplace was fixed; it did not change: Prime followed Matins, Terce Prime, and Brother Edgar carried supplies to the hermit on the Sabbath. That this should not be so was like saying water might be dry or air edible. So it was that, even as I wanted more than anything else in the world to get down to the crag, see if I could determine why Edgar had failed to appear, still there was a part of me anxious about what I might find there.

It was nearly None by the time I convinced myself Brother really wasn't coming, and by that time Father had already taken his nap. But, thankfully, I was able to persuade him otherwise (the man passed from waking to sleeping easily in those days, as though sleeping itself were his natural state and waking a condition difficult to maintain), and once I had him safely bedded down again, I hurried to the crag as fast as my legs would carry me.

Truth be told, I don't know what I had expected to find there. Redestone entirely gone? The valley flooded perhaps or afire, an enemy host encamped upon our fields? Who knows what childish fantasies my mind had invented to explain Brother's absence? But surely nothing could have been less expected (or more disappointing?) than that which did greet my eyes, Redestone sitting quiet and peaceful beneath an overarching sky, no writhing, no blushes, just the familiar intimate cluster of red-brown buildings, green garth, surrounding fields. Why even God Himself seemed to smile upon the place, not a cloud in sight after all that rain.

And then I saw Father.

Thinking back on it now I realize he must have waited for just that moment, must have stood waiting for who knows how long beneath the eaves so that, when he saw me walk out onto the crag (as he must have known I would), he could step out into the sunlight of the garth and be certain his emergence would catch my eye. As of course it did. The man appeared (immediately recognizable in figure and gait as Father Dagan), moved purposefully to the center of the garth, and then—in a movement that sent a chill up my spine—cocked his head back and looked directly at the place where I stood. After all those years spent spying on the valley, someone had finally returned my gaze.

At first he did nothing. For what seemed a long while but in truth could not have been more than a moment or two, the two of us just stared across the distance separating us, our roles in a sense reversed, the one on high meek and trembling, the one below awful and mighty. Then, as if it were the most natural thing in the world, as if it were the reason he'd gone out there, stood at the center of the garth, Father raised his hand, raised his hand and shook it in the air like a man trying to shake water from his fingers. And as if there really had been water on his fingers, something glinted in the air, something caught the light, glinted in the air just beyond Father's outstretched hand. And I saw what it was.

But my mind rejected that.

My mind rejected that, began immediately to turn the thing Father brandished into something else, a pot perhaps or a lamp or maybe even (could it have been?) the distended and glistening stomach of a lamb. But then Father swung the thing again and I could no longer fool myself. The censer. Yes, yes of course it was. Which could mean only one thing. On only one other occasion had I seen them cense the garth, cense, for that matter, anything outside the church. They did it to ward off evil, to replace an evil air with that which was good, pure, holy. And instantly I knew why Brother Edgar hadn't come, why, doubtless, Brother wouldn't be coming again for some time, would, perhaps, never come again. The pestilence was among us. Father Dagan was censing the garth which meant—could only mean—one thing: *the pestilence was among us again.*

XXXVIII

It was a slow walk I made that day back up to the hermit's camp. There was so much to be done, and, so far as I could see, almost no way to do any of it. Father's message had, of course, been unequivocal. After making a show of censing the garth, he had pointed up at me and then, emphatically, displayed the palm of his hand. Knowing how susceptible I was to the disease, Father was ordering me to remain upon the mountain, hoping thereby to keep me above contagion's reach. But what Father didn't know, couldn't know, was that I was the cause of this illness, that if I could but descend, confess my sin, reverse the course of my prayer, Redestone might be saved. But how could I descend? If I went down now, who would care for Father? And once my crime had been revealed, once I had been expelled from the abbey, forgotten, what were the chances anyone would be sent back up the mountain to replace me? Prior Maban hadn't wished to send someone when the community was healthy and Redestone comparatively well manned. How would he feel now when any brother still fit must seem indispensable? No, no I could not fool myself. If I went down now, Father would die. Father would die alone and confused and afraid.

Unless, of course, *I* came back.

The thought, at first, struck me, naturally enough, as absurd. I mean I would be anathema, an excommunicate, someone all good people shunned, a rim-walker, an outcast, the mark of Cain upon my head. But, then again, given that status, who was going to bother with me? I would be—in a very real sense and for the first time in my life—free, free to do whatever I wanted, go wherever I wanted. And where of course I would want to go would be to the hermit. Forget the Rule, forget the Rule and forget Redestone; I would be able to climb back up the mountain and save Father, save and care for him for the rest of his life!

The rest of his life.

For that, of course, was what I had forgotten, what I had forgotten and now recalled. Behind me, back down the path I now trod, below the crag, below all that belonged to this mountain world, lay the valley, and in that valley lay disease. If I descended and then came back up, who was to say what I might not bring with me? Instead of saving the hermit I might be killing him, might be guaranteeing him a death I had witnessed too many times, a death I would not wish on my greatest enemy. Oh if only I'd never heard of Wilfrid, if only I'd never prayed those prayers, if only there was some way I could undo what I had done without having to go back down the mountain!

And it was then—as if I were a child again in the heat of the peas, the mountain clear and beckoning above me—that my thoughts rose to the hermit, rose as of old to the man who waited for me at the end of this path. Was it possible? Could *he* save me? And despite myself, despite the ban I had placed on all such thoughts, I remembered my first morning back on the mountain, what it had been like to wake up like that, to find the Host already raised, Father's face contorted, struggling to remember the words, the *exact* words, and then the look of relief that washed over him when he realized he was not alone, a look of relief that changed quickly into something else, a sly, almost mischievous invitation, the child enticing his father, cajoling him to help with a chore that by rights was the child's alone, Father asking for my help, pleading with his eyes that I make it better, fix this problem, this familiar thing we both knew and only he seemed to have forgotten the words for. And it was, I believe, as I was thinking this, remembering that wretched moment, that I knew, knew for certain: *I could have helped him.*

Though of course I hadn't. I mean, after all, it was the Mass— Father's face crestfallen when I took the vessels from him. But I could have. I mean I did know the words, had heard them who knows how many times before. And if that were possible, if I could have walked him through the Mass—the introit, the offertory, the great Amen— well, how much easier still the shorter rite of confession?

Of course Brother Baldwin wouldn't approve, and certainly not Brother Prior, but what harm could there be in it? If the phrases were the same, if they got said, what did it matter if someone prompted the priest, reminded him of what needed to be said next, needed to be done? So long as Father actually said them, even if only parroting me, he was saying the words, a priest was saying them; and I would respond from the depths of my heart, my contrition real, genuine, true. How many times had we been taught that the priest was only a channel for God's love, God's forgiveness? And so he would be in this case. I would be his servant, nothing more, acting as his memory when needed. Even if you tried to claim the sanctity of the confessional had been violated, there being, in a sense, three people present—penitent, priest, and servant—I could claim it remained whole as both penitent and servant existed in the one person—me—just as, in a sense, Christ and man existed in the priest. Yes. Yes, the more I thought about it, the more reasonable it became. With Father supplying the holiness and I the words, together we might approximate one half-way decent priest. An inattentive priest perhaps, but what did that matter? How many times had I (and how many others?) hurried to Father Beorhtfrith's confessional for just that reason, knowing full well that any sin dropped down that well would sink forever unnoticed beneath Father's blissful self-regard? And besides, this was an emergency. Redestone stood in danger of destruction, and I—and I alone—held the power to save her.

Doubtless I ran that last little stretch up to the hermit's camp. I'm not sure, I have no memory of it, but I can imagine myself doing so, happy, exultant, sure of my course now, anxious to get on with it. And then the inevitable disillusionment: the old man awake when I got there (always a bad sign) and clearly distracted, looking for something. I glanced over at the camp's stores but, thankfully, could see no evidence of the usual fumbling depredations. Then he noticed me, Father noticed me, turned what I had come to think of as his oblate face upon me, the one that gave nothing away, that appeared neither too friendly (in case I was a stranger) nor too shocked (in case I was his son). He looked at me. He didn't say anything. He smiled a careful smile.

I said, "Are you hungry Father?" reminding him of both his position and mine, that I was the purveyor of food.

The smile grew large, real; the old man blinked, seemed to think about it. "Yes," he said. "Yes, you know I think I am."

I smiled. "Maybe you'd like some biscuits and honey?"

The smile extended to the cheeks, threatened to overwhelm Father's face. "Biscuits and honey!" he said, the phrase itself a superlative.

I nodded. "But first we have to do something. First you have to hear my confession."

"Your *confession*?!" Father said the word as if I'd suggested something obscene.

"Yes, my confession. You're a priest and I need someone to hear my confession."

"Well, yes, of course…." Father adopted a thoughtful air, the wise man pondering a particularly thorny problem. "But…well, you know, it's been a long time. I'm not sure…."

"I'll help you."

Father looked at me as if he'd forgotten I was there. "Are you a priest?" he asked.

"No," I answered, trying to keep the feeling out of my voice. "I'm not a priest, but I know the words. I can help."

Father blinked, "Oh, well, that would be nice. A confession." Again the word sounded strange on his tongue.

"Yes. A confession."

"Well where would we do it?"

"Here. Now."

"Now!" Father tossed a frightened glance at the surrounding wood.

"It'll be all right." I reached out, touched him on the arm, and immediately it was as if some power had gone out of me: Father's shoulders relaxed; he looked up at me, smiled. "Well, all right," he said, "if you think it'll be all right."

"I do," I said, never having felt less sure of anything in my life. "I do."

Father nodded. "Here?" he asked again, this time perfectly trusting, more than willing to sit down wherever I suggested and do whatever it was I wanted him to do.

"Let's move down by the stream," I said, "you know, where we used to do it…"—my voice breaking on this last, the distance between the real and the remembered suddenly clear, manifest.

Father just looked at me, no more cognizant of my feelings than he was of my name. I took him by the hand and led him down to the stream, my eyes brimming uselessly.

That was, by any lights I suppose, a strange confession, halting, broken, following the prescribed order but only just. We began, as I remember it, with the usual exchanges, the ritual request, the ritual declaration, Father nodding absently all the while, watching the stream, so that I couldn't tell if he was really listening to my voice or only lulled by it, eyes glazed, red-rimmed, lids drooping. I think I must have passed over the customary list of minor offenses—the initial offerings with which we propitiate our God, toughen Him for what is to come—for the next thing I remember clearly is the way Father jumped, roused himself from stupor. "What?!" he demanded. "What did you say you did?"

"I said I prayed for the destruction of our bishop."

"You didn't!"

I had to look away, pretend to study something downstream, all the while telling myself I'd been mistaken, that I hadn't heard it, hadn't detected the note of glee in Father's voice, the fishwife exclaiming over a particularly choice bit of gossip. "Yes Father," I said, still not looking at him, "that is what I did. I prayed for the destruction of our bishop."

Nothing, silence.

I looked back around at the hermit only to discover that he was now staring off up-stream as if expecting something, a boat perhaps.

"Did you hear me?"

The hermit's head swung around turtle-like. "Were you…? I'm sorry," he said. "Did you say something?"

"My confession. You're hearing my confession, Father."

"Oh yes, of course." Father nodded, assumed a neutral air.

"I was telling you I had prayed against Bishop Wilfrid, prayed that he might die."

Father's face became serious. "You prayed *against* someone?"

"Yes Father, our bishop."

"Oh, that's bad, very bad."

"Yes I know; I am sorry Father."

The old man lowered his gaze, noticed something on his knee, a patch, fingered it, managed to pull a stitch loose.

"Father?"

Again the questioning eyes, the innocent look, the face somehow smaller than I remembered it, reduced, contracted, a face caving in on itself, collapsing beneath the weight of years.

"You were hearing my confession. I was telling you that I had committed a grave sin, that I have prayed for the death of Bishop Wilfrid."

"You prayed for someone's death!?"—the information news to Father all over again, a cause for shock this time, perturbation.

"Yes, that's right."

"But why would you do that? Why would anyone do something so dangerous, so…so…."

"Foolhardy?"

Father smiled. "Yes! So *foolhardy*. Why would you…. I'm sorry, what were we talking about?"

This was impossible—Father's debility becoming in and of itself a penance, forcing me to confess my sin over and over again, relive the shame, the guilt, without any hope of resolution. "We've been over all this before," I said. "This is my *confession*. You're hearing my *confession*. And you've just asked why I was so stupid as to pray for the death of our bishop."

"Oh, yes…"—Father's look of sobriety a sham, his lower lip quivering, giving him away.

I shook my head. "It was for my father, for Ceolwulf. He asked me to do it."

"Your father asked you to do something?"

"Yes, no." Again I shook my head. "No, that's not right, it was for me. I did it for me, because I was angry. Because I didn't like Abbot Godwin, didn't like what he'd done to me."

"The abbot did something to you?" Father was appalled.

I smiled. It was a little smile, meaning something quite different from what Father thought, but he took it seriously. He smiled. I shook my head. "Yes," I said. "Yes, he took away my right to come here, to visit you."

"You don't mean it!" Father making conversation now, inserting an exclamation where his mind told him exclamation was required.

"Yes, Abbot Godwin took away my right to…. He assigned the task of supplying you to Brother Edgar. That's when Brother Edgar began coming here."

"Brother Edgar?"

"Yes, you remem…. It doesn't matter. I wanted to come here. I missed you, I missed this place."

"And I missed you too!" the old man serious now, the part of him that remained Father Hermit flaring up, recognizing a need in me and responding to it whether or not he knew my name, had any idea who I was.

I smiled.

Father smiled. He'd already forgotten what had led to these expressions but he liked smiling, always had. It was remarkable really. You could destroy the man's body, ruin his mind, and still the holiness endured, still it glowed from within him, alive, pure, inextinguishable. I suppose I should have taken off my sandals and covered my head in its presence. I suppose I should have knelt down before it, worshipped at its feet. Instead, stubbornly, I went on.

"My penance," I said, as if nothing had happened. "You need to give me a penance, Father."

And the light went out. Leaning out over the stream, trying to get a better look at me, eyes cloudy with years, the smile vanished from Father's face, disappeared, was as quickly replaced by something else—the blinking eyes, the trembling lip, the shaking head of old and vacuous age.

"You've heard my confession and now you have to give me a penance," I said, trying to hurry him along, embarrassed now by what sat before me, the part I had played in its creation. "You know, a penance, something I can do to atone for my sin."

"A penance." Father nodded. "Yes, of course, a penance."

I waited.

The old man didn't say anything.

"Father?"

"You know I think I'm getting hungry." He glanced up at the sky. "Isn't it about time to eat?"

I shook my head. "In a moment Father, first we have to finish this. Remember, you're hearing my confession? I've just confessed that I prayed for Bishop Wilfrid's death and now you're going to give me a penance."

"Say a Pater Noster and be mindful of the phrase 'Thy Kingdom come'." Father blinked, looked at me, clearly as surprised as I by the ease with which this chestnut had sprung from him. It happened sometimes; if you poked and prodded hard enough, the coals of Father's mind would produce a little light.

"But Father," I protested, "a Pater Noster...? I mean I prayed for someone's *death*, the death of my rightful superior. I need more than a mere Pater Noster, give me something really hard to do."

"There's nothing *mere* about a Pater Noster. And besides," Father less certain here, "that's the penance I always assign, isn't it?"

Well, yes. I couldn't argue with him there. But still....

"Now make an act of contrition so we can eat."

"But...?"

The eyes grew large, Father's hunger brooking no dissent.

"Lord Jesus Christ, Son of the living God, have mercy on me a sinner."

Father smiled. "'Lord Jesus Christ, Son of the...' What was the rest of that?"

"You taught me that prayer, Father."

"I did?"

I nodded, smiled.

Father looked down at his lap. "So…" he said, noticing the patch again, picking at it experimentally, "may we eat now?"

I almost laughed. He was like a child really, a little boy, and at that moment I felt an almost paternal regard for him. "Yes, we can eat Father. But first you have to absolve me of my sin."

The face came up, looked worried.

"It's all right, I'll help you. Remember, 'God, the Father of mercies'?"

"God, the Father of mercies…."

"'Through the death and the resurrection of His Son….'"

"Through the death and…."

"Resurrection."

"Through the death and resurrection of His Son…."

"Has reconciled…."

"Has reconciled the world to Himself and sent…and sent the Holy Spirit among us for the forgiveness of sins…."—this last said quickly, Father spitting it out before he could forget it again.

"That's right, very good! Now, remember the rest? 'Through the ministry of the Church….'"

A small frown. "Through the ministry of the Church…." Another smile. "Through the ministry of the Church may God give you pardon and peace, and I…and I absolve you from your sins in the name of the Father, and of the Son and of the Holy Spirit."

And it was done, the Names invoked, my confession made, Father's absolution given. It might not have been canonically correct but, under the circumstances, it was—I honestly believed—the best I could hope for.

XXXIX

anflæd. Eanflæd. Do you have any idea what it is like for
me to commit that name to writing, to finally confess to the
fact of her existence, to the fact of our.... Well, what name
should I give the utter nothing that has connected us all these years,
the meetings that never took place, the messages that never got sent,
the gestures that figure—wild and fantastic—only in my mind? Like
some anxious spirit I have hovered over her life, caught glimpses
from the terrace of someone who might or might not be she, listened
for reports of her in Chapter, celebrated her successes, mourned her
losses, prayed for her soul. And is it possible...? Do you suppose Eanflæd has ever thought of me?

Yes. Yes I know, I am a silly old man, the worst kind of monk—a
dreamer, a mountebank, one whose vocation is little more than façade.
Yet I cannot help myself, I do wonder.... Does she ever think of the
boy she visited once beneath a cherry tree, the oblate with whom she
shared, if not an afternoon, at least a portion of one? Does she fare
well? Does her husband love her? Does he care for her as he should?
Is her larder well-stocked? Does her complexion remain, as it does in
my mind, soft, pure, lit from within? Does she sleep well? Or, now
that we have drawn so much closer to its door, does the house of the
dead once more figure in her dreams? If it does, I hope that it has
become less frightening, less dramatic with age. I hope that, were the
two of us to meet again, sit beneath a cherry tree, share its fruit, we
might laugh over the things that bother us now, our knees, how they
refuse to bend, our eyes, how they fail to see, our friends, how they
insist upon dying. She would tell me about her children. She would

cry, perhaps, over the two she lost. I would share with her that I have prayed—and continue to pray—for all five of them. And then, maybe, if the moment suited, we would talk again of her dream, that place, the house where bodies refuse to lie still, where the dead turn and trouble one another, trouble us, and how, with age, even that agitation loses some of its terror, seems, if just as real, less awful, more familiar, a bogeyman grown almost, if not quite, ridiculous with time.

The other day a novice said something to me about the "forest path" and it took me a moment to realize what he was talking about, that somewhere along the line he'd mistaken the word "forest" for "furnace" and now that path which once signified so much to me, means nothing to him, has become only a way through a wood. How long before such a mistake becomes common usage, before all that we have known and loved passes, arcane and archaic, into dead and empty past?

So many stories are told now of the death of Father Gwynedd, of how he asked to be carried down to the stream where it had been his habit to pray, and how, sitting there, singing God's praises, meditating upon the blessings he had received in this life, the good man passed peacefully into the next. And I would not deny such an account for, in its essentials, it is true, and has doubtless set a pious and helpful example for many that have followed after him. Still, as with most such tales, the event itself was both simpler and more complicated.

It was not long after Father heard my confession that his health took a turn for the worse. His feet began to swell, which (though it seemed a minor complaint at the time) clearly made the hermit uneasy. Indeed, if I did not watch him closely, the old man was liable to remove his sandals to relieve the pressure they caused him and wander thereafter barefoot about his camp. This I should not have minded were it not for the fact that, as unsteady as he was, I worried he might veer toward the fire and step upon a coal. Now it was a peculiar feature of this illness that whenever Father lay down, and especially if he lay down with his feet raised, the swelling subsided. But even this afforded the poor man little comfort for, just as the pressure in his feet abated, Father would begin to experience difficulty breathing—the two events falling so quickly one upon the other that one could believe them related, that whatever ailed Father's feet ran— when those parts were elevated—down to contaminate and congest his lungs. Needless to say this inability to lie down comfortably made sleeping difficult. Many's the night I moved seamlessly from night-mare to nightmare, one moment the furnace huffing and hissing at me dangerously, the next the hermit himself, lips drawn back in a sort of snarling rictus, eyes staring big at me over the fire, uncomprehend-ing and child-like, desperate, afraid. At such times the only remedy was open air. I would gather up our blankets and lead Father down to the little stream that ran below his camp. There, the night's terror already behind him, forgotten, Father would fall into a fast and easy sleep. But not I. For then it was that I lay awake, my memory sound, triumphant, teasing me with visions of things to come.

As any of you know who have nursed a brother through such an illness, the evil that first dares enter your patient only at night, soon grows bold and advances upon him by day. And so it was that, within a very short time indeed, the hermit began to have difficulty breath-ing regardless of the hour. Then, as if he retained some physical mem-ory of the solace it had provided the night before, Father would repair to his little stream. At the time I assumed he found the air down there more congenial to his lungs, the waters soothing to his feet, but it may well be that the associations he had with the place, the prayers he had prayed there, also played some role in the comfort it now gave him. Whatever the cause, sooner or later, no matter where he had begun the day, I would find the old man sitting down there, staring contentedly at the little flow of water, apparently finding its vagaries as diverting as you or I might those of a mighty stream. Sometimes I would join him and—though by this time Father had as much diffi-culty remembering the names for things as he did those for people— still he would point out those that caught his eye, a pretty leaf, a shiny stone, the object likely as not called by a quality as its name—"green" perhaps or "slippery"—the man unable, even suffering from a deficit of words, to keep the silence, stifle his desire to share, to teach, to communicate his fascination with all that went on in the world around him.

Those were good days. When I look back on them now, I realize they were very good days indeed. But they did not seem so then. Then I followed a strange round, my hours devoted not so much to praise as to worry, my intervals to endless desperate calculation. Would our food last? Had my confession worked? And if it had, did that mean the prayers I now prayed daily also worked? Did He relent? Was it possible that, even now, the livid stream cooled, withdrew back up the valley whence it had come, the pestilence in turn slinking off down river, its source, its inspiration, dissipated, gone? And if that were true, if everything had turned out as I wished (realizing even as I considered the possibility how immodest and unlikely a proposition it was), did that mean that the most crucial of our needs would also be met, that at this very moment someone might be climbing up to relieve us, climbing up the mountain to bring us food, to feed and save us? For if someone did not come soon—come very soon I prayed—we would begin to starve.

It's interesting, isn't it, what God sends us in our extremity? We cry out for a religious, some priest or brother to come help us, come save us from the dangers we face, and instead of the grown-up we've prayed for—the man of mettle, the abba, the *rabboni*, the hero, the saint—we get Stuf—Stuf the charcoal-maker, Stuf the heathen, Stuf the clown.

I'll never forget the day he wandered into our camp, what it felt like to look up and see him standing there, the scare it gave me. Looking back on it now I realize this must have been Stuf's intention, that the man must have enjoyed causing these little sensations, for he seemed always to arrive like that: suddenly, mysteriously, as if materializing out of thin air. I wonder, did he study his approaches? Do you suppose he sat and waited for just the right moment, the instant when he knew he could really startle a person, catch him with his guard down? Whatever, he was certainly good at it. Normally, at that time of year, when the leaves lie thick upon the ground, you can hear someone coming long before he actually trudges into view. But that day I heard nothing. I was working down by the stream as I remember it, cleaning a pot maybe, maybe some bedclothes, when Father moved in a way that caught my attention, made me look up, follow his glance toward the wood. At first I saw nothing—saplings still dark from last night's rain, leaf litter fawn-colored, glowing faintly— and then suddenly, too abruptly, unrelated things began to move, join, commingle, so that what had seemed to be nothing, an emptiness between edges, became instead something, extricated itself from its surroundings, tree becoming trunk, limb leg, leaf eye, Stuf stepping from among the saplings like a man stepping from behind a wall—a little spin to celebrate the fact, a wink to say I told you so.

I was, as I remember it, appalled—appalled and overjoyed. It was everything I could do to keep from running to the man, running to him and bowing down before him, washing his very feet.

Which, as it turned out, was—at least according to Stuf—exactly how the hermit had greeted him when first he'd visited that place.

I never did find out if that was true. You know you have to be careful with the hill people: they'll lie to you just for the sake of lying, just to make a story sound pretty or give it a fancy ending. And Stuf was no different from any other. The man loved to put on airs, affect a station and dignity out of all proportion to his own. Yet, truth be told, it wouldn't surprise me if the hermit really had greeted him that way, greeted him as he would have Christ. Pagan or not, Stuf was a man; and I never saw Father deny any man his company or the comfort of his hearth.

For his part, Stuf treated the hermit with an elaborate and uncharacteristic respect. If Father stood, Stuf stood (and could not be prevailed upon to sit again). If Father did not care for his food, Stuf did not care for his either (and looked at me as if I had done something wrong). And then there was the way he listened to the man. By that time, by the time the charcoal-maker found us, began to deliver us from our hunger, Father had reached a point where language itself was now often beyond him. He would look at you, eyes alert, brow creasing and uncreasing as he spoke, for all intents and purposes the image of a man making some difficult but important point, yet what he said, what actually came out of his mouth, was little more than noise, a series of sounds that in form and cadence mimicked speech but, in truth, never attained anything like its meaning. And Stuf loved it. When Father spoke like that, utterly nonsensically, the charcoal-maker would sit up and pay attention as you or I might sit up and pay attention to a great prophet or holy man.

At first (I will admit it here), I was taken in by this. When Stuf explained that men like Father were, quite literally, *touched*, that some one or some thing had reached down from heaven and dealt them a glancing blow, granting them in the process a vision so astonishingly clear, so utterly at odds with our own, that they were rendered incapable of ordinary speech, I wanted to believe him, wanted to believe that the Father I had known still existed, that if I but listened to him closely, attended to what he had to say, I might regain that which I had lost, find again the Father I had known, the Father I had loved, the Father I missed so much.

But of course it wasn't true. Again and again I did as Stuf bade me, and, again and again, sitting by the hermit, listening to his garbled speech, I heard not wisdom but dementia, saw not a prophet but an old and feeble man. For Father had taught me too well. I knew his sign, could not ignore it, and where Stuf saw meaning in the creasing of that brow, I saw worry, a glimmer of the reason that as yet resided there; and it frightened me, it frightened me to think that somewhere deep inside him, somewhere so deep it could not get out, a part of Father did in fact still exist, and, existing, knew, understood, that the sounds coming from his mouth were not right, that they did not mean what he wished them to mean, meant, in fact, nothing at all.

I went often to the crag in those days. There was no need for me at the camp now; Stuf was there, Stuf could watch over Father. So I went to the crag. I would sit and look out over the valley and I would think about things. I would think about Father and I would think about the things he had said to me, the things we had done together, the places he had shown me. And sooner or later, no matter how much I tried to avoid it, I would think about the day he had taught me to love tracking, the day when we had lain together and awaited a vixen's return, what it had been like to curl up beneath his arm, to know myself safe there, the feel of his woolens rough against my face, the smell of cook-fires embedded in them, the smell of cook-fires and breakfast and, further down, faint but real, the smell of Father himself, the aroma of the man, his hair, his skin, his sweat, the heart that kept it warm, the heart that kept me warm.

Once, years before, the hermit had spoken to me of death. I had been talking to him about the pestilence as I remember it, what it had been like for us down in the valley during that first visitation, and, in particular, I had been telling him about Oftfor, what it had been like to watch my fellow oblate die—making of course the most of myself in the telling, turning myself into the uncomplaining hero of my tale. But, as he always did, Father took me at my word. His brow softened, I remember, and he reached for me, touched my hand. There was, I believe, something in the man that responded to suffering, bent toward it as a physician bends to a wound; and it embarrassed me. I was ashamed to see my invented grief taken for real, the bereavement I affected worried over, commiserated with. But looking back on it now...well, who's to say? Maybe he was right. Maybe I felt the boy's death more keenly than I realized. Certainly I've never forgotten what Father said to me that day, the way he refused to explain away what had happened to me, what had happened to poor little Oftfor. "God is wild," he told me. "God is uncontrollable. We cannot appease Him with our prayers or drive Him with our sacrifices. He does as He pleases. And what pleases Him is beyond our ken. He takes what we love most—mother, father, friend, child—and rips them from us brutally, without warning or care. There is no succor. They are gone. He has taken them. And He is silent. You stare across the field and the wind plays at your face and there are no answers, only wildness. We are helpless. We either accept Him as He is—wanton, willfull—or we lose all hope and grow bitter and sad. We continue to live and love at the whim of an unknowable Being. We take comfort in the beliefs and rituals we have built up over the years to placate Him but, in the final analysis, they are like straws before the wind. The first blow and they are gone. The wind roars where it will."

Of course, at the time, I was terribly shocked by this. I even, I remember, considered reporting the hermit. I had only recently begun visiting him then, and the picture of myself standing before Faults, denouncing the man's heterodoxy as I had been taught to do, an oblate true to his station and the Rule, pleased me. But of course I didn't report him. I had, I believe, even as early as that, begun to love the hermit a little, to love him and to appreciate the way he sometimes spoke to me as an equal—however much what he said might frighten me. And besides, I could always tell myself it was just his grief talking, the sadness he felt over the death of Brother Ælfhelm. You must remember that this was a time when the horror of the pestilence, the memory of it, was still fresh in our minds. It was not at all uncommon in those days to see grown men beating their breasts as they prayed, to hear an eerie wailing rise up at night from the village. Once, I remember, I even saw a brother overtaken as he walked upon the garth. He was near the church as I remember it, and, despite the fact he turned his face to the wall, pulled his hood up over his head, you could tell the man was in the grip of some strong emotion, that his shoulders went up and down like that because something was happening inside him, something was perhaps breaking inside him, something deep and dark and irreplaceable. So it seemed acceptable to think the hermit's outburst had been just that, an outburst, the expression of a perfectly natural and even humble grief.

Or at least that was what I told myself when first I heard the hermit's speech. But later, later when he was dying, later when I sat upon the crag, looked out over the valley (the green of the garth disturbed by fresh diggings), I wondered. Maybe Father had been right. Maybe the God I knew, the God of the cloister, of order and discipline, *was* just a human invention, that we followed the Rule so assiduously not that we might conform ourselves to His image but that He might be conformed to ours. I thought about the times I had prayed as Father prayed, the prayers of silence and emptiness, and I thought about the God I had encountered in those prayers, and there was no denying He was different from that of the cloister. Truly, He was wild and free and utterly unknowable. And now that Mystery had cast a pall over the man who had brought me to Him, had rendered all I had ever learned or loved of Him suspect, doubtful—His herald, His envoy, ruined like this, destroyed. I sat upon the crag and stared out over the valley, and, as promised, there were no answers, only the bite of the wind, its icy taste, the feral scent of distant weather.

At other times my mind seemed of its own accord to turn from such a view of things. I would be sitting there, looking out over the valley, thinking my sober thoughts, when suddenly and without warning I would find myself diverted, would find myself remembering for some reason my confession, the way Father had leaned out over his little stream to get a better look at me, the image floating before me once more effigy-like, the absurd bob of the head, the dreamy eyes, that silly hopeless smile. And as if it were all real, as if Father really did float on the air before me, really did approve of what he saw, I would find myself smiling back—pleased, happy to remember Father pleased, the man taking pleasure in my company, the man taking pleasure in anybody's company, enjoying himself. The one thing all us hermits have in common, he used to say, the one trait all hermits share, is their love of company. And then he would laugh and laugh, laugh that big laugh of his, the one that went so deep and carried so far, the laugh that both frightened me (for surely it must draw the entire Cumbrogi nation down upon us) and convinced me I had nothing to fear (for how could anyone be afraid of anything in the company of a man who could laugh like that?).

Once, a year or two before the coming of Godwin, Father had said something that, at the time, surprised me. I no longer remember the exact circumstances—the time of day, the part of the mountain we were on—but I do remember that we were in a good mood, that there had been a fresh fall of snow the night before and, as a result, we were both feeling happy, light-hearted, the tracking easy, full of interest. Then, quite unexpectedly, we came upon a spot where six or seven deer had congregated beneath a cedar tree. For a moment I remember we didn't say anything, struck dumb as it were by the obvious meaning of the place, the crush of print, the cedar stripped of needles, the stains upon the snow, the bristly-looking scat. It was Father who finally broke the silence. "Who knows the deer better," he asked, "the man who sees a picture of one in a book, or the man who never sees the animal at all but follows its track through a snowy wood, finds a place like this, sees, knows, what it means, the hunger that drove these animals, the food they were willing to eat?" I didn't say anything. There was no need to answer Father (we both knew who knew the deer better), and, moreover, there was something about the scene before us, its quiet gravity, that made all talk seem suddenly superfluous, even cruel. As if he understood this, knew what I was thinking, Father spoke again. "The world is God's sign," he said, "you must look at it, observe it, without fear or judgment. If you're brave enough to do that, Winwæd, if you can really see the world as it is…. Well, then you touch *His* print, smell *His* musk, hold *His* spoor in the palm of your hand."

So what then was I to make of this sign, this spoor—on the one hand the God who gave me Father, gave me the man who laughed and played, the man who loved me, cared for me, watched over me from his mountaintop; and, on the other, the God who took that man away, took Father away, killed him, killed everyone?

I was working by the fire when it happened, I'm sure of that, for I remember noticing the wind shift, the flames flickering in a new direction, the jolt of presentiment that sent through me; and then I remember turning and seeing—as I had known I would see—that it had found him, that once again the smoke had found Father, and that despite this, despite the fact that smoke now streamed over and around the man as water will stream over and around a rock, he wasn't coughing, despite all that smoke Father wasn't coughing, was, in point of fact, just sitting there, apparently indifferent, immune; and if such vigor wasn't frightening enough, there was also something about the way he was sitting there, something about his attitude, the tilt of his head, that did not look right, that did not look right at all.

By the time I got to him he was of course gone, had, doubtless, been gone for some time now. But his eyes were still open. Glassy, sightless, they stared at the water, stared at the little trickle of water that was Father's stream, had always been his stream, his place. For a moment I remember I did nothing, just stood there, taking it all in, trying not so much to undo it as to understand it, to actually see what I was seeing. Then I sat down. I sat down and, absently, I began to stroke Father's hand. Of course a part of me must have known what would happen, what my fingers would find there, but still I remember it coming as a shock, the scar that rode the back of Father's hand, the scar that had ridden the back of Father's hand ever since a little boy, an oblate, had sought to test him, to see if, in his ecstasy, the old man could feel anything, know anything of the world around him. Finding it, touching it, remembering everything, I began to cry.

XL

Of course Father showed up the very next day. As if God had wanted to make it perfectly clear who was in charge, had wished to leave no doubt as to His purpose, that He had been waiting for just this moment to answer my prayer, to lift His siege, send relief, it was the very next day, the day *after* Father Gwynedd died, that Father Beorhtfrith appeared at the edge of our camp bearing his weight of news and supplies. And how equally suspicious, when you think about it, that they should have sent Beorhtfrith. I mean Brother Edgar must have had to draw him a map. So far as I know, until that day, the furthest Father Beorhtfrith had ever ventured from the abbey was the occasional walk down to the fish ponds, and even then he probably had to be led. Certainly he'd never climbed Modra nect before. Yet he is the one they chose. Doubtless they were thinking about the harvest. Doubtless they were thinking they could spare him, that, at a time when every able-bodied man was needed to salvage what could be salvaged from the remains of that pitiful harvest, they thought they could spare Beorhtfrith, that poor perpetually ineffectual Beorhtfrith was perfect for this task. As, of course, he was. For who else could have delivered that news with such aplomb? Who else could have told me what had happened below— who had lived and who had died—without for a moment thinking of anything other than himself, listening, as I believe he must always have listened, to only his own voices, the ones that told him what *he* thought of this, how *he* felt about what had happened. And so it was that, however poorly I may have dissembled, however much I may have grown pale at what he had to tell me, Father never noticed a thing, remained, throughout his report, blithely ignorant of all but his own internal mutterings. And I was left to digest the news on my own, spared the curiosity and questions I might have endured had God chosen to send someone else.

Abbot Godwin was dead. Prior Maban was dead. Everyone was dead. Everyone, that is, who was new, all those that had never known the old days, the days of Agatho and Folian, all those that had come only after Godwin had come, had sworn allegiance only to him and his master; they were all dead. My prayer had cut through them like a scythe. Moreover, they were the only ones dead. No one who had survived the pestilence the first time it struck Redestone had succumbed to this its second visitation. Or, in other words, the old world, the world my wicked prayer had sought to resurrect, the world of Dagan and Waldhere, Osric and Baldwin, this was the world that had survived, this the world that had, indeed, in however perverse a sense, been resurrected. And not only was it resurrected, but In-Hrypum herself now lay in a state of near ruin. As if to leave no doubt as to the cause of all this, Wilfrid's seat at In-Hrypum, which previously had always escaped the pestilence, was, this time, brought low by it, the community there decimated, reduced, it was said, to gleaning for its food.

Father Beorhtfrith, I remember, told me this last as if it somehow bore upon his character that such a malady, one that had claimed even a bishop's see, should have spared him. Then, whispering lest he wake the monster, provoke it to still further mischief, the good father went on to assure me the worst was now over, that we could all breathe easier for the miasma was most certainly gone, had drained (forever, he prayed) back into whatever fetid swamp had first produced it.

Which meant God *had* heard my confession, *had* placed His bow in the sky, sent His dove, His Spirit, to redeem the face of the earth. But only after He had killed everyone, killed all of them, all those associated with my removal from the hermit's service, all those associated with that first and lasting fall from grace. All of them, that is, but Wilfrid. Some final justice in that, I suppose, that the one I had

sought first, the one I had most wished to destroy, should be the only
one left standing.

We buried Father on a piece of high ground overlooking his little
stream. They tell me the place is well marked now, that there is even a
sort of unofficial shrine on the site, but at the time there was nothing
special about it, just a quiet place with a good deposit of soil. Good
soil is hard to come by on the mountain, soil deep enough to bury a
man. But we found it there. As, of course, had the trees. I remember
we had to wrest Father's grave from the grasp of a particularly large
and tenacious oak. Doubtless those roots have long since grown back,
long since encircled the man, their tendrils now his winding sheet.
For some reason I find the image strangely comforting.

After we closed the grave, Stuf left. He had no reason to tarry,
Beorhtfrith having made it perfectly clear he did not care for the man,
crossing himself whenever Stuf so much as brushed against him. And
of course our Christian rites had been a trial for the charcoal-maker.
Not that he hadn't tried to appear respectful, hadn't tried to stand up
straight, nod now and then as if following the service closely. But unlike
Beorhtfrith, I had been able to see where Stuf hid his hands behind his
back, the way they jogged up and down as we chanted, the one finger
tapping against the others as if ticking off the moments till he could be
gone. I find it interesting now, when I think back on it, that he should
have been in such a hurry. Was he really anxious to be off, or merely
anxious to seem so? You must remember you are dealing with a hill
person here. Their concerns, their motives, must always remain obscure.
Thinking about it now, and bearing in mind what I knew of the man,
I believe it quite possible Stuf crept back there after Father and I left,
that he said his own obsequies, performed quite probably his own rites,
his own office, over Father Hermit's grave. Not that it really matters.
Such devilry, I have long since grown convinced, can only find itself
helpless before the benign indifference of a soul like Father's.

So Stuf left. As soon as the last of the earth had been replaced, the
charcoal-maker set aside his spade, turned and, without so much as
a fare-thee-well, walked off up into the wood. I remember I watched
that small back grow smaller still and, watching it, found myself

strangely reluctant to see him go, reluctant to see our time here come to an end like this, Stuf wandering off by himself into the wood. And so I ran after him. Like some overwrought postulant, I ran after the charcoal-maker, caught up with him, walked with him for a distance. And, incredibly, I think Stuf himself, even poor benighted Stuf, may have felt something like what I was feeling, for he greeted my appearance at his side that day with none of his usual mischief. Indeed, as I remember it, he showed an almost monastic decorum, inviting me to join him with a small bow and a nod of his head, the two of us walking on together in companionable silence, heads down, arms at our sides, for all intents and purposes just two old friends out for a stroll.

Of course it couldn't last, and, interestingly, I think it was Stuf who brought the thing to a close. Certainly he was the one who spoke, he the one who tried to sum it all up, give the day a proper benediction. "Remember how he used to laugh?" he said, not really looking at me, looking at something else, hearing, I think, something else. Then, shaking his head once, still clearly in awe of what he had remembered, he turned and walked away—no dancing, no spins, no winks of the eye, just that final question, the last shake of his head, and Stuf the charcoal-maker, his business with Redestone complete, disappears from this and all histories of our land.

As for myself, I was in for a surprise. For weeks I had watched Father's decline, watched as, again and again, Death had come to take his measure, lean upon his door. And with each of those visits, with each step in that decline, I had grown ever more frightened, ever more unsure. For this was Father Hermit. I was watching the man I loved more than any other, needed more than any other, fall toward something unimaginable, the place from which no one I knew had ever returned; and I was powerless to stop that descent, powerless to help him, to save him; powerless, finally, to do anything other than watch as (unwitting and innocent of all that lay before him) Father fell toward his doom.

And then it happened. The thing I dreaded more than any other actually happened; and I found myself on the other side of it alive and well and feeling unaccountably good.

Of course there is nothing like a death to make us think of life. We watch the one thing become the other as quietly and unobtrusively as thought, and we marvel at the ease with which it is done. Small wonder we grow giddy round the deathbed, for there we know—however momentarily, *we know*—how close we stand, how thin the wall that separates us. And that may be all the explanation necessary for the strange sense of exhilaration I experienced in the days following Father's death. But I think there was more to it as well. I think there was something about Father's death, something about death itself, that I had not known before, had not understood, probably could not have understood until I saw that death, watched that man die.

Of course it all seems rather banal now. How many times had I been taught that death was just a door, how many times had I watched the community gather round the bed of a brother about to cross over? But this was the first time I had stood so close, this the first time it had been my Father Hermit doing the crossing, and though I shouldn't have been, I was unprepared for the power of the metaphor. He was here. A moment ago he was here, a man complete and whole unto himself, and now, in an instant, he was gone. And there was something about that, something about standing there looking at that dead and empty body, that called out to me, declared itself. I knew this, recognized it. No one could look at those staring eyes, that heedless yawn, without seeing them for what they were. This was sign. This was a body stunned and staggered by the speed of its abandonment. *I could read this.* I was unalone.

Yes. Yes I know, one does not necessarily follow from the other. Yet at the time it did. Somehow—looking at those unseeing eyes, that jaw hanging loose as if broken—I knew, knew, that what half-sat, half-slumped, on the ground before me wasn't Father, that this was merely rain-shadow—the proof, the evidence, that someone had been here. Father wasn't here. Father was somewhere else. Father was. God was. The goose flesh ran unimpeded up and down my arms.

And it didn't go away. Unlike the shameless glee that sometimes disgraces deathbed scenes, the sense of exhilaration I experienced upon seeing Father Hermit dead persisted. All through that winter it stayed with me. I stepped onto the cold floor of the dortoir and it bothered me not; my stomach growled for want of food and it was all I could do to keep from laughing. Reality was changed, transformed, transfigured: God and Father Hermit *with me*, carrying me, buoying me up. I exulted. I gave thanks. Life was good, life was holy, life was chant.

And then, slowly, as spring bled into winter, stained and eventually overcame it, the work once more imposing itself upon our lives—the aches and pains, the fatigue—this happiness, this near-euphoria, naturally enough began to fade, and, with it, the feeling that Father was ever with me. And I let him go. With very little regret, I let the hermit go. Father had himself taught me that I should, that such consolations are only distractions, that Creation in and of itself must suffice, prove miracle enough. Still, I never was the contemplative he was, never will be; and so I do enjoy my memories, the smiles that, from time to time, rise of their own accord to my lips. Which, of course, does not go unnoticed. On more than one occasion Father Abbot has had to point a finger at me in Chapter. But that doesn't matter. Father Hermit doesn't mind. He just leans out over his silly little stream, bobs that big old head at me and smiles and smiles.

ALPHABETICAL LISTING OF
IMPORTANT CHARACTERS

Ælfhelm, poet, monk of the monastery at Redestone, and courier to Gwynedd.

Agatho, Roman priest and abbot of the monastery at Redestone (supplanted Abbot Folian).

Alcfrith*, under-king of Deira (southern half of Northumbria), son of King Oswiu.

Baldwin, monk and sacristan of the monastery at Redestone.

Botulf, monk and kitchen master of the monastery at Redestone.

Ceolwulf, Anglo-Saxon warrior and father of Winwæd.

Cuthwine, priest and cellarer of the monastery at Redestone, dies of the plague.

Dagan, priest and prior of the monastery at Redestone.

Eadnoth, monk of the monastery at Redestone, dies of septicemic plague.

Ealhmund, oblate of the monastery at Redestone.

Eanflæd, a young girl who lives in the village at Redestone.

Edgar, replaces Winwæd as courier to Gwynedd.

Ecgfrith*, King of Northumbria, successor to his father, King Oswiu.

Folian, Northern (Celtic) priest and founding abbot of the monastery at Redestone.

Godwin, third abbot of the monastery at Redestone, replaces Agatho.

Gwynedd, priest and hermit.

Maban, replaces Dagan as prior of the monastery at Redestone.

Oftfor, oblate of the monastery at Redestone, dies of the plague.

Osric, monk of the monastery at Redestone and cellarer after Cuthwine dies of plague.

Oswiu*, king of Northumbria and Bretwalda (overlord) of lands beyond its borders.

Paulinus*, Roman priest sent as missionary by Pope Gregory to England in 601 A.D. Is credited with converting large numbers to the Christian faith.

Penda*, pagan king of Mercia.

Stuf, a pagan (one of the hill people) who makes charcoal for the furnace at Redestone.

Tatwine, monk of the monastery at Redestone who shows Winwæd the way to Father Gwynedd's hermitage.

Victricius, monk and furnace master of the monastery at Redestone.

Waldhere, oblate of the monastery at Redestone.

Wilfrid*, Roman priest and bishop.

Winwæd, oblate of the monastery at Redestone.

*Historical figure (Note: The spelling of these names may vary.)

ACKNOWLEDGMENTS

A book like *The Oblate's Confession* owes a very real debt to all the anonymous people who, over the course of human history, have taken time to record something of their lives and the lives of those that preceded them. Without them, neither history nor life as we know it would be possible.

In addition, there are any number of professional historians who have made the writing of this book possible. First and foremost among these must be the Venerable Bede. Any scholar of seventh century England will recognize the many borrowings and out-and-out thefts I have made from the life and work of this brilliant, humble man. I owe a similar, if somewhat less extensive, debt to the Roman historian, Tacitus. As for modern historians, there are any number whose works have informed my own. I would like to express my special thanks to the late Gerald Bonner, whose encouragement and advice convinced me that a book like *The Oblate's Confession* could actually be written. Though I never had the good fortune to meet the archaeologist Rosemary Cramp, her work at Bede's monastery of Monkwearmouth-Jarrow taught me a great deal about the material culture of seventh century Northumbria.

Among the monks whose work has influenced and made possible my own, I must mention Thomas Merton, Thomas Keating, Thich Nhat Hanh, and, of course, the anonymous author of *The Cloud of Unknowing*. I would also like to thank the brothers of Our Lady of the Holy Cross Abbey (Berryville, Va.) and St. Anselm's Abbey (Washington, D.C.), who helped me with advice, encouragement, and the loan of works from their libraries. From time to time, they also heard my own confession.

I am indebted to the staff and board of the Talbot County Free Library, who, in addition to paying my salary over the last several years, have given me permission to play at will among their stacks. Can there be any greater source of inspiration than unfettered access to a library?

I also want to thank my publisher, Ron Sauder, who, from the beginning, has believed in this book. Scripture tells us "to be hospitable to strangers for some have thereby entertained angels unawares." Ron may have been a stranger when he first walked into my life, but it didn't take long to notice the wings and halo.

I have been blessed with any number of friends and family members whose care and affection have made this book possible, but I want to especially single out five. When an artist as serious and accomplished as S. A. Jones tells you the book you've written is good, it gives you faith in yourself and the work. I will never be able to thank her enough. Jean-Pierre LeDru and his late wife Winnie offered me sound counsel, a Gallic perspective on my research, and loving friendship; I thank them both. During all the years when I thought no one would ever publish my book, my mother re-read it annually, and then spent the rest of her time telling me how much she loved it. This may be a book about "fathers," but it is one that I would have given up on long ago were it not for my mother. And, finally, Melissa. What can I say? You're it, kid.

To all of these I owe a debt beyond paying. *The Oblate's Confession* would not have happened without you. Its faults are all my own, its strengths I owe to you.

William Peak
Easton, Maryland
June 3, 2014